HARRAP'S

P9-APC-923

BROKEN PROMISE

LINWOOD BARCLAY

First published in Great Britain in 2015 by Orion Books, an imprint of the Orion Publishing Group Ltd

Orion Books Limited
Carmelite House
50 Victoria Embankment
London EC4Y 0LS

This educational edition of *Broken Promise* by Linwood Barclay is published by arrangement with the Orion Publishing Group Ltd, London.

Pour les notes en marge du texte :
© Larousse, 2018
21, rue du Montparnasse
75283 Paris CEDEX 06

HARRAP's® est une marque de Larousse SAS
www.harrap.com

ISBN 978 2 81 870 523 0

About the author

Linwood Barclay was born in the United States but moved to Canada just before turning four years old, when his father accepted a position with an advertising[1] agency north of the border.

He is a former columnist[2] for the *Toronto Star*. His first standalone[3] thriller, *No Time for Goodbye*, was published in 2007 to critical acclaim[4] and great international success.
The book has been sold around the world and been translated[5] into nearly thirty languages.

Broken Promise is now part of a gripping[6] Promise Falls trilogy (book 2 is *Far From True*, book 3 *The Twenty-Three*).

1. publicitaire

2. chroniqueur
3. en un seul ouvrage
4. et salué par la critique

5. traduit

6. captivante

DIRECTION DE LA PUBLICATION : Carine Girac-Marinier

NOTES EN MARGE : Mathilde Rojinski-Sadot

RÉVISION DES NOTES : Marianne Mouchot

RELECTURE : F. Le Dantec

INFORMATIQUE ÉDITORIALE ET MISE EN PAGES :
Philippe Cazabet, Marie-Noëlle Tilliette

CONCEPTION GRAPHIQUE : Uli Meindl

FABRICATION : Rebecca Dubois

Mot de l'Éditeur

Vous aimeriez lire en langue originale, mais le vocabulaire, les expressions figurées ou la syntaxe vous arrêtent parfois ?

Cette collection est faite pour vous !

Vous trouverez en effet, en note dans la marge, une traduction de certains mots et expressions qui vous permettra d'avancer facilement dans votre lecture.

Nous n'avons pas cherché à vous donner une traduction littéraire de l'ouvrage et nous nous sommes parfois écartés du sens littéral pour vous fournir le sens qui convient le mieux à l'histoire. Aussi les mots sont-ils traduits dans le contexte du texte original.

Les expressions figées anglaises sont, bien entendu, rendues par une expression équivalente en français.

Les allusions à des réalités culturelles du monde anglo-saxon sont expliquées également dans la marge, pour vous aider à mieux comprendre la trame de l'histoire.

Vous aurez ainsi, en regard du texte original, tout le savoir-faire d'un dictionnaire rien que pour vous et adapté à ce livre !

Notre objectif est de vous mener jusqu'au mot FIN en vous donnant les clés nécessaires à la compréhension du récit.

Laissez-vous gagner par l'angoisse, l'humour et le suspense qui règnent chez les maîtres de la littérature anglo-saxonne.

Lire en VO ? You can indeed!

For Neetha

Acknowledgments

Authors need help, and I had plenty. Thanks go to Susan Lamb, Heather Connor, John Aitchison, Danielle Perez, Bill Massey, Spencer Barclay, Helen Heller, Brad Martin, Nick Whelan, Kara Welsh, Graeme Williams, Gaby Young, Paige Barclay, Ashley Dunn, Kristin Cochrane, Juliet Ewers, Eva Kolcze and D. P. Lyle.

And, as always, the booksellers.

Coup de pouce pour vous aider
à bien comprendre le début de l'histoire...

Le premier jour de cette histoire s'ouvre sur la déconfiture de David Harwood, jeune veuf, jeune père et jeune journaliste au chômage.

Difficile d'affronter cette nouvelle journée avec un optimisme serein quand on a dû retourner vivre chez ses parents et quitter Boston pour sa petite ville natale... une ville pas si tranquille.

ONE

I hate this town.

THE FIRST DAY

TWO

David

A couple of hours before all hell broke loose[1], I was in bed, awake since five, pondering the[2] circumstances that had returned me[3], at the age of forty-one, to my childhood home.

It wasn't that the room was exactly the same as when I'd moved out almost twenty years ago. The Ferrari poster no longer hung over the blue-striped wallpaper, and the kit I built of the starship *Enterprise*—hardened amberlike[4] droplets of glue visible on the hull[5]—no longer sat[6] on the dresser[7]. But it was the same dresser. And it was the same wallpaper. And this was the same single bed.

Sure, I'd spent the night in here[8] a few times over the years, as a visitor. But to be back here as a resident? To be *living* here? With my parents, and my son, Ethan?

God, what a fucking state of affairs.[9] How had it come to this[10]?

It wasn't that I didn't know the answer to that question. It was complicated, but I knew.

The descent had begun five years ago, after my wife, Jan, passed away[11]. A sad story, and not

1. avant l'apocalypse

2. à réfléchir aux

3. m'avaient ramené

4. couleur d'ambre

5. coque

6. n'était plus

7. commode

8. dormi ici

9. Quelle merde.

10. en était-on arrivé là

11. était décédée

17

one worth rehashing[1] here. After half a decade[2], there were things I'd had no choice but to put behind me[3]. I'd grown into[4] my role of single father[5]. I was raising Ethan, nine years old now, on my own[6]. I'm not saying that made me a hero. I'm just trying to explain how things unfolded[7].

Wanting a new start for Ethan and myself, I quit my job as a reporter for the *Promise Falls Standard*—not that hard a decision[8], considering the lack[9] of interest by the paper's management[10] in actually[11] covering anything approaching news—and accepted an editing position[12] on the city desk at the *Boston Globe*. The money was better[13], and Boston had a lot to offer Ethan: the children's museum, the aquarium, Faneuil Hall Marketplace, the Red Sox[14], the Bruins[15]. If there was a better place for a boy and his dad, I couldn't think where it might be. But …

There's always a *but*.

But most of my duties as an editor took place in the evening, after reporters had handed in[16] their stories. I could see Ethan off[17] to school, sometimes even pop by[18] and take him to lunch, since I didn't have to be at the paper until three or four in the afternoon. But that meant most nights I did not have dinner with my son. I wasn't there to make sure Ethan spent more time on his homework than on video games. I wasn't there to keep him from watching countless[19] episodes of shows[20] about backwoods duck hunters[21] or airheaded[22] wives of equally airheaded sports celebrities or whatever the latest celebration of American ignorance and/or wretched[23] excess happened to be. But the really troubling thing was, I just wasn't *there*. A lot of being a dad amounts to being around[24], being available[25]. *Not* being at work.

Who was Ethan supposed to talk to if he had a crush on some[1] girl—perhaps unlikely[2] at nine, but you never knew—or needed advice on dealing with a bully[3], and it was eight o'clock at night? Was he supposed to ask Mrs. Tanaka? A nice woman, no doubt about it, who was happy to make money five nights a week looking after a young boy now that her husband had passed away. But Mrs. Tanaka wasn't much help[4] when it came to[5] math questions. She didn't feel like[6] jumping up and down with Ethan when the Bruins scored in overtime[7]. And it was pretty hard to persuade her to take up a controller[8] and race a few laps[9] around a virtual Grand Prix circuit in one of Ethan's video games.

By the time I stepped wearily through[10] the door—usually between eleven and midnight, and I *never* went out for drinks after the paper was put to bed[11] because I knew Mrs. Tanaka wanted to return to her own apartment eventually[12]—Ethan was usually asleep. I had to resist the temptation to wake him, ask how his day had gone, what he'd had for supper, whether he'd had any problems with his homework, what he'd watched on TV.

How often had I fallen into bed myself with an aching heart[13]? Telling myself I was a bad father? That I'd made a stupid mistake leaving Promise Falls? Yes, the *Globe* was a better paper than the *Standard*, but any extra[14] money I was making was more than offset by[15] what was going into Mrs. Tanaka's bank account, and a high monthly rent[16].

My parents offered to move to Boston to help out[17], but I wanted no part of that[18]. My dad, Don, was in his early seventies now, and Arlene, my mother, was only a couple of years behind him. I was not going to uproot them[19], especially

1. était amoureux d'une

2. peu probable

3. tenir tête à une brute

4. n'était pas d'une grande aide

5. pour ce qui était des

6. n'était pas chaude pour

7. marquaient aux prolongations

8. console

9. faire quelques tours de piste

10. À l'heure où, épuisé, je franchissais

11. après le bouclage,

12. à un moment

13. le cœur gros

14. supplémentaire

15. ne faisait pas le poids comparé à

16. loyer

17. m'aider

18. n'avais pas voulu en entendre parler

19. les déraciner

after a recent scare Dad put us all through[1]. A minor heart attack. He was okay now, getting his strength back, taking his meds[2], but the man was not up to a move[3]. Maybe one day a seniors' residence in Promise Falls, when the house became too much for him and Mom to take care of, but moving to a big city a couple of hundred miles away[4]—more than three hours if there was traffic[5]—was not in the cards[6].

So when I heard the *Standard* was looking for a reporter, I swallowed my pride[7] and made the call.

I felt like I'd eaten a bucket of Kentucky Fried Crow[8] when I called the managing editor and said, "I'd like to come back."

It was amazing there was actually a position[9]. As newspaper revenues declined, the *Standard*, like most papers, was cutting back[10] wherever it could. As staff[11] left, they weren't replaced. But the *Standard* was down to[12] half a dozen people, a number that included reporters, editors, and photographers. (Most reporters were now "two-way[13]," meaning they could write stories and take pictures, although in reality, they were more like "four-way" or "six-way," since they also filed[14] for the online edition, did podcasts, tweeted[15]—you name it[16], they did it. It wouldn't be long before they did home delivery[17] to the few subscribers who still wanted a print edition[18].) Two people had left in the same week to pursue nonjournalistic endeavors[19]—one went to public relations, or "the dark side[20]," as I had once thought of it, and the other became a veterinarian's assistant—so the paper could not provide its usual inadequate coverage of goings-on[21] in Promise Falls. (Little wonder that many people had, for years, been referring to the paper as the *Substandard*.)

It would be a shitty[1] place to go back to. I knew that. It wouldn't be real journalism. It would be filling the space between the ads[2], at least, what ads there were. I'd be cranking out[3] stories and re-writing press releases[4] as quickly as I could type them.

But on the upside,[5] I'd be back to working most-ly days[6]. I'd be able to spend more time with Ethan, and when I did have evening obligations, Ethan's grandparents, who loved him beyond measure[7], could keep an eye on him.

The *Standard*'s managing editor offered me the job. I gave my notice to the[8] *Globe* and my land-lord[9] and moved back to Promise Falls. I did move in with my parents, but that was to be a stopgap measure[10]. My first job would be to find a house for Ethan and myself. All I could afford in Boston was a rented apartment, but back here, I'd be able to get us a proper home. Real estate prices[11] were in free fall[12].

Then everything went to shit[13] at one fifteen p.m. on Monday, my first day back at the *Standard*.

I'd returned from interviewing some folks who were petitioning for a crosswalk[14] on a busy street before one of their kids got killed, when the publisher, Madeline Plimpton, came into the newsroom[15].

"I have an announcement," she said, the words catching in her throat[16]. "We won't be publishing an edition tomorrow."

That seemed odd. The next day was not a holiday[17].

"And we won't be publishing the day after that," Plimpton said. "It's with a profound sense of sad-ness that I tell you the *Standard* is closing."

1. merdique

2. remplir les trous entre les pubs

3. Je devrais pondre

4. des communi-qués de presse

5. le bon côté, c'était que

6. de jour

7. par-dessus tout

8. J'ai démis-sionné du

9. résilié mon bail

10. devait être provisoire

11. Les prix de l'immobilier

12. en chute libre

13. tout dérapa

14. passage piéton

15. salle de rédaction

16. la gorge nouée

17. férié

She said some more things. About profitability, and the lack thereof[1]. About the decline in advertising, and classifieds[2] in particular. About a drop in market share[3], plummeting readership[4]. About not being able to find a sustainable business model[5].

And a whole lot of other shit.

Some staff started to cry. A tear ran down Plimpton's cheek, which, to give her the benefit of the doubt, was probably genuine[6].

I was not crying. I was too fucking angry. I had quit the goddamn *Boston Globe*. I'd walked away from a decent, well-paying job to come back here. As I went past the stunned[7] managing editor, the man who'd hired[8] me, on my way out of the newsroom, I said, "Good to know you're in the loop[9]."

Out on the sidewalk, I got out my cell[10] and called my former[11] editor in Boston. Had the job been filled[12]? Could I return?

"We're not filling it, David," he said. "I'm sorry."

So now here I was, living with my parents.

No wife.

No job.

No prospects[13].

Loser.

It was seven. Time to get up, have a quick shower, wake up Ethan, and get him ready for school.

I opened the door to his room—it used to be a sewing room for Mom, but she'd cleared her stuff out[14] when we moved in—and said, "Hey, pal[15]. Time to get cracking[16]."

He was motionless[17] under the covers, which obscured all of him but the topsy-turvy[18] blond hair atop his head.

"Rise and shine[19]!" I said.

He stirred[1], rolled over, pulled down the bed-spread[2] enough to see me. "I don't feel good," he whispered. "I don't think I can go to school."

I came up alongside the bed, leaned over[3], and put my hand to his forehead. "You don't feel hot[4]."

"I think it's my stomach," he said.

"Like the other day?" My son nodded. "That turned out to be nothing[5]," I reminded him.

"I think this might be different." Ethan let out a small moan[6].

"Get up and dressed and we'll see how you are then." This had been becoming a pattern[7] the last couple of weeks. Whatever ailment[8] was troubling him, it certainly hadn't been troubling him on weekends, when he could down[9] four hot dogs in ten minutes, and had more energy than everyone else in this house combined. Ethan didn't want to go to school, and so far I'd been unable to get him to tell me why[10].

My parents, who believed sleeping in[11] was staying in bed past five thirty—I'd heard them getting up as I'd stared at that dark ceiling—were already in the kitchen when I made my entrance. They'd have both had breakfast by this time, and Dad, on his fourth coffee by now, was sitting at the kitchen table, still trying to figure out[12] how to read the news on an iPad tablet, which Mom had bought for him after the *Standard* stopped showing up at their door[13] every morning.

He was stabbing at the device with his index finger hard enough to knock it off its stand[14].

"For God's sake, Don," she said, "you're not trying to poke its eye out[15]. You just tap it lightly[16]."

"I hate this thing," he said. "Everything's jumping around all over the place[17]."

1. remua

2. couvre-lit

3. me penchai

4. Tu n'as pas le front chaud

5. C'était rien, finalement

6. gémissement

7. régulier

8. Quelle que soit la maladie qui

9. s'enfiler

10. n'avais pas su lui faire dire pourquoi

11. faire la grasse matinée

12. piger

13. d'arriver chez eux

14. pointait si fort de l'index que la tablette en tombait de son socle

15. tu n'es pas censé enfoncer le doigt dedans

16. tapotes, simplement

17. Y a tout qui saute dans tous les sens

Seeing me, Mom adopted the excessively cheerful tone she always used when things were not going well. "Hello!" she said. "Sleep well?"

"Fine," I lied[1].

"I just made a fresh pot[2]," she said. "Want a cup?"

"I can manage[3]."

"David, did I tell you about that girl at the checkout[4] at the Walgreens[5]? What was her name? It'll come to me[6]. Anyway, she's cute as a button[7] and she's split up[8] with her husband and—"

"Mom, please."

She was always on the lookout[9], trying to find someone for me. It was *time*, she liked to say. Ethan needed a *mother*. I'd grieved[10] long enough, she was forever[11] reminding me.

I wasn't grieving.

I'd had six dates in the last five years, with six different women. Slept with one. That was it. Losing Jan, and the circumstances around her death, had made me averse to commitment[12], and Mom should have understood that.

"I'm just saying," she persisted, "that I think she'd be pretty receptive if you were to ask her out[13]. Whatever her name is. Next time we're in there together, I'll point her out[14]."

Dad spoke up. "For God's sake, Arlene, leave him alone[15]. And come on. He's got a kid and no job. That doesn't exactly make him a great prospect[16]."

"Good to have you in my corner[17], Dad," I said.

He made a face[18], went back to poking at his tablet. "I don't know why the hell I can't get an honest-to-God goddamn paper[19] to my door. Surely there are still people who want to read an actual paper[20]."

"They're all old," Mom told him.

"Well, old people are entitled[1] to the news," he said.

I opened the fridge, rooted around[2] until I'd found the yogurt Ethan liked, and a jar of strawberry jam. I set them on the counter and brought down a box of cereal from the cupboard.

"They can't make money anymore," Mom told him. "All the classifieds went to craigslist and Kijiji[3]. Isn't that right, David?"

I said, "Mmm." I poured[4] some Cheerios into a bowl for Ethan, who I hoped would be down shortly[5]. I'd wait till he showed before pouring on milk and topping it with a dollop[6] of strawberry yogurt. I dropped two slices of white Wonder bread[7], the only kind my parents had ever bought, into the toaster.

My mother said, "I just put on a fresh pot. Would you like a cup?"

Dad's head came up.

I said, "You just asked me that."

Dad said, "No, she didn't."

I looked at him. "Yes, she did, five seconds ago."

"Then"—with real bite in his voice—"maybe you should answer her the first time so she doesn't have to ask you twice."

Before I could say anything, Mom laughed it off[8]. "I'd forget my head if it wasn't screwed on.[9]"

"That's not true," Dad said. "I'm the one who lost his goddamn wallet[10]. What a pain in the ass it was getting that all sorted out[11]."

Mom poured some coffee into a mug and handed it to me with a smile. "Thanks, Mom." I leaned in and gave her a small kiss on her weathered[12] cheek as Dad went back to stabbing at the tablet.

"I wanted to ask," she said to me, "what you might have on[13] for this morning."

---

1. ont droit

2. farfouillai

3. [sites de petites annonces en ligne]

4. versai

5. descendrait bientôt

6. grosse cuillerée

7. [pain de mie industriel]

8. désamorça la situation d'un rire

9. Un jour j'oublierai ma tête !

10. portefeuille

11. Qu'est-ce qu'on en a bavé pour régler ça

12. usée

13. si tu avais quelque chose de prévu

"Why? What's up?"

"I mean, if you have some job interviews lined up, I don't want to interfere with that at all or—"

"Mom, just tell me what it is you want."

"I don't want to impose," she said. "It's only if you have time."

"For God's sake, Mom, just spit it out[1]."

"Don't talk to your mother that way," Dad said.

"I'd do it myself, but if you were going out, I have some things I wanted to drop off[2] for Marla."

Marla Pickens. My cousin. Younger than me by a decade[3]. Daughter of Mom's sister, Agnes.

"Sure, I can do that."

"I made up a chili, and I had so much left over[4], I froze some of it, and I know she really likes my chili, so I froze a few single servings[5] in some Glad containers[6]. And I picked her up a few other things. Some Stouffer's frozen dinners. They won't be as good as homemade, but still. I don't think that girl is eating. It's not for me to comment[7], but I don't think Agnes is looking in on her often enough[8]. And the thing is, I think it would be good for her to see you. Instead of us old people always dropping by. She's always liked you."

"Sure."

"Ever since this business[9] with the baby, she just hasn't been right[10]."

"I know," I said. "I'll do it." I opened the refrigerator. "You got any bottles of water I can put with Ethan's lunch?"

Dad uttered an indignant "Ha!" I knew where this was going[11]. I should have known better than to have asked[12]. "Biggest scam[13] in the world, bottled water. What comes out of the tap[14] is good enough for anybody. This town's water is fine, and I should know[15]. Only suckers[16] pay for it. Next

1. accouche

2. déposer
3. de dix ans

4. tellement de restes
5. portions individuelles
6. [boîtes en plastique]

7. ça ne me regarde pas
8. aille la voir assez souvent

9. cette histoire
10. elle n'est plus la même
11. ce que ça présageait
12. Pas malin de ma part de demander ça
13. arnaque
14. robinet
15. je suis bien placé pour le savoir
16. Seuls les couillons

thing you know[1], they'll find a way to make you pay for air. Remember when you didn't have to pay for TV? You just had an antenna, watched for nothing. Now you have to pay for cable. That's the way to make money. Find a way to make people pay for something they're getting now for nothing."

Mom, oblivious to my father's rant[2], said, "I think Marla's spending too much time alone, that she needs to get out, do things to take her mind off[3] what happened, to—"

"I said I'd do it, Mom."

"I was just saying," she said, the first hint of an edge entering her voice[4], "that it would be good if we all made an effort where she's concerned."

Dad, not taking his eyes off the screen, said, "It's been ten months, Arlene. She's gotta move on[5]."

Mom sighed. "Of course, Don, like that's something you just get over[6]. Walk it off[7], that's your solution to everything."

"She's gone a bit crackers[8], if you ask me." He looked up. "Is there more coffee?"

"I just said I made a fresh pot. Now who's the one who isn't listening?" Then, like an afterthought, she said to me, "When you get there, remember to just identify yourself[9]. She always finds that helpful."

"I know, Mom."

"You seemed to get your cereal down okay[10]," I said to Ethan once we were in the car. Ethan was running behind[11]—dawdling[12] deliberately[13], I figured[14], hoping I'd believe he really was sick—so I offered to drop him off[15] at school instead of making him walk.

"I guess[16]," he said.

"There something going on[17]?"

---

1. Tu vas voir

2. sourde aux vociférations de mon père

3. se distraire de

4. montrant de l'agacement pour la première fois

5. Faut qu'elle tourne la page

6. comme si c'était le genre de choses dont on se remet comme ça

7. Qu'on fait passer en allant se promener

8. a viré un peu barge

9. à lui dire qui tu es

10. Tes céréales sont bien passées, on dirait

11. était en retard

12. à traînailler

13. exprès

14. à mon avis

15. le déposer

16. Mouais

17. Y a un problème

He looked out his window at the passing street scene. "Nope."

"Everything okay with your teacher?"

"Yup[1]."

"Everything okay with your friends?"

"I don't have any friends," he said, still not looking my way[2].

I didn't have a ready answer for that. "I know it takes time, moving to a new school. But aren't there some of the kids still around[3] that you knew before we went to Boston?"

"Most of them are in a different class," Ethan said. Then, with a hint of accusation in his voice: "If I hadn't moved to Boston I'd probably still *be* in the same class with them." Now he looked at me. "Can we move back there?"

That was a surprise. He wanted to return to a situation where I was rarely home at night? Where he hardly ever saw his grandparents?

"No, I don't see that happening[4]."

Silence. A few seconds went by, then: "When are we going to have our own house?"

"I've gotta find a job first, pal[5]."

"You got totally screwed over[6]."

I shot him a look[7]. He caught my eye, probably wanting to see whether I was shocked.

"Don't use that kind of language[8]," I said. "You start talking like that around me, then you'll forget and do it front of Nana[9]." His grandmother and grandfather had always been Nana and Poppa to him.

"That's what Poppa said. He told Nana that you got screwed over. When they stopped making the newspaper just after you got there."

"Yeah, well, I guess I did. But I wasn't the only one. Everybody was fired[10]. The reporters, the

1. Ouais

2. toujours en m'évitant du regard

3. encore là

4. ça m'étonnerait

5. bonhomme

6. t'es fait complètement baiser

7. lui décochai un regard

8. Parle pas comme ça

9. Mamie

10. s'est fait virer

pressmen[1], everyone. But I'm looking for something[2]. Anything[3]."

If you looked up "shame"[4] in the dictionary, surely one definition should be: *having to discuss your employment situation with your nine-year-old.*

"I guess I didn't like being with Mrs. Tanaka every night," Ethan said. "But when I went to school in Boston, nobody ..."

"Nobody what?"

"Nothin'." He was silent another few seconds, and then said, "You know that box of old things Poppa has in the basement[5]?"

"The entire basement is full of old things." I almost added, *Especially when my dad is down there[6].*

"That box, a shoe box? That has stuff[7] in it that was his dad's? My great-grandfather? Like medals and ribbons and old watches[8] and stuff like that?"

"Okay, yeah, I know the box you mean. What about it?"

"You think Poppa checks that box every day?"

I pulled the car over to the curb[9] half a block down[10] from the school. "What on earth are you talking about?"

"Never mind," he said. "It doesn't matter."

Ethan dragged himself out[11] of the car without saying good-bye and headed in the direction of the school like a dead man walking[12].

Marla Pickens lived in a small one-story house[13] on Cherry Street. From what I knew, her parents—Aunt Agnes and her husband, Gill—owned the house and paid the mortgage on it[14], but Marla struggled[15] to pay the property[16] taxes and utilities[17] with what money she brought in[18]. Having spent a career in newspapers, and still having

1. journalistes
2. autre chose
3. N'importe quoi
4. À l'article « honte »
5. cave
6. y est
7. des trucs
8. montres
9. garai la voiture contre le trottoir
10. à une rue
11. sortit péniblement
12. très abattu
13. maison de plain-pied
14. dont ils payaient le crédit
15. avait du mal
16. foncières
17. l'eau et le gaz
18. le peu d'argent qu'elle gagnait

some regard for truth and accuracy[1], I didn't have much regard[2] for how Marla made her money these days. She'd been hired[3] by some Web firm to write bogus online reviews[4]. A renovation company seeking to rehabilitate and bolster[5] its Internet reputation would engage the services of Surf-Rep, which had hundreds of freelancers who went online to write fictitious laudatory reviews[6].

Marla had once shown me one she'd written for a roofing company[7] in Austin, Texas. "A tree hit our house and put a good-size hole in the roof. Marchelli Roofing came within the hour, fixed[8] the roof, and reshingled it[9], and all for a very reasonable cost. I cannot recommend them highly enough."

Marla had never been to Austin, did not know anyone at Marchelli Roofing, and had never, in her life, hired a contractor of any kind to do anything.

"Pretty good, huh[10]?" she'd said. "It's kind of like[11] writing a really, really short story."

I didn't have the energy to get into it[12] with her at the time.

I took the bypass[13] to get from one side of town to the other, passing under the shadow of the Promise Falls water tower[14], a ten-story structure that looked like an alien mother ship on stilts[15].

When I got to Marla's, I pulled into the driveway beside her faded red, rusting[16], mid-nineties Mustang. I opened the rear hatch[17] of my Mazda 3 and grabbed[18] two reusable grocery bags[19] Mom had filled with frozen dinners. I felt a little embarrassed doing it, wondering whether Marla would be insulted that her aunt seemed to believe she was too helpless to make her own meals[20], but what the hell[21]. If it made Mom happy …

Heading up the walk, I noticed weeds and grass coming up¹ between the cracks in the stone.

I mounted the three steps to the door, switched² all the bags to my left hand, and, as I rapped on it³ with my fist⁴, noticed a smudge⁵ on the door frame⁶.

The whole house needed painting or, failing that,⁷ a good power-washing⁸, so the smudge, which was at shoulder height and looked like a handprint⁹, wasn't that out of place¹⁰. But something about it caught my eye.

It looked like smeared blood¹¹. As if someone had swatted¹² the world's biggest mosquito¹³ there.

I touched it tentatively¹⁴ with my index finger and found it dry.

When Marla didn't answer the door after ten seconds, I knocked again. Five seconds after that, I tried turning the knob¹⁵.

Unlocked¹⁶.

I swung it wide enough¹⁷ to step inside¹⁸ and called out, "Marla? It's Cousin David!"

Nothing.

"Marla? Aunt Arlene wanted me to drop off a few things. Homemade chili, some other stuff. Where are you?"

I stepped into the L-shaped¹⁹ main room. The front half of the house was a cramped²⁰ living room with a weathered couch²¹, a couple of faded easy chairs²², a flat-screen TV, and a coffee²³ table supporting an open laptop²⁴ in sleep mode²⁵ that Marla had probably been using to say some nice things about a plumber in Poughkeepsie²⁶. The back part of the house, to the right, was the kitchen. Off to the left was a short hallway²⁷ with a couple of bedrooms and a bathroom.

1. que de l'herbe et des mauvaises herbes sortaient
2. j'ai passé
3. en frappant à la porte
4. du poing
5. tache
6. chambranle
7. au moins
8. grand lavage
9. trace de main
10. ne se voie pas autant
11. une tache de sang
12. écrasé
13. un moustique géant
14. avec méfiance
15. poignée
16. Pas fermé à clef
17. l'ouvris juste assez
18. pour entrer
19. en forme de L
20. plein à craquer
21. canapé décati
22. fauteuils
23. basse
24. [ordinateur] portable
25. en veille
26. [ville de l'État de New York]
27. couloir

31

1. poussette pliable

2. glissée

3. C'est quoi ça ?!!

4. grommelai-je

5. miaulement

6. gargouillis

7. si choquant que ça

8. posai

9. pour jeter un coup d'œil

10. en avait fait une Déchetterie

11. des meubles au rebut

12. moquette

13. démodés

14. avait visiblement l'étoffe d'une entasseuse

15. emmitouflé

16. des bruits de tétée

17. tétine

18. biberon

19. en tenant tendrement

20. fauteuil rembourré

21. couches

22. lingettes

As I closed the door behind me, I noticed a fold-up baby stroller[1] tucked[2] behind it, in the closed position.

"What the hell?[3]" I said under my breath[4].

I thought I heard something. Down the hall. A kind of... mewing[5]? A gurgling sound[6]?

A baby. It sounded like a baby. You might think, seeing a stroller by the door, that wouldn't be all that shocking[7].

But here, at this time, you'd be wrong.

"Marla?"

I set[8] the bags down on the floor and moved across the room. Started down the hall.

At the first door I stopped and peeked[9] inside. This was probably supposed to be a bedroom, but Marla had turned it into a landfill site[10]—disused furniture[11], empty cardboard boxes, rolls of carpet[12], old magazines, outdated[13] stereo components. Marla appeared to be an aspiring hoarder[14].

I moved on to the next door, which was closed. I turned the knob and pushed. "Marla, you in here? You okay?"

The sound I'd heard earlier became louder.

It was, in fact, a baby. Nine months to a year old, I guessed. Not sure whether it was a boy or girl, although it was wrapped[15] in a blue blanket.

What I'd heard were feeding noises[16]. The baby was sucking contentedly on a rubber nipple[17], its tiny fingers attempting to grip the plastic feeding bottle[18].

Marla held the bottle in one hand, cradling[19] the infant in her other arm. She was seated in a cushioned chair[20] in the corner of the bedroom. On the bed, bags of diapers[21], baby clothes, a container of wipes[22].

"Marla?"

She studied my face and whispered, "I heard you call out, but I couldn't come to the door. And I didn't want to shout. I think Matthew's nearly asleep."

I stepped tentatively into the room. "Matthew?"

Marla smiled, nodded. "Isn't he beautiful?"

Slowly, I said, "Yes. He is." A pause, then: "Who's Matthew, Marla?"

"What do you mean?" Marla said, cocking her head in puzzlement[1]. "Matthew is Matthew."

"What I mean … Who does Matthew belong to? Are you doing some babysitting for someone?"

Marla blinked[2]. "Matthew belongs to me, David. Matthew's my baby."

I cleared a spot[3] and sat on the edge[4] of the bed, close to[5] my cousin. "And when did Matthew arrive, Marla?"

"Ten months ago," she said without hesitation. "On the twelfth of July."

"But … I've been over here a few times in the last ten months, and this is the first chance I've had to[6] meet him. So I guess I'm a little puzzled."

"It's hard … to explain," Marla said. "An angel brought him to me."

"I need a little more than that[7]," I said softly.

"That's all I can say. It's like a miracle."

"Marla, your baby—"

"I don't want to talk about that," she whispered, turning her head away from me, studying the baby's face.

I pressed on gently[8], as if I were slowly driving onto a rickety bridge[9] I feared would give way beneath me[10]. "Marla, what happened to you … and your baby … was a tragedy. We all felt so terrible[11] for you."

1. penchant la tête d'un air perplexe

2. cligna des yeux

3. me fis un peu de place
4. au bord
5. près de

6. c'est la première fois que je

7. Il va falloir m'en dire un peu plus
8. J'ai insisté doucement
9. pont branlant
10. que je craignais de voir s'écrouler sous mon poids
11. On a tous eu énormément de peine

Ten months ago. It had been a sad time for everyone, but for Marla it had been devastating.

She lightly touched a finger to Matthew's button nose[1]. "You are so adorable," she said.

"Marla, I need you to tell me whose baby this really is." I hesitated. "And why there's blood on your front door."

1. petit nez rond

THREE

DETECTIVE[1] Barry Duckworth, on this, the twentieth anniversary of his joining the Promise Falls Police Department, was thinking he was facing the[2] greatest challenge of his career.

Would he be able to drive past the doughnut[3] shop on his way to the station[4] without hitting the drive-through[5] for a coffee and a chocolate frosted[6]?

After all, if there was ever a day where he felt entitled to a treat[7], this was it. Twenty years with the department, nearly fourteen of them as a detective. Wasn't that a cause for celebration?

Except this was only the second week of his latest attempt[8] to lose weight[9]. He'd tipped the scales at two hundred and eighty pounds[10] in the past month and decided maybe it was time to finally do something about it. Maureen, bless her[11], had stopped nagging him[12] about his size, figuring[13] the choice to cut back had to be his[14]. So, two weeks earlier, he decided the first step would be to forgo the[15] doughnut he inhaled every morning. According to the doughnut chain's Web site, his favorite pastry[16] was about three hundred calories. Jesus. So if you cut out[17] that doughnut, over five days you were eliminating fifteen hundred calories

1. L'inspecteur
2. se croyait confronté au
3. de beignets
4. poste
5. passer par le libre-service
6. beignet glacé au chocolat
7. en droit de se faire plaisir
8. tentative
9. perdre du poids
10. passé les 140 kg
11. la brave femme
12. de l'asticoter
13. considérant que
14. la décision de maigrir devait venir de lui
15. renoncer au
16. pâtisserie
17. on supprimait

from your diet. Over a year, that was seventy-two thousand calories.

It would be like going without food for something on the order of[1] three weeks.

It wasn't the only step[2] he was trying to take. He'd cut out dessert. Okay, that wasn't exactly right[3]. He'd cut out his *second* dessert. Whenever Maureen made a pie—especially if it was lemon meringue—he could never limit himself to one slice. He'd have one regular wedge[4] after dinner, then go back and tidy up the edge[5] of the last cut. That was usually just a sliver[6], and how many calories could there be in a sliver? So he would have a second sliver.

He'd been making a concerted[7] effort to give up the slivers.

He was a block away[8] from the doughnut place. *I won't pull in[9].*

But Duckworth still wanted a coffee. He could drive through and just order a beverage[10], couldn't he? Was there any harm in that[11]? He could drink it black, no sugar, no cream. The question would be, once he was in the line[12] for the coffee, would he be able to resist the—

His cell[13] phone rang.

This car was equipped with Bluetooth, so he didn't have to go reaching into his jacket pocket for the phone. All he had to do was touch a button on the dash[14]. Another bonus was that the name of the caller came up on the screen.

Randall Finley.

"Shit," Duckworth said under his breath.

The former mayor[15] of Promise Falls. Make that[16] the former *disgraced*[17] mayor of Promise Falls. A few years back, when he was making a run for a Senate seat[18], it came out that he had, on at least

Notes (margin):
1. à peu près
2. mesure
3. vrai
4. une part
5. se recouper un petit bout
6. fine tranche
7. résolu
8. à une rue
9. m'y arrêter
10. boisson
11. Quel mal y avait-il à ça
12. file d'attente
13. portable
14. tableau de bord
15. ancien maire
16. Ou plutôt
17. déchu
18. pendant sa campagne sénatoriale

one occasion, engaged the services of an under-age prostitute[1].

That didn't play so well with[2] the electorate.

Not only did he lose his bid[3] to move up the political food chain[4], he got turfed[5] as mayor in the next election. Didn't take it well, either. He made his concession speech[6] after downing[7] the better part of a bottle of Dewar's[8], and referred to those who had abandoned him as "a cabal of cocksuckers[9]." The local news stations couldn't broadcast[10] what he said, but the uncensored[11] YouTube version went viral[12].

Finley vanished from public view for a time, nursed his wounds[13], then started up a water-bottling company after discovering a spring[14] on a tract of land[15] he owned north of Promise Falls. While not quite as big as Evian—he had named it, with typical Randall Finley modesty, Finley Springs Water—it was one of the few around here that was doing any hiring[16], mainly because they did a strong export business. The town was in economic free fall of late[17]. The *Standard* had gone out of business[18], throwing about fifty people out of work[19]. The amusement park, Five Mountains, had gone bankrupt, the Ferris wheel[20] and roller coasters[21] standing like the relics of some strange, abandoned civilization.

Thackeray College[22], hit by a drop in enrollment[23], had laid off[24] younger teaching staff who'd yet to make tenure[25]. Kids finishing school were leaving town in droves[26] to find work elsewhere, and those who stayed behind could be found hanging around[27] local bars most nights of the week, getting into fights, spray-painting mailboxes[28], knocking over gravestones[29].

1. prostituée mineure
2. C'était mal passé auprès de
3. perdu son pari
4. monter dans la hiérarchie politique
5. s'était fait jeter
6. discours de défaite
7. s'être enfilé
8. [whisky]
9. enfoirés
10. diffuser
11. non censurée
12. avait fait un tabac sur internet
13. avait pansé ses plaies
14. source
15. terrain
16. qui embauchaient
17. ces derniers temps
18. coulé
19. au chômage
20. grande roue
21. les montagnes russes
22. L'université
23. baisse des inscriptions
24. licencié
25. n'étaient pas encore titulaires
26. en masse
27. traînaient dans
28. à taguer des boîtes aux lettres
29. des pierres tombales

The owners of the Constellation Drive-in[1], a Promise Falls–area landmark[2] for fifty years that had engaged in combat with the VCR[3], DVD player, and Netflix, were finally waving the white flag[4]. A few more weekends and a small part of local history would be toast[5]. Word had it that[6] the screen would be dropped[7], and the land turned into some kind of housing development[8] by developer Frank Mancini, although why anyone wanted to build more homes in a town where[9] everyone wanted to leave was beyond Duckworth's comprehension.

This was still the town he'd grown up in, but it was like a suit[10], once new[11], that had turned shiny and threadbare[12].

Ironically, it had gotten worse since that dickhead[13] Finley had stopped being mayor. For all his embarrassing shenanigans[14], he was a big booster for the town of forty thousand[15]—actually, more like[16] thirty-six thousand, according to the latest census[17]—and would have fought to keep failing industries afloat[18] like he was hanging on[19] to his last bottle of rye[20].

So when Duckworth saw who wanted to talk to him, he opted, with some regret, to take the call.

"Hello," he said.

"Barry!"

"Hey, Randy."

If he was going to turn into the doughnut place, he'd have to hit his signal[21] and crank the wheel[22] now, and he knew if he entered the drive-through he wouldn't be able to stop himself from ordering a soft, doughy circle of heaven[23]. But Finley would hear his exchange at the speaker[24], and even though the former mayor did not know he'd embarked[25] on a diet, Barry didn't want anyone gaining insight into[26] his dietary indiscretions[27].

So he kept on driving.

"Where are you?" Finley asked. "You in your car?"

"I'm on my way in."

"Swing by[1] Clampett Park. South end. By the path."

"Why would I want to do that?"

"There's something here you should see."

"Randy, maybe, if you were still mayor, I'd be at your beck and call[2], and I wouldn't mind you having[3] my private cell phone number, but you're *not* the mayor. You haven't been for some time. So if there's something going on, just call it in[4] the way everybody else does."

"They're probably going to send you out here anyway," Finley said. "Saves you[5] going into the station and then back out again."

Barry Duckworth sighed. "Fine."

"I'll meet you at the park entrance. I got my dog with me. That's how I came across it[6]. I was taking her for a walk."

"It?"

"Just get over here."

The trip took Duckworth to the other side of town, where he knew Finley and his long-suffering wife[7], Jane, still lived. Randall Finley was standing with his dog, a small gray-haired schnauzer. The dog was straining at the leash[8], wanting to head back into the park, which bordered a forested area and beyond that, to the north, Thackeray College.

"Took you long enough[9]," Finley said as Barry got out of his unmarked cruiser[10].

"I don't work for you," he said.

"Sure you do. I'm a taxpayer[11]." Finley was dressed in a pair of comfort-fit jeans, running

1. Faites un saut à

2. je vous obéirais au doigt et à l'œil

3. ça ne me gênerait pas que vous ayez

4. faites un signalement

5. Ça vous évite

6. suis tombé dessus

7. son épouse d'une patience à toute épreuve

8. tirait sur sa laisse

9. Vous en avez mis un temps

10. voiture de patrouille banalisée

11. contribuable

shoes, and a light jacket that he'd zipped up to his neck. It was a cool[1] May morning. The fourth, to be exact, and the ground was still blanketed with[2] dead leaves from the previous fall[3] that had, up until six weeks ago, been hidden by snow.

"What did you find?"

"It's this way[4]. I could just let Bipsie off the lead and we could follow her."

"No," Duckworth said. "Whatever you've found I don't want Bipsie messing with[5]."

"Oh, yeah, of course," Finley said. "So, how ya been[6]?"

"Fine."

When Duckworth did not ask Finley how he was, the ex-mayor waited a beat[7], and said, "I'm having a good year. We're expanding at the plant[8]. Hiring another couple of people." He smiled. "You might have heard about one of them."

"I haven't. What are you talking about?"

"Never mind," Finley said.

They followed a path[9] that led along the edge of the woods[10], which was separated from the park by a black chain-link fence[11] about four feet high[12].

"You lost weight?" Finley asked. "You're looking good. Tell me your secret, 'cause I could stand to lose a few pounds myself." He patted his stomach with his free hand.

Duckworth had lost all of two pounds[13] in the last two weeks, and was smart enough to know it didn't show[14].

"What'd you find, Randy?"

"You just have to see it, is all[15]. It must have happened overnight[16], because I walk along here with Bipsie a couple times a day[17]—early in the morning, and before I go to bed. Now, it was getting dark when I came by last night, so it might

---

1. frais
2. couvert de
3. automne dernier
4. par ici
5. que Bipsie l'abîme
6. comment va
7. marqua une pause
8. usine
9. chemin
10. lisière du bois
11. clôture à mailles métalliques
12. de 1,20 m de haut
13. royalement perdu 1 kg
14. que ça ne se voyait pas
15. c'est tout
16. durant la nuit
17. deux fois par jour

have been there then and I didn't notice, but I don't think so. I might not have even noticed it this morning, but the dog made a beeline for[1] the fence when she caught a whiff of it[2]."

Duckworth decided not to bother[3] asking Finley anymore what it was he wanted to show him, but he steeled himself[4]. He'd seen a few dead people over the years, and figured he'd see plenty more before he retired[5]. Now that he had twenty years in[6], he was better than halfway there[7]. But you never really got used to it. Not in Promise Falls, anyway. Duckworth had investigated several homicides over the years, most of them straightforward domestics or bar fights[8], but also a few that had garnered[9] national attention.

None had been what you'd call a good time[10].

"Just up here," Finley said. Bipsie started to bark. "Stop it! Settle down[11], you little fucker!"

Bipsie settled down.

"Right there, on the fence," Finley said, pointing.

Duckworth stopped and studied the scene before him.

"Yeah, pretty weird[12], huh? It's a goddamn massacre. You ever seen anything like this before?"

Duckworth said nothing, but the answer was no, he had not.

Randall Finley kept on talking. "If it had been just one body, or even two, sure, I wouldn't have called. But look how many there are. I counted. There's twenty-three of them, Barry. What kind of sick fuck[13] does something like that?"

Barry counted them himself. Randy was right. One short of two dozen[14].

Twenty-three dead squirrels[15]. Good-size ones, too. Eleven gray ones, twelve black. Each one with a length of white string, the kind used to secure

1. ma chienne s'est jetée sur

2. a repéré l'odeur

3. de ne pas prendre la peine

4. s'attendait au pire

5. avant la retraite

6. d'expérience

7. il en avait fait une bonne moitié

8. des cas classiques de violence domestique ou de baston

9. attiré

10. spécialement agréable

11. Couchée

12. super bizarre

13. cinglé

14. Deux douzaines, à un près

15. écureuils

1. fermer des colis

2. barre

3. sur 3 m

4. une cordelette de 30 cm

parcels[1], knotted tightly around its neck, and hung from the horizontal metal pole[2] that ran across the top of the fence.

The animals were spaced out along a ten-foot stretch[3], each of them hanging on about a foot of string[4].

"I got no love for them," Finley said. "Tree rats, I call them, although I guess they don't do that much harm. But there's gotta be a law against that, right? Even though they're just squirrels?"

FOUR

David

"**MARLA**, I'm serious. You need to talk to me here," I said.

"I should put him down for a nap[1]," she said, cradling[2] the baby in her arms, lightly touching[3] the nipple[4] of the baby bottle to his lips. "I think he's had all he's going to have for now."

She set the bottle on the bedside table. The baby, eyes closed, made soft gurgling noises of contentment[5].

"He wasn't like this at first," Marla said. "He cried a lot yesterday. Making strange and all[6]."

I was going to ask why a baby who she would have me believe had been with her[7] for months would make strange, but let it pass[8].

She continued. "I sat with him all night and we've made a strong bond[9], the two of us." She gave a weak laugh. "I must look a fright[10]. I haven't had a shower this morning or put on my makeup or anything. Last night I put him down for a sleep once he stopped crying, and ran out to the store[11] to get a few things. I know I shouldn't have left him alone, but there was no one I felt I could call,

1. sieste
2. berçant
3. en posant légèrement
4. tétine
5. des gargouillis d'aise
6. Il était tout bizarre
7. soi-disant avec elle
8. je ne relevai pas
9. tissé des liens très forts
10. avoir une mine à faire peur
11. supérette

43

1. pas encore

2. avais vraiment des choses à acheter

3. incohérences

4. [talk-show]

5. de ne pas la voir comme ça

6. me décocha un regard dur

7. comme si elle répugnait à l'admettre

8. blessée

9. que je n'ai pas la mémoire des visages

10. la revois dans ma tête

not just yet[1], and I was desperate for supplies[2]. The angel only brought a few things."

"Who else knows about Matthew?" I asked. "Does Aunt Agnes—does your mother know?"

"I haven't told her the good news yet. It's all happened pretty quickly."

The inconsistencies[3] persisted. "How quickly?"

Marla, her eyes still on the baby, said, "Okay, I haven't exactly had Matthew for ten full months. Yesterday, late in the afternoon, around the time *Dr. Phil*[4] comes on, I was doing some reviews for an air-conditioning company in Illinois when the doorbell rang."

"Who was it?"

A weak smile. "I told you. The angel."

"Tell me about this angel."

"Well, okay, she wasn't a real angel, but it's hard not to think of her that way[5]."

"It was a woman."

"That's right."

"The mother?"

Marla looked at me sharply[6]. "I'm the mother now."

"Okay," I said. "But up until the moment she gave you Matthew, *she* was the mother?"

Hesitantly, as though unwilling to make the admission[7], she said, "Maybe."

"What did she look like? How did she seem? Was she injured[8]? Did you see any blood? Was there blood on her hand?"

Marla shook her head slowly. "You know I'm not good with faces[9], David. But she was very nice, this woman. All dressed in white. That's why, when I picture her[10], all I see is an angel."

44

"Did she say who she was? Did she give you her name? Did she leave any way for you to contact her?"

"No."

"You didn't ask? You didn't think it was strange? A woman just coming to your door and handing you a baby?"

"She was in a hurry," she said. "She said she had to go." Her voice drifted off[1]. She put Matthew in the middle of the bed and surrounded him with pillows[2], creating a kind of berm[3] around him.

"Until I get a crib[4], I have to do this. I don't want him rolling off the bed and hitting the floor. Would you be able to help me with that? Getting a crib? Is there an IKEA in Albany? Or maybe Walmart[5] would have one. They're closer. I don't think I could fit a crib, even one that wasn't put together[6], into the Mustang, and I don't think I'd be very good at putting it together. I'm pretty clueless[7] about that sort of thing. I don't even have a screwdriver[8]. Well, I might in one of the kitchen drawers, but I'm not sure. Doesn't IKEA put a little thingy[9] in with the pieces? So you can build it even if you don't have a bunch of tools[10]? I don't want to get a used[11] crib at a secondhand shop[12] or an antique store[13], because all kinds of safety improvements have been made on them. I saw this thing on TV once where you could make the side of the crib go up and down, and this one dropped by accident on the baby's neck." She trembled. "I don't want anything like that."

"Of course not."

"So is that something you could help me with? Getting a crib?"

"I imagine so. But there are a few things we need to sort out[14] first."

1. s'évanouit
2. des oreillers
3. muret
4. berceau
5. [chaîne d'hypermarchés]
6. en pièces détachées
7. nul
8. tournevis
9. bidule
10. même sans être équipé
11. d'occasion
12. dépôt-vente
13. brocante
14. régler

Marla wasn't paying much attention to me. I wondered whether she was on any kind of medication[1], whether that would explain her apparent detachment from reality. If she'd been seeing a psychiatrist since losing her baby, and been prescribed anything to deal with depression or anxiety, I wasn't aware of it[2]. There was no reason why I would be. And I wasn't about to start rooting about[3] in her medicine cabinet[4], because I wouldn't know what to make of[5] what I might find.

Maybe she wasn't on anything[6], and this was just the way she'd been since giving birth to a lifeless child[7]. Dad had more or less nailed it[8], in his own tactless way[9], when he said she'd gone "a bit crackers." I'd only heard bits and pieces[10] of the story. How Marla's mother, Agnes, who way back in her twenties[11] had been a midwife[12] before becoming a nurse[13], had been there at her side, along with the family physician[14], a doctor named Sturgess, if I remembered right. Mom had talked about their sense of horror when they realized something was wrong. How Marla had been able to hold the child, briefly, before it had to be taken away.

How it had been a girl.

"Such a sad, sad thing," Mom said whenever her niece crossed her mind[15]. "It did something to her. Something just snapped[16]; that's what I think happened. And where was the father? Where was he? Did he help her through this at all[17]? No, not one bit."

The father was a Thackeray College student. Seven or eight years younger than Marla. I didn't know much else about him. Not that any of that mattered now[18].

Did the police have any reports of a missing baby[19]? If the paper[20] were still in existence, if I still carried around press credentials[1], I'd just call headquarters[2], ask if they'd heard anything. But for a private[3] citizen it was a little trickier[4]. Did I want to alert the authorities to anything before I'd found out what, exactly, was going on? It was possible Marla really was babysitting for someone, but had allowed some kind of fantasy to envelop her[5].

I mean, an angel coming to the door?

"Marla, did you hear me? There are things to sort out."

"What things?" Marla said.

I decided to play along[6], as if this were a normal situation we were dealing with here. "Well, I'm sure you want everything to be legal and aboveboard[7]. So if Matthew is going to be yours, there will be some papers to sign. Legal matters to resolve."

"I don't think that's necessary," she said. "When he gets older, like when he goes to school, or even older than that, and has to get a driver's license or something, I'll just tell them I lost his birth certificate, that I can't find it. They'll just have to deal with that[8]."

"It doesn't work that way, Marla. The town keeps records[9], too."

She looked unfazed[10]. "They'll just have to accept that he's mine. You're making it into a much bigger deal than it is[11]. Society's too wrapped up[12] in documenting every little thing."

"But we still need to know who bore[13] this child," I persisted. "Like, medical history[14]. You need to know about his real mother and father, what diseases or conditions[15] they might have."

"Why don't you want me to be happy, David? Don't you think, after all I've been through[16], I deserve some happiness?"

1. ma carte de presse
2. le commissariat
3. simple
4. plus compliqué
5. s'était abandonnée à une sorte de fantasme
6. jouer le jeu
7. régulier
8. devront bien faire avec
9. des archives
10. resta imperturbable
11. Tu te fais une montagne d'un rien
12. a la manie
13. a donné naissance à
14. Par exemple, ses antécédents médicaux
15. quelles maladies
16. tout ce que j'ai subi

I didn't know what to say, but it turned out I didn't have to come up with something[1]. Marla said, "I'm going to freshen up. Now that you're here, I can have a shower, put on some clean clothes. I was thinking Matthew and I would go out and get a few things."

"The stroller, behind the door," I said. "Did you buy that yesterday?"

"No, the angel brought that," she said. "Did your mom send over some more goodies[2] for me?"

"She did," I said. "I'll put everything into the freezer for you."

"Thanks," she said. "I won't be long." She slipped into the bathroom and closed the door.

I took a quick look at the child, saw that he was sleeping peacefully and unlikely[3] to roll out of his pillow prison. I put the frozen food Mom had sent with me into Marla's freezer—I am nothing if not practical[4]—and then went to the living room to check out the stroller. It was in the folded position, making it easy to drop into a car trunk[5], or stow away in a closet[6].

On the right handle[7] were more smudges[8] that looked like the one I had seen on the doorjamb[9].

I opened up the contraption[10], tapped a small lever[11] with my foot to make sure it was locked into position. The stroller had seen some use[12]. The once-black rubber wheels were rough with wear[13]. Stale[14], dry Cheerios were stuck in the crevices[15] of the seat pad[16]. A small zippered[17] pouch[18] was attached to the back. I opened it, reached inside. I found three rattles[19], a small wooden car with thick wooden wheels, a flyer[20] for a store that sold baby supplies, a half-full package of predampened wipes[21], and some tissues[22].

Something about the flyer caught my eye. A few words printed on one side, on a label[1].

It was an address. This was not a general piece of junk mail[2], but a targeted[3] flyer for Baby Makes Three, a Promise Falls clothing store for infants[4]. And even more important, the label had a name attached to the address.

Rosemary Gaynor. She lived at 375 Breckonwood Drive. I knew the street. It was in an upscale neighborhood[5]—certainly nicer than Marla's—a couple of miles[6] from here.

I got out my cell, tapped on the app that would allow me to find a number[7] for the Gaynor household. But once I had it under my thumb, I considered[8] whether making the call was the smartest thing to do[9].

Maybe it made more sense to go over there[10].

Right fucking now[11].

I heard water running in the bathroom. The shower. The phone still in my hand, I called home.

It picked up on the first ring. "Yeah?"

"Dad, I need to talk to Mom."

"What's up?"

"Just put her on[12]."

A fumbling sound, a muted[13] "He wants to talk to you." And then: "What is it, David?"

"Something's happened here at Marla's."

"Did you give her the chili?"

"No. I mean, I brought it. But … Mom, there's a baby here."

"What?"

"She's got a baby. She says it's hers. She says some woman came to the door and just gave it to her. But the story, it's just not holding water[14]. Mom, I'm starting to wonder[15] … I hate to say this, but I'm wondering—God, this sounds totally crazy

1. étiquette

2. pub
3. ciblé
4. tout-petits

5. quartier chic
6. à env. 3,2 km

7. numéro de téléphone
8. me demandai
9. si les appeler était la meilleure chose à faire
10. me rendre sur place
11. Sans perdre une minute

12. Passe-la-moi
13. frottement, une voix étouffée :

14. ça ne tient pas la route
15. à me demander

1. a volé

—but I'm wondering if she snatched[1] this kid from someone."

"Oh, no," Mom said. "Not again."

FIVE

BARRY Duckworth wanted officers[1] dispatched[2] to the neighborhoods surrounding the park to canvass[3] residents in case anyone had noticed anything suspicious the night before. A person carrying a heavy sack, maybe, hanging[4] around the fence long enough to string up[5] nearly two dozen squirrels.

The first uniformed cop on the scene, a six-footer[6] by the name of[7] Angus Carlson, saw the assignment[8] as an opportunity to perfect his stand-up act[9].

"This case could be a tough nut to crack[10]," Carlson said to Duckworth. "But I'm feeling bright eyed and bushy tailed[11] and ready to get at it[12]. But if we don't find a witness[13] soon I'm gonna go squirrelly.[14]"

Duckworth had encountered Carlson at several crime scenes in recent months. He seemed to think he'd been assigned the role of Lennie Briscoe, the *Law & Order*[15] detective played by Jerry Orbach, who always had some clever quip[16] to make before the opening credits[17]. From the few conversations Duckworth had had with the man, he knew that he'd come here four years ago after working as a cop[18] in some Cleveland suburb[19].

1. que des agents
2. soient envoyés
3. interroger
4. traînant
5. enfiler
6. type de 1,80 m,
7. du nom de
8. mission
9. numéro de comique
10. risque de nous casser les noix
11. plein de panache
12. à m'y attaquer
13. un témoin
14. j'ai peur de m'y casser les dents !
15. de *New York, Police judiciaire*
16. trait d'esprit
17. générique de début
18. flic
19. banlieue

"Spare me[1]," Duckworth told him.

He put in a call to the town's animal welfare[2] department, spoke to a woman named Stacey, brought her up to speed[3]. "I got a feeling this may fall more into your bailiwick[4], but I've got some people working the scene right now. The type of person who does this, it'd be kind of nice to know who it is before people's cats and dogs start hanging from the streetlights[5]."

Duckworth walked back in the direction of his car. Ex-mayor Randall Finley had hung in[6] to watch other police[7] arrive, take pictures, search the area, but when he saw Duckworth leaving, he followed him, dragging Bipsie along on her leash.

"You want to know what I think?" Finley asked.

"You bet I do[8], Randy."

"I bet it's some kind of sicko cult[9]. This is probably an initiation ritual."

"Hard to say."

"You'll keep me posted[10], now[11]."

Duckworth shot Finley a look as he opened the door to his unmarked cruiser[12]. Did the ex-politician really think he had some kind of authority?

"If I have any questions I'll be sure to get in touch[13]," he said, then got behind the wheel[14] and closed the door.

Finley evidently wasn't finished[15]. He'd made no move to step back[16] from the car. Barry powered down the window. "Still got something on your mind[17]?"

"Something I wanted you to know. I'm not telling a lot of people about this, not yet, but I think you're somebody who should be in the loop[18]."

"What?"

"I'm gonna run again[19]," Finley said, then paused for effect. When neither shock nor delight

52

crossed Barry's face, he continued. "Promise Falls needs me. Things have gone to shit since I was in charge[1]. Tell me I'm wrong[2]."

"I don't follow politics," Duckworth said.

Finley grinned[3]. "Don't give me that[4]. Politics has everything to do with how you do your job. Elected officials fuck up[5], let jobs disappear; people get desperate, they drink more, get into more brawls[6], break into[7] more homes. You telling me that's not true?"

"Randy, really, I have to go."

"Yeah, yeah, I know; you're on the trail[8] of a squirrel serial killer. All I'm saying is, when I get back in—"

"If."

"*When* I get back in, I'll be looking to make some changes, and that could include the chief of police. You strike me as the[9] kind of man who'd be good for a job like that."

"I'm happy doing what I'm doing. And if you don't mind my pointing this out[10], the voters may not have forgotten your habit of engaging the services of fifteen-year-old prostitutes."

Finley's eyes narrowed[11]. "First of all, it was just *one* underage[12] prostitute, and she'd told me she was nineteen."

"Oh, okay. Sure, run[13]. There's your slogan right there. 'She told me she was nineteen. Vote Finley.' "

"I got fucked over[14], Barry, and you know it. I was a good mayor. I got shit done[15]; I worked to save jobs. This personal stuff was irrelevant[16], and the media made a much bigger deal of it than it deserved[17]. I'm thinking, now that that Plimpton bitch[18] has shut down the *Standard* and I don't have to worry about a lot of negative press, I got a real shot[19]. I can control the message. It's not

1. depuis que je ne suis plus aux commandes

2. Osez me contredire

3. sourit largement

4. Me prenez pas pour un con

5. Les élus merdent

6. se bastonnent plus

7. cambriolent

8. sur la piste

9. Vous me faites l'effet du

10. si je peux me permettre une remarque

11. Le regard de Finley se fit perçant

12. mineure

13. soyez candidat

14. me suis fait baiser

15. étais vachement efficace

16. n'avait pas d'importance

17. en ont fait tout un foin

18. cette salope de Plimpton

19. j'ai toutes mes chances

like[1] the Albany media gives a shit[2] what goes on around here, unless I get caught fucking a goat[3] or something. What I'm trying to tell you is, your being something of an insider for me in the department[4] is something I would look upon with gratitude, and someday I'd be looking to repay the favor[5]."

"You think being kept up to speed[6] on a squirrel torturer is your key to victory?" Barry asked.

Finley shook his head. "Course not. But I'm just saying, generally, anything that's going on you think might be in my interest to know about, you give me a call. That's all. That's not asking a lot. It's good to have an ear on the inside. Like, say Her Royal Highness[7] Amanda Croydon, I dunno[8], gets pulled over[9] for drunk driving[10]."

"I don't think our current mayor[11] has the same issues as you do, Randy."

"Okay, not drunk driving, but whatever. She gets a city road crew[12] to shovel her driveway[13]." He grinned. "That almost sounds dirty[14]. Anyway, you hear anything about her taking advantage of the taxpayer[15] or cutting legal corners[16], you could pass it along[17]. Same goes for the chief. There's got to be stuff on her[18]. Can you believe we got a woman mayor and a woman police chief? They should rename this town Beaver Falls[19]."

"I have to go, Randy."

"Because, let's face it"—and the former mayor leaned in closer[20]—"we've all got things we like to keep hidden. Some of us—I mean, I'm the perfect example—have nothing left to hide[21]. It's already out there. But there are others who'd be happy for the world not to know all their business."

Duckworth's eyes narrowed. "I'm not sure what you're getting at[22]."

Finley smiled slyly[1]. "Who said I'm getting at anything?"

"Jesus, Randy, are you ... Tell me this isn't some lame[2] attempt to threaten me."

Finley moved back as though slapped in the face, but kept smiling. "How could you say such a thing? I'm just making conversation. As far as I know, you have an impeccable record with[3] the Promise Falls police. Ask anyone. It's an unblemished[4] career." He leaned back in again. "You're a good cop, and a good family man."

He put the emphasis on *family*.

"I'll see you later, Randy," Duckworth said. He raised the window and put the car in drive[5].

Finley offered up a friendly wave good-bye, but Duckworth wasn't looking.

Duckworth headed for[6] Thackeray College.

The campus was close enough to the[7] park that[8] students often walked through it, jogged through it, did drugs in it[9], made out in it[10]. A Thackeray kid could have killed those squirrels. Or if not, a Thackeray kid might have seen it happen.

Maybe this was a waste of his time and energy. A couple dozen squirrels would get run over[11] on the streets of Promise Falls before the day was over, and the police wouldn't exactly be going around charging[12] drivers with leaving the scene of[13] an accident.

Duckworth fully expected that when he got back to the station, there'd be a pack of nuts[14] on his desk. If not from Angus Carlson, then from someone else.

After all, it was legal to hunt squirrels much of the year[15] in New York State. A couple years ago, in fact, over in Holley, the local fire department[16]

---

1. d'un air finaud

2. foireuse

3. états de service à
4. sans tache

5. enclencha la première [boîte automatique]

6. prit la direction de
7. assez proche du
8. pour que
9. s'y droguent
10. s'y câlinent

11. se feraient écraser

12. à dresser des PV aux
13. pour avoir pris la fuite après
14. sachet de noisettes

15. une bonne partie de l'année
16. les pompiers du coin

had a fund-raiser[1] that awarded a prize[2] to whoever shot the five heaviest squirrels. Finding the killer of a couple dozen of the critters[3] was not exactly something the Promise Falls police force was going to devote[4] all its resources to.

What troubled Duckworth was, What kind of person found entertainment value in[5] killing twenty-three small animals and stringing them up for all to see[6]?

What inspired him—okay, maybe a *her*, but most likely a *him*—to do such a thing?

And what would this person's next stunt[7] be? The literature[8] was full of convicted[9] killers who got their start[10] snuffing the life out[11] of house pets[12] and other creatures[13].

He steered the car off the main road and through the gates into the grounds of Thackeray College. Handsome, stately[14] redbrick buildings with imposing white columns, many of them dating back more than a century. There were some architectural exceptions. The chemistry[15] building was five years old, and the athletic center was constructed ten years ago.

As he drove along the road to the administrative buildings, past Thackeray Pond, the college's own miniature lake that was about a quarter mile wide[16], Duckworth noticed a work crew[17] installing a six-foot post[18] with a red button, and a small sign attached. He was driving by[19] too quickly to make out[20] what it said, but it reminded him of an old-fashioned[21] fire alarm call box[22].

He parked in a visitor spot[23] and once inside the building consulted a directory[24] to locate the office of the head[25] of campus security.

Heading into the building, he thought about what Randall Finley had said, and what he might have been intimating[1].

Did Randy think he had something on him[2]? Was he trying to blackmail[3] the detective into giving him dirt on[4] what was going on inside the department so he'd have something to campaign on[5] if he really did take another run at the mayor's job?

If that was his plan, he could goddamn well forget it, Duckworth thought. Because the man had no leverage[6]. Just like the former mayor said, Duckworth had had an exemplary career. He'd kept his nose clean[7].

Pretty much[8], anyway.

Sure, he'd cut the odd corner[9] here and there over the years. There wasn't a cop in the department who hadn't. But he'd never taken a bribe[10]. Never planted evidence[11], or held on to[12] some, like cash from a drug deal, for himself[13].

Maybe years ago, before he met Maureen, he'd let a couple of pretty girls off[14] with a warning when they[15]'d been driving over the limit.

Maybe he'd even gotten a phone number or two that way.

But he chalked that up[16] to youth and inexperience. He'd never pull a stunt like that[17] now. Surely Finley hadn't gone back twenty years[18] to get some dirt on—

"Can I help you?"

Barry found himself at a desk just outside the campus security offices. A young man with several studs[19] in one ear who looked as though he might still be a student had just offered to be of assistance.

"I want to see your boss," Duckworth said.

"Do you have an appointment[20]?"

1. avait pu sous-entendre

2. des infos sur lui

3. faire chanter

4. pour qu'il rapporte

5. lui donnant ainsi de quoi alimenter sa campagne

6. n'avait pas de moyen de pression

7. avait les mains propres

8. À peu près

9. filouté à l'occasion

10. accepté de pot-de-vin

11. fabriqué des preuves

12. ni caché

13. pour son propre compte

14. laissé de jolies filles s'en tirer,

15. leur signalant juste qu'elles

16. attribuait ça

17. Pas question de jouer un jeu pareil

18. n'était pas remonté 20 ans en arrière

19. clous

20. rendez-vous

1. montra rapidement sa carte

2. avait la quarantaine bien mûre
3. pas loin de 1,80 m
4. 85 kg
5. mâchoire carrée
6. Svelte
7. de beaux biscotos
8. Dus aux haltères

9. opina d'un air sombre

10. La rumeur court
11. garder le secret
12. indéfiniment
13. les choses bien en main
14. J'ai une main de fer
15. mon équipe
16. inquiétude
17. mesures

Duckworth flashed his ID[1], and within seconds he was sitting across the desk from Clive Duncomb, Thackeray College chief of security.

He was in his mid to late forties[2]. Just shy of six feet[3], about a hundred and seventy pounds[4], a hard, square jaw[5] and thick, dark eyebrows that matched his hair. Trim[6], and wearing a shirt that looked one size too small, as if he knew it would draw attention to his biceps. The guy had a decent set of guns[7]. Weights[8], Duckworth guessed. Probably didn't have a doughnut every morning on the way to work, either.

"Nice to meet you," Duncomb said. "What'd you say your name was again?"

Duckworth told him.

"And you're a detective?"

"Yes."

"What can I do for you?"

"I need to talk to you about an incident last night."

Duncomb nodded grimly[9] and sighed. He leaned back in his chair, arms extended, palms flat on his desk.

"I can't say I'm surprised to see you. I've kind of been expecting someone from the Promise Falls police. Word gets around[10]; I understand that. Hard to keep a lid[11] on these things forever[12]. But I want you to know, I've got matters well in hand[13] here. I run a tight ship[14], and I've got my people[15] working on it. But I can understand your concern[16], and don't mind bringing you up to speed on the steps[17] we've been taking."

Duckworth wondered what sorts of steps the college might be taking to protect the squirrel community, and was more than a little surprised to learn this was already a high priority. "Go on," he said.

"Maybe you noticed, driving in, some of the emergency posts[1] they're installing on the grounds."

"Emergency posts?"

"All you do is hit[2] the button; that sends a message to the security team, tells them where you are, and we dispatch[3] someone right away[4]. Kind of like a fire alarm, or one of those panic strips[5] they put in the subway cars[6] in the big cities."

"And you're doing this why?"

Duncomb took his hands off the table and leaned forward in the chair. He eyed Duckworth suspiciously.

"You telling me you're not here about the attempted rapes[7] we've had? We got some nutcase[8] running around[9], got every woman on campus scared half to death[10]."

1. panneaux d'urgence

2. appuyer sur

3. on envoie

4. sur-le-champ

5. sonnettes d'alarme

6. wagons de métro

7. tentatives de viol

8. un taré

9. en liberté

10. à moitié mortes de peur

SIX

David

"**WHAT** are you talking about, Mom?" I said. "What do you mean, 'not again'? Marla's grabbed a baby before[1]?"

"While you were in Boston," she said. "There was an incident."

"What kind of incident?"

"At the hospital. She snuck[2] into the maternity ward[3] and tried to walk out with someone else's baby."

"Oh, my God. You're not serious."

"It was just awful. Marla almost made it to the parking lot[4] before someone spotted her[5], stopped her. Probably someone recognized her, given that[6] she's in the hospital pretty often, not just to see your aunt, but I think she goes there to see a psychologist or psychiatrist or something. I think his name is … I just can't remember it. It was right on the tip of my tongue[7]. Oh, that's so annoying[8]."

"Don't worry about it. Just tell me what happened."

"Well, the police got called, but Agnes and Gill explained what had happened, that Marla'd lost a

1. a déjà enlevé un bébé

2. est entrée en douce
3. service maternité

4. était presque arrivée au parking
5. ne la voie
6. vu qu'

7. Je l'avais sur le bout de la langue
8. énervant

60

child, that she was, you know, mentally unstable, that she shouldn't be held accountable for[1] her actions because of the state she was in, that she'd been getting help[2]."

"I never heard a word about this."

"Agnes didn't want anyone to know. You know what she's like. And, of course, she was in a position[3] to keep it quiet for the most part, but things do get out[4]. People at the hospital talked. Even so, your father and I, we never told a soul[5], except for now I'm telling you. But something like that, you can't stop the rumor mill[6]. Agnes, of course, made sure the hospital didn't take any action against her, and the parents were persuaded not to press charges[7]. Agnes made sure[8] the hospital picked up[9] all the costs that their insurance didn't cover. Thank God Marla didn't hurt the baby. It was only two days old, David. We've been so worried about her, wondering whether she's pulling herself together[10]. I didn't think she'd do anything like this again. This'll just kill Agnes. She'll go off the deep end[11] for sure. You know how concerned[12] she is about what people think."

"I don't think she took this baby from the hospital. It's not a newborn. It's probably nine, ten months old. You need to call Agnes, get her over here[13]."

"Some mother somewhere must be going out of her mind[14] right now, wondering where her baby is. Hang on[15]." She raised her voice. "Don!"

"Huh?" Sounding like he was in another room.

"Was there anything on there about a missing[16] baby?"

"What?"

"Didn't you have the radio on? Did they say if the police were looking for a missing baby?"

1. tenue responsable de

2. se faisait soigner

3. en mesure

4. finissent par se savoir

5. on ne l'a dit à personne

6. on n'arrête pas la rumeur

7. de ne pas porter plainte

8. a fait en sorte que

9. prenne en charge

10. va bien

11. va piquer une crise,

12. inquiète

13. dis-lui de rappliquer

14. folle d'inquiétude

15. Ne quitte pas

16. porté disparu

"Jesus Christ, she hasn't done it again, has she?"

"Was there or not?"

"I didn't hear anything."

To me, Mom said, "Your father says he didn't—"

"I heard. I think I may know where the baby came from. I'm going to go over there."

"You know whose baby it is?"

"You know anyone named Rosemary Gaynor?"

1. ça ne me dit rien

"No, it doesn't ring a bell[1]."

"It might to Agnes. She might know Marla's friends."

2. cloîtrée chez elle

3. faire des courses

"I don't think Marla has any friends. She just stays cooped up in her house[2] most of the time except to go out and run errands[3]."

"Call Agnes. Tell her to get over here as fast as possible. I want to go over to the Gaynors' house, but I feel a little uneasy about[4] leaving Marla alone with the baby." I paused. "Maybe I should just call the police."

4. ne tiens pas tellement à

5. prudemment

6. régler ça

7. discrètement

8. Si ça se trouve

"Oh," Mom said cautiously[5], "I wouldn't do that. I know Agnes will want to try to sort this out[6] quietly[7]. And you don't really know what's going on. For all you know[8], Marla's just babysitting for someone, with their permission."

"I asked Marla that. She says no."

"But it's possible! Maybe she's babysitting, and while she's looking after this child, she's imagining that he's her own baby. When you think of what she's been through[9]—"

9. ce qu'elle a vécu

10. Je te tiendrai au courant

The shower stopped. "I gotta go, Mom. I'll keep you posted[10]. Get Agnes over here."

I slipped the phone back into my jacket.

"David?" Marla called from behind the closed door. I moved to within a foot of it[11].

11. m'approchai à 30 cm

"Yeah?"

"Did you say something?"

62

"No."

"Were you on the phone?"

"I had to take a call."

"You weren't talking to my mom, were you?"

"No," I said honestly.

"Because I do *not* want her coming over. She's just going to make a big deal about this."

I didn't want to lie[1], or even mislead her[2]. "I called my mom, but I told her to call Agnes. You could use[3] your mom's help. She knows all about babies. She was a midwife[4] before she went into nursing[5], right?"

The second I'd said it, I regretted it, thinking it might remind Marla of the day she lost her child. Agnes had been present not only because she was Marla's mother, but because she had expertise in delivering a child[6].

Not that it did any good.[7]

"You had no right!" Marla shouted. She threw open[8] the door, wrapped in a towel. "I don't want to be here when she shows up[9]." She stomped[10] into her bedroom and slammed[11] the door.

"Marla," I said weakly. "You need to—"

"I'm getting dressed. And I have to get Matthew into something. We'll go look for a crib[12]."

I had no safety seat[13] for an infant. It had been several years since I'd needed any version of one for Ethan. But at this moment, that seemed a minor problem compared to everything else. If Marla was determined to leave the house, but still willing to[14] be in my company, then I'd put her and the baby in the car, ostensibly[15] to go looking for a crib, drive like I had a bowl of goldfish[16] on the front seat, but head for the Gaynor home instead of[17] a furniture store.

See how Marla reacted.

1. mentir
2. la duper
3. as besoin de
4. sage-femme
5. de devenir infirmière
6. était experte en accouchements
7. Mais pour ce que ça avait servi...
8. ouvrit violemment
9. arrivera
10. se rua
11. claqua
12. berceau
13. siège auto
14. d'accord pour
15. en faisant mine
16. bocal de poissons rouges
17. mais direction chez les Gaynor, et non

"Five minutes!" Marla said.

She was out in four, dressed in jeans and a rat-
ty pullover sweater[1], her hair still wet. She had
the baby in her arms. It was hard to see what he
was wearing, she had him wrapped up in so many
blankets.

"Grab the stroller[2]," she said. "I don't want to
have to carry him when we're shopping. Oh, and
let me get another bottle[3] from the fridge."

I didn't feel I could call my mother back in front
of Marla to tell her we were on the move[4]. I figured the moment Agnes arrived and found no
one here, my cell would start ringing. I folded the
stroller, and as we stepped outside and Marla put
her key in the door to lock it, I took another look
at the bloody smudge on the door frame.

Maybe it wasn't blood. It could be dirt[5]. Someone who'd had their hand in the garden. Except
Marla wasn't much of a gardener[6].

"I think you should sit in the back," I told her.
"If the air bag went off in the front and crushed
the baby into you, well, that wouldn't be a good
thing."

"Just drive real careful," Marla said.

"That's what I'll do."

I got her settled into the backseat, behind the
front passenger seat, with Matthew in her arms. I
opened the back hatch[7], tossed in the stroller, then
got behind the wheel.

"Where are we going to look?" she asked.
"Walmart? Or maybe the Sears[8] at Promise Falls
Mall[9]?"

"I'm not sure," I said, heading west. Even though
I'd grown up in this town, it wasn't until I was a
reporter for the *Standard* that I really got to know
all corners of it. I could find Breckonwood without

---

1. vieux pull
miteux

2. Prends la
poussette
3. biberon

4. qu'on partait

5. de la terre

6. jardinait peu

7. coffre

8. [chaîne
de grands
magasins]

9. centre
commercial

the help of a navigation system. "Walmart might be a good place to start."

"Okay," she said placidly.

It didn't take long to reach the Gaynors' neighborhood. Breckonwood was in one of the town's tonier[1] enclaves. Houses here cost much more than the average Promise Falls bungalow[2], but they weren't fetching the same kind of money they might have ten years ago, when the town was prospering. Madeline Plimpton lived around here. She'd thrown a party[3] for *Standard* staff at her home eight or nine years ago, back when there were things to celebrate in the newspaper business.

"I don't see any stores around here," Marla said.

"I have to make a stop," I said.

I turned onto Breckonwood, worried that I might see half a dozen police cars and a news van from Albany. But the street was quiet, and I found some comfort in that. If someone had called in a report of a missing child, the street would have been abuzz[4]. I found 375, then steered the car over to the curb.

"This look familiar to you?" I asked, twisting around[5] to get a look at Marla and Matthew, who had a tiny smile on his face.

She shook her head.

"You know anyone named Rosemary Gaynor?"

Marla eyed me suspiciously. "Should I?"

"I don't know. Do you?"

"Never heard of her."

I hesitated. "Marla, it has to have occurred to you[6] that this baby—Matthew—came from somewhere."

"I told you where he came from. The woman who came to my door."

1. plus proprettes
2. pavillon

3. fait une fête

4. en ébullition

5. en me retournant

6. tu as bien dû te dire

65

"But she had to get Matthew from someplace[1], right? Someone had to give him up[2] for you to have him[3]."

She was nonplussed[4]. "It must have been someone who couldn't look after him. They asked around[5] and realized I could provide a good home for him." She offered up a smile that seemed as innocent as Matthew's.

I didn't see the point[6] of pursuing this any further. At least not right now. I said, "You sit tight[7]. I'll be back in a minute."

I got out of the car, pocketing the keys, and took in[8] 375. The structure was newer than many on the street, suggesting an older house had been torn down[9] and this built in its place. Well landscaped[10], two stories[11], double garage, easily five thousand square feet[12]. If anyone was home, there was probably a high-end SUV[13] sitting[14] behind that garage door.

I went to the door and rang the bell. Waited.

I glanced back at[15] the car. Marla's head was bent down as she talked to the baby. About ten seconds had gone by[16] without anyone answering, so I leaned[17] on the doorbell a second time.

Another twenty seconds went by. Nothing. I got out my phone, reopened the app that had brought up the phone number for the Gaynors, tapped the number, and put the phone to my ear. Inside the house, I could hear an accompanying ring.

No answer.

Nobody home.

I heard a car approaching and turned around. A black four-door Audi sedan[18]. It turned, quickly, into the driveway and stopped within an inch of the closed garage door, the brakes giving out a loud, sharp squeal[19].

A slim man in his late thirties[1], dressed in an expensive suit, jacket open, tie askew[2], threw open the door and stepped out.

"Who are you?" he snapped[3], striding toward me, his keys hanging from his index finger.

"I was looking for Rosemary Gaynor. Are you Mr. Gaynor?"

"Yeah, I'm Bill Gaynor, but who the hell are you?"

"David Harwood."

"Did you ring the bell?"

"Yes, but no one—"

"Jesus," Gaynor said, fiddling with his keys, looking for the one that would open the front door. "I've been calling all the way back from Boston. Why the hell hasn't she been answering the goddamn phone?"

He had the key inserted, turned it, and was shouting, "Rose!" as he pushed the door open. "Rose!"

I hesitated a moment at the front door, then followed Gaynor inside. The foyer[4] was two stories tall[5], a grand chandelier[6] hanging down from above. To the left and right, a dining room and living room. Gaynor was heading straight for the back of the house.

"Rose! Rose!" he continued shouting.

I was four steps behind the man. "Mr. Gaynor, Mr. Gaynor, do you have a baby, about—"

"Rose!"

This time, when he called out her name, it was different. His voice was filled with anguish and horror.

The man dropped to his knees. Before him, stretched out on the floor, was a woman.

1. la trentaine bien sonnée

2. sa cravate de travers

3. lança sèchement

4. vestibule

5. allait jusqu'au premier

6. lustre imposant

She lay on her back, one leg extended, the other bent awkwardly[1]. Her blouse[2], which from the collar appeared to be white, was awash in red[3], and ripped[4] roughly straight across[5] near the bottom.

A few feet away, a kitchen knife with a ten-inch blade[6]. Blade and handle covered in blood.

The blood, Jesus, it was everywhere. Smudged bloody footprints[7] led toward a set of sliding glass doors[8] at the back of the kitchen.

"God oh God Rose oh my God Rose oh God!"

Suddenly the man's head jerked[9], as though something horrible had just occurred to him[10]. Something even more horrible than the scene before him.

"The baby," he whispered.

He sprang to his feet, his pant legs[11] stained with blood that had gone thick and tacky[12], and ran from the kitchen, trailing bloody shoeprints in his wake[13]. He nearly skidded[14] on the marble flooring[15] in the foyer as he turned to run up the stairs.

I shouted, "Wait! Mr. Gaynor!"

He wasn't listening. He was screaming: "Matthew! Matthew!"

He tore up the stairs two steps at a time[16]. I stayed by the bottom of the stairs. I had a feeling he'd be back in a matter of[17] seconds.

Gaynor disappeared down a second-floor hallway[18]. Another anguished cry: *"Matthew!"*

When he reappeared at the top of the stairs, his face was awash with[19] panic. "Gone. Matthew's gone. The baby's gone." He wasn't looking at me. It was as if he were speaking more to himself, trying to take it in[20].

"The baby's gone," he said again, nearly breathless[21].

Trying to keep my voice calm, I said, "Matthew's okay. We have Matthew. Matthew is fine."

He glanced back over his shoulder, out the front door that remained wide-open, to my car parked at the curb.

Marla had remained in the backseat, Matthew still in her arms. She was looking at the house now instead of him.

No expression on her face whatsoever.

"What do you mean, *we*?" Gaynor said. "Why do you have Matthew? What have you done?" His head turned toward the kitchen. "You did that? You? Did you—"

"No!" I said quickly. "I can't explain what happened here, but your son, he's okay. I've been trying to find out—"

"Matthew's in the car? Is that Sarita with him? He's with the nanny[1]?"

"Sarita?" I said. "Nanny?"

"That's not Sarita," he said. "Where's Sarita? What's happened to her?"

And then he started running toward my car.

1. nounou

SEVEN

AGNES Pickens was very not happy with the muffins.

There were two dozen, arranged on the platter in the center of the massive boardroom[1] table. Coffee and tea had been set up on a table along the wall, and everything there looked fine. Decaf, cream, sugar, milk, sweeteners[2]. Plus, copies of the hospital's latest progress report[3] had been distributed around the table where everyone would be sitting. But when Agnes scanned[4] the muffin selection, she did not find bran[5]. She found blueberry[6] and banana and chocolate—and let's face it[7], a chocolate muffin was just cake shaped like a muffin—but bran was noticeable by[8] its absence. At least there was fruit.

When you were a hospital administrator and called an early morning board meeting[9], you had to at least make an effort to offer healthy choices[10]. Even if the bran muffins were passed over[11] in favor of the chocolate, she could at least say they had been made available[12].

The meeting was set to[13] begin in five minutes, and Agnes had stopped in here to make sure everything was as it was supposed to be. Find-

1. de la salle de conférence

2. des sucrettes

3. rapport d'avancement

4. examina

5. n'en vit aucun au son d'avoine

6. myrtilles

7. regardons les choses en face

8. brillait par

9. qu'on réunissait un conseil d'administration à l'aube

10. des options saines

11. négligés

12. proposés

13. devait

ing it was not, she went to the door and shouted, "Carol!"

Carol Osgoode, Agnes's personal assistant, popped her head out a room down the hall. "Yes, Ms. Pickens?"

"There are no bran muffins."

Carol, a woman in her late twenties with shoulder-length brown hair and eyes to match[1], blinked hurriedly[2]. "I just asked the kitchen to send up a selection of—"

"I specifically told you to make sure that there were some bran muffins."

"I'm sorry; I don't recall—"

"Carol, I told you. I remember quite clearly. Call Frieda and tell her to send up half a dozen. I know they have some. I saw them down in the cafeteria twenty minutes ago. Steal them from there if you have to."

Carol's head disappeared.

Agnes set her purse[3] on the table, removed her phone, and realized it was not on[4]. Her HuffPost[5] app had been loading slowly that morning, as well as some of her other programs, so she'd turned the phone off with the intention of turning it back on immediately. A quick reboot[6]. But then her rye[7] toast had popped[8], and she'd neglected[9] to restart it. So now she pressed and held the button at the top right, but flipped the tiny switch on the left side to mute the ring[10].

Agnes set the phone on the table, then tapped her red fingernails impatiently on the polished surface. This was not going to be a pleasant meeting. She had not been looking forward to it. The news was distressing. The latest hospital rankings[11] were in[12], and Promise Falls General had come in below average[13] for the upstate New York region[14].

1. assortis
2. cligna vivement des yeux

3. sac à main
4. allumé
5. du Huffington Post

6. redémarrage
7. au seigle
8. sauté du grille-pain
9. oublié
10. le mettre sur silencieux

11. classement
12. était arrivé
13. tombait sous la moyenne
14. nord de l'État de New York

71

The closest[1] hospitals in Syracuse and Albany had ranked in the high seventies and low eighties, but PFG had been saddled with[2] a sixty-nine. A totally unfair[3] and arbitrary figure[4], in Agnes's estimation. Much of it had to do with perception. The locals[5] figured[6] that if you needed top-quality health care, you had to go to a hospital in a big city. Bigger, at least, than Promise Falls. That meant Syracuse or Albany, or even New York.

Sure, PFG had some trouble eleven months ago with an outbreak[7] of *C. difficile*[8]. Four elderly[9] patients contracted the bacterial infection, and one of them had died. (Too bad[10] the *Promise Falls Standard* was still printing at the time; it was front-page material[11] for the better part of[12] two weeks.) But that was the sort of thing that could happen to any hospital, and almost invariably did. Agnes Pickens had instituted even more rigorous hand-washing and cleaning procedures, and had gotten the outbreak under control. And where was the *Standard's* front-page story on that?

Ask anyone in town if they'd be happy to be treated at Promise Falls General, and invariably they'd say, "Uh, if you think there's even a chance of one in a hundred you can get me to Syracuse or Albany before I die, I'll take a pass on[13] PFG." Changing that perception was proving to be a challenge[14] for Agnes.

A woman in a pale green uniform and a hairnet[15] walked into the room with a plate of bran muffins.

"Here you go, Ms. Pickens," she said.

"Frieda, take them off that plate and arrange them[16] with the others," Agnes said. "And I hope to God you washed your hands before you touched the food."

"Of course, ma'am." She added the new muffins to the platter and slipped out of the room as Carol entered.

"They're here," she said.

"Send them in," Agnes said.

Ten people filed in[1], nodding greetings[2], making small talk[3]. Local businesspeople, two doctors, the hospital's chief fund-raiser.

"Morning, Agnes," said a silver-haired man in his early sixties.

"Dr. Sturgess," she said, shaking his hand. Then added, "Jack."

Jack Sturgess, as if anticipating a rebuke[4], smiled and said, "I've started entering my notes into the system this week. Honest. No more paper."

A few others heard the comment and chuckled[5] as they helped themselves[6] to coffee and tea and settled into the cushioned high-backed[7] chairs around the table's perimeter. Several helped themselves to muffins, and Agnes noticed at least three of them reaching for[8] a bran.

She liked vindications[9], no matter how small.

She also liked being in charge[10]. Liked it very much. Here she was, someone who'd never been a doctor, in charge of all this. After graduating nursing school[11], she'd tried her hand at being a[12] midwife in Rochester for a couple of years, then returned to school for business[13]. Applied[14], and got, a job in this hospital's administrative department and, over the years, worked her way right to the top[15].

Agnes Pickens took her seat at the head of the table and kept her welcome short. "I want to get straight to business[16]," she said, setting her cell phone, screen up, on the table next to her copy of the hospital report. "You'll notice on the first page

1. entrèrent en file indienne

2. se saluant de la tête

3. papotant

4. réprimande

5. rirent discrètement

6. tout en se servant

7. à haut dossier

8. tendant le bras vers

9. que les faits lui donnent raison

10. aux commandes

11. être sortie diplômée de l'école d'infirmières

12. avait exercé comme

13. pour étudier les affaires

14. Elle avait postulé à

15. avait gravi tous les échelons

16. entrer directement dans le vif du sujet

of the document before you that the rankings are in and they are not satisfactory. They are a disgrace[1]. They do not reflect the quality of the work that we are doing here at Promise Falls General."

A woman at the far end of the table said, "You have to take those things with a grain of—[2]"

"Dr. Ford, I'm speaking. While this ranking is grossly unfair[3], the only way we're going to deal with it is to work even harder in every department. We need to look at every single thing we do here and find a way to do it even better. For example, we're still not where we need to be on computerization of records[4]. It's vitally important that all relevant patient information be entered[5] into the system to avoid any potential allergy and medication mix-ups[6]. But some staff[7] are still recording information on paper, and leaving it to others to input this data[8]."

"Not guilty," Jack Sturgess said. "I've gone totally computer."

"You're an inspiration to us all," Agnes said.

Her phone buzzed. She glanced down, saw that it was her sister, Arlene Harwood, calling. She also noticed, for the first time, that she had a couple of voice-mail messages. Agnes felt that whatever they were could wait. The phone buzzed six times, the vibrations traveling the length of the table like a minor earth tremor[9].

"I'm getting pushback[10] from some staff on this computer filing issue, and I want to get the message out that no one is so special as to be exempt from this[11]. No one. And it's not the regular rank and file[12] who are resisting. It's the doctors and surgeons and specialists who seem to think that somehow this duty is beneath them[13]. In part, it's

1. abominables

2. Il faut en prendre et en...
3. d'une injustice criante

4. l'informatisation des dossiers
5. soit saisie

6. confusions
7. membres du personnel
8. rentrer ces données

9. tremblement de terre
10. de la résistance
11. n'a lieu d'en être dispensé
12. le gros des troupes
13. indigne d'eux

74

a generational issue[1]. Younger physicians who've grown up with technology are not—"

The phone buzzed again. Arlene trying a second time.

Agnes Pickens hated to be thrown off her game[2] when she was in the middle of something. She picked up the phone, pressed a button to immediately decline[3] the call.

"As I was saying, just because some people who work here, or have privileges here, may not be as computer-savvy[4] as some of their younger colleagues is not an excuse. They are going to have to—"

A text appeared on her phone. From Arlene:

CALL ME!!! IT'S ABOUT MARLA.

Agnes studied the screen for several seconds. "Excuse me," she said finally, pushing back her chair. "I want five ideas on how to get this ranking up by the time I come back." She grabbed her phone, exited[5] the boardroom, and closed the door behind her. She entered her sister's home number and put the phone to her ear.

"Agnes?"

"I'm in the middle of a board meeting," she said. "What's this about Marla?"

"My God, I've been calling and calling."

"What is it?"

"She's done it again," Arlene said. "David just called. I sent him by to see her with some chili and—"

"Done what, Arlene?"

"David found her looking after a baby."

1. problème

2. déconcentrée

3. refuser

4. au point en informatique

5. sortit de

Agnes closed her eyes and touched her free hand to her temple, as if she could magically ward off[1] the headache she knew was coming.

1. repousser

"There's been no incident here," Agnes said. "If someone had taken a baby from the hospital I would have been notified instantly. David must be mistaken."

"I don't know where she got it," Arlene said. "But I trust David on this. If he says there's a baby, there's a baby."

"Dear God," Agnes said. "That child, I swear."

2. une adulte

"She's not a child. She's a grown woman[2], and she's been traumatized. It's not her fault."

3. Ne me fais pas la morale

"Don't lecture me[3], Arlene." It never ended, Agnes thought. Once an older sister, always an older sister.

Agnes wasn't just younger than Arlene. She was her *much* younger sister. Their mother had Arlene at the age of twenty, and didn't get pregnant with Agnes until she was thirty-five. There was one other child, a boy named Henry, a couple of years after Arlene, and then a gulf of thirteen years. Everyone figured Agnes must have been an accident. Surely their parents hadn't planned to have her. But once they knew she was on the way, they went ahead and had her[4]. The thought of terminating the pregnancy[5] never even occurred to their parents, and not because they were at all religious or were staunchly prolife[6].

4. l'avaient gardée

5. avorter

6. farouchement anti-avortement

They just figured, What the hell[7]. Let's have another kid.

7. Et pourquoi pas

Despite having an older brother and sister, Agnes felt as though she were an only child[8]. The age difference meant her siblings[9] had very little to do with her. They were either in or just starting high school[10] when she came along[11]. So they

8. fille unique

9. frère et sœur

10. le lycée

11. à sa naissance

were never playmates[1], never went to school together. Arlene and Henry, being two years apart, had a bond[2] Agnes could only dream of. She resented it[3] for years, until Henry was killed in a car accident nearly two decades earlier. Only then, it struck Agnes, did Arlene begin to take a greater interest in her.

Well, it was too late by then.

Arlene seemed to believe she had some kind of family monopoly on wisdom[4]. Did *she* run[5] a hospital? Had *she* had that kind of responsibility? Had Arlene worked her way up from nothing[6] to oversee[7] a multimillion-dollar budget? And had David ever been the source of worry to Arlene and Don that Marla had been to her and Gill? Marla had been a challenge from the get-go[8]. The teenage years were a nightmare. Sleeping around[9], drinking, drugs, ignoring school.

Agnes and Gill had figured that once Marla hit her twenties[10], things would settle down. But troubles remained. Hints[11] of a personality disorder[12], difficulty recognizing people, mood swings[13]. One doctor thought she might be bipolar. But at least, with her parents' financial help, she was living independently in a small house of her own, getting the odd job here and there[14], and then, more recently, this thing where she reviewed businesses on the Internet.

It gave Agnes hope. Maybe, just maybe, Marla was getting her life back on track[15]. So long as there were no setbacks[16], she might be able to move on to a more conventional kind of job. Agnes would have tried to find her something at the hospital, but after the incident with the baby, that wasn't possible.

1. n'avaient pas joué ensemble

2. lien affectif

3. en avait souffert

4. la sagesse

5. dirigeait

6. était partie de rien

7. administrer

8. dès le début

9. Coucheries

10. quand Marla atteindrait la vingtaine

11. Les signes

12. trouble de la personnalité

13. des sautes d'humeur

14. faisant des petits boulots

15. reprenait le contrôle de sa vie

16. rechutes

Agnes might be able to pull some strings[1] somewhere. She knew people in this town. The mayor, the head[2] of the chamber of commerce, the police chief. All of them, as it turned out[3], women. They understood how important it was to help a child find her way in the world[4].

But then Marla met that boy.

A *student*, for God's sake. From Thackeray College. A local boy, the son of, if you could believe it[5], a landscaper[6].

And he'd gotten her pregnant[7].

What had Marla been thinking, getting involved with someone so young, someone who wasn't even finished with school? Someone who had no prospects[8], other than to help his father cut lawns and plant shrubs[9]? Agnes had done some checking up on him[10]. A few years ago he'd even been a suspect in the murder of a local lawyer[11] and his family. The boy turned out to[12] be innocent, but you had to wonder, would the police have even looked at him in the first place if there hadn't been something off about him[13]? He was getting a degree[14] in English or philosophy or something else equally useless[15].

Yes, Agnes conceded, what had happened with the baby had been tragic for Marla, and she was more than entitled to grieve[16]. She'd needed time to get over her loss[17], and Agnes believed she herself had been a good mother through this period, helping to get Marla back on her feet[18]. But who could have predicted what Marla would do? That she would sneak into Agnes's own hospital and kidnap a newborn?

Several months had passed since then, and Agnes now believed Marla was getting better. She was back doing her Internet reviews from home.

78

The next step would be getting her out of the house, out into the *world*.

But now *this*.

Marla with another baby.

"Are they at the house?" Agnes asked Arlene.

"Last time I talked to him, yes," Arlene said. "I think David was wondering whether to[1] call the police."

"Tell me he has not done that," Agnes said sternly[2]. "This does *not* have to be a police matter. We can sort this out[3]. Whatever's happened, we can deal with it[4]. Did you call Gill?"

"I called the house and left a message. I don't seem to have his cell phone number."

Gill, a management consultant who worked from home[5], had said something about meeting with a client that morning, Agnes recalled[6].

"Okay, I'm heading over[7]," she said, and ended the call.

The boardroom door opened and Jack Sturgess emerged. "Is anything the matter, Agnes?"

Her eyes locked briefly on his[8]. "Marla," she said.

"What?" he asked. "What's happened?"

She brushed past him as she returned to the conference room. The board members had the look of guilty children who'd been throwing spitballs[9] while the teacher had been down to the office[10].

Pickens stood behind her chair. "I'm afraid we'll have to reschedule[11]," she said evenly[12]. "Something has come up that demands[13] my immediate attention."

She tossed[14] her phone into her bag and left the room, passing her office and heading straight for the stairs. The elevator could take forever[15], especially if a patient transfer was under way[16]. Once

1. s'il devait
2. sévèrement
3. On peut régler ça nous-mêmes
4. gérer
5. faisait du télétravail
6. se rappelait
7. j'y vais
8. croisèrent les siens
9. boulettes de papier
10. chez le proviseur
11. reporter
12. calmement
13. exige
14. jeta
15. prendre un siècle
16. en cours

Agnes was out of the building, she had her phone out again, brought up a contact, tapped it.

It rang nine times before someone answered. "Yeah?" A man, sounding both surprised and annoyed.

"Gill, we've got a problem with Marla," she said.

"Jesus, when don't we[1]," her husband said. "Hang on[2], let me just … Okay, I was with a client. What's happened?"

"She's done it again. She's taken another baby."

"Fucking hell[3]," he said.

"I'm on my way."

"Let me know what you find," Gill Pickens said.

"You're not coming?"

"I'm right in the middle of something," he said.

"You're unbelievable[4]," she said, and dropped the cell back into her purse.

Agnes wondered what, exactly, Gill was really in the middle of. More than likely, some slut's legs[5].

1. pour changer
2. Ne quitte pas
3. Bordel de merde
4. hallucinant
5. les jambes d'une salope

EIGHT

David

I ran after Bill Gaynor as he sprinted toward my car. Marla had worn a blank expression[1] up to now, but as Gaynor charged in her direction, her face changed. Her eyes widened with fear. I saw her glance down, probably checking to see that the car's back door lock was set[2]. Then she scooped[3] Matthew into her arms and held on to him tightly.

"Matthew!"

"Mr. Gaynor!" I shouted. I reached out, tried to grab his shoulders to slow him down.

Gaynor spun around[4], tried to throw a punch[5], and in the process[6] tripped over his own feet[7]. As he hit the lawn[8] I stumbled[9] over his ankle[10] and hit the ground next to him. I scrambled over[11] before he could get up, leaned over him[12], and said, "Just listen! Listen to me."

All I really wanted now was to keep[13] Gaynor from hurting or frightening Marla. I wanted to bring some calm to the situation, as unrealistic as that might sound[14]. Only moments earlier, Gaynor had found his murdered wife in their home, and he

1. gardé un air absent

2. enclenché

3. prit vite

4. fit volte-face

5. lancer un coup de poing

6. ce faisant,

7. se fit un croche-pied

8. s'écrasait sur la pelouse,

9. trébuchai

10. cheville

11. me relevai tant bien que mal

12. me penchai sur lui

13. empêcher

14. si improbable que cela puisse paraître

had every reason to be acting the way he was. But I was afraid, in his state, anything could happen.

He brought himself up to a sitting position, then launched himself at[1] me. Two broad palms against my chest. I went flying backward[2].

He was on his feet in a second, and heading toward the car again. When he got to it, he was moving so quickly he had to brace himself[3]. His outstretched hands hit the top of Marla's door, and the car rocked. He reached down for the handle, yanked[4] on it, but found it locked.

Marla screamed.

Gaynor yanked on the door handle two more times, maybe thinking he could bust it open.

"Go away!" Marla shouted.

Gaynor shielded his eyes with his hand long[5] enough to peer[6] through the window and get a good look at the baby. He made a fist and banged on the glass. "Open the goddamn door!"

Marla screamed a second time for him to go away.

I was to the car now, fumbling[7] in my pocket for the keys. I'd be able to unlock the doors as quickly as Marla could lock them, but I wasn't sure that doing so was a good idea. Marla and the baby were better off[8] in that car, at least until the police arrived.

"Matthew!" Gaynor shouted. He ran around to the other side of the car, but before he could reach the back door, Marla leaned over awkwardly[9], baby still in her arms, and locked it, too. He yanked on the handle a second too late.

"He's mine!" Marla yelled, her voice muffled[10] by the cocooning effect of the glass.

A woman who'd no doubt heard all the commotion[11] was coming out of a house on the other

1. se jeta sur
2. en arrière
3. se retenir des bras
4. tira violemment
5. se mit la main devant les yeux
6. voir
7. à fouiller
8. plus en sécurité
9. se pencha comme elle put
10. étouffée
11. raffut

side of the street. She took two seconds to take in[1] what she was seeing, and ran back inside.

Make the call[2], I thought.

Gaynor banged on Marla's window twice with the flat of his hand, then decided to try the driver's door.

Shit.

Marla hadn't been able to reach into the front to lock that one.

I raised the remote[3], hit the button, but I was too late.

Gaynor got the door open and dived in[4], putting his knees on the driver's seat so he could reach into the back. As he lunged for[5] Matthew, Marla freed one hand and slapped at his arms.

"Stop!" I shouted. "Stop it!"

I wasn't sure which of them I was yelling at. I just wanted everything to stop before anyone got hurt.

I got behind Gaynor and put my arms around his waist, tried to pull him back out of the car. He kicked back at me, catching me on the front of the leg, below the knee. It hurt like a son of a bitch[6], but I kept my hold on him[7].

"Stop!" I yelled. "We're trying to help!"

Although, as I said it, I had to wonder at the truth[8] of my words. Maybe I was trying to help, in the sense that I was trying to figure out[9] what had happened here.

But Marla was another story.

Marla had Bill Gaynor's child, and I was not yet in a position to explain how that had come to pass.

And in that instant, in that millisecond, in the midst of all this chaos, I recalled the bloody smudge on Marla's door.

Oh, no.

1. comprendre

2. Appelle-les

3. télécommande

4. s'engouffra

5. plongeait vers

6. me fit un mal de chien

7. je ne lâchai pas

8. m'interroger sur la véracité

9. piger

"Give him to me!" he shouted at Marla, who was still hitting any part of him she could catch. She landed[1] a couple of blows on his head.

"Marla! Stop it! Stop it!"

While I struggled with Gaynor, managing to drag him almost all the way out of the car, Marla tucked[2] Matthew under one arm like a football[3], threw open the back door on the other side, got out, and started to run.

Gaynor managed to turn around—he was younger and in better shape[4] than I was—so that he could push me up against the inside of the driver's door and drive a fist into my stomach. I let go of him[5] and my knees hit the pavement.

The wind was gone from me[6]. I gasped for air[7] as Gaynor tore around the back of the car and caught up to Marla as she ran across the lawn. As I struggled to my feet[8], I saw him grab Marla by one arm.

"Go away!" she screamed, twisting her body, shielding the baby from the baby's father.

Again I yelled, "Wait!"

Gaynor kept his focus on Marla, and his hand on her arm. He was digging his fingers into her flesh, and she was screaming in pain.

"I'll drop him!"

That did it. Gaynor released his grip on her, took half a step back. For several seconds, everything froze. All you could hear was breathing. Shallow[9] and rapid from Gaynor, his tie askew[10], hair tousled[11], arms down at his sides. Marla, jaw dropped[12], inhaling huge gulps[13] of air. And then there was me, still struggling to get my breathing back to normal after that punch to the gut[14].

1. réussit à lui envoyer
2. se cala
3. ballon
4. en meilleure forme
5. lâchai prise
6. ne pouvais plus respirer
7. reprenais ma respiration
8. tentais de me relever
9. Brève
10. de travers
11. les cheveux en bataille
12. bouche ouverte
13. avalant de grandes bouffées
14. poing dans le ventre

Half doubled over[1], I came around the car, one arm raised, palm out[2], in some weak kind of conciliatory gesture.

Gaynor's wild eyes went from Marla to me and back to Marla. There were tears running down her face, and Matthew was starting to cry, too.

"Please," Bill Gaynor said to her. "Don't hurt him."

Marla shook her head, stunned[3] by the request. "Hurt him? You're the one who's trying to hurt him."

"No, no, please," he said.

I managed to stand fully upright[4] as I stepped over the curb[5] and walked onto the lawn.

"Marla," I said. "What matters now, more than anything, is that nothing happen[6] to Matthew. Right?"

She studied me warily[7]. "Okay."

"He's our number one concern, agreed?"

"That's my son," Gaynor said. "Tell her to give me my—"

I raised a hand in his direction and nodded[8]. "We all want the same thing, and that's for Matthew to be safe."

In the distance, for the first time, sirens.

"Of course," she said.

"Marla, something's happened in the house, and the police are coming, and it's all going to get very busy here in a few minutes, and the cops are going to want to ask all of us lots of questions, and we don't want to subject[9] Matthew to that, do we? Some people are going to believe one thing and some people are going to believe something else, but the bottom line is,[10] Matthew needs to be safe."

She said nothing, but tightened her grip on[11] the baby.

1. plié en deux
2. la paume vers le haut
3. abasourdie
4. me redresser complètement
5. en descendant du trottoir
6. qu'il n'arrive rien
7. d'un air méfiant
8. acquiesçai
9. soumettre
10. ce qui compte, c'est que
11. serra plus fort

1. Tu me fais confiance

2. à passer de l'un à l'autre

3. très légèrement

4. voiture de patrouille

5. me scruta
6. figée

7. fait apparaître

8. une seule pour le moment
9. s'arrêta dans un crissement de freins
10. agents

11. sortit son arme

12. aboya

"Do you trust me[1], Marla?"

"I don't know," she said.

"We're cousins. We're family. I wouldn't do anything to hurt you. I want to help you, and I want to help you through this. You have to trust me."

Gaynor's eyes continued to bounce between us[2].

"I guess I do," she said. I could see her grip on Matthew, who was continuing to cry through all of this, relax ever so slightly[3].

The sirens grew louder. I took my eyes off Marla for half a second, saw a Promise Falls cruiser[4] turn the corner a long block away, lights flashing.

"Give him to me," I said. I looked at Gaynor. "Is that okay with you, if she gives him to me?"

He searched my eyes[5]. "Okay," he said slowly.

Marla stood frozen[6]. She'd taken a quick look up the street, too, and the imminent arrival of the police had prompted[7] a more frightened look in her eyes.

"If I can't have him …"

"Marla."

"If I can't have him, then maybe no one …"

"Don't talk that way, Marla." Jesus, what might she do? Run into the street, throw herself in the path of the police car, baby in her arms?

The cruiser—only the one so far[8]—screeched to a halt[9] and two male officers[10], one black and one white, jumped out. I was pretty sure I recognized both of them from my time reporting for the *Standard*. The black officer was Gilchrist, the white guy Humboldt.

"Give him to me!" Gaynor yelled at Marla, and advanced threateningly toward her.

Gilchrist drew his weapon[11], but kept it pointing toward the ground. "Sir!" he barked[12], his sharp voice a thunderclap[1]. "Back away from the woman!"

Gaynor looked at the cop, pointed to Marla. "That's my son! She has my son!"

Christ on a cracker[2], this very bad situation was milliseconds away from getting a fuck of a lot worse[3]. The cops had no idea what they'd walked into. They probably thought it was some kind of custody[4] dispute. A full-scale domestic disturbance[5].

"Officer Gilchrist?" I said.

The man's head snapped my way. "I know you?"

"David Harwood. Used to work for the *Standard*. This is my cousin, Marla. She's under a lot of ... stress right now, and she was just about to hand the baby to me. And I think that's okay with Mr. Gaynor here, right?"

"Everyone just stay right where they are," Gilchrist said as his partner came alongside. "Would you like to bring us up to speed[6], Harwood?"

"It'd be easier to explain once Marla hands me[7] the baby."

"That work for you?" Humboldt, speaking for the first time, asked Bill Gaynor.

Gaynor nodded.

"How about you, Marla?" Gilchrist asked.

Marla took four slow steps in my direction. Carefully she handed the crying child to me. I supported him against my chest with one arm, wrapped the other around him. Felt his warmth. The stirring of his small limbs[8].

Gilchrist holstered[9] his weapon.

"In the house," I said, my voice feeling as though it might break. "You have to go ... into the house."

"What's in the house, sir?" Humboldt asked.

---

1. d'une voix tonitruante

2. Doux Jésus

3. sacrément pire

4. pour la garde du gosse

5. grosse engueulade de couple

6. nous mettre au parfum

7. m'aura remis

8. Ses bras et jambes bouger

9. rengaina

It was Gaynor who spoke. "My … wife." The way he said it, the way the two words came out so brittle[1], neither of the cops seemed to feel the need to ask what her situation was.

Humboldt drew a weapon and slowly approached the open front door. The house swallowed him up[2] as he entered the foyer.

Gilchrist spoke into the radio attached to his shoulder, said he was going to need more units[3] on Breckonwood. Probably a detective and a crime-scene unit.

Marla's red eyes looked my way. I wondered whether she would ask me what was in the house, but she didn't.

Instead, she slowly melted to the grass[4]. Once she was on her knees, she put her hands over her eyes and began to weep[5] so hard her body shook.

My phone rang. Tucked[6] into my inside jacket pocket, against my chest, it felt like I'd been hit by one of those paddles[7] paramedics use[8]. With a wailing[9] Matthew pressed against me, I worked[10] my free hand into my jacket to retrieve[11] the phone. I saw who it was before I put the phone to my ear.

"Agnes," I said.

"I'm at Marla's and there's no one here. What the hell is going on?"

Matthew cried. "We're not there," I said.

"Who is … Oh, dear God, is that the baby?"

"Yeah. Look, Agnes—"

"Where are you? Where the hell are you?"

I couldn't even remember where I was. I was numb[12]. I glanced at the house, read the number to her.

"A street, David? That would be enormously helpful."

The footnotes in the left margin:

1. Vu sa voix bri-sée en le disant
2. l'engloutit
3. des renforts
4. s'effondra lentement dans l'herbe
5. pleurer
6. Comme il était
7. électrochocs
8. qu'utilisent les équipes de secours
9. en pleurs
10. glissai
11. attraper
12. tétanisé

I had to think a moment. "Breckonwood. You know where that is?"

"Yes," Agnes snapped. "What are you doing there?"

"Just come," I said.

"Your mother said you had some wild idea that you might call the police. Whatever's happened, you are not[1] to call the police."

"Aunt Agnes, we're way past that now[2]."

1. je t'interdis
2. on n'en est plus là

NINE

"SO let me see if I have this right[1]," Barry Duckworth said, sitting across the desk from Thackeray College security chief Clive Duncomb. "You've got a sexual predator wandering[2] the campus, and you've decided the Promise Falls police are the last people who need to know about this."

"Not at all," Duncomb said.

"That's how it looks to me."

"We're well equipped to deal with all manner[3] of situations," Duncomb said. "I have a staff of five[4]."

"Oh, well," Duckworth said. "And I suppose you can call on[5] your students to pitch in[6] as needed[7]. Do the chemistry majors[8] do your forensic work[9]? You have an interrogation room somewhere, or do you just use one of the lecture halls[10]? I guess your art students can do the fingerprint work[11]. They'd have plenty of ink on hand[12]."

Duncomb said nothing. Instead, he opened the bottom drawer of his desk and brought out a file folder[13] stuffed with about half an inch[14] of paperwork[15]. He opened it and began to read:

" 'January fourteenth, ten seventeen p.m., vandal throws brick though dining hall window. Call put in[16] to Promise Falls police, told they have no one available[17], ask Thackeray security to e-mail

90

them a report. February second, twelve-oh-three a.m.[1], inebriated[2] student shouting and taking his shirt off on steps of library. Security puts in call to Promise Falls police, told to send them a copy of the report.' You want me to go on?"

"You think a broken window and a drunk kid equate with rape[3]?"

Duncomb waved a finger at him. "There hasn't been an actual rape[4]. Which is one of the reasons why we chose not to bother[5] the Promise Falls police." He smiled. "We know how busy you are."

"These things can progress[6]," Duckworth said.

"I'm aware of that[7]. I was with[8] the police in Boston before I took this position[9]."

Duckworth was about to tell Duncomb that he should know better then, but stopped himself. He knew he was getting off on the wrong foot[10] with this guy, that he might need his cooperation with whatever was going on here, but, boy, he was steamed[11].

"On behalf[12] of the Promise Falls police, please accept our heartfelt apologies[13] for our lack of attentiveness[14] in those matters."

Duncomb offered up a small *hmmph*. "Okay." He cleared his throat. "You have to understand where I'm coming from[15], what my position here is. I'm getting a lot of heat[16] from those farther up the food chain[17]. The admin, the president's office."

"Go on."

"There's a lot of competition out there when it comes to deciding where to send your kid to school."

"Sure," Duckworth said.

"And Thackeray had some bad press a few years back—this was before I got here—with the college

1. à minuit 03

2. en état d'ébriété

3. sont comparables au viol

4. de viol à proprement parler

5. déranger

6. évoluer

7. J'en suis conscient

8. dans

9. de prendre ce poste

10. partait du mauvais pied

11. purée, il était en pétard

12. Au nom

13. sincères excuses

14. manque d'écoute

15. mon point de vue

16. pression

17. mes supérieurs

president and that plagiarism scandal and the shooting[1]. You remember that?"

"Yes."

"That's mostly water under the bridge now[2]. I mean, people remember it, but they've moved on[3]. It was nearly a decade ago. If anyone was ever thinking of sending their kid to a college other than Thackeray because of that, it's likely no longer an issue[4]. But what we don't need around here is more bad press. News of some pervert preying on[5] young girls is all it might take for[6] Mom and Dad to decide to send little Susie somewhere else to find a future husband."

Barry Duckworth did not like this man.

Duncomb took a breath and continued. "So before we bring in the marines—or the local police—we're doing everything we can to find this fucker. I've got my people patrolling at night, and one of them, a woman—Joyce, who's in her thirties, and pretty hot[7]—has been acting as a kind of decoy[8], trying to draw this guy out."

Duckworth sat up in his chair. "You can't be serious."

"What? Isn't that what you'd do?"

"Has Joyce been trained in proper policing methods? Does she know self-defense? Do you have her in radio contact with other members of your security team at all times? Are they shadowing her[9]?"

Duncomb had both hands in the air, palms forward. "Whoa. First of all, I've been a cop, and I was a damn good one. And I've been giving Joyce the benefit of my training and experience. Second, Joyce has taken an accredited security guard course[10]. And all that other stuff you mentioned, I wouldn't get too hung up about it[11], because I'm not sending her out there empty-handed[12]."

1. fusillade

2. De l'eau a coulé sous les ponts depuis

3. sont passés à autre chose

4. ce n'est probablement plus un problème

5. s'en prenant à

6. peut suffire à ce que

7. très sexy

8. appât

9. Est-ce qu'ils la suivent dans ses déplacements

10. des cours

11. me prendrais pas la tête avec ça

12. les mains vides

92

"She's armed?"

Duncomb grinned, then made a gun sign with his hand, pulled the trigger[1]. "Oh, yeah. It's not like I'm telling her to shoot the bastard, but she sure shouldn't have any trouble persuading him to behave himself[2]."

Duckworth was imagining the countless[3] ways this approach could go horribly wrong.

"How many attacks?" the detective asked.

"Three," Duncomb said. "In the last two weeks. All late at night. Girls walking home alone from one part of the campus to another, heading back to the residence. Lot of wooded areas, places where someone can hide. Man jumps out, grabs them from behind[4], attempts to drag them into the bushes, manages to cop a few good feels[5]."

Duckworth wondered whether Duncomb's decision to leave the Boston force was his own[6].

"In each case, the girl's managed to break free[7], run away. Nobody's been hurt."

"Not physically," Duckworth said.

"That's what I said," the college security chief said.

"Suspect?"

"Just partial descriptions, although what we have from the three he went after[8] is consistent[9]. Man about six feet tall[10], slender build[11]."

"White? Black?"

Duncomb shook his head. "Wearing a ski mask. Plus a hoodie[12]. Like a big football one, with a number on it."

"Did he say anything?"

"Nope[13]. At least, not that any of the girls recalled[14]. But like I said, we're on this[15], and those posts with the panic buttons will all be in place by the end of the day, so I got a good feeling we're

1. tirant sur une gachette imaginaire

2. bien se tenir

3. innombrables

4. les chope par-derrière

5. bien la peloter

6. venait de lui

7. se dégager

8. qu'il a attaquées

9. concorde

10. 1,80 m

11. mince

12. sweat à capuche

13. Nan

14. pas qu'aucune se souvienne

15. on est sur le coup

not only going to get this shithead[1], but make the girls around here feel a whole lot safer."

"I want their names," Duckworth said.

"Say what?"

"The three women who were attacked. I want their names and contact information[2]. They need to be interviewed."

"I suppose we could do that."

"This isn't a Thackeray College issue," Duckworth said. "This is a Promise Falls issue. Your attacker may not be a student. He may be someone from town. And vice versa. If it's a student, or even a member of the faculty—"

"Oh, Jesus, don't even go there[3]," Duncomb said.

"—or even a member of the faculty, there's nothing to stop him from heading into town and attacking someone there. You need our resources and expertise. We need to talk to those women."

"Fine, fine, I'll get those to you." He put his hands flat on the desk. "We done[4]?"

"No," Duckworth said. "I came here to ask you about something else."

"Okeydoke.[5]"

"Have you had any acts of animal cruelty on campus?"

"Animal cruelty?" He shook his head slowly. "I guess they still dissect frogs over in the biology building. Has Kermit filed a complaint?[6]"

"No poisoned dogs or cats? No cutting the heads off the Canada geese[7] I see wandering around here?"

Duncomb shook his head one last time. "Nothing like that at all. Why?"

Duckworth felt a buzzing in his jacket. "Excuse me," he said. He took out the phone and put it to his ear. "Duckworth."

He listened for several seconds, reached into his pocket for a small notebook and a pen. He scribbled down[1] a Breckonwood Drive address, then put the phone away.

He stood. "Do *not* send your Joyce out there as a decoy. And I want those names."

Duckworth dropped a business card on the man's desk, and found his way out.

1. griffonna

TEN

David

1. d'accord pour
que je porte

2. qu'on calmait
la situation

3. il n'allait
sûrement pas

4. garder

5. grouillait de
flics

6. policière

7. le passer

8. Services
sociaux

9. regard

10. chemisier
déchiré

BILL Gaynor had been okay with my holding[1] the baby while the situation was being defused[2], but damned if he was going to[3] let me hang on to[4] Matthew now that Breckonwood was swarming with police[5].

He did agree to Officer Humboldt's suggestion, however, that the baby be placed in the arms of a uniformed female officer[6], who in turn was going to hand him over[7] to the first person who showed up from the Promise Falls Department of Children's Services[8].

Besides, I couldn't imagine Gaynor wanted to be holding on to a crying child while he attempted to answer questions about what had happened to his wife, Rosemary, back in that kitchen. Especially if that meant going back into that house.

I couldn't get the image out of my head. Her lifeless gaze[9] upward. The ripped blouse[10]. The blood.

So much blood.

Gaynor wasn't the only one who had to be persuaded that Matthew needed to be left in someone else's care[1], at least for now.

"They'll never give him back to me," Marla said. "Once they take him away they'll never give him back."

We were over by my car, and I had taken my cousin into my arms, held her as she went from one crying jag[2] to another.

"We'll just have to wait and see how things go," I told her, even though I knew we were more likely to be struck by a meteor than to see the Gaynors' baby handed back to Marla.

I had few doubts that Matthew belonged to the Gaynors.

It wasn't as if it had actually been spelled out for me[3], but it wasn't hard to put it all together[4]. Marla had a child in her house that was not hers. She had some crazy story about an "angel" dropping him off like a FedEx parcel[5]. There was the addressed flyer in the stroller. When Bill Gaynor returned home from some business trip, he went into a panic about his missing baby, Matthew.

And he instantly recognized his son in my car. The dots were not that hard to connect[6].

So I didn't think the odds of[7] Marla going home with Matthew were particularly good. But I couldn't help but wonder[8] what the odds were that Marla had something to do with Rosemary Gaynor's death. Was it possible, I wondered, as I tried to comfort her, that my cousin was capable of something like that?

I honestly had no idea.

The cops had asked us a few preliminary questions, then told us to wait for a detective to arrive. Not long after that, I saw Barry Duckworth

1. aux soins de quelqu'un d'autre

2. crise de larmes

3. on me l'avait dit explicitement

4. à reconstituer

5. colis

6. Ce n'était pas sorcier à reconstituer

7. les chances pour que

8. m'empêcher de me demander

1. débarquer
2. fait sa connaissance
3. mal ajusté
4. incessante
5. balance
6. étonnement
7. s'était peut-être dit
8. le saurait bien assez tôt
9. s'entretenir
10. devait endurer
11. poignardée
12. Je te parie que

show up[1]. I'd gotten to know him[2] a few years ago, not just through my work at the *Standard*, but through a personal matter. Dressed in an ill-fitting[3] gray suit, he didn't appear to be winning his perennial[4] battle with his bathroom scale[5].

He glanced in my direction on his way into the house, a brief look of puzzlement[6] on his face. At first he might have assumed[7] I was here covering the story, but with the *Standard* out of business, there had to be some other reason.

He'd find out soon enough[8].

Once inside the house, I saw Duckworth confer[9] with Officer Gilchrist, who had been talking to Gaynor.

God, what that man had to be going through[10].

Duckworth shook Gaynor's hand, and then the door was closed.

"What did you see in the house?" Marla asked me. She already knew the big picture. There were enough police here now to figure out that something very bad had happened in there.

"His wife," I said. "In the kitchen. She's been stabbed[11]. She's dead."

"That's horrible," Marla said. "Just horrible." She paused. "You know what I think?"

"What do you think, Marla?"

"I'll bet[12] he did it. That man. Her husband. I'll bet he killed her."

I looked at her. "Why would you say that?"

"Just a feeling. But I bet he did it. And when they figure out he did it, they won't let him keep the baby."

I could see where this was going.

"Marla, did you know that woman?"

"You already asked me that. At my house. I told you. I've never heard of her."

"Could you have met her, but not known that was her name?" It wasn't like I had a picture of the woman I could show Marla, so the question was kind of pointless[1]. And even if I'd had a picture, it wouldn't have done much good[2]. So Marla's answer was not surprising.

"I don't think so. I don't go out all that much[3]."

"Have you ever been here?" I asked. "To this house?"

Marla raised her head and studied the house for a moment. "I don't think so. But it's a very nice house. I'd like to have a house like this. It's so big, and my house is so small. I'd love to go inside and look around[4]."

"Not now, you wouldn't," I said.

"Oh, yeah," she said.

"So you're telling me you didn't come to this house, yesterday or maybe the day before, for Matthew? You didn't find him here?"

"I already told you how he came to me," she said tiredly[5]. "Don't you believe my story?"

"Sure," I said. "Of course I do."

"It doesn't sound like it[6]."

I happened to glance down the street, which had been taped off[7] in both directions. A woman lifted up the police tape, ducked under[8], and strode purposefully[9] toward us. When an officer attempted to stop her she brushed him aside[10].

"It's your mom," I said to Marla, and I felt her stiffen[11] in my arms.

"I don't want to talk to her," she said. "She'll just be mad[12]."

"She can help you," I said. "She knows people. Good lawyers[13], for one[14]."

99

1. un peu absurde
2. n'aurait pas servi à grand-chose
3. tant que ça

4. jeter un coup d'œil

5. d'un ton las
6. On dirait pas

7. barrée au ruban de sécurité
8. passa en dessous
9. d'un pas déterminé
10. l'écarta d'un geste
11. se raidir
12. furieuse

13. avocats
14. déjà

1. d'un air triste-
ment éberlué

2. lui rendre la
pareille
3. subitement

4. suis passé voir
5. s'occupait d'
6. bout de lettre

7. La mine
d'Agnès
s'allongea

8. ai cru
comprendre

9. la forcer à lui
donner

10. ne s'adresse à
nouveau à moi

Marla looked at me with sad wonder[1]. "Why would I need a lawyer? Am I in some kind of trouble?"

"Marla!" Agnes said. "Marla!"

Marla pulled away from me and turned to face my approaching aunt. Agnes took her into her arms, gave her a three-second hug, barely giving her daughter enough time to respond in kind[2]. Then Agnes looked at me sharply[3] and said, "What's going on here?"

Marla said, "It's all … it's kind of hard to explain, Mom, but—"

"That's why I'm asking your cousin," Agnes said, her eyes still fixed on me.

My mouth was dry. I licked my lips and said, "I dropped in on[4] Marla. She was looking after[5] a baby. An address on a piece of mail[6] tucked into the stroller led me here. The husband had been away on business, showed up at the same time; we went in, found his wife." I paused. "She's dead."

Agnes's face fell[7].

"And there's something about a nanny they had. Mr. Gaynor, he was asking about someone named Sarita. I got the idea[8] he was expecting she'd be at the house, but she wasn't."

"Good God," Agnes said. "Who are these people? Who's the woman, the one who was killed?"

"Rosemary Gaynor," I said.

Agnes abruptly turned away from me, looked at the house, as if by staring at it hard enough she could make it provide[9] some answers. I was given a view of her back for a good ten seconds before she engaged me again[10].

"The baby?"

"It's being looked after by the police or the child welfare people[1], at least for now. Mr. Gaynor's being interviewed by the cops."

"His name is Matthew," Marla said, moving closer to[2] us so she could be part of the conversation.

Agnes was ready now to question her instead of me. "What were you thinking? How did this happen? How did you end up with that baby? Did you learn nothing after what you did at my hospital? Nothing at all?"

"I—"

"I simply can't believe it. What on earth possessed you?[3] What did you do? Did you grab him at the mall[4]? Had she taken the baby out for a stroll?" She put a hand to her own mouth. "Tell me you didn't snatch[5] him here, at their house. Tell me you had nothing to do with this."

Marla's eyes filled with tears. "I didn't do anything wrong. He was given to me. Someone came to my door and asked me to look after him."

"Who?" Agnes snapped[6]. "The mother? This Gaynor woman?"

"I don't know who she was. She never said."

"Honestly, Marla, no one in the world is going to believe a story like that."

More to herself than to us, she said, "We're going to have to come up with something better than that[7]."

Agnes gave me a look of exasperation. "Have the police talked to her?"

"Briefly," I said. "They're trying to sort out the scene[8], I think, and told us not to leave. There's a detective here already, and probably a forensics unit[9], too."

"She doesn't say a word, not to anyone," Agnes said. "Not one word." She raised a finger

---

1. les gens de la protection de l'enfance

2. s'approchant de

3. Non mais qu'est-ce qui t'a pris ?!

4. centre commercial

5. enlevé

6. dit avec rudesse

7. On va devoir inventer mieux que ça

8. d'y voir plus clair sur place

9. équipe de la scientifique

to her daughter's face. "You hear that? You don't say one thing to the police. If they so much as ask you your birthday, you tell them to talk to your lawyer."

Agnes rooted through her purse[1], brought out a phone. She went through her contacts, found a number, and tapped it with her thumb. "Yes, this is Agnes Pickens. Put me through to Natalie. I don't *care* if she's with a client; put her on the phone *right this second.*"

Natalie Bondurant was my guess. One of Promise Falls' sharpest legal minds[2]. She'd helped me in the past.

"Natalie? Agnes Pickens here. Whatever you're doing, drop it[3]. I have a situation[4]. No, not with the hospital. I'll explain when you get here." She told Natalie where she could find her and ended the call before she could get an argument.

Agnes said to me, "That goes for you, too[5]."

"What?" I asked.

"Not a word to the police. You have nothing to say."

The first thing that popped into my head was a childish, *You're not the boss of me.* But what I said was "I'll decide what I tell the police, Agnes."

She didn't like that. "David," she said, in a whisper so Marla could not hear, "can't you see what's happened here?"

"I don't think we know that yet."

"We know enough to know Marla needs to be protected. Whatever she's done, it's not her fault. She's got problems; she's not responsible for her actions. We all have to look out for her[6]."

"Of course," I said.

"She hasn't been right for a long time, but losing the baby, it did something to her, to her mind."

Marginal notes:

1. fouilla dans son sac
2. L'une des juristes les plus futées de Promise Falls
3. arrête tout de suite
4. problème
5. Ça vaut pour toi aussi
6. veiller sur elle

"What are you saying?" Marla asked.

"It's all right, dear. I'm just talking to David."

"I'll keep what you have to say in mind," I told my aunt. "But I don't think my role in this entitles me to clam up[1] when the police start asking questions."

Agnes shook her head. "You really are Arlene's boy, aren't you? Stubborn to the end[2]." She scanned[3] the various police vehicles. "I'm going to find out who's in charge[4] here."

She went off in search of authority[5].

My cousin looked at me and said, "You have to help me."

"Your mom's doing that," I said. "That was probably Natalie Bondurant she was talking to on the phone. She's a good lawyer."

"Don't you get it?" Marla asked. "Didn't you hear what she said? She said 'I' have a situation."

"Marla, she just meant—"

"I know what she meant. She's worried about her own reputation first."

"Even if that were true, anything she does to protect herself will end up protecting you[6]."

Marla's eyes darted about[7], as if looking for some safe place to run to, and finding none[8]. "I think … maybe I am in trouble."

I leaned in close to her, rested my hands on her shoulders. I'd already asked her the big question, but felt it was time to try again. "Marla, look at me. Tell me. Did you do anything to that woman? To Matthew's mother? Maybe, just for a moment, something snapped[9]? You did something you didn't mean to do[10]?"

Even as I asked this, I wondered whether I wanted to know the answer. If Marla confessed to me that she'd killed Rosemary Gaynor and then

1. me donne le droit de la boucler

2. Têtu jusqu'au bout

3. passa en revue

4. qui commande

5. d'un responsable

6. te protégera aussi

7. allaient de gauche à droite

8. n'en trouvaient pas

9. tu as craqué

10. sans le vouloir

1. s'était enfuie
2. cacher à

run off[1] with her baby, would that be something I could withhold from[2] the police?

I knew how Agnes would answer that question.

"David, I could never do a thing like that," she said, a voice barely above a whisper. "Never."

"Okay, okay, that's good," I said.

"You'll help me, won't you?"

"Sure, of course. But really, I know you don't always trust your mother's motives[3], but once she gets Natalie on board[4], then—"

3. les intentions
4. de son côté
5. suppliant

"No, no," Marla said, her eyes pleading[5]. "You. *You* have to help me. It's what you do, right? You ask questions and find out things[6]."

6. tu découvres des choses
7. tu sais faire

"Not anymore," I told her.

"But you know how[7]. Find the woman who gave me Matthew. Find her. She'll tell you what I'm saying is the truth."

"Marla, just—"

"Promise," she said. "Promise you'll help me."

8. cherchais les mots justes
9. de ton côté
10. se décomposa instantanément
11. visiblement inconsciente
12. du caractère complètement évasif de ma réponse

I was hunting for the right words[8]. I held her tightly, looked her in the eye, and said, "You know I'm in your corner[9]."

Her face shattered like a dropped teacup[10] as she slipped her arms around me. "Thank you," she said, her voice muffled against my chest, clearly not appreciating[11] how totally noncommittal my response had been[12].

ELEVEN

"I wonder what's going on," said Arlene Harwood, standing at the top of the stairs to the basement[1]. "I want to phone David, but I figure[2], if he has something to tell us, he'll call. What a terrible situation. Just terrible."

Don Harwood, seated at his workbench[3], had just tightened the vise[4] on a lawn-mower blade[5] that he wanted to sharpen[6]. His basement[7] workshop—as opposed to the other one he had in the garage—was more crowded[8] than it once was, ever since he'd set up a Lionel train layout[9] on a four-by-eight sheet of plywood[10] for Ethan to play with before he and his father had moved away to Boston. Ethan had lost interest in it, but Don had not, and could not bring himself[11] to tear it down. He'd put a lot of work into it. The O scale station[12], the miniature people waiting on the platform[13], the crossing signal that flashed[14] when the train raced by, even a replica of the town's water tower[15], with the words "Promise Falls" printed on the side.

"I don't know," he said, not looking in Arlene's direction, but staring at the blade, wondering where he'd put his grinder[16]. That'd be just the ticket[17] to make this blade sharp enough to shave with. "She's trouble[18], that girl. Always has been,

1. escalier de la cave
2. me dis
3. établi
4. étau
5. lame de tondeuse à gazon
6. aiguiser
7. à la cave
8. encombré
9. maquette de petit train
10. plaque de contreplaqué
11. se résoudre
12. station d'aiguillage miniature
13. quai
14. lumière qui se déclenchait au passage à niveau
15. château d'eau
16. affûteuse
17. pile ce qu'il lui fallait
18. un nid à emmerdes

always will be. Your sister should have committed her to a mental ward for a while[1] after she tried to run off with that baby in the hospital."

Arlene descended halfway down the stairs, far enough that[2] Don would be able to see her from the waist down[3], if he chose to take his eyes off the blade. "That's a horrible thing to say."

"Is it? Maybe if she had, she wouldn't be having more trouble with her today. Damn it, where's my grinder?"

Don suddenly raised his head, sniffed the air. "Arlene, you got somethin' on the burner[4]?"

"What?"

"Something sure smells like it's burning[5]."

"Oh, Lord!" she said, turned and started running up the stairs. But two[6] from the top, she stumbled[7], pitched forward[8], and yelped[9].

"Shit," Don said, then hopped off his stool[10] and bolted up[11] the stairs to help her.

"I'm so stupid!" she said, trying to get upright[12].

Don knelt next to her. "What hurts? What did you hit?"

"Just my leg. Below my knee. Damn it. Go turn off the stove[13]!"

Don edged around her[14] and entered the kitchen. Smoke was billowing up[15] from a frying pan. There were half a dozen breakfast sausages burning to a crisp[16]. Don grabbed the handle, slid the pan over to another burner[17], then opened a lower cupboard door to look for the biggest lid[18] he could find. He grabbed one and slammed it on top of the pan, smothering[19] the smoke and the flame that was just beginning to erupt.

He could feel his heart pounding,[20] stood leaning[21] against the counter[22] to catch his breath. He hadn't run up a flight of stairs[1] in a long time, certainly not since his cardiac incident.

He heard some shuffling[2], looked to see Arlene framed in the doorway[3] to the basement. She'd managed to climb the rest of the stairs, but there was blood on her beige slacks[4], below her right knee.

"Oh, honey, you've really hurt yourself," he said.

"I'm okay, I'm okay. I was cooking up some sausages so I could slice them and put them in toast for our lunch. I can't believe I did that."

"It's okay," he said. "I'll make us something else. Some soup. I'll open a can of soup."

Arlene limped over[5] to the kitchen table, dropped herself into a chair. "Look what I've done to these pants. I just bought these. I don't know if I can get that out[6]. They'll never be the same."

"Don't worry about that," Don said. "Let me have a look."

He pushed himself away from the counter and went carefully down to one knee, rolled up the pant leg to just over Arlene's knee, and examined the wound[7]. "Those things always hurt like hell, right on the bone there. You've scraped the skin[8], and it's gonna swell up good[9]. Does it feel like it's broken?"

"I don't think so."

"Stay here." With effort, he stood, using the table for leverage[10], feeling his bones creak as he did so, and rummaged around in the drawer where they kept a first-aid kit[11]. He cleaned the wound, put a bandage on it, then got a pliable ice pack[12] from the freezer.

"Hold this on it," Don said. "Here, let's prop your leg up[13] on another chair. Then the pack won't slide off[14]."

1. volée de marches

2. un bruit de pas traînant

3. dans l'encadrement de la porte

4. pantalon

5. boita

6. nettoyer ça

7. blessure

8. t'es éraflée

9. gonfler

10. pour s'appuyer

11. trousse de secours

12. sac de glace souple

13. te poser la jambe

14. ne glissera pas

He rolled her pant leg back down so the ice pack wouldn't be right on her skin[1], then set it into position.

"Damn, that's cold," she said.

"Yeah, well, you'll get used to it. Gotta leave it on there for a bit."

Arlene reached out and touched his arm. "I'm losing my marbles[2]."

"No, you're not."

"I'm forgetting things," she said. "More and more."

"We all do," he said. "I forget stuff all the time. Remember the other night I was trying to remember the name of that actor, the one from that movie?"

"Which movie?"

"You know, the one where they were fighting that thing, and that actress was in it? The one you like? You know."

She smiled sadly. "You *are* as bad as me."

"I'm just saying, we're forgetting things that aren't that important, like movie stars' names, but we still remember the stuff that matters[3]."

"Remembering I have something on the stove matters," she said. "I can't find my keys half the time; the other day I thought I'd lost my Visa card and I found it in the drawer. Why would I put my Visa card in a drawer and not in my wallet?"

Don pulled up a third chair so that he could set himself down right next to her[4]. He put an arm around her shoulder. "You're fine[5]. We get older; we forget things. But you're fine. Don't worry about the sausages. If you're okay walking, we'll go out for lunch[6] today."

"You can't," Arlene said suddenly.

"And why not?"

1. directement sur la peau

2. Je perds la boule

3. trucs qui comptent

4. à côté d'elle

5. C'est pas si grave

6. déjeuner dehors

"Because you're meeting Walden. I shouldn't even have been making the sausages. You're not going to be here at lunch."

"What? What are you talking about? Walden Fisher?"

"Do you know any other Waldens?"

"He's coming over to see me?"

"At eleven. I think he said coffee, not lunch, but when you go out at eleven, there's a good chance it'll turn into lunch."

"This is all news to me," Don said, an edge in his voice[1].

"Oh, no," Arlene said. "I don't believe it."

"What?'

"He called here yesterday. I'm pretty sure it was yesterday. He said he was going to drop by[2]. Didn't I tell you? Are you sure I didn't tell you?"

"It doesn't matter."

"I wrote it down. I'm sure I wrote it down. Look on the calendar."

By the phone was a promotional calendar from a local florist that came in the mail[3] every December. They kept a record of their appointments[4]—mostly medical these days—in the tiny squares[5].

"Here it is," he said. " 'Walden, eleven.' "

"I knew I wrote it down. I was sure I told you." The ice pack slid off her leg and hit the floor. "Oh, Christ almighty[6]."

Don bent over, carefully retrieved it, and put it back on his wife's leg. "Feeling any better?"

"What hurts most is my pride[7]."

"Why the hell does Walden want to see me? I haven't talked to him in years."

Arlene shook her head. "Well, he's going to be here in a few minutes. You get ready. I'm fine, really."

1. d'un ton contrarié

2. passer

3. par la poste
4. rendez-vous
5. petites cases

6. Seigneur

7. fierté

1. de quoi il s'agissait

2. on n'a plus le droit de passer

3. ait pris sa retraite d'inspecteur en bâtiment

4. se croisaient de temps en temps

5. comme rapporteur

6. avait débuté

7. dans les années 1960

8. mort depuis longtemps

9. avait eu son diplôme d'ingénieur

10. l'avait recommandé auprès de

11. la DRH

12. sans lien de parenté

13. attribuait à Don le mérite

14. avantages sociaux

15. se faire virer

16. répliqua-t-il sèchement

17. Pas la peine de m'agresser

"Did he say what it was about[1]?"

"For heaven's sake, Don, a man can't get together[2] for coffee? He's a friend of yours."

"That's kind of debatable," Don said.

Walden Fisher, a good fifteen years younger than Don, was still employed by Promise Falls. Before Don retired from his position as a building inspector[3], he and Walden occasionally crossed paths[4], even though Walden worked in the town's engineering department as a draftsman[5]. It was there, however, where Don had gotten his start[6] when he went to work for the town back in the sixties[7].

Don had worked with Walden's father—long since passed away[8]—and when Walden graduated college with an engineering degree[9], Don put in a good word for him with[10] personnel[11]. Walden's dad had figured a recommendation would be better coming from someone who was not a relative[12]. Walden always credited Don with[13] getting him into a decent job with decent benefits[14], where the risk of getting laid off[15] was minimal.

"It wouldn't kill you to have a social life," Arlene said.

"I suppose," Don said. "But I haven't talked to him since I retired."

"You heard, I guess," Arlene said.

"About his daughter?" he snapped[16], almost defensively. "Of course. Who the hell hasn't heard about that? It was only three years ago. Who could forget that?"

"You don't have to bite my head off[17]. And I'm not talking about her. Walden's wife. She passed away a couple of months back."

"How do you know that?" Don asked, his voice softening.

"I read the paper[1]. Or I did, when there still was one. It was in the death notices[2]."

"Oh," Don said. "Didn't know."

"Maybe he's just looking to get out there[3], get out of the house, now that his wife is gone."

"You know what happened to her?" Don asked.

"Cancer, I think," she said. "Go on, he's likely to be here any—[4]"

The doorbell rang.

Don was frozen[5]. He didn't want to leave Arlene. "It's okay," she said. He told her one more time to keep the ice on her leg, and left the kitchen.

He swung open the front door, and there was Walden Fisher. Looking older and grayer[6] than the last time he'd seen him, that was for sure, although there was less hair to turn gray than there used to be. A bit more padding around the middle[7], but he wasn't a heavy man[8]. Had to be about fifty-five now, Don figured.

"I'll be damned," Don said. "Look who it is."

Walden smiled awkwardly[9]. "Hello, there, Don. Long time."

Back in the kitchen, he could hear the phone start to ring.

"You retired?"

"No, I got nearly five more years to go. But I've built up so much overtime[10], I'm taking a day here and there. Taking the better part of this month off[11]. I get you at a bad time[12]? You knew I was coming, right?"

The phone rang a second time.

"Of course, yeah. What's on your mind?"

"I wanted to pick your brain some[13]. It'll take five years, but all the town's planning and engineering is going to computer[14]. Most of the infrastructure was built before computers, so it's all on

1. journal	
2. avis de décès	
3. veut juste sortir un peu	
4. peut arriver à tout...	
5. se figea	
6. plus grisonnant	
7. plus de rembourrage à la taille	
8. gros	
9. gauchement	
10. tellement d'heures de récup à prendre	
11. Presque tout le mois, là	
12. te dérange	
13. ai besoin de tes lumières	
14. devient informatisé	

paper. Blueprints[1], schematics[2], everything. Details of every water main[3], bridge support, sewer grate[4] are on huge sheets rolled up with rubber bands[5], and God knows where they've all gone to. If you can believe it, some guys retired and took their work home with them when they did."

"I never did that," Don said.

"Not saying you did," Walden said. "But I've been getting together with some of the older guys, no offense intended[6], to see if they know where some of that stuff ended up. Once we find it, we can get it all transferred onto computer."

"Thought you said you were taking some time off[7]."

Walden shrugged. "When I'm actually[8] in the office, I don't have time to do what I'm doing now."

Don let out a breath he'd been holding[9]. "Like I said, I never took anything home, but I might be able to fill in some of the gaps[10] if there's stuff you don't know. I worked on the water tower, for one thing." It was why he wanted to have a model of it on the model railroad[11].

The phone started to ring a third time, then stopped abruptly.

Don said, "Listen, let me grab my jacket and we'll go over to Kelly's. I could go for[12] a BLT[13], maybe a piece of pie."

Don left Walden standing on the front step[14], but before going to the hall closet for his coat, he returned to the kitchen. He was worried Arlene probably got up to answer the phone, and that was exactly what she had done.

The ice pack was on the floor. Arlene was leaned up against the counter, one foot off the floor[15], receiver[16] in hand.

---

1. Les plans
2. les schémas
3. canalisation
4. grille de tout-à-l'égout
5. des élastiques
6. sans vouloir te vexer
7. des vacances
8. vraiment
9. lâcha un soupir de soulagement
10. te filer un coup de main
11. circuit miniature
12. me ferais bien
13. sandwich au bacon
14. perron
15. levé
16. le combiné

She looked at Don and said, "I thought it would be David calling with news about Marla. But it's the school, and it's David they're looking for. They had a cell[1] number for him but it was his Boston number, and he changed his phone since then and must not have told them and why wouldn't he think to do that[2]?"

"What *is* it?" Don asked.

"Ethan. Something's happened with Ethan."

1. de portable

2. qu'est-ce qui lui a pris d'oublier

TWELVE

1. amena
2. porte
donnant sur

BARRY Duckworth steered[1] Bill Gaynor into the dining room, making sure the connecting door to[2] the kitchen was closed. He pulled out two chairs that were tucked under the dining room table and turned them to face each other.

"Mr. Gaynor, have a seat."

"Tell me again, where's Matthew?"

"Matthew is fine; don't worry. Please sit."

Gaynor settled into a chair, and when Duckworth sat, their knees were a foot apart[3].

3. à 30 cm
d'écart

"They won't give him back to that crazy woman," Gaynor said.

"Don't worry about that. Do you know that woman, Mr. Gaynor?"

"No, I've never seen her before in my life."

"I'm told her name is Marla Pickens. Mean anything to you[4]?"

4. Ça vous dit
quelque chose

The man shook his head tiredly. "No."

Duckworth noticed a photo on the serving table[5] against the wall. He pointed to it. "That's you and your wife?"

5. desserte

Gaynor looked older than the man in the picture. "That was taken when we were married."

Duckworth took a longer look at[6] the picture. Rosemary Gaynor's straight black hair hung to her

6. s'attarda sur

114

shoulders[1]. She'd still been wearing it in the same style. Her eyes were dark brown, her skin pale, no rouge[2] or lipstick to give herself some color.

Gaynor asked, "What's going to happen to my Rosemary?"

"I'm sorry?"

"My wife." He tipped his head in the direction of the door to the kitchen. "What's going to happen with her? What are they going to do with her?"

"She'll be taken to the forensic examiner's office[3]," Duckworth said. "An autopsy has to be conducted. Once that's done, she can be released to you[4] so that you can make arrangements."

"Why?"

"Why what?"

"Why does there have to be an autopsy? For Christ's sake, all you have to do is look at her to know …" He put his face into his hands and cried. "Hasn't she been through enough[5]?"

"I know," Duckworth said gently. "But an examination of your wife may yield[6] a lot of helpful information that will help us find out who did this. Unless you already have some idea."

Without looking up, he shook his head. "No, I have *no* idea. Everyone loved Rose. This is the work of some crazy person. That woman. She's crazy. She had Matthew, for God's sake." He raised his head, looked at Duckworth with red eyes. "It had to be her[7]. She kidnapped Matthew and when Rose tried to stop her, she … she did that."

Duckworth nodded. "That's something we're going to be looking into[8], Mr. Gaynor. But right now, I need to get a sense[9] of when things happened."

A timeline[10], the detective was thinking. He needed to get a timeline. "When did you last

---

1. lui tombait jusqu'aux épaules
2. fard
3. cabinet du médecin légiste
4. vous être rendue
5. assez souffert
6. fournir
7. C'est forcément elle
8. investiguer
9. me faire une idée
10. chronologie

speak with your wife? When you left for work this morning?"

"No, it was yesterday."

"Sunday?"

1. en déplacement

"That's right. I've been out of town[1]. On business."

"Where were you?"

"I was in Boston. Since Thursday."

"What were you doing there?"

2. au siège
3. dans les assurances
4. venait

"I ... I was at a meeting at our head office[2]. I'm in insurance[3]. Neponset Insurance. I spend a lot of time there. Sometimes Rose comes—would come[4] with me. Before we had Matthew. If I was going to be there for a while."

"Where did you stay?" Duckworth asked, scribbling in his notebook.

5. qu'on me prend une chambre
6. d'un maximum d'infos
7. enverrait vérifier

"The Marriott Long Wharf. That's where they always put me up[5]. Why does this matter?"

"I need to get a full picture[6], Mr. Gaynor." Duckworth was thinking that before he walked out of this house, he'd have someone onto[7] the Marriott and Neponset Insurance to check Gaynor's story. Even though there was nothing so far to suggest Gaynor had murdered his wife, spouses[8] were always high on the suspect list. Boston was only a couple of hours away by car, if you really pushed it[9]. The man could have left Boston yesterday afternoon, returned home, killed Rosemary Gaynor, then hightailed it back to the city[10], pretending to have been there the whole time.

8. les conjoints

9. en allant à fond

10. refilé en ville

11. peu probable

It seemed unlikely[11] to Duckworth, but if he didn't check it out, it would always remain a possibility.

He asked, "When did you leave Promise Falls for Boston?"

"Like I said, Thursday. Very early, so I could be there by ten. We finished up this series of meetings last night, but I was too tired to drive home then, so I decided to get up early this morning. I was calling Rose all the way home[1]. The house phone, her cell. She wasn't answering."

"But you talked to her yesterday. On Sunday."

The man nodded. "Around two? There was a lunch. We had a keynote speaker[2], a funny motivational talk. When that was over, I had a few minutes before the next session I had to attend[3], so I called Rose on my cell."

"And you reached her."

He nodded.

"What did you talk about?"

"Nothing, really. I told her I missed her. I asked how Matthew was. I told her I'd probably drive home in the morning, but if I decided to come back that night I'd call and let her know[4]."

"So you didn't call her again?"

"Not till I was on my way this morning." He bit his lip. "I should have come home last night. Why the hell didn't I just come back then? I could have been here, could have stopped this from happening[5]."

"We'll know more as the investigation proceeds[6], Mr. Gaynor, but it appears this attack happened yesterday afternoon. Coming home last night … it's unlikely it would have made any difference."

Bill Gaynor closed his eyes and breathed in[7] slowly.

"I noticed you have a security system," Duckworth said.

He opened his eyes. "Yes. But Rose only turned it on at night when she went to bed. She didn't have it on through the day[8]. Every time she'd

1. pendant toute la route du retour

2. conférencier d'honneur

3. à laquelle je devais assister

4. pour la prévenir

5. empêcher ça

6. au cours de l'enquête

7. inspira

8. dans la journée

117

go out, to go to the store, or take Matthew for a walk in his stroller, she'd have to disengage it[1] before she opened the door. So she only put it on at night."

"Okay. What about just locking it?"

A fast nod. "That she almost always did. She'd turn the dead bolt[2] every time she came back in the house."

"What about friends? Did your wife belong to any clubs? Like a university women's club or a gym[3]? Anything like that?"

"No," he said, shaking his head.

"And I have to ask, Mr. Gaynor, whether it's possible there could have been anyone else."

"Anyone else?"

Duckworth said nothing, just let the question sink in.

"Oh, no, God. I mean, we were devoted to each other[4], and she just had a baby. She's hardly— That's a terrible thing to ask."

"I'm sorry. Any kind of trouble with the law?"

"Are you serious? Of course not. Okay, she got a speeding ticket[5] a week or so ago, but I'd hardly call that being in trouble with the law."

"Nor would I," Duckworth said gently. "Do you have family in town?"

"No. We don't really have any extended family at all. I was an only child and my parents passed away when I was in my teens[6]. And Rose, she did have an older sister, but she died years ago."

"How'd that happen?"

"Horseback riding. She fell off a horse and broke her neck."

Duckworth winced[7]. "Parents?"

"Like me, Rose's mother and father passed away fairly early[8]. I think she lost her mother when

1. ça aurait voulu dire l'éteindre

2. verrou

3. salle de sport

4. tout l'un pour l'autre

5. amende pour excès de vitesse

6. adolescent

7. grimaça

8. assez jeunes

118

she was nineteen, and her father when she was twenty-two."

"So there's no parents, in-laws[1], who might have keys to the house."

1. beaux-parents

"No, just Sarita."

"Who's Sarita?"

2. nounou

"The nanny[2]. I don't know where she is. She should be here. I'm pretty sure this is the day she comes in the morning."

"What's Sarita's last name[3]?"

3. nom de famille

Gaynor's mouth opened but nothing came out.

"Her name?" Duckworth repeated.

"I don't … I don't think I've ever known Sarita's last name. Rose, she took care of that end of things[4]." His face reddened with embarrassment. "I know I should know this."

4. ces questions-là

"That's okay," Duckworth said, keeping his disapproval to himself. "But what can you tell me about her?"

"When we had Matthew, I thought it would be a good idea for Rose to have some help. She's had … health problems over the years. So if we had someone come in a few times a week to help out[5] … Sarita isn't exactly a nanny, although she's got training[6] and has worked with children. But even if she could be here just to spell[7] Rose. Give her a chance to get out of the house. Do some shopping without having to lug[8] Matthew and the car seat and all that. Plus, Sarita helped out with other things. Cleaning, getting the laundry caught up[9]. Cooking. That kind of thing. All before she headed off[10], if she had a shift[11]."

5. l'aider
6. est formée pour
7. soulager
8. traîner
9. se mettre à jour en lessive
10. avant de repartir
11. allait prendre son service

"A shift?" Duckworth asked.

"Yeah. She pulled a few shifts[12] at a nursing home[13] or a hospital or something. I don't know exactly what it was."

12. faisait quelques gardes
13. maison de retraite

"How did you find Sarita? To hire her[1]?"

"It wasn't me who did it. I told Rose I thought it'd be a good idea for her to have help, but she did the actual looking[2]. I think she saw an ad[3] online somewhere; there was a phone number. She called and Sarita came out for an interview and Rose liked her and that was that[4]."

"And you're sure you don't know her last name."

Gaynor shook his head.

Duckworth was thinking that Rosemary Gaynor would probably have a number for[5] the nanny in the contacts in her phone. Failing that[6], it would probably be written down somewhere. Then he had another thought.

"How's Sarita paid? You must have some canceled checks[7]. There'll be a name on those."

"It was … cash," he said. "We always pay Sarita in cash. She's not, strictly speaking … I'm not sure whether Sarita is here legally[8]."

"Okay. Where's she from?"

"I didn't even think people from Mexico came this far north[9], but she might be from there. Or she might be from the Philippines. She doesn't look really, you know, that foreign[10], like maybe one of her parents was an American. Like, a white American."

Duckworth said nothing, made a note.

"I'm sorry, I'm not sure about this. Does it matter where she's from? I mean, you've got that insane woman[11] who had Matthew. That's who you need to be talking to."

Duckworth said, "Can you excuse me for five seconds?"

He left the dining room, waved over Officer[12] Gilchrist. "Find out where Marla Pickens lives and seal that house off[13]. No one gets in. Right now[14]."

"Got it[1]," he said.

Duckworth went back to his living room chair. Gaynor had a cell phone in his hand. He wasn't making a call or checking mail. He was simply staring at it.

"I feel like I should be calling someone," he said. "But I can't think who[2]."

"Let's get back to Sarita. You say she should have been here today. Is that right?"

"Yes. I'm certain this is her morning to come. And yesterday. She was supposed to be here yesterday."

"Okay," Duckworth said. "If she's supposed to be here, and she isn't, that raises a couple of possibilities, Mr. Gaynor. One is that she may have something to do with this, or know something about what happened here. And ..." Duckworth hesitated a moment. "And it may mean that she's in some kind of trouble herself."

Bill Gaynor blinked[3]. "Oh, my God. This Marla woman didn't just kill Rose. She's killed Sarita, too, hasn't she?"

1. Compris

2. ne sais pas qui

3. cilla

THIRTEEN

David

1. à l'avant
2. au volant

3. lui remettre

4. transmettre
5. resta à surveiller qu'on restait sur les lieux
6. jusqu'au bout du périmètre de sécurité
7. guetter l'arrivée

8. ne rendait pas justice à cet endroit

I'D put Marla back in my car, up front[1] in the passenger seat. I got behind the wheel[2], but we weren't going anywhere. Officer Gilchrist had ordered me to surrender[3] my keys earlier, and then he was back asking to see Marla's driver's license, as if he wanted to know where she lived. He got on his radio to pass along[4] some information, then kept watch on us to make sure we didn't leave the scene[5]. Agnes had gone down the street, to where they'd strung the police tape[6], to watch for[7] lawyer Natalie Bondurant.

"Remember coming up to the cabin?" Marla asked. The question came out of nowhere.

"Wow, that was a long time ago," I said. "I only went up half a dozen times, when I was sixteen or seventeen? Eighteen maybe?"

Marla was referring to a place her parents owned on Lake George, barely an hour's drive north of Promise Falls. And to call it a cabin was to do the place a disservice[8]. It was a beautiful home. The property had been in Gill Pickens's family for several generations, and long ago there had been a simple cabin and an outhouse[1] on the site. Gill's parents tore it down[2] and built a house in its place, but it never stopped being called "the cabin."

Back when Agnes and my mother were getting along[3] better than they were now, my family was invited up there for a few weekends. I swam and waterskied[4] and went searching up and down the lake in Gill's boat for teenage girls. Marla was a little kid then, probably six or seven.

"I had a crush on you[5]," she said quietly, looking down into her lap.

"What?"

"I mean, even though you were my cousin, and, like, ten years older, I really liked you. Don't you remember me following you around all the time?"

"You were my shadow," I said. "I remember anytime I wanted to go anywhere, you wanted to go with me."

She smiled weakly[6]. "Remember that time I found you[7]? With what's-her-name[8]?"

I cocked my[9] head. "I don't know what you're talking about."

"In the boathouse. I went in there and caught you making out[10] with that girl. I think her name was Zenia or something. You had your hand right under her shirt."

"Yeah, I remember that. I begged you[11] not to tell anyone."

Marla nodded. "I made you take me to the marina, in Dad's boat, and get me something at the snack bar. I was bought off[12] for the price of a milk shake."

I shot her a smile. "Yeah. I remember that, too."

"I should have asked for more, considering what I'd end up[13] doing for you later."

"What?" I asked.

1. remise
2. l'avaient fait démolir
3. s'entendaient
4. faisais du ski nautique
5. en pinçais pour toi
6. faiblement
7. le jour où je t'ai surpris
8. Machine
9. penchai la
10. en pleine action
11. t'ai suppliée
12. me suis laissée acheter
13. vu ce que j'allais

"That same summer?"

"I don't … I don't think I know what you're re-ferring to[1]."

She waved a hand, dismissed it. "All my mem-ories of the cabin used to be good. It was my hap-py place, you know? But I don't think I can ever go back there." She went silent for several seconds, then said, "That's where I lost her, you know. Where I lost Agatha."

"Agatha," I repeated.

"That's what I would have named her. I had a name all picked out[2]. Agatha Beatrice Pickens. A mouthful[3], I know." Her eyes, which hadn't had much of a break[4] from crying in the last couple of hours, moistened yet again[5].

"I didn't know it happened up there," I said.

"There was this outbreak[6] at the hospital then, *C. diff* or whatever they call it, and Mom was wor-ried about me having the baby there. Although she didn't want anyone to know she was choos-ing to keep her own daughter out of the hospital. She knew how that would play[7], sending me else-where at the same time she was telling the press that the hospital was perfectly safe, that all precau-tions were being taken. But she was trained as a nurse and was a midwife for a while years ago— you knew that, right?"

"Yeah."

"So she said she could look after me[8] as well as anybody could. Although she didn't want to take too many chances[9], so she got Dr. Sturgess to help out. So they got me all set up at the cabin. I mean, it was a good idea, and it was really nice up there. Relaxing, you know?"

"Sure," I said.

Marginal notes:

1. à quoi tu fais allusion
2. tout trouvé
3. Dur à prononcer
4. ne s'étaient pas beaucoup arrêtés
5. redevinrent humides
6. épidémie
7. ça serait interprété
8. s'occuper de moi
9. risques

"Mom stayed up there with me. She had Dr. Sturgess on standby[1]. Like, if the contractions started getting really close together, she'd call him and get him up there. Since she's the head of the hospital, people, even the doctors, jump when she tells them to[2]."

"I've noticed," I said.

"So, when it looked like the baby was about to be born, she texted him[3] and he got up there real fast. And things were going okay at first, although I had a lot of pain, you know? *Lots* of pain." Her voice drifted off[4].

I didn't know what to say. Maybe there wasn't anything she wanted me to say. Marla just wanted to talk.

"They gave me something for it[5]; Dr. Sturgess did. And that helped. But then things started going wrong. Something really bad. And when the baby—when Agatha—came out, she wasn't breathing."

"Was it the cord[6]? The umbilical cord?" I didn't know a lot about the subject, but I had heard of newborns dying that way.

She looked away and nodded. "Yeah. I've read about it online, and it happens a lot, but it's rare for it to actually threaten[7] the baby. But that's what happened. It was all kind of surreal, because I was sort of in and out[8], but even so, I'll never forget it. Not as long as I live."

"I'm sorry, Marla. I can't imagine how horrible that must have been."

"At least I got to hold her[9]," Marla said. "To see her perfect little fingers." The tears were coming now. "Mom says I held her for a couple of minutes before they had to take her away. You have any Kleenex?"

1. à sa disposition au cas où

2. lui obéissent au doigt et à l'œil

3. lui a fait un SMS

4. s'éteignit

5. contre la douleur

6. cordon

7. que ça menace vraiment
8. à demi consciente

9. ai pu la tenir

1. boîte à gants
2. mouchoirs en papier
3. s'en est voulu

4. en a vraiment souffert
5. passe pour une sacrée peau de vache

6. paraissait logique
7. étais d'accord
8. le plus intelligent

9. faire face à
10. tourne mal

11. furax

12. de s'être faite à l'idée

I pointed to the glove box[1]. She opened it, grabbed three tissues[2], dabbed her eyes, and blew her nose. "Mom blamed herself[3]," she said.

"What do you mean?"

"After, she said it was all her fault. That if I'd had the baby at the hospital, maybe they could have done more to save her. She took it pretty hard[4]. I know she comes across as a total bitch and a half[5], but she took it almost as bad as I did."

"What about you?" I asked.

"What about me?"

"Do you blame her?"

She took several seconds to answer. "No," she said finally. "It made sense[6], doing things that way. I mean, I went along with it[7]. Dr. Sturgess said it was the smartest thing[8] to do. It was just … it was just the way it happened. If I blame anyone, I guess I blame God. That's who Mom says she blames, after she's done blaming herself."

I nodded.

"And I'm not a religious person. I mean, I didn't really believe in God until I needed Him to blame. Does that make any sense?" She searched my face.

"I think so," I said. "It's hard to know how to handle[9] these things."

"And up until everything went to shit[10], it was kind of a good time up there. I mean, just being there with Mom. She was okay. She was really nice to me. She wasn't judging me the way she usually does, even though I know she was pretty pissed[11] when she found out I was pregnant. But close to the end, she seemed to come to terms with it[12]."

"How about the father?" I asked. "How'd he react?"

"Derek?" she said.

"Yeah. I've never known his name."

126

"Derek Cutter."

The name rang a bell[1]. From my days as a reporter for the *Standard*.

"I didn't tell him right away[2]. I hadn't talked to him much in the last few weeks I was pregnant. She didn't want me to have anything to do with him. I don't think I was really in love with him or anything."

"He's a student?"

Her head went up and down twice. "He's local[3]. He didn't leave town to go to college like a lot of kids do. He started out living at home[4], but then his parents split up[5], and they sold the house and his mom moved away, I think. His dad moved into an apartment, and then Derek started sharing a house close to the college[6] with some other students."

"Sounds kind of rough[7] for him."

"Yeah. His dad runs a gardening service or something. When Derek was a teenager, he worked for him. Cutting lawns and doing landscaping and stuff like that. But when the house got sold, he had to rent a garage or something to store his lawn mowers and everything. Mom never liked Derek. She figured I should be finding someone whose parents were lawyers or owned Microsoft or invented Google. Someone like that. But Derek was okay."

"Where'd you meet him?"

"At a bar in town. We just kind of bumped into each other[8]. I might have sort of lied about how old I was[9]. I told him I'd just gotten out of school, so he'd think I was only a year or two older than him, instead of seven. But I don't think age really matters that much[10], do you?"

My phone rang. "Hang on[11]," I said.

1. me disait quelque chose

2. tout de suite

3. du coin

4. Au début, il vivait chez ses parents

5. se sont séparés

6. près de la fac

7. dur

8. s'était rencontrés par hasard

9. un peu menti sur mon âge

10. que l'âge ait tant d'importance

11. Attends

It was home calling. That could mean Mom or Dad, but I was betting Mom.

"Hello?"

"David?"

I was right. "Yeah, Mom."

"What's happening?"

"It's a long story. I can't really get into it[1] right now. I'm with Marla, and Agnes has arrived."

"Because I don't know if this is something you want your father to handle[2]. I'd do it myself but I fell on the stairs."

I gripped[3] the motionless steering wheel with my free hand. "Mom, what's going on?"

"I was coming up the stairs and slipped, but it's nothing. But the school called about Ethan."

Jesus, when it rained, it poured[4]. "What about Ethan? Is Ethan hurt?"

"I don't think so, but he got into some kind of fight[5]. With another boy. He got sent to the office[6] and they called here for you. You gave them your old cell phone number when you enrolled him[7] and you must have forgotten to give them your new one, so if there's an emergency[8]—"

"Mom!" I shouted. "What about Ethan?"

"They want you to pick him up[9]. They're sending him home."

I closed my eyes and exhaled[10]. "I can't do that right now. I can't leave the scene[11]."

"The scene?"

"Let Dad go. He can pick up Ethan, and I'll sort things out[12] when I get home. Okay?"

"I'll tell him. What did Marla do, David? Did she really take another baby?"

"Later, Mom."

1. te raconter

2. dont tu veux que ton père s'occupe

3. serrai

4. la loi des séries

5. bagarre

6. chez le directeur

7. l'as inscrit

8. en cas d'urgence

9. que tu ailles le chercher

10. soupirai

11. les lieux

12. réglerai tout ça

I ended the call, put the phone away, and lowered my head until it was touching the top of the wheel.

"Trouble?" Marla asked.

"Seems to be a lot of it going around[1]," I said. "But it's okay."

I looked at the Gaynor house. The front door was being opened from the inside. Detective Duckworth emerged, locked eyes on[2] my car, and headed our way[3]. But before he could reach the car, two other people appeared by Marla's open window.

Agnes and Natalie Bondurant.

Agnes said, "Everything's going to be okay, child. Everything is going to be okay."

Duckworth reached the car and asked Agnes and Natalie to step aside. "Marla Pickens? Would you step out of the car?[4]"

"She has nothing to say," Agnes said as Marla started to push open the door. Agnes pushed it back.

"Ms. Pickens," Natalie said, addressing Agnes, "let me take it from here[5]. Hello, Barry."

"Natalie," he said.

"I'm representing Marla Pickens. I'm afraid she won't be taking any questions at this time."

Duckworth eyed her tiredly[6]. "I'm investigating a murder[7] here, Natalie. I've got things to ask."

"I can appreciate[8] that. But right now my client's in shock[9] and in no position to handle questions[10]."

"And just when[11] do you think your client *will* be taking questions?"

"I'm not able to say at this time[12]."

"Well, whether she wants to answer questions or not, you're going to have her at the station[13] in exactly one hour."

1. que c'est pas ça qui manque

2. fixa
3. vint vers nous

4. Veuillez sortir du véhicule !

5. prendre le relais

6. la regarda d'un air las
7. j'enquête sur un meurtre
8. comprendre
9. sous le choc
10. n'est pas en état de répondre
11. quand au juste
12. pour l'instant
13. au commissariat

1. prit un air moqueur

2. ne rien me dire

Natalie's tongue poked the inside of her cheek[1]. "She's not going to have anything to tell you."

"Then she can not tell me anything[2] at the station."

Now Agnes opened the door, took Marla by the arm, and helped her out. With Natalie on one side and Agnes on the other, they escorted her down the street, leaving me alone behind the wheel.

"You got a lawyer, too?" Duckworth asked, looking at me through the open door.

"Not yet," I said.

He glanced into the back of my car. "Where'd you get that stroller?"

"It belongs to the Gaynors," I said.

3. Doux Jésus

4. coffre

"Christ on a cracker[3]," Duckworth said. "Open the hatch[4]."

5. allais prendre

6. me claqua la

I got out and did so. I went to reach for[5] the stroller but Duckworth slapped my[6] hand.

"Don't touch that," he said. "Have you already touched that?"

"Yes."

Duckworth sighed. "Let's you and me have a talk."

FOURTEEN

"**YOU** sure you don't mind[1] my tagging along[2]?" Walden Fisher asked Don Harwood.

"Nah, it's okay. I just got to go to the school and pick up my grandson, bring him home," Don said, walking down the front steps in the direction of his blue Crown Victoria that he'd had forever. "Hop in[3]."

The passenger door creaked[4] as Fisher opened it.

"Gotta put some WD-40[5] on that," Don said.

"Your grandson sick?"

"No. He got into some kind of scrap[6] with another kid."

"He okay?"

"Well, they weren't calling from the hospital, so I guess that's a good thing," Don said. "Truth is, the boy could use some toughening up[7]. Getting in the odd fight[8] probably be a good thing for him. I'll scoop him up[9], bring him home, and we can go grab a coffee. Just want to check in on[10] Arlene when I get back, though."

"What's wrong with her?"

"She just took a little trip[11] on the stairs, banged up her leg. I want to make sure she's okay."

1. que ça ne t'ennuie pas

2. que je t'accompagne

3. Monte

4. grinça

5. du dégrippant

6. une bagarre

7. aurait besoin de s'endurcir

8. Une bagarre de temps en temps

9. vais passer le prendre

10. voir comment va

11. gamelle

131

1. En sortant de la voie de garage en marche arrière

2. assombrir

3. sale crabe

4. comme condoléances

5. de l'avoir croisée

6. sujet

7. dont Don ne voulait surtout pas parler

8. n'était peut-être pas autant au fait des décès qu'Arlene

9. poignardée à mort

10. du pied de la cascade

11. à l'aube de sa vie

12. obtenu

13. décroché

Walden nodded understandingly. Backing out of the driveway[1], Don glanced over and thought he saw a look of sadness wash over[2] the man's face. "Arlene was telling me … she saw the notice in the paper about …"

"Beth?" Walden said.

"Right, yeah, Beth. I couldn't remember her name. Arlene was telling me she passed away recently."

"Nine weeks," he said. "The big C[3]."

"Sorry," Don said. He didn't know what else to offer in the way of condolences[4]. He wasn't good at that sort of thing. "I'm not sure whether I ever met her[5]."

"Probably at some Christmas party, a million years ago," Walden said. "A different time." A pause. "She was never really the same, after."

"After the diagnosis?"

Walden shook his head. "Well, yeah, that's true. But what I meant was, after what happened to Olivia."

There was a topic[6] Don didn't want to touch with a barge pole[7]. Don might not keep up with the death notices the way Arlene did[8], but there wasn't anyone in Promise Falls who didn't know about Olivia Fisher and what happened to her. Three years ago—Don was thinking it was three years ago this month—the twenty-two-year-old woman was fatally stabbed[9] one night in the downtown park, just steps away from the base of the falls[10] from which the town got its name.

Olivia Fisher was a young, beautiful woman just starting out on life's journey[11]. She'd recently completed[12] a degree in environmental science at Thackeray, had lined up[13] a job with an oceanic institute in Boston that was dedicated to preserving sea life, and was about to marry a young man from Promise Falls.

The world was waiting for her to make it a better place.

No one had ever been arrested for the crime. The Promise Falls police brought in help from the state, even an FBI profiler[1], but never made any real headway[2].

Don felt uncomfortable, not sure what to say. The best he could come up with was,[3] "It must have been devastating for Beth. But ... you, too."

Walden said, "Yeah, but I finally went back to work. Had to. Didn't have any choice. The grief[4]'s always with you, but sometimes you throw yourself into something; you just go on autopilot. It becomes mechanical, you know?"

"Sure," Don said, although he wasn't sure he did know. Certainly not in this context. Maybe his son, David, would. He'd been to hell and back[5] over his late wife[6], Jan, a few years ago.

"But Beth, she was a stay-at-homer[7], you know? Took the odd part-time job[8], and when Olivia was little she did babysitting, ran a day care out of the house[9]. But she gave that up[10] once Olivia was around ten. So every day I went to work, Beth was home alone with nothing but Olivia's ghost as company. I know there's probably no way to prove this, but I think that's why she got sick. She was so depressed, it just poisoned her. You think something like that could happen?"

"I guess[11]," Don said.

"It was almost as bad for Vick. Maybe worse."

"Vick?"

"Oh, sorry, I just keep thinking everybody knows all the details. Victor Rooney. The one who nearly became our son-in-law. They were going

1. psychologue expert du profilage

2. n'avait jamais rien trouvé

3. Il ne trouva rien de mieux à dire que :

4. chagrin

5. avait vécu l'enfer

6. lors de la mort de sa femme

7. femme au foyer

8. un boulot de temps en temps

9. gérait une garderie

10. avait arrêté

11. Je suppose

1. a plus ou moins sombré

2. à picoler

3. chez les pompiers

4. centres de désintoxication

5. se reprendre en main

6. ne s'en est jamais remis

7. l'ont viré

8. a démissionné

9. Je l'aperçois de temps en temps

10. avais fait sa connaissance

11. prendre sa retraite

12. Dans l'équipe de nuit

13. risque de faire le moins de dégâts

14. n'a pas inventé la poudre

15. place

16. devant

17. éraflée

18. accroc

19. surpris

20. est très occupé

to get married in three more months. He kind of went off the deep end[1], too. Started drinking hard[2]. Never finished his degree in chemical engineering, got a job with the fire department[3]. But the drinking got worse. They did their best for him, considering the circumstances and all. Sent him a couple of times to one of those places to dry out[4], get himself straightened up[5], but he never did pull it together[6]. I think they finally fired him[7], or he quit[8], don't know which, and if he ever found any other work I don't know. See him the odd time[9] just driving around town in his van. Too bad. Seemed like a good kid. I met him[10] back when he had a summer job once with the town, working in the water treatment plant."

"They still got Tate Whitehead working there? See him around town once in a while. He must be due to retire[11] soon."

"On the night shift[12], I think," Walden said. "Where he can do the least damage[13]."

"Yeah, well, Tate has a good heart but he's no nuclear physicist[14]," Don said. "The school's just up here."

"I'll wait in the car," Walden said.

"Sure."

Don found a parking spot[15], left the keys so Walden could listen to the radio if he wanted, and went into the building, following the signs to the office. As soon as he walked in, he saw his grandson seated in a chair this side of[16] a raised counter. Ethan's face was scraped[17], and there was a tear[18] in one knee of his jeans. His eyes were red.

The boy was startled[19]. "I didn't know you were coming," Ethan said. "I thought it would be Dad."

"He's got his hands full[20]," Don said.

"A job interview?"

134

Don shook his head. "I wish[1]."

A woman seated at a desk behind the counter got up and approached. "May I help you?"

"I'm Ethan's grandfather. Who are you?"

"I'm Ms. Harrow. I'm the vice principal[2]."

"There was some kind of trouble?"

"He and another boy got into a fight. They're both suspended[3] for the rest of the day."

"Who's the other kid? Where's he?" Don asked.

"That'd be Carl Worthington."

"Who started it?" Don asked.

"That's not really the issue[4]," Harrow said. "We have a zero-tolerance policy[5] about fighting. So they're both being disciplined[6]."

"You start it?" Don asked his grandson.

"No," Ethan said meekly[7].

"There," he said to the vice principal. "If he didn't start it, why's he being suspended?"

"Carl says it was Ethan who started it. I just got off the phone with Sam Worthington having this very same discussion."

"That's the father of the kid that started it?"

The vice principal started to speak but Don held up his hand. "Save it[8]. I'll take him home. In my day[9], we'd just let the kids sort it out[10] and didn't get so goddamn involved[11]. Let's go, Ethan."

Don tried to get some details out of Ethan on the way to the car, but he didn't want to talk about it. But when he saw someone sitting in the front seat of the Crown Victoria, he asked, "Who's that?"

"Friend of mine. Well, sort of[12]. Someone I worked with a long time ago, before I retired. Don't be asking him anything[13] about anybody."

"What would I ask him?"

"I don't know. But just don't, okay?"

1. Hélas non

2. directrice adjointe

3. renvoyés

4. la question
5. politique de tolérance zéro
6. punis
7. humblement

8. Laissez tomber
9. De mon temps
10. régler leurs affaires
11. on ne s'en mêlait pas comme ça

12. si on veut
13. Ne lui pose aucune question

Ethan got into the back of the car. Walden Fisher turned in his seat and extended a hand.

"I'm Walden," he said.

Ethan accepted the handshake[1] warily[2]. "I'm Ethan. I don't have anything else to say."

"Okay, then," Walden said.

When they got back home, Ethan burst out of[3] the car like it was rigged to explode[4] and ran in ahead of his grandfather. He found Arlene on the living room couch watching CNN, an ice pack on her leg. She tried to ask him what had happened, but he ran up to his room and closed the door.

Don asked his wife how she was doing[5], said he didn't have to go have a coffee with Walden if she needed his help, but she said she was fine, which was not the answer he was hoping for[6].

So, with some reluctance[7], Don Harwood went to Kelly's, where he had a coffee and a piece of cherry pie with whipped cream on top, and spent the better part of an hour[8] talking to Walden about blueprints and water-main bursts and buried[9] electrical lines, and when it was all over he came home and plunked down[10] in his reclining chair[11] with the intention of taking a nap[12].

But he could not sleep.

1. poignée de main
2. avec méfiance
3. se jeta hors de
4. bourrée d'explosifs
5. comment elle allait
6. qu'il escomptait
7. à contrecœur
8. près d'une heure
9. enterrées
10. s'écroula
11. siège inclinable
12. faire un somme

FIFTEEN

David

"**HOW** are you involved in all this[1]?" Barry Duckworth asked me.

We'd moved to his unmarked cruiser[2]. He was behind the wheel and I was up front next to him.

"Marla's my cousin," I explained. I told him about dropping by[3] that morning with some food my mother had prepared.

"Why would your mother do that?"

"Because she's nice," I said.

"That's not what I mean. Marla Pickens is a grown woman. Why does your mother think she needs to send her food? Is Marla out of work[4]? She been sick?"

"She's had a rough few months."

"Why?"

"She ... she lost a child. At birth. A little girl. She hasn't been quite right since." I didn't get into details, and I didn't volunteer the story about[5] Marla trying to kidnap a baby from Promise Falls General. I had no doubt he'd find that out[6] sooner or later, but I wasn't going to be the one who told him.

1. Quel est votre rôle dans cette histoire

2. voiture banalisée

3. que j'étais passé

4. au chômage

5. je ne lui parlai pas de

6. l'apprendrait

It wasn't that I feared my aunt's wrath[1] at divulging that. Okay, maybe a little. But it really was Marla I was looking out for[2]. What she'd done at the hospital was hugely damning[3] in the current circumstances, and I wasn't sure Duckworth or anyone else with the Promise Falls police would feel the need to pursue a very broad investigation[4] once they had that tidbit[5]. Marla killed Rosemary Gaynor and made off[6] with her baby. Simple as that. Case closed[7], let's go get a beer.

I didn't know that it was that simple[8]. Then again[9], maybe it was.

There was no denying[10] Marla had Matthew Gaynor. And even though her story of how he'd come into her life seemed unlikely, I wasn't convinced Marla had it in her[11] to have committed the kind of savagery I'd seen—if only for an instant—inside that house.

I hoped to God she didn't.

"What do you mean, hasn't been quite right?" Duckworth asked.

"Depressed, withdrawn[12]. Maybe not taking as good care of herself as she could. Which was why my mom wanted to send some food over."

"Why you?"

"What do you mean, why me?" I asked.

"Why didn't she take it over herself?"

I licked my upper lip. "I had the time. I'm back home living with my folks[13]. I'm out of work. Maybe you heard, the *Standard* went under[14]."

"And the Gaynors' baby was there? At Marla's house?"

I nodded.

"And this didn't seem right to you? Because you knew she didn't have a child?"

---

1. la colère

2. que je protégeais

3. jouait lourdement en sa défaveur

4. mener une enquête très approfondie

5. info

6. s'était taillée

7. Affaire réglée

8. doutais que ce fût si simple

9. Mais cela dit

10. On ne pouvait nier

11. était du style

12. renfermée

13. revenu vivre chez mes parents

14. a fait faillite

138

"That's right. She told me a woman handed her the baby yesterday."

"Just out of the blue[1], someone knocked on the door and said, 'Here, have a kid[2].' "

"Yeah."

Duckworth ran a palm over his[3] mouth. "That's quite a story."

"That's what she says happened."

He shook his head slowly, then said, "I thought I'd heard you'd moved to Boston."

"I had." I guessed it wasn't that[4] strange that Duckworth would take notice of what I was up to[5], given that we knew each other from my troubles[6] five years earlier. "But I moved back. Things weren't working out at the *Globe*. I was working nights most of the time and never got to see Ethan. You remember Ethan."

"I do. Good boy."

Even with everything that was going on, I couldn't stop worrying about what had happened with Ethan at school.

"I wanted to be close to my parents," I told Duckworth. "They're a great help. I got rehired at the *Standard* just as the paper closed."

Duckworth wanted to know how I'd made the connection with the Gaynors. I told him, and about arriving[7] at the same time as the husband. Duckworth wanted to know how Bill Gaynor seemed, before we'd found his wife.

"Agitated. He said he'd been trying to raise her[8] on the phone, couldn't."

He asked me whether I knew anyone named Sarita.

"No. But I heard Gaynor say the name. That she's the nanny. Haven't you talked to her?"

1. Comme ça, sans crier gare

2. Tiens, je te donne un gosse

3. se passa une main sur la

4. Ce n'était sans doute pas si

5. suive ce que je devenais

6. les problèmes que j'avais eus

7. comment j'étais arrivé

8. l'avoir

"Not yet." He paused. "You're not getting your car back."

"I kind of figured[1]."

"Eventually[2], but not for a while."

"You're going to find my prints[3] on that stroller."

"Uh-huh[4]," Duckworth said.

"I just thought I should mention it[5]. I put it in the car when we came over here."

"Okay."

"And probably in the house, too," I added. "I was inside, briefly, with the husband. So on the door, maybe some other places. I don't remember. I might have touched something."

"Right," Duckworth said. "Thanks for filling me in[6]."

I thought maybe, in retrospect, that pointing those things out didn't do me the service[7] I was hoping it would.

1. m'en doutais un peu
2. Ça viendra
3. empreintes
4. oui, OK
5. vous prévenir
6. de m'avoir prévenu
7. ne plaidait pas en ma faveur

SIXTEEN

JACK Sturgess had two patients currently in the hospital[1] he felt obliged to check in on[2] before he left Promise Falls General and went back to the medical building a few blocks away, where he kept his office. But he couldn't get his mind off what Agnes had told him at end of the canceled[3] board meeting.

That there was trouble, again, with Marla. Just when you think things are settling down[4], another bomb goes off.

His first patient was an elderly woman who'd fallen and broken her hip. She'd taken a tumble[5] at the nursing home where she lived[6], and Sturgess was recommending she be kept here another couple of days[7] before sending her back to let the home staff look after her.

Next was a seven-year-old girl named Susie who'd had a tonsillectomy[8] the day before. Back around the dawn of time[9], a child who'd had this procedure would be kept for three or four days in the hospital, but now it was usually a day surgery[10]: Arrive in the morning, go in for surgery, home by suppertime. Not that the patient would feel much like eating anything.

1. actuellement hospitalisés
2. de passer voir
3. annulée
4. que ça se tasse
5. fait une grosse chute
6. sa maison de retraite
7. qu'on la garde encore deux ou trois jours
8. été opérée des amygdales
9. Aux temps anciens
10. une opération en ambulatoire

But Susie had lost a lot of blood during the operation, so she'd been kept overnight.

"How's the princess doing today?" the doctor asked as he approached her bedside.

Struggling, she said, "Okay."

"Hurts, huh?" he said, touching his own throat.

Susie nodded[1].

"They tell you you'll get to eat all this ice cream after the operation, but once it's over, the last thing you want to do is eat anything, am I right?"

The little girl nodded again.

"Even ice cream will hurt going down that throat of yours. But I'm betting by this afternoon you'll want a bowl. That's a promise. I'm sending you home today. You're going to be just fine."

He placed his palm on the girl's cheek and smiled. "You're a brave one, you are."

Susie managed a smile. "I'm missing school," she whispered.

"You like that?"

An enthusiastic nod.

"Maybe what we could do," Sturgess said, "is next week, we put the tonsils back in[2]; then we'll take them out again so you can miss even more school."

That brought a smile. "You're joking," she said hoarsely. "I don't hate school that much[3]."

"You get better," Sturgess said.

As he walked back to the car, his thoughts returned to Marla Pickens. He wondered what the problem was this time. If she'd kidnapped another baby from the hospital, surely everyone in the building would have been talking about it.

He figured sooner or later he'd learn the details. He was, after all, the family's GP[4].

1. acquiesça

2. on remet les amygdales

3. à ce point-là

4. médecin traitant

His car was parked in the multilevel[1] garage that had been built four years ago. The hospital still had some ground-level lots[2], but over the last decade it had become nearly impossible to find a spot[3], even in the area reserved for staff, so a five-story[4] parking building had been erected. The doctors were given exclusive access to the north end of the first level.

Sturgess had his remote out[5], pressed the button, saw the lights on[6] his Lincoln SUV flash. He was reaching for[7] the door handle when someone behind him, by one of the pillars, said, "Dr. Sturgess?"

There was no time to react.

The fist drove its way into his stomach[8] the second he turned around. It felt as though it went in far enough to touch his spine. He dropped to his knees immediately, head down, a pair of worn sneakers[9] in front of him.

Sturgess didn't bother to look up. He didn't know who this person was, but he didn't have to guess who had sent him.

"Hey, Doc," said the man standing over him. "I guess you can figure out what that's about."

Sturgess's chest heaved[10] as he struggled to get his breath back[11]. The punch[12] had been well placed. He didn't believe anything had been broken. The man hadn't caught a rib[13]. He figured he'd be able to[14] walk in another minute or two.

"Yeah," he croaked[15].

"It's a message," the man said.

"I know."

"What do you think it means?"

"It means … you want your money."

"Not me."

"The man … who sent you."

1. à plusieurs niveaux
2. des parkings au rez-de-chaussée
3. une place
4. à 4 étages [+ le RDC]
5. sorti sa clé télécommandée
6. phares de
7. tendait le bras vers
8. Le coup de poing le percuta au ventre
9. vieilles baskets
10. haletait,
11. luttant pour reprendre sa respiration
12. coup de poing
13. touché de côte
14. se dit qu'il pourrait
15. articula d'une voix étranglée

"That's right. He says you're nearly paid up, but not quite. Until your debts and the interest are dealt with, he's gonna keep sending me around to visit you."

"I understand."

"I'm not sure you do," the man said. "Next time there will be blood." He chortled[1]. "And it'll be coming from the little stump[2] where one of your fucking fingers used to be[3]."

"I hear you," the doctor said, most of his wind back[4] now. "I gave him a hundred grand[5]. You'd think he'd be fucking happy with that."

"If a hundred grand was all you owed[6], I'm guessing he would be." And then in a slightly more conciliatory tone, "You know, have you ever considered that maybe you've got a problem?"

"What?" Sturgess said; he had one knee up, and was slowly coming to a standing position. Now he was able to look his attacker in the eye. The thug[7] was about thirty, bearded, pushing three hundred pounds easy.

The man rested a hand gently on the doctor's shoulder. "You think I enjoy this? You think I like beating the shit out of people[8] to get them to pay up[9]?" He shook his head. "Not at all. I'm telling you, maybe you should get help. Gamblers[10] Anonymous or something like that. Don't go telling my boss I said this, because he likes the business he's in, but hey, if you got your act together[11], there's always some other dumb asshole willing to[12] throw away his paycheck on the horses or blackjack or whatever. But you're a doctor, right?"

Sturgess nodded.

"You help people. You probably work with your hands, doing surgery, shit like that. So when I see you next, and have to relieve you[13] of one of your

1. ricana
2. moignon
3. d'un doigt qui sera plus là
4. qui avait repris sa respiration
5. mille dollars
6. Si tu devais pas plus de cent mille balles

7. voyou

8. casser la gueule de quelqu'un
9. pour le faire raquer
10. Aux Parieurs
11. te prends en main
12. un autre couillon prêt à

13. te débarrasser

144

fingers, that's kind of bad for society[1], you know? Like, imagine this. I chop your finger off[2]; then I get in a car accident or something, and you're the only doctor on call[3], but you can't operate on me[4] because your hand is fucked[5]. That would be ironic, right?"

"It would," Sturgess said.

"Well, then," the man said, giving the doctor's shoulder one more friendly pat[6], "you better pay up, because I'm one fucking lousy driver[7]."

He chuckled[8], turned, and walked away.

Sturgess got his door open and collapsed[9] into the driver's seat. The man was right. He needed to get his problem under control.

But first he had to pay off the rest of his debts. Otherwise he might not live long enough to get his act together[10].

1. ça serait con pour la société
2. te coupe le doigt
3. de garde
4. m'opérer
5. naze

6. tape amicale
7. je conduis super mal
8. rit
9. s'affala

10. se reprendre en main

SEVENTEEN

David

1. en eut fini

ONCE Detective Duckworth was done[1] with me, I had to find a way home. I considered calling my father, but he'd already been pressed into service[2] to pick Ethan up at school, and I didn't want to have to answer all the questions he'd have if he picked me up at a crime scene. And Mom, according to the brief chat I'd had with her, had hurt her leg, so I wasn't going to trouble her, either.

2. réquisitionné

3. taxi

So I called a cab[3].

4. On ne hèle pas

You don't hail[4] a taxi in Promise Falls the way you do in New York. Unlike in the big city, most people here have a car and use it to go everywhere, so cabbies aren't wandering suburban streets looking for a fare[5]. You call in[6], and they send one out to you. Once I'd phoned in, I waited on the corner where I said I would be.

5. il n'y a donc pas de taxis en maraude

6. On appelle

And thought.

What a morning.

Mom just had to send me to Marla's with chili.

7. pour finir

Of course, even if she hadn't, we'd have all been drawn into Marla's problems eventually[7], because we were family. We'd have been concerned[8]; we'd

8. On se serait inquiétés

have offered support[1]; we'd have followed developments with interest.

But we wouldn't be involved[2]. Not like this.

I felt I was involved in this as much as I wanted to be[3].

I'd promised Marla my support, but not a lot beyond that. I supposed I could start asking around on my own in the hopes of finding something that would hold up[4] her version of events, but just how obliged was I to do that? And there seemed little doubt Agnes would be doing everything she could, starting with the hiring of Natalie Bondurant, to make sure Marla didn't get charged with[5] Rosemary Gaynor's murder.

The cab showed up[6].

I was home ten minutes later. Mom was stretched out[7] on the couch[8]; Dad was in his recliner[9], not reading, not watching TV, just staring off into space[10]. I felt like I'd wandered into an old-folks'-home lobby[11].

"Where's Ethan?" I said.

"I didn't hear you pull up[12]," Dad said, his voice low and weary. "Where's your car?"

"What happened with Ethan?" I asked.

Mom said, "Is Marla okay? Did she give the baby back?"

"Something wrong with the car?" Dad asked.

I had to find a job. I had to move out of here. I raised both hands. "I'll fill you in[13], in a minute. Right now, I'm asking about Ethan."

"He's up in his room," Mom said.

"What happened?"

Dad spoke up. "He got into some fight with a kid. Don't know much more than that, but Ethan says he didn't start it, and that's good enough for me. I didn't get a chance to see the other kid, but I

1. notre aide

2. impliqués

3. À mon avis, j'étais déjà assez impliqué comme ça

4. corroborer

5. ne soit pas accusée du

6. arriva

7. étendue

8. canapé

9. fauteuil inclinable

10. le regard dans le vide

11. Je crus arriver dans un foyer de vieux

12. t'arrêter

13. Je vous raconte tout

1. lui a balancé
un ou deux
coups de poing

2. ne put se
retenir

3. toquai

4. Bien tenté

5. marmonna

6. Plus fort !

7. à m'embêter

8. à la récré

hope Ethan landed a couple of good ones on him[1]. I got his name if you want it, and the father's. In case you and me want to go over there and have a word with them."

The hands went up again. "Thanks for that, but let me just talk to Ethan. Okay?"

Mom couldn't help herself[2]. "What about Marla?"

"In. A. Minute."

I climbed the stairs, rapped lightly[3] on Ethan's door, but did not wait for an answer before I opened it.

He was facedown on his bed, on top of the covers, his head buried in his pillow. He rolled onto his side and said, "Where were you?"

"Excuse me?"

"Why did Poppa have to get me?"

"Because I was busy. And nice try[4], trying to make this an interrogation of *me* from the get-go, but I'm the one who's got the questions. What happened?"

"Nothing."

I pulled Ethan's computer chair over next to the bed and sat down. "That's not the way this is going to go. Who'd you get into a fight with?"

He mumbled[5] something.

"Speak up.[6]"

"Carl Worthington."

"He's in your class?"

Ethan nodded.

"How did the fight start?"

"He's always picking on me[7]."

"How'd the fight start?"

"He … he took something from me at recess[8] and I tried to get it back."

"What'd he take?"

"Just something."

"I'm not in the mood[1], Ethan. Spill it[2]."

"Poppa's watch. I mean, one of his dad's watches."

"What?"

"From that box of old stuff that he has in the basement. My great-grandfather's things. Like ribbons and medals and old letters and postcards and stuff. There was a watch, but not like a regular watch[3]. It was big and didn't have a strap[4]?"

"A pocket[5] watch," I said. "A long time ago, men would keep a watch in the front pocket of their vest[6]. You took that?"

"Sort of."

"Did you ask your grandfather if you could take it?"

"Not exactly," Ethan said.

"So the answer is no," I said.

"I'd just never seen anything like it and I wanted to show it to my friends. Or show it to some kids so they might want to be my friend."

I felt my heart sinking. I should be angry but it wasn't in me.

"So you took it to school. Then what happened?"

"There was a bunch of us[7] passing it around to look at it, and Carl said he really liked it and put it in his pocket. When I told him to give it back he wouldn't[8]."

"Why didn't you just tell a teacher he took it from you and make him give it back?"

"I started to get scared, because I might have to tell the teacher how I got it, and then Poppa would find out and I'd be in trouble. So I just grabbed Carl and tried to get it out of his pocket, and he punched me in the head and we fell down together and everyone was watching, and then Mr. Appleton came over."

1. d'humeur
2. Crache le morceau
3. montre standard
4. de bracelet
5. à gousset
6. gilet
7. On était un petit groupe,
8. n'a pas voulu

"Your teacher?"

Ethan shook his head. "He's not my teacher. He was just on yard duty[1]. We got sent to the office." Ethan's lip began to tremble. "When Poppa came to pick me up I thought somehow he knew."

"I don't think he does," I said.

"But next time he looks in that box and can't find the watch—"

I gestured for Ethan to sit and put my arms around him as he started to cry. "It's okay," I said. "We'll sort it out[2]. So this kid, he still has the watch?"

I felt him nod into my shoulder.

"And the school doesn't know anything about it?"

"They don't know."

"Okay," I said.

"I have some money saved up. Maybe we can go to a store where they sell old things and buy another watch just like that."

I patted his back. "Like I said, we'll sort it out."

"Don't tell him. Don't tell Poppa. He'll kick us out before you have a chance to find a job and get us a place to live."

That cut in more ways than I could count. "He wouldn't do that," I said. "He would never do anything like that. I can't promise you he won't find out, but I'll see what I can do. Okay?"

He nodded, broke free[3] and grabbed a tissue[4] from the box on his bedside table, and blew his nose[5].

"Is this why you've been acting sick[6] in the morning?" I asked him.

Ethan didn't say anything.

"Because you don't want to go to school and run into this kid?"

1. de surveillance

2. On va arranger ça

3. se dégagea

4. prit un mouchoir

5. se moucha

6. fait semblant d'être malade

"Sort of," he said quietly. "Maybe. He's been picking on me ever since I came back here. But he's not the only one. Some of the other kids are meaner[1]."

I rested my hand on his shoulder. "Okay. Listen, why don't you hang out here for a while longer."

"Am I grounded?[2]"

"No. Just give me fifteen minutes before you come down."

I knew I was going to have to fill my parents in on[3] what was happening with Marla and the police and the body I'd found. I didn't want Ethan to hear all of that, although I knew, what with the Internet and everything, he'd probably know the broad strokes[4] before the end of the day.

"Well?" Dad said when I entered the living room.

"Just a fight," I said. "No big deal[5]. Did you say you had the name of the kid's father?"

"Sam Worthington," he said. "Heard the name when I was in the office. Whatcha[6] going to do?"

"Nothing. I just wondered."

I could tell there was something wrong with Mom, the way she was lying down. "Tell me again what happened to you."

She told me about tripping on the stairs. She pulled up her pant leg and showed me her injury.

"Jesus, Mom, you should go to the hospital."

"Nothing's broken. It'll be okay. Now tell us what's going on."

I did. They let me tell the story pretty much all the way through without interruptions, aside from the occasional "Oh, dear" or "Good heavens" from Mom. Dad's first question, not surprisingly, was, "When they going to give you back your car?"

"This is so terrible," Mom said. "What can we do to help, do you think?"

1. encore plus méchants

2. Je dois pas sortir de ma chambre ?

3. raconter à mes parents

4. les grandes lignes

5. Rien de grave

6. [= What are you]

151

"I don't know," I said. "I really don't."

I told them I had to go out, and asked Mom if I could borrow her old Taurus. She didn't drive much anymore, but she still had her car, and the plates were up-to-date[1].

"Keys are in the drawer," she said.

I knew this was probably a bad idea. Getting involved in your kids' disputes, especially when it brought you face-to-face with other parents, wasn't always such a good move[2].

I felt the best way to handle Mr. Worthington when I saw him would be to tell him there was a misunderstanding. I wouldn't accuse Carl of stealing anything. I'd say something along the lines that[3] Ethan had agreed to let Carl hang on to[4] the watch for a while, but the watch wasn't his to lend[5]. I'd explain that it was a family heirloom[6], that it had been Ethan's great-grandfather's. I'd embellish. I'd say that once Ethan's grandfather found out it was missing, the boy was going to be in for a good whoopin'[7].

No, I could not say that. That was ridiculous.

The important thing was not to lay blame[8]. Be nice. Just get the damn watch back.

I opened the address app and looked for S. WORTHINGTON. There was one, on Sycamore[9].

It wasn't that far from where my parents lived[10], which made sense[11], since Ethan and Carl were going to the same school, but it seemed a great distance. The block[12] where the Worthingtons lived was a stretch of low-income town houses jammed together like upended shoe boxes on a shelf[13]. Cars in varying stages of disrepair[14] were parked in short driveways[15], back ends hanging over the sidewalk[16].

This might not have been something I'd ordinarily have felt up to[1], but after the morning I'd had, there was a part of me that just didn't give a shit[2]. I'd be nice, but I was going to get back that damn watch that little bastard had stolen from my son.

I found the right door, climbed the three cement steps, one hand on the rusted metal railing[3], and knocked.

From behind the door, a muffled[4] shout.

"Who is it?" Didn't sound like a man to me.

"I'm looking for Sam Worthington!" I shouted back. "I'm Ethan's dad!"

"Who?"

"Ethan's a friend of my son! I just came by to—"

Suddenly the door swung wide.

It was a woman.

"I'm Samantha," she said flatly[5]. "Most people call me Sam." About thirty, short brown hair, wearing a tight[6] white tee[7] and jeans just as snug[8]. They fit her well.

She was a nice-looking woman, but if I'm honest, I'd have to say the first thing I noticed was the shotgun[9] she had in her hands, and the fact that it was pointed right between my eyes.

---

1. eu le cran de faire
2. qui s'en foutait
3. rambarde rouillée
4. étouffé
5. tout net
6. moulant
7. T-shirt
8. tout aussi serré
9. fusil

EIGHTEEN

1. De quoi auriez-vous besoin

2. pour remettre Five Mountains sur pied

3. C'était loin d'être aussi bien que

4. en tant que maire de la ville

5. À l'époque,

6. des rideaux

7. usine de mise en bouteilles

8. terrain

9. manquait de

10. du contreplaqué éraflé

11. empilables

12. encadrées

13. Un faux combat contre

14. l'ancien boxeur

15. puis

16. Oh, la barbe

17. comme si

"WHAT would it take to get you[1] to get Five Mountains up and running again[2]?" Randall Finley asked Gloria Fenwick as they sat in the offices of Finley Springs Water. It was a far cry from[3] the office he had when he presided over the small empire of Promise Falls as its mayor[4]. Back then[5] he had a broad oak desk, leather armchairs for guests, velvet drapes[6] at the windows. Well, at least they looked like velvet.

But his office at the Finley Springs bottling plant[7], five miles north of Promise Falls on a tract of land[8] that had been in his family for five generations, lacked[9] charm. A cheap metal desk topped with chipped fake-wood laminate[10]. Plastic stackable[11] chairs. He'd rehung a few framed[12] photos that had adorned the walls of his mayoral office. Shaking hands with Fox News commentator Bill O'Reilly. Fake fisticuffs with[13] former wrestler[14] and onetime[15] governor Jesse Ventura.

There'd never been a *Penthouse* calendar on the wall of the mayor's office, however. Finley was thinking maybe he should have taken that down before inviting Fenwick to drop by. What the hell[16]. It wasn't like[17] it showed anything she hadn't already seen herself. In the mirror.

Gloria Fenwick, forty, pencil thin[1], blond hair to her shoulders and decked out in[2] Anne Klein, had been the general manager of the theme park, and was still in charge of the place, winding things down[3] for the parent corporation[4]. That meant dealing with creditors, selling off bits and pieces of the place, entertaining[5] offers for the property. As far as that went[6], there had been none.

"I don't even know why I agreed to this meeting," Fenwick said, standing, looking at the closest[7] plastic chair. The seat was cracked[8], and looked as though it would pinch her in a delicate place[9] if she dared sit in it[10].

"You agreed to it because you know if an opportunity presented itself that would make you look good to your superiors, you'd go for it."

Fenwick picked up a plastic bottle of Finley Springs Water that was sitting[11] on the man's desk. She held it up to a flickering overhead fluorescent light and squinted[12]. "This looks a little cloudy[13] to me."

"We had a few quality issues[14] with the last batch[15]," Finley said. "Perfectly safe to drink despite a few contaminants."

"You should put that on the label[16]," she said.

Finley's desk phone rang. He glanced at who the caller was, but ignored it. "Won't you sit down?"

"This chair is cracked."

Finley came from behind his desk and found another chair that looked less likely to pinch Fenwick's very pleasant butt[17]. She sat, and Finley returned to the chair behind his desk.

"Your park was a huge shot in the arm for[18] Promise Falls."

"Five Mountains is not reopening," she said.

---

1. ultra-svelte
2. en habits chics de chez
3. gérant la fermeture
4. société mère
5. recevant
6. Quant à ce dernier point
7. la plus proche
8. fendillé
9. semblait pouvoir lui pincer les fesses
10. osait s'asseoir dessus
11. posée sur
12. plissa un œil
13. opaque
14. problèmes
15. lot
16. étiquette
17. fessier
18. dopait

"I think your corporate overlords[1] are not taking the long view[2]. A park like that, it needs time to develop, build an audience, as it were[3]."

"What's this to you[4]?"

He leaned back[5], laced his fingers[6] behind his head, a posture that made his stomach loom in front of him[7] like an upturned wok[8].

"I'm looking to[9] get back into politics," Finley said. "I want back in the game[10]. Promise Falls has hit the skids[11]. This town is broken. Businesses closing, people moving away. Paper's gone under[12]. That private prison—which would have meant a shitload of jobs[13]—didn't get built here. A plant[14] that was making parts[15] for GM and Ford lost its contract to[16] Mexico. And as if all that weren't bad enough, the local theme park has folded up its tent[17]. That'd be you[18]."

"It was not a viable operation," Gloria Fenwick said. "Building in that location[19] was a miscalculation. Traffic patterns were misjudged[20]. Promise Falls is too far north of Albany. There are no other attractions, like a discount outlet mall[21], to make this a logical destination point. People had to go too far out of their way[22] to get here. People don't pass Promise Falls on their way from point A to point B. So the place has been mothballed[23]."

"Every time I drive by, it kind of freaks me out[24]," Finley said. "Seeing that Ferris wheel, the roller coaster[25], everything just sitting there, not moving[26]. Abandoned like that. It's creepy[27]."

"Try being there[28]," Fenwick said. "My office is still on the property[29]. It's like living in a ghost town. Especially late at night."

"Anyway, when I get back in[30]," Finley said, putting his hands on his desk and leaning forward, "I can make it so Five Mountains pays no local business taxes or property taxes for five years. And in five years' time, if the park is still not financially viable, that could be reexamined. Make it ten years. People having jobs is more important than filling local tax coffers[1]."

The phone rang again. He let it go, but seconds after it stopped ringing, his cell went off[2]. "Goddamn it," he said. "It's like having flies[3] buzzing around your head all the time."

"Maybe you need an assistant," Fenwick said. "Interested?"

"No," she said.

"Because I've actually been scouting around[4], getting some names. What with[5] running a business, restarting my political career, I'm kind of drowning[6]."

"Is that a joke?" Fenwick asked.

"What do you mean?"

"You being in the water business."

"Oh." He grinned[7]. "I missed that one[8]."

"When did you get into this?"

"Three years ago. This has been Finley land for seventy-three years. We always knew there was a natural spring[9] on the property, but I was the one who decided to look into its financial potential. I set up a plant, and now we're going gangbusters[10]."

"So what do you care about getting back into politics? You have a good business going here."

"I like to contribute," Finley said. "I like to make a difference[11]."

Fenwick wondered whether the man could keep a straight face[12]. Finley managed it. But it didn't stop her from pursuing the matter.

"A man like you always has an angle[13]. You don't want to get back in to help the people. You want to get back in to help yourself. You get in,

---

1. remplir les coffres de la ville

2. portable sonna

3. des mouches

4. en fait, j'ai cherché un peu

5. Entre

6. je me noie

7. fit un grand sourire

8. n'avais pas vu

9. source

10. on marche du tonnerre

11. pouvoir changer les choses

12. ne pas rire en le disant

13. un intérêt

you do people favors, they pay you back. That's how it works."

"A cynical theme-park operator," Finley said. "It's like finding out Willy Wonka hated[1] chocolate." He rubbed his[2] hands together. "Here's the thing. I'm not asking Five Mountains to reopen. I know that may not be feasible. But if you could find a way to say, after having a meeting with me, that you are at least considering taking another look at reopening, I'd really appreciate that."

"You mean lie[3]," she said.

Finley waved a hand in the air. "Call it what you will[4]. But just in this room."

"What's in it[5] for Five Mountains?" she asked. "Say[6] I go to my superiors and make your pitch[7]. What's in it for me?"

"All the free[8] springwater you want?" he said, and grinned.

Gloria took a second look at the clouded bottle. "If it comes with some antibiotics."

"And," Finley said, taking a white letter-size envelope from his desk and placing it on top, "this."

The envelope was a quarter of an inch thick. Fenwick glanced at it, but did not touch it.

"You must be kidding[9]," she said. "Who are you? Tony Soprano[10]?"

"It's a consulting fee[11]. I've been consulting you about your firm's plans. Don't you at least[12] want to see how much it is?"

"No, I don't," she said, standing.

Finley slid the envelope off the desk and back into the drawer. "I know you can't sell the place." He chortled. "If I was you, I'd tell my bosses to torch the whole operation[13] and collect the insurance. Only way you'll get a fraction of your money back out of it."

1. découvrir qu'un chocolatier [d'après un personnage de Roald Dahl] a horreur du
2. se frotta les
3. mentir
4. voudrez
5. intérêt
6. Si
7. relaie votre baratin
8. gratuite
9. rigolez
10. La Mafia [d'après le personnage d'une célèbre série]
11. votre cachet en tant que consultant
12. au moins
13. tout torpiller

Fenwick shot him a look. "What the hell made you say that?"

Finley's smile broadened. "I touch a nerve there?"

"Good-bye, Mr. Finley. I can find my way out[1]."

Finley didn't bother getting up as she left the office.

"Bitch[2]," he said.

He wondered if maybe he could have handled that better. Maybe it was the *Penthouse* calendar. Maybe he'd never had a chance at winning over Fenwick once she'd seen that woman with her bush hanging out[3].

The phone rang again. He looked at it and shouted, "Shut up![4]" He lifted the receiver an inch and slammed it back down[5]. It was only then that he realized, from the call display[6], that the call had come from his home. Which meant it was his wife, Jane, or Lindsay, who did double duty as[7] housekeeper and care worker[8].

"Shit," he said, then picked up the phone and dialed[9] the number.

"Hello?" It was Lindsay.

"Did you call?" he asked.

"It must have been Jane," she said. "Hang on." The line was put on hold[10], then a pickup on an extension[11].

"Randy?" Jane asked, her voice tired.

"Hello, love. What's up?"

"Would you have time to go by the bookstore[12] today? I finished the one I was reading."

"Of course," he said. "I'd be happy to."

"Anything else by the same author. His name is, hang on[13], his name … what is his name?"

"Leave it with me[14]. I'll see you soon."

1. Inutile de me raccompagner

2. Sale garce

3. dont on voyait le pubis

4. La ferme !
5. raccrocha violemment
6. par l'affichage du numéro
7. était à la fois
8. femme de ménage et aide-soignante
9. composa

10. en attente
11. quelqu'un prit la ligne

12. passer à la librairie

13. attends
14. Laisse, je chercherai

Finley hung up the phone, sighed[1], cast his eye across his empty office. Thank God he had Lindsay's help on the home front[2], but he needed assistance here just as much.

As he'd told Fenwick, he had too much on his plate[3]. He needed help. Someone to keep him organized, manage a campaign, deal with media out of Albany. Talk to local business leaders[4], get them behind his candidacy[5].

Finley knew he could sometimes rub people the wrong way[6].

Trouble was, he'd burned a lot of bridges[7]. People who'd worked for him in the past had sworn they'd never work for him again. Like Jim Cutter, who used to drive him around[8] back when he was the mayor[9]. Fucking[10] Cutter had broken his nose while working for him. Finley, looking back, knew he probably had it coming[11], and if he thought there was a chance in[12] a million Cutter would work for him again, put the landscaping business on hold[13], Finley'd have him back in a minute. Cutter was a smart[14] guy. Too smart, Finley realized, to ever work for him again.

So Finley had been asking around, looking for someone he hadn't already pissed off[15]. Someone with media savvy[16].

He had a name. Someone who'd gotten turfed[17] when the *Standard* went tits-up[18]. Guy by the name of David Harwood.

Finley had a number for him.

What the hell? he figured, and picked up the phone.

NINETEEN

"WHAT'S happening?" Gill Pickens asked his wife, Agnes, in the police station lobby. "What's going on?"

"She's in there being interrogated like some common criminal[1]; that's what's going on," she told him, hands on her hips. "Where the hell were you?"

"Why aren't you in there with her?"

Agnes rolled her eyes[2]. "They won't *let* me. But Natalie Bondurant's with her. I just hope she knows what the hell she's doing[3]."

"Natalie's good," Gill said.

"You talking professionally, or is she one you've bagged[4] I don't know about?"

Gill sighed. "Honest to God, Agnes."

"That's not an answer," she said.

"She's a good lawyer. A very good lawyer. And that's all I know about her. You know it, too[5]."

Agnes ran her tongue along the inside of her cheek[6]. "Again, where the hell have you been?"

"I told you. I was with a client. I met with him at the Holiday Inn Express in Amsterdam. He runs[7] an industrial cleaning service, and he's looking for ways to make it more efficient. Baldry. Emmett Baldry. Call him if you don't believe me."

1. un simple délinquant

2. leva les yeux au ciel

3. ce qu'elle fiche

4. une de tes conquêtes

5. d'ailleurs
6. fit « Mon œil ! »

7. dirige

"Why'd you meet at the Holiday Inn?" she asked. "Were you planning on some *other* business there?"

Gill shook his head as he whispered angrily, "Is this really the time? When we've got another crisis with Marla? This is what you want to talk about? I swear, Agnes, you've become fixated on this notion that I'm being unfaithful to you[1], which is complete and utter bullshit[2]. I'm telling you, I had a meeting with Emmett Baldry, and I got here as fast as I could. Could we talk about what really matters? What does Natalie say? Does she think Marla's in real trouble here?"

"She's still getting up to speed[3]," Agnes said, implicitly agreeing to her husband's request to move on. At least for now. "But this isn't like what happened before. I could control that. It happened under my roof. This time it's different."

"Where did she grab this baby?"

Agnes's eyes went up, as though heaven would provide an answer. "I don't know. She's saying someone came to the door and just handed the kid over[4]."

"And the mother? The real mother? She's dead?"

Agnes nodded gravely. "Our girl's really done it[5] this time."

"My client has nothing to say," Natalie Bondurant said.

She was sitting next to Marla Pickens at a metal table in an interrogation room of the Promise Falls Police Department. Across from them[6] sat Detective Barry Duckworth.

"I understand," he said. "Really, what I'm looking for here is some assistance. I'm not out to get you[7], Marla." He looked directly at her instead of

1. te fais des infidélités
2. de la connerie pure

3. n'est pas complètement briefée encore

4. lui a remis le gosse

5. déconné

6. En face d'eux,

7. Je ne cherche pas à vous accuser

talking through Natalie. "I'm really not. I just want to find out what happened, and I think you may be in a position to help me with that. Fill in some of the blanks[1]."

"Barry, please," Natalie said.

"I'm serious, Natalie. Right now no one is talking about kidnapping charges[2] against Ms. Pickens or anything like that."

"Kidnapping?" Marla said.

Duckworth nodded. "We don't fully understand how Matthew Gaynor came into your care[3], Marla. That's something I hope will come clear in time. Right now I'm trying to find out what happened to Matthew's mother. I'm sure you'd like to do everything you can to help us in that regard[4]."

"Sure," Marla said.

"Don't answer him," Natalie said, resting her[5] hand on Marla's arm.

"But I do," she said. "I want them to find out who did that. That was a terrible thing somebody did."

"It sure is," Duckworth said. "Have you ever met Rosemary Gaynor before?"

"You don't have to answer that," Natalie said.

"But I haven't. At least, I don't think so. The name isn't familiar to me."

Duckworth slid a picture across the table. A blown-up profile shot[6] from Rosemary Gaynor's Facebook page.

"You've never seen this woman before?"

Marla studied it. "I don't recognize her."

"Okay. You know what, let me just get a few other things out of the way[7]. What's your address, Marla?"

"You already know that," Natalie said. "You took her driver's license[8]."

---

1. À compléter un peu mes infos

2. une accusation de kidnapping

3. s'est retrouvé à votre garde

4. sur ce point

5. posant la

6. photo agrandie

7. réglons quelques formalités

8. permis de conduire

1. maître
2. débita
3. seule

"Please, Counselor[1]."

Marla rattled off[2] her address and phone number. "I live by myself[3]," she added.

"And what do you do?"

"What do I do?"

"What's your job? Are you employed?"

4. des critiques
5. Sans blague
6. de films

"Yes," Marla said, nodding. "I write reviews[4]."

Duckworth's eyebrows went up. "No kidding[5]? What sort of reviews? Movie[6] reviews? Book reviews? Do you review restaurants?"

"Not movies or books. Some restaurants. But mostly businesses."

Natalie, not sure where this was going, looked uncertain. "Maybe we should—"

7. des commentaires

"No, it's okay," Marla said. "I do write-ups[7] about businesses on the Internet."

"How does that work, exactly?" Duckworth asked.

"Well, let's say you run a—I don't know—a paving company. You go around paving people's driveways. I write a review of your company saying what a good job you did." She smiled tiredly. "I don't get paid a lot for each review, but I can get a lot done in an hour, so it adds up[8] pretty fast."

8. chiffre
9. perdu

"Wait a sec," Duckworth said. "I'm confused[9]. You use the services of enough businesses that you can[10] write lots of reviews in an hour?"

10. pour pouvoir

Marla shook her head. "No, no, I haven't used *any* of them."

11. à voir avec notre affaire

"I don't think this has any bearing on anything[11]," Natalie said.

12. attendez
13. dont vous n'avez jamais utilisé les services

"But hang on[12]," Duckworth said, holding up a hand. "I'm just curious, personally, how you can review businesses whose services you've never engaged[13]?"

Marla said, "The way it works is, if you're the paving guy, you get in touch with[1] the Internet company I work for, and you say you need lots of good customer reviews so that when people are looking for a paver, they pick you[2]. So then the company sends me the info and I write the review. I've got, like, half a dozen online identities I can use so it doesn't look like they're all from the same person. So even though I don't know a lot about paving, I can kind of figure it out, and say they gave me a good price, they were on time[3], the driveway was really smooth[4], like that."

"No more," Natalie said, gripping Marla's arm tighter[5].

"That's fascinating," Duckworth said. "So you just completely make it up[6]. You say a few good words about a business you know nothing about and have never used. I'm guessing it wouldn't even have to be in Promise Falls. It could literally be anywhere."

Marla nodded.

"So, in other words, Marla, you lie," Duckworth said.

Her head snapped back[7] as though she'd been slapped[8]. "Not really," she said. "It's the Internet."

"Well, let me ask you this, then. Why did you try to take a baby out of Promise Falls General?"

Natalie blinked[9]. She said, "Whoa, hold on. If you've got anything to substantiate the idea that Ms. Pickens took Matthew Gaynor from the hospital, then I'd like to see—"

He raised a hand. "No, not Matthew." He reviewed some paperwork in front of him. "The child's name was Dwight Westphall. He was just a couple of days old when your client snuck[10] into the maternity ward[11] and—"

1. contactez

2. c'est vous qu'ils choisissent

3. dans les temps

4. bien lisse

5. serrant plus fort le bras de Marla

6. inventez de bout en bout

7. Elle se redressa net

8. reçu une gifle

9. tiqua

10. est entrée en douce

11. service maternité

165

1. évitiez
d'employer

"I would ask that you refrain from[1] a word like 'snuck,' Detective."

"We're not in front of a jury, Ms. Bondurant." He paused. "Not yet. As I was saying, Ms. Pickens here was stopped by hospital security before she could exit the building. Police were notified[2], but an accommodation[3] was reached between the Westphalls and the hospital and no further action was taken[4]. Would that accommodation have anything to do with the fact that your mother is the hospital administrator, Ms. Pickens?"

2. a été informée
de l'incident

3. accord

4. il n'y a pas eu
de suites

Her eyes were welling up with tears[5].

5. se gonflaient
de larmes

"Strikes me," Duckworth said to Natalie, "that you haven't been fully informed of your client's previous activities." He leaned over the table and eyed Marla sympathetically. "It's a good thing Matthew's okay, Marla. You looked out for[6] him and that's good. Maybe, when you tried to take him, Mrs. Gaynor came at you[7]. Threatened to hurt you. Is that what happened? Were you just acting in self-defense?"

6. avez veillé sur

7. est devenue
agressive

"It was the angel," Marla said.

"Excuse me?"

"I didn't take Matthew. It was the angel that brought her."

"We're done here[8]," Natalie said.

8. ne restons pas

"Can you describe this angel?" Duckworth asked.

Marla shook her head. "I can't."

Duckworth slid the photo of Rosemary Gaynor toward her again. "Was this your angel?"

Marla gave the picture another look[9]. "I don't know."

9. regarda de
nouveau la
photo

"What do you mean, you don't know? Either this is her or it isn't."

"I … have trouble," Marla said. "With faces."

"But this only just happened in the last twenty-four hours."

"It's the prosopagnosia," Marla said.

Confusion flashed across the faces of both lawyer and detective.

"I'm sorry. Proso- what?" Duckworth said.

"I have it," Marla said. "Not real bad, but bad enough. Prosopagnosia." She paused. "Face blindness[1]."

"What's that?" Duckworth asked.

"I can't remember faces. I can't remember what people look like." Marla pointed to the picture. "So it might have been that woman who gave me Matthew. But I just don't know."

[1]. Un trouble de la reconnaissance des visages

TWENTY

David

1. en m'écartant de

2. en levant les mains en l'air

3. disons

"WHOA," I said, backing away from[1] the door, putting my hands in the air[2]. The last thing I wanted to do was appear threatening as Sam—make that[3] Samantha—Worthington pointed that shotgun at my head.

"Who'd you say you were?" she asked. "What are you doing asking about my boy? Did they send you?"

"I think there's some kind of misunderstanding here," I said, slowly lowering my arms, but still keeping lots of space between my hands and my body. For all I knew, she thought I was carrying a gun and might reach for it. Why else would you show up at the door with a shotgun?

I continued, trying to keep my voice even. "My name's David Harwood. I'm Ethan's dad. Our boys go to school together. Ethan and Carl."

"What's the name of the school?" Sam asked.

"What?"

"Name it. Name the school."

"Clinton Street Elementary," I said.

"What's the teacher's name?"

I had to think. "Ms. Moffat," I said.

The shotgun began to lower. If she shot me now, it'd be my chest that got blown away and not my head. A slight improvement[1], perhaps.

"Did I pass the test[2]?" I asked. Because that was certainly what it felt like[3].

"Maybe," she said.

From inside the house, someone shouted, "Who is it, Mom?" A boy. Carl, presumably.

Sam whirled her head around[4], no more than a second. "Stay in the kitchen!" she said. There wasn't another peep out[5] of Carl.

"Brandon's folks[6] didn't send you?" Sam asked me.

"I don't know a Brandon," I said.

She studied me another five seconds, breathing through her nose. Finally she lowered the shotgun all the way[7], pointing it at the floor. I let my arms go limp[8], but I didn't move any closer[9] to the door.

"What is it you want?" she asked.

"Right now, a change of shorts," I said. I looked for any hint of a smile[10] and did not find one. "My son gave your boy an antique watch[11]. It was a mistake. It wasn't his to give. It belongs to his grandfather. Actually[12], it was his father's. It's kind of a family memento."

"A watch?"

"A pocket watch." I made a circle with my thumb and forefinger. "A little bigger than an Oreo[13]."

"Just a minute," she said. "Stay right there." She closed the door. I heard a chain slide into place.

So I cooled my heels out front[14]. Put my hands into my pockets. Smiled as an elderly woman wheeled past with a small grocery cart[15]. She ignored me.

---

1. légère amélioration

2. réussi mon examen

3. l'impression que j'avais eue

4. tourna vivement la tête

5. signe

6. Les parents de Brandon

7. complètement

8. baissai complètement les bras

9. ne m'approchai pas

10. l'ombre d'un sourire

11. montre ancienne

12. En fait

13. [biscuit rond]

14. Je restai donc à poireauter dehors

15. passa en faisant rouler son petit Caddie à provisions

Here it was, only midafternoon. I'd found a body[1], been interrogated by the police, and now had been threatened with a shotgun. I was afraid to wonder what the rest of the day would bring.

My phone rang.

I dug the cell out[2] of my pocket and looked at the number. It was not one I recognized. Maybe it was Detective Duckworth with more questions. I accepted the call and put the phone to my ear.

"Hello?"

"Is this David Harwood?" It was a man's voice. Gruff[3], and louder than it needed to be.

"Who's calling?" I asked.

"Randall Finley. You know who I am?"

It would have been hard not to, particularly in my line of work. The former mayor, whose bid for higher office crashed and burned[4] when it got out[5] that he had used the services of an underage prostitute.

"Yeah, I know who you are," I said.

"I used to read your stuff[6] in the *Standard*. You were a good reporter. Think you interviewed me more than once in the past."

"Yes," I said.

"So anyway, why I'm calling. I hear you got hired back by the paper just as it went down the toilet[7]."

I said nothing.

"That had to be a hell of a thing. You'd gone to Boston, am I right?"

"That's right," I said slowly.

"And then came back. Raising a boy on your own, that's what I hear. After that business with your wife a few years ago."

"What can I do for you, Mr. Finley?"

1. cadavre

2. sortis mon portable

3. Une voix brusque

4. qui, lorsqu'il briguait un mandat de sénateur, s'était rétamé

5. ça s'était su

6. vos articles

7. pile quand il a mis la clé sous la porte

"I don't know if you know what I'm up to these days[1]."

"Not really."

"Since I got out of serving the people I started up a business. Bottling springwater. Pure, delicious, chemical-free water," Finley said. "It's a thriving business[2]."

"Great."

"But I'm also thinking of getting back into public service. Going to take another try running[3] Promise Falls."

What a thought.

"Well," I said. "That's something. But the thing is, I'm not a reporter these days. The *Standard* is gone. I'm not freelancing for anyone, either. Freelance has totally dried up[4]. If you want publicity for your plans, if you're putting out a release[5] or something, you're probably best contacting media in Albany. They still cover stories up this way if they're interesting enough, and I think I can say a comeback bid by you would get their attention."

"No, no, you're way off[6]," Finley said. "I'm offering you a position[7]. A job."

I couldn't think of a thing to say.

"You there?"

"Yeah," I said. "I'm here."

"You sound pretty excited," he said.

"I don't think I'm your guy," I said.

"I haven't even told you what the job entails[8]. Thing is,[9] I can't manage everything. I can't manage this company, run a campaign, do PR[10], answer phone calls, field media inquiries[11], get the word out[12], all that shit, without my fucking head blowing up. You know what I'm saying?"

"Sure."

1. ce que je fais ces temps-ci	
2. affaire florissante	
3. retenter la mairie de	
4. ne se fait plus du tout	
5. voulez faire une annonce	
6. n'y êtes pas du tout	
7. un poste	
8. en quoi consiste le boulot	
9. Le problème est que	
10. m'occuper des relations publiques	
11. répondre aux journalistes	
12. envoyer des infos	

"I need an administrative assistant, I guess you would call it. Handle the media, do publicity, put shit up on Facebook and Twitter, which I totally fucking don't understand, but I get that these days you have to use everything that's out there. Am I right?"

"Like I said, I don't think I'm your guy."

"Why?" Finley asked. "Because I'm an asshole[1]?"

He caught me again at a loss for words[2].

"Because that's what I am. Ask around. Hell, you don't need to ask around. You worked for the paper. You know what I'm like. I'm an asshole. So what[3]? Do you know how many people would have jobs if they refused to work for assholes? The whole fucking country would be unemployed. So what if I'm an asshole? I'm an asshole willing to pay you a thousand bucks a week[4]. How does that sound[5]?"

The door opened. Sam was back.

"I have to go," I said, raising an index finger at Sam.

"You'd start right away[6] if you're interested," Finley said. "Tell you what. Think on it overnight and let me know tomorrow. You're not the only guy from the *Standard* who's out of work, you know. But from asking around, sounded like you might be the best. A grand[7] a week. Think about it. It'll be fun. We'll be stirring up some major shit[8]."

Randall Finley ended the call.

Dumbfounded[9], I put the phone back into my jacket and looked apologetically at Samantha Worthington.

"Sorry about that," I said.

"My kid doesn't have that watch," she said, and closed the door.

Marginal notes:
1. connard
2. Une fois de plus, je ne sus que lui répondre
3. Et alors
4. mille dollars par semaine
5. Qu'en dites-vous
6. tout de suite
7. Mille balles
8. On va secouer la baraque
9. Sidéré

TWENTY-ONE

BARRY Duckworth didn't have enough on Marla Pickens to hold her[1]. He had no choice but to let her leave with Natalie Bondurant. But he didn't think it would be long before he had her back in that interrogation room. The techs[2] were at her house, looking for evidence[3]. He'd already heard they'd found blood by the front door, and on the handle of the stroller. A DNA analysis[4] wouldn't be coming overnight[5], but if that blood matched[6] Rosemary Gaynor's, Marla Pickens was going down[7]. And with any luck, Duckworth thought, he'd have something on her even before that.

The fact that she had Rosemary's baby[8]—Jesus, it just hit him that he'd stumbled[9] into a horror movie—was not in itself proof that Marla had killed the woman. Damning, yes, but not proof. Her story about an angel coming to the door and handing over Matthew was pure and utter bullshit, with no supporting evidence[10], so it didn't worry him much. It wasn't that he had to disprove[11] that story. He just had to prove Marla was at that house on Breckonwood Drive.

And he had to find the nanny.

Sarita.

1. la mettre en garde à vue

2. gars de la scientifique

3. cherchant des éléments de preuve

4. L'analyse ADN

5. ne serait pas prête demain matin

6. correspondait à

7. plongeait

8. [c'est aussi le titre d'un film d'horreur psychologique, 1968]

9. avait fait irruption

10. sans preuve à l'appui

11. réfuter

1. sac à main
2. posé,
3. bien visible,

4. lieux du crime

5. nom de
famille

6. composant le
numéro

7. sonneries

Bill Gaynor had been no help there, but they had found his wife's cell phone in her purse[1], which was sitting[2] in plain view[3] on the kitchen counter. If Rosemary Gaynor's killer had taken anything from it, and there was nothing to suggest he had, he'd apparently had no interest in her cash or credit cards.

He? Duckworth thought. More likely *she*.

When Duckworth was finished with Marla Pickens, he checked his own phone, which he'd felt vibrate during the interrogation. An e-mail from one of the officers on the scene[4] informed him that there was a contact listing for "Sarita" in the Gaynor woman's phone.

No last name[5].

So Duckworth tapped on the number, automatically dialing it[6], and listened.

After three rings[7]: "Hello?"

The voice sounded female, so he asked, "Is this Sarita?"

"Sarita?"

"That's right. Are you Sarita?"

"Sarita who?"

Duckworth sighed. "I'm trying to get in touch with Sarita. Am I talking to Sarita?" Bill Gaynor had suggested Sarita was an illegal immigrant, but the detective did not detect any kind of foreign accent.

"I don't have a last name. I'm looking for Sarita. She works as a nanny."

"Who is calling?"

He hesitated. "Duckworth. Detective Duckworth, with the Promise Falls police."

"I don't know any Sarita. There is no Sarita here. You have the wrong number."

"I don't think so," he said. "It's very important that I speak to Sarita."

"Like I said, I don't know how you got this number."

"If you're not Sarita, then do you know her? Because I—"

The call ended. Duckworth had been hung up on[1]. "Shit," he said. He never should have identified himself[2] as being with the police[3].

He returned to his desk, and just as he'd suspected, word had gotten around about his first call of the day[4]. Placed in front of his computer monitor[5] was a jar of salted peanuts[6], with a yellow sticky note[7] attached that read[8], *For paying your informants.*

The twenty-three dead squirrels. Was that actually today? It seemed like a week ago.

He cracked the lid[9], poured out a handful[10] of nuts, tossed[11] them into his mouth. Then he entered the phone number he'd just dialed[12] into the Google search field on his computer. If it was a landline[13], there was a good chance the name of the person who owned that phone would come up[14].

No such luck.

But not all was lost, even if the phone was a cell. Unless it was a throwaway[15], they'd be able to attach a name to it in no time[16]. Duckworth could get someone on that. The Internet abounded with firms offering to track down cell-phone identities for a price[17], but they often promised more than they could actually deliver[18].

Duckworth forwarded[19] the officer's e-mail containing Sarita's number to Connor Stigler, in communications[20], with the words: *Whose number is this?*

1. On lui avait raccroché au nez
2. se présenter
3. comme policier
4. sa première visite du jour était visiblement connue
5. écran d'ordinateur
6. bocal de cacahuètes salées
7. Post-it
8. disait
9. dévissa le couvercle
10. sortit une poignée
11. lança
12. qu'il venait de composer
13. une ligne fixe
14. apparaîtrait dans les résultats
15. jetable
16. très vite
17. contre paiement
18. fournir
19. transféra
20. au service télécoms

Then he phoned his wife, Maureen.

"Did you have one?" she asked him.

"Have one what?"

"On the way to work. A doughnut."

"I did not." It was nice not to have to lie for once. "It was a close one[1], though."

"You sound like you're eating something right now[2]."

"Peanuts," he said. "What's for dinner?"

"Gee[3], I don't know," she said. "What are you making?"

"Seriously?"

"Why is it always my responsibility? Maybe you didn't get the memo[4]. I work, too."

"Okay. I'm bringing home a bucket of fried chicken, mashed potatoes, and gravy."

"Well played," Maureen said. "I'm serving fish. Pickerel[5]." She paused. "And some greens[6]."

"Greens," Duckworth said. "Maybe I *will* pick up fried chicken."

Maureen ignored the threat. "Will you be late?"

"Maybe. I'll keep you posted[7]. Heard from[8] Trevor?"

Their son. Twenty-four years old, looking for work. He didn't live with them, or anyone else, for that matter[9]. Not anymore. The love of his life, a girl named Trish, who'd traveled across Europe with him, had recently broken things off[10]. Trevor, devastated, now had a two-bedroom apartment all to himself. Barry and Maureen didn't hear from him as often as they'd like, and they worried about him.

"Not today," Maureen said. "Maybe I'll give him a call. See if he wants to come for dinner."

"For fish? Good luck with that."

"It doesn't have to be today."

1. J'ai bien failli
2. en ce moment même
3. Mince
4. l'info
5. Du maquereau
6. Avec des légumes
7. Je te tiens au courant
8. Des nouvelles de
9. d'ailleurs
10. rompu

"Okay, do that. Listen, gotta go."

He'd noticed that he already had an e-mail back from Connor.

It read[1]: *L SELFRIDGE 209 ARMOUR ROAD*.

As he was pushing his chair back from the desk, uniformed officer[2] Angus Carlson walked past, glanced at Duckworth and the jar of peanuts, and smiled.

Before Duckworth could level an accusation[3], Carlson said, "Wasn't me." Paused, then added, "I'd have to be nuts to mock a[4] superior officer."

The Armour Road address was a rooming house[5], a three-story[6] Victorian home that had been broken down[7] into apartments. There was a buzzer[8] by the front door labeled MANAGER. Duckworth buzzed. Moments later, a short, heavyset[9] woman with little more than a few wisps[10] of hair came to the door and opened it a few inches.

"Yeah?"

"Ms. Selfridge?" he asked.

"Mrs. But the mister died a few years back. We don't have any vacancies[11], but you can leave your name if you'd like."

"I'm not looking for a room," he said. "That was pretty rude of you[12], cutting me off like that."

Her eyes danced. "Huh?"

"On the phone, a few minutes ago. When I was asking for Sarita."

"How'd you find where I live?"

"You pay the bill on that cell phone[13], Mrs. Selfridge. There are some things you don't need Homeland Security for[14]."

"I told you before, I don't know any Sarita."

"I'm thinking you do."

1. disait
2. l'agent
3. ait pu l'accuser
4. C'est une idée à la noix, je me moquerais pas d'un
5. pension de famille
6. à deux étages [+ le RDC]
7. découpé
8. Interphone
9. trapue
10. mèches
11. rien de libre
12. grossier de votre part
13. votre facture de téléphone
14. qu'on peut trouver sans l'antiterrorisme

She started to close the door but Duckworth got his shoe in.

"You got no right[1]," she said.

"I'm guessing Sarita likes to keep under the radar[2], so you let her use your phone. That way she doesn't need to get one in her own name. You tack on a little to the rent[3] every month for the service?"

"I don't know what you're jawin' about[4]."

Duckworth looked around, like a would-be buyer[5] appraising[6] the house. "When's the last time you had a fire[7] inspection, Mrs. Selfridge? Someone to go through, room by room, make sure everything's up to code[8]?"

"You're talking crazy talk."

"I could give them a call right now if you'd like. Invite them over to—" He stopped midsentence, his nose in the air. "What's that I smell?" he asked.

"That's chocolate-chip banana bread[9]," she said. "I just took it out of the oven[10]."

Duckworth gave her his warmest smile. "My God, that smells wonderful. I have this theory that when you arrive in heaven, the first thing you smell will be something like that."

"I make it whenever I've got a lot of old bananas that are too ripe[11] to eat. But you mush them all up and bake 'em and[12] they're good to eat."

"My mother used to do that. She'd even put black bananas in the freezer until she got around to making banana bread."

"I do that, too." Anxiously, she said, "This business with the fire inspection. I'm pretty up to code here, smoke[13] detectors and all that. There's no need for them to come in here and get their shorts all in a knot[14] about little picky things[15]."

1. n'avez pas le droit
2. clandestine
3. lui rajoutez un chouïa au loyer
4. de quoi vous me causez
5. acheteur potentiel
6. jaugeant
7. anti-incendie
8. que tout est bien aux normes
9. un cake à la banane et aux pépites de chocolat
10. du four
11. mûres
12. si on les réduit en bouillie pour en faire un gâteau,
13. de fumée
14. se mettent dans tous leurs états
15. pour des détails

"They can be picky[1]," Duckworth said. "I suppose we could talk about it over some of that banana bread."

The woman gave him a withering look[2], sighed, and opened the door wide.

"You don't even have to tell me where your kitchen is," he said. "I can follow the scent, like a dog chasing down a rabbit."

Seconds later he was parked[3] at the woman's small kitchen table.

"This is asking a lot," Duckworth said, "but would you mind cutting me off an end piece[4]? Where it's crustier[5]? It's never better than when it's still warm."

Mrs. Selfridge obliged[6]. She cut him a slice off the end, and one more, set it on a chipped pale green plate, and placed it in front of him.

"You want it buttered?" she asked.

"No, no, that's fine," Duckworth said. "I'm trying to cut back[7]."

"You want milk with it?" she asked. "That's the way my Leonard would have it. And I got a splash of coffee left[8] in the pot if you'd like that."

"Coffee'd be just fine," he said. She set a mug in front of him and sat down. Watched him bite into the end piece.

"Dear God," he said. "That's wonderful."

"Thank you," she said. She paused, then asked, "So what is it you want to know about Sarita?"

Duckworth held up a hand. "Nothing just yet." He took another bite of banana bread, then sipped his coffee. "I really needed this. And I don't even feel guilty, because I haven't had any other treats[9] today."

"You trying to lose weight? I'm not saying you should. I'm just asking."

1. pénibles
2. regard furieux
3. installé
4. l'entame
5. plus croustillant
6. s'exécuta
7. perdre du poids
8. un reste de café
9. douceurs

He nodded. "I could stand to lose a few. But it's hard when you love to eat."

"You're telling me[1]," she said. "Some days I look down and wonder where my feet is."

Duckworth laughed. "Aren't we entitled[2] to a little pleasure in life? And if good food gives us pleasure, can we not be forgiven for enjoying it?"

Mrs. Selfridge nodded slowly, rested her hands on the table.

"And I'll let you in on[3] a little secret," he said.

"What's that?"

"Today is twenty years."

"You've been married twenty years?"

He shook his head. "Twenty years with the police. It's my anniversary[4] today."

"Well, congratulations. They do something special for you today at the police station?"

"Not one damn thing," Duckworth said, taking another bite[5].

The woman watched him eat. She said, "I don't know where she's gone."

"Hmm?" the detective said, like he'd forgotten why he was here.

"Sarita. I don't know where she's at."

"When did you see her last?"

"Yesterday. Late afternoon."

"What's her name? Her last name?"

"Gomez. Sarita Gomez."

"And she rents a room here from you."

"Yeah."

"Does she live here alone?"

The woman nodded.

"Since when?"

"She's been renting from me going on three years now. Never a speck of trouble from her[6]. She's a good girl."

1. À qui le dites-vous !
2. On a bien droit
3. vais vous confier
4. la date anniversaire
5. bouchée
6. un souci avec elle

"How old?"

"Twenty-six? Seven? Something like that. She makes money and sends it home to help her family."

"Her family where?"

"Mexico, I think. Don't know where exactly. It's never been any of my business[1]. But she told me that much[2]."

"You know how she makes a living[3]?"

"She did some work looking after some lady's baby, and she also did shifts[4] at a nursing home[5] or two, I think. She couldn't afford a cell phone, so I always let her use mine, just so long as she didn't run up long-distance charges[6] to Mexico on it[7]."

"You know which nursing home?"

Mrs. Selfridge shook her head. "Beats me[8]. But the people she did nannying for[9] are named Gaynor. Lady's name is Rosemary. But I don't know much more than that. But Sarita must have had a shift yesterday, 'cause she was dressed for it. In like a nurse's uniform."

"And tell me about yesterday. The last time you saw her."

"I heard the front door open real hard[10] and then running up the stairs. Her room's right over mine and I could hear her banging about, so I went up to see and she was stuffing[11] some things into a suitcase[12]. I says, 'What's up?'[13] And she says she's going away."

"Going away where?"

"She didn't say."

"She say for how long?"

Mrs. Selfridge shook her head. "But she didn't say she was giving up the apartment or anything. But I'll tell you this, she was rattled pretty good[14]."

"Did she say why?"

1. Ça ne me regarde pas

2. au moins ça

3. gagne sa vie

4. des gardes

5. maison de retraite

6. du moment qu'elle passait pas d'appels longue distance

7. avec

8. Aucune idée

9. qui l'employaient comme nounou

10. violemment

11. fourrait

12. valise

13. « Qu'est-ce qui se passe ? », que j'y ai demandé

14. toute chamboulée

"Nope. But I says to her, 'You okay? You've got some blood on your sleeve[1] there.' And she looks at it and starts taking her uniform off and putting on something else and she's running around like a chicken with its head cut off, right? And she runs downstairs with her bag and there's a car waiting for her out front[2]."

"A car?"

"I didn't get a look at it[3]. Just black. And it took off[4]. It might have been a boyfriend. I think she might have had a boyfriend, but she never had him here, not overnight[5]. But the last thing she says is not to tell anybody anything about her, not to say where she went, but I don't even know, so I guess I'm really not doing anything wrong by telling you."

"I appreciate it," Duckworth said. He finished off the second slice of banana bread and downed the last of[6] his coffee. Smacked his lips with flourish[7].

"Whaddaya say we go have a look at[8] Sarita's room," he said.

1. sur la manche
2. devant la maison
3. J'ai pas vraiment regardé
4. la voiture est partie
5. pour passer la nuit
6. finit d'un trait
7. Fit un ah ! de contentement
8. Et si on allait voir

TWENTY-TWO

"I want something done about that man," Agnes Pickens said as she, her husband, Gill, and their daughter, Marla, entered the Pickens family home.

"Agnes," Gill said, "the detective is just doing his job."

"Why am I not surprised that you would take his side?[1]"

"For Christ's sake[2], it's not a question of taking sides," Gill said. "Duckworth has a murder to investigate, and he follows things where they lead[3]."

"He's got no business following them[4] to our daughter."

"She had their goddamn baby!"

His voice bounced off[5] the walls of the oversize[6] foyer. Marla stood behind them, arms limp[7] at her sides, her eyes dead.

"For God's sake, Gill," Agnes said, taking her daughter into her arms, shielding her[8] as though her husband's words might physically strike her. "That really helps."

Marla's arms remained motionless[9].

Agnes said, "You go up to your room, sweetheart. Why don't you lie down? It's been an exhausting[10] day for you. We're going to take care of

1. C'est curieux, je ne suis pas surprise que tu prennes sa défense

2. l'amour du ciel

3. le mènent

4. n'a pas à les suivre

5. On entendit l'écho de sa voix sur

6. trop grand

7. ballants

8. la protégeant de son corps,

9. immobiles

10. épuisante

this." Turning to Gill, she said, "I just hope Bondurant knows what she's doing."

"I liked her," Marla whispered. "I thought she was nice."

"Yeah, well, she needs to be a lot more than nice," Agnes said.

"When can I go back to my house?" Marla asked.

"That'll be up to[1] the police," Gill said. "I'm guessing they'll tear the place apart[2]."

"Can you go get my computer?" she asked. "So I can do my work?"

"Yes," Agnes said. "Look into that[3], Gill."

"They're not going to give her back her computer," her husband said, exasperated. "They'll be reading all her e-mails and checking her browsing history[4]. That's what they do in these kinds of investigations."

"You're some sort of expert?" his wife asked.

He shook his head. "Have you watched *any* television?"

Agnes looked at her daughter. "Is that going to be a problem, sweetheart? Are they going to find anything you'd rather they didn't[5] on your computer?"

She looked into her mother's eyes. "Like what?" she asked.

"Well, we won't worry about that right now. Are you hungry? Do you want something to eat?"

"I could use a drink[6]," Gill said, and started heading for the kitchen.

"Maybe some toast," Marla said.

"Okay, we can—"

The doorbell rang.

Agnes Pickens let go of[7] Marla and opened the front door. Standing there was Dr. Jack Sturgess, who had been among those at the hospital board meeting that morning.

1. dépendra de
2. vont passer la maison au peigne fin
3. Renseigne-toi là-dessus
4. historique de navigation
5. que tu ne voudrais pas qu'ils voient
6. boirais bien un coup
7. lâcha

"Agnes," he said.

"Oh, Jack, thank you for coming."

Gill stopped and turned. "Jack?"

"I called and asked him to stop by," Agnes said. "I filled him in[1] on the phone. I thought he should have a look at Marla, make sure she's okay."

"I'm fine," Marla said.

"Gill, take Marla into the kitchen and get her something to eat while I talk to Jack."

Gill mumbled[2] something, then took his daughter by the arm and led her away. Once he and Marla were out of earshot[3], the doctor said, "It's a horrible thing. Just horrible."

"Yes," Agnes agreed.

"How on earth[4] did she come into possession of that baby?" he asked.

"I have no idea. My God, there are only two possibilities, and they're both unimaginable. One is that she actually[5] killed that woman and ran off with the child, or she's actually telling the truth and someone delivered the baby right to her[6]. I mean, how could that happen?"

"How's she now? Did she believe the child was really hers?"

Agnes shook her head. "No more than she did when she tried to take that baby out of the hospital the other time. But we need to get to the bottom of this[7]."

"I wonder if I need to prescribe something, to calm the nerves."

"For her, or me?" Agnes asked.

"Agnes, I—"

"You should have anticipated this, Jack. That there would be lasting trauma from what she went through[8]. Losing a child, that's an absolutely devastating thing for a person to deal with."

1. l'ai mis au courant

2. marmonna

3. trop loin pour entendre

4. diable

5. vraiment

6. lui a vraiment mis le bébé dans les bras

7. tirer les choses au clair

8. Qu'elle serait longtemps traumatisée par ce qu'elle a subi

1. tu n'y as
jamais pensé
toi-même

2. as fait suivre
Marla par un psy

3. reste de

4. ne sais trop

5. avis
6. Au pire
7. la met en
examen

8. aura son rôle
à jouer

9. membre
10. de l'hôpital
de Promise Falls
11. finit au
tribunal
12. Le
témoignage
13. invalidé

"For God's sake, Agnes, that never occurred to *you*[1]? You've had Marla seeing someone[2]; you've done all you could. No one could have predicted Marla would react this way, going around stealing babies and—"

Gill reappeared. "Jack, a drink?"

The doctor shook his head. "No, that's okay, but thank you, Gill."

"How is she?" Agnes asked her husband.

"I showed her the leftover[3] spaghetti Bolognese that was in the fridge and she said she'd like some of that. It's one of her favorite things. It's warming up now in the microwave. So, Jack, what do you think?"

"I hardly know[4] what to think," he said. "It might be a good idea to get another psychiatric assessment[5]. God forbid[6], if the police charge her[7], you want to start planning a strategy, and her state of mind will play into that[8]."

"I'll talk to Dr. Frankel," Agnes said. "She's been seeing him for nearly ten months now. I'm sure he'll say whatever we need him to say."

"It might be better to get someone who's not connected to your hospital," Gill said. "Frankel's part[9] of the PFG[10] psychiatric unit. That might work against Marla if this, as Jack says, ends up before the courts[11]. Frankel's testimony[12] could be tainted[13] by his connection to you."

There was a *ding* from the kitchen microwave.

"I'll be back," Gill said, and disappeared.

Dr. Sturgess had his mouth open to say something when he and Agnes heard Gill shout, "Jesus, Marla!"

The two of them ran to the kitchen, where they found Gill on one side of the table, Marla on the other. She was standing, holding a steak knife

186

in her right hand, poised[1] over her upturned left wrist[2].

"Stay away from me," she said.

"Marla!" Agnes said. "Put that down! Right now."

Marla did not obey. Her cheeks were tearstained[3] as she looked at her mother and Dr. Sturgess.

"Why?" she asked.

"Sweetheart, just put that knife down," Agnes said.

"Why did you have to let my baby die?"

Sturgess cleared his throat. "Marla," he said quietly, "we did everything we could. We truly did."

"I'm so sorry," Agnes said. "You have no idea how sorry I am."

"You should have saved her."

"There was nothing we wanted more," her mother said. "It was just ... all I can tell myself is that it was God's will[4]."

Gill was slowly moving around the end of the table, trying to close[5] the distance between himself and his daughter.

"Why wouldn't God want me to have her?" Marla asked. "Why would He be so mean[6]?"

"There are things we can never understand," Gill said. "Horrible things happen, I know. But we have to try to move forward[7]. It's hard. But we can help you. We can help you do that. I love you very much."

"We *both* love you," Agnes said.

"She was so beautiful," Marla said. "So perfect. Wasn't she, Mom? Wasn't she perfect? I close my eyes and try to picture her[8] and it's hard."

"She was. She truly was."

Marla glanced at her father. "Don't."

1. figé
2. la face interne de son poignet gauche
3. barbouillées de larmes
4. la volonté
5. réduire
6. méchant
7. aller de l'avant
8. l'imaginer

1. ma chérie
2. parie
3. m'enfermer
4. engagerons
5. On fera tout pour t'éviter ça
6. agrippa
7. arracher
8. claqua par terre
9. de justesse
10. recouvrit
11. perla de ses doigts
12. se précipita
13. saisit un torchon
14. le serra
15. la soutenait
16. le SAMU
17. composa
18. qu'on lui avait retiré Matthew

He stopped. "Please, honey[1]. Just put that down. I'm betting[2] Dr. Sturgess can give you something that will make you feel better."

"I can help you," the doctor said. "Let us all help you, Marla."

"They're going to put me away[3]," she said. "I'm going to go to jail."

"No," Agnes said. "We won't let that happen. We'll hire[4] the best lawyers there are. If Natalie isn't the best, we'll get someone else."

"That's right," Gill said. "Whatever it takes[5]."

"I don't think so," Marla said, then brought the blade down on her wrist and drew it across.

"No!" Agnes screamed, her hands going to her mouth.

Gill rushed forward and clutched[6] Marla's right arm to wrest[7] the knife from her, but she made no effort to hold on to it. It clattered to the floor[8], narrowly[9] missing Gill's shoe.

Marla allowed her left arm to drop. Blood emerged from her wrist, coated[10] her hand like dark red paint, and dripped off the tips of her fingers[11].

Dr. Sturgess raced forward[12], grabbing a tea towel[13] hanging from the oven door handle along the way, and bound it tightly[14] around Marla's bleeding wrist while Gill held on to her[15]. Agnes was frozen, hands still over her mouth, watching the scene in front of her in horror.

"Call nine-one-one[16]!" the doctor screamed at her. "Agnes! Call an ambulance!"

She ran to the wall phone, picked up the receiver, and punched in[17] the number.

Marla, for the first time since she'd had Matthew taken away from her[18], allowed herself a smile.

TWENTY-THREE

David

ETHAN must have been watching from his bedroom window and seen me pull into the driveway[1] in his grandmother's ancient[2] Taurus, because he was waiting for me at the door when I came into the house. Mom and Dad were in the kitchen, so he didn't have to worry about interrogating me in front of them.

1. me garer dans l'allée
2. vénérable

"Did you get it?" he asked. "Did you get the watch?"

I shook my head solemnly. "No."

"Was nobody home?"

"They were home. Carl's mother talked to him and told me he said he didn't have it."

"He's lying!"

"I know," I said.

"Didn't you tell his mom that he was lying?"

"Come on out front[3]," I said. I led him onto the porch and directed him to the white wicker chairs[4]. I put him in one and I took the other. "It's complicated," I said.

3. dehors

4. fauteuils en rotin

"But he has it. He's lying."

189

1. n'aurait servi à rien

"If I'd told his mother that, it wouldn't have helped[1]. She wouldn't have believed me. Look, if someone came here and said you'd stolen something, and you said you hadn't, I wouldn't believe them; I would believe you."

2. répliqua-t-il
3. as quand même

"But I would never steal anything," he countered[2].

"Yeah, well, you did kind of[3] take that watch without permission," I reminded him.

That stopped him for a second. "But that wasn't really stealing. I was going to put it back."

I nodded, rested a hand on his shoulder. "What I'm trying to say is, parents don't like to think their kids have done things they shouldn't. We just naturally defend you. And that's what Carl's mom did with him."

"Did you talk to Carl?"

"No."

"Why not?"

I'd already decided not to mention Samantha

4. a pris des mesures

Worthington's shotgun. "His mother took steps[4] to make sure that didn't happen."

5. démoralisé

Ethan looked defeated[5]. "What about Poppa?"

"You're going to have to tell him," I said.

"Me?"

I nodded. "Yup."

"Can't you tell him?"

I shook my head. "I didn't take it. I tried to save

6. de te rattraper le coup
7. mon pote
8. assumer

your bacon on this one[6], buddy[7]. But I couldn't. So you're going to have to own up to[8] what you did."

"Will he kick us out[9]?"

9. nous mettre à la porte

"No, he won't do that. Let's go find him."

Mom was in the kitchen, her weight mostly on one leg as she stood by the counter peeling potatoes.

"Where's Dad?" I asked.

"I think he's out in the garage," she said. "He's gotten awfully quiet this afternoon. He was okay at first, but as the day's gone on, I don't know. Something's not right."

"Is he sick?" I asked. "His heart's not acting up[1], is it?"

Mom shook her head, downplaying the seriousness[2]. "Nothing like that. I thought maybe he was mad at[3] me for being such an idiot and tripping on the stairs, but I don't think that's it. I'm wondering if it has something to do with Walden."

"Walden?" I asked.

"Walden Fisher. He called your father out of the blue[4], wanted to go get coffee. You remember him?"

I did not.

"Your father helped him get a job with the town[5] years ago. I'm betting you remember that horrible business with Olivia Fisher?"

"The woman who was ..." I might have finished the sentence if Ethan hadn't been standing there. The woman who was fatally stabbed[6] in the park by the falls[7].

Even though I'd never finished the sentence, Mom knew where I was going[8]. "That's the one[9]. She was Walden's daughter. Anyway, Walden's wife just died, too, poor man. He still works for the town, and he wanted to ask your father some questions about all these things that went on back when[10] your father worked there. Don't ask me what because I don't know and I don't care." She looked at Ethan. "What's with the face[11]?"

"Nothing," he said.

"You want a cookie?"

"No, thank you."

"Come on," I said to him. "Let's go find Poppa."

1. ne fait pas des siennes

2. pour dédramatiser

3. très fâché contre

4. à l'improviste

5. auprès de la municipalité

6. tuée à coups de poignard

7. près des chutes

8. ce que j'allais dire

9. Celle-là même

10. à l'époque où

11. C'est quoi cette tête

He was, as Mom had said, in the garage. It was a separate building in back of the house that was a second workshop[1] for Dad. It was hard to keep it warm in the winter, so he'd set up a place to work in the basement, too. But when the weather was nice, he spent a lot of time out here puttering[2].

1. atelier

We found him standing at the workbench[3], sorting screws[4] and dropping them into a drawer made up of dozens of small plastic cubicles[5]. Dad was a good sorter[6].

2. à bricoler
3. devant l'établi
4. à trier des vis
5. cases
6. fort en tri

"Hey," I said.

"Hmm," he said, barely acknowledging us[7]. Ethan shot me a worried look, one that said, *Maybe this isn't a good time.*

7. nous saluant à peine

"Dad, you got a sec[8]?"

8. seconde

He half turned to look at us, and I don't know how this could be, but he looked older than when I'd seen him earlier in the day. I thought about his heart.

"What is it?" he asked.

I nudged Ethan's shoulder[9].

9. bousculai gentiment Ethan

"I have to tell you something," my son said. "You promise not to get mad?"

My father eyed him curiously[10]. "I know you haven't wrecked[11] my car. You can't reach[12] the pedals. There can't be anything much worse than that. So, okay."

10. d'un drôle d'œil
11. cassé
12. ne touches pas

"You know the fight I had with Carl Worthington?"

"Yup."

"It was about your dad's watch. The one you had in a box downstairs with other stuff[13]."

13. d'autres trucs

"Okay," Dad said.

"I kind of took it from the box and took it to school to show people, and Carl took it and wouldn't give it back, and I'm really sorry and I know I shouldn't have done it and I should have asked you if I could take it to school, and I'll pay you back[1]."

Dad's eyes softened[2]. "That's what the fight was about."

"I grabbed him to try to get it back but he kept it. And Dad went over there to get it back but Carl lied and said he didn't have it." He paused for a breath[3]. "But I know that none of this would have happened if I hadn't taken it in the first place[4]."

Dad said nothing for several seconds. Then: "Well, it didn't keep time[5] anyway. There's people done[6] worse things than what you did."

He put his hand to Ethan's cheek, held it there for a moment, then went back to sorting screws.

Ethan looked like a death row inmate[7] who'd gotten a call from the governor at two minutes to midnight[8]. I nodded toward the house, indicating he should take off[9]. He did.

"Everything okay, Dad?" I asked.

"Yeah, sure," he said, his back to me[10].

"You let Ethan off pretty easy[11]."

"He's a good boy," Dad said. "He screwed up[12]." A pause. "We all do."

"Mom said you met up with an old friend from work today."

"Not really," he said. "His dad was a friend of mine."

"Was it good to see him?"

A shrug[13], his back still to me as he separated Robertsons from Phillips[14]. "Yes and no. I don't really keep up[15] with folks I worked with. Say hello if I see them on the street is all, like Tate."

I had no idea who Tate was.

Dad continued. "I've got enough to do without living in the past. It's not good for you, dwelling[16]

---

1. te rembourserai

2. s'adoucirent

3. pour reprendre son souffle

4. je ne l'avais pas pris, déjà, pour commencer

5. ne marchait pas

6. qu'ont fait

7. condamné à mort

8. minuit moins deux

9. ferait mieux de nous laisser

10. en me tournant le dos

11. as été cool avec Ethan

12. a fait une bêtise

13. haussement d'épaules

14. [marques de vis]

15. ne suis pas vraiment resté en contact

16. de s'appesantir

1. contre lesquelles on ne peut foutrement rien

2. gêné
3. s'ensuivit
4. faute de sujets de conversation
5. ne pouvais me défaire de

6. lancer un autre sujet de

7. fronça les sourcils

8. directeur de cabinet
9. Directeur de campagne
10. a assez à faire
11. des relations publiques

12. Pourquoi tu hésites

on things that happened a long time ago that you can't do a damn thing about[1]."

"What are we talking about here, Dad?" I asked.

"Nothing," he said. "Absolutely nothing."

An awkward[2] silence ensued[3], but it wasn't for lack of things to talk about[4]. Marla and the baby and Rosemary Gaynor. I still couldn't shake[5] the image of that dead woman on the floor. As hard as I tried to mentally push it away, it kept coming back.

I figured even if I could block it out, it would be replaced with the image of a shotgun in my face.

I decided to go with something else to make[6] conversation.

"I got offered a job today," I said.

That prompted Dad to turn and face me. "Hey, that's great news, son. That's terrific."

"I haven't said yes. In fact, I'm not sure I want to say yes."

He frowned[7]. "What is it?"

"Remember Randall Finley?"

"Yeah, of course. Good man, Finley."

"What?" That took me by surprise.

"Oh, yeah, he was a good mayor. You telling me *he* offered you a job?"

"Yeah. A kind of executive-assistant[8] thing. Campaign manager[9], maybe. He's thinking about running again, but he's got his hands full[10] overseeing his water-bottling company. Needs someone to do PR[11] for him, deal with media, stuff like that."

"Pay good?"

"Thousand a week."

"What's there to think about[12]?" my father asked. "That's good money."

"Dad, he's an asshole."

Dad shrugged. "He's a politician."

194

"Remember the underage-hooker thing[1]?"

Dad nodded. "But he didn't *know* she was underage."

Was this my father I was talking to? "You mean if she was just old enough, that made it okay?"

He looked down at the floor. "No, I'm not saying that. I'm just saying there are degrees. Look at Clinton back in the nineties[2]. Look at our own Spitzer, a few years back. They get a little bit of power and they think they can do anything; then they find out they can't and get cut down to size[3]. They learn. Does that mean we cut 'em off from ever[4] making a contribution again?"

I said nothing.

"Let me tell you a story," he said. "After your mother and I got married, but before I got a job with the town, I was out of work[5]. There was a guy building houses on the south side of town who was looking to hire[6]. I knew something about him. I knew he was a drunk[7], that he abused[8] his wife, that he beat his kids. He was a total shit[9], this guy. And I had a wife to look after, rent[10] to pay. I had responsibilities. I took that job. I wasn't proud of myself, but looking after your mother came ahead of[11] my pride. I decided I'd work that job, and keep looking for something better in the meantime[12]. And as soon as I found something with the town, I gave that bastard my notice[13] and left. But through it all, your mother never went hungry, and she never spent a day without a roof over her head."

I swallowed[14]. "I hear you."

"Yeah, Finley's an asshole. But I think he loves this town, and maybe he's what Promise Falls needs right now. Someone to shake things up[15]."

1. scandale de la prostituée mineure

2. dans les années 1990

3. se font remettre à leur place

4. qu'on doive définitivement les empêcher

5. au chômage

6. cherchait quelqu'un à embaucher

7. poivrot

8. maltraitait

9. salopard

10. un loyer

11. comptait plus que

12. pendant ce temps-là

13. démission

14. avalai ma salive

15. qui fasse bouger les choses

I nodded. We stood there facing each other. I put my arms around him and patted his back.

"You're a good man," I said as he returned the hug[1].

"Don't be so sure," Dad said.

1. répondait à mon étreinte

TWENTY-FOUR

IT didn't freak out[1] Gloria Fenwick to be working in a deserted amusement park[2]. At least, not in the daytime.

She'd worked for the corporation that owned Five Mountains and several other parks across the country, and she'd been posted[3] at some of those other locations[4] through the years. And that had meant being there in the off-season[5], winding things down[6] after the children had gone back to school, their parents back to the drudgery of their jobs[7].

Fenwick was accustomed[8] to strolling past[9] riderless[10] horses stuck in their tracks[11] on the merry-go-round[12]. She could never bring herself[13] to ride any of the parks' roller coasters[14], so the stillness[15] of the Five Mountains Super Collider Coaster actually gave her comfort[16]. She couldn't stand close to it[17] when it was in operation[18], feeling the supporting structure tremble and vibrate, always fearing the apparatus would collapse[19], sending dozens of people to their deaths.

The empty concession stands[20], the driverless bumper cars[21], the deserted parking lot. It was all just fine with[22] Fenwick.

In the daytime.

1. lui fichait vraiment les jetons

2. sans mauvais jeu de mots

3. à écluser

4. proposait

5. démonté

6. expédié là-bas

7. reconstruction en cours

8. licenciés

9. reçues

10. flic au carrefour

11. orientant les gens selon le renseignement qu'il leur fallait

12. d'innombrables autres tâches

13. la fermeture du parc

14. procès en cours

15. le dentier

16. lui en aurait racheté un

17. réclamait une compensation morale

18. s'éclipsait

19. surveiller

20. que des sans-abri

21. ne s'installent pas dans les attractions

But at night, well, that was a different story. At night, the place really did creep her out[1].

She felt reasonably secure in the park's administrative offices, where she was now, as darkness fell. She had a mountain of work—no pun intended[2]—still to deal with[3]. There were several offers from different amusement parks for some of the Five Mountains rides. An Italian firm was putting up[4] several million dollars for the Super Collider, which could be dismantled[5], shipped overseas[6], and reassembled. A group involved in the ongoing rebuilding[7] of the Jersey Shore after Hurricane Sandy was interested in some of the concession stands. A representative from Disney wanted information on laid-off[8] employees. They might have work for them at one of their theme parks.

Fenwick not only had to reply to all of them, but let the head office know about incoming[9] offers. All the big decisions were made there. She was just the traffic cop[10], directing inquiries this way and that[11].

Plus, there were countless other duties[12] involved in winding the place down[13]. Dealing with creditors. One pending lawsuit[14] from a woman whose dentures[15] flew out while on the coaster. If all she'd wanted was some new teeth, Five Mountains would have bought her a set[16], but the woman was claiming emotional distress[17], too.

What a fucking world, Fenwick thought.

She didn't work here entirely alone. She had an assistant most days, but he took off promptly[18] at five, whether there was work left to deal with or not. And Five Mountains had engaged a security firm to watch[19] the place, keep it from being vandalized, make sure homeless folks[20] weren't camped out in the inner workings of the log ride[21].

Usually it was a guy named Norm through the day, who did three rounds[1]: one at nine, another at one, and his last at five. In the evenings it was Malcolm. She knew for sure[2] he inspected the park at ten[3], because she'd been here working that late[4] on more than one occasion. He was supposed to come through again[5] at two in the morning, and then four hours later at six.

Gloria was thinking she wouldn't see Malcolm tonight. She hoped to get out of here around half past nine at the latest.

She was making a list of things she had to do the next day when her cell rang. She smiled. It was Jason. From the head office. Hundreds of miles away. When he called this late[6], it was not to talk business.

"Hey," she said.

"Whatcha doin'[7]?"

"I'm still here."

"Oh, go home. You're working too hard[8]." A pause. "And speaking of hard …"

"Stop it," she said, grinning, putting down her pen and running her fingers through her hair.

"Are you going to get here this weekend?"

"I'm going to try," she said, picking up the pen again, writing, *Call denture lawyer*[9]. "What about Memorial Day?" The May holiday weekend, a little more than two weeks away. "You coming here for that?"

"Oh, yeah. But I need to see you before then. I *really* need to see you."

"Oh, yeah?"

"I had this idea of something new we could try," Jason said.

"Go on."

1. tournées

2. avec certitude

3. 22 h

4. à cette heure tardive

5. repasser

6. aussi tard

7. Qu'est-ce tu fais

8. bosses trop

9. *avocat dentier*

"Okay, so picture this. You're on the bed, on your back, and—"

"What am I wearing?" she asked, scribbling[1], *Review[2] offer on bumper cars*.

"A pair of high heels," he said. "The black pumps[3]."

"I like those," Gloria said. "They make me feel dirty[4]. But they're hard to walk in."

"You won't be doing any walking," Jason said.

"Okay, so I'm on my back, in heels, and then what? Tell me this[5]. Are you there with me? Because, the way this is sounding, I just might be getting off[6] without you." Underlining, with a question mark at the end, *Tell head office about Finley?*

"Oh, I'm there, and my cock[7] is very, very—"

There was a flash of light outside Gloria Fenwick's window.

"Hold that thought[8]," she said, and put the cell phone on her desk. She got up and walked to the window. The light remained constant, but was somehow[9] *moving*.

"No," she said.

The light, which was being cast on a row[10] of gift-shop buildings[11] across from the admin offices, was coming from behind the building Fenwick worked in, where most of the rides were[12].

The rides that had all been powered down, that were in the process of being decommissioned[13].

She went back to her desk, picked up the phone, and said, "I'll have to call you back."

"What's—"

She ended the call, then contacted the security company. "Yeah, hey, it's Gloria at Five Mountains. There's something going on here. You need to get someone here[14] now. Yeah, right."

---

1. tout en griffonnant

2. *Examiner*

3. escarpins

4. cochonne

5. juste un truc

6. jouir

7. queue

8. Attends une seconde

9. semblait

10. rangée

11. boutiques de souvenirs

12. se trouvaient la plupart des attractions [à émotions fortes]

13. mis hors service

14. envoyer quelqu'un

Gloria, keeping the phone in her pocket, left the office, went down a flight of stairs[1], and exited onto the park's main street. To the left, the admission gates[2]. Heading right[3] would take her deeper into the park.

When she rounded the corner of the building, she could not believe what she was seeing.

The six-story-tall Ferris wheel[4] was alive.

Fully lit[5], it was a low-hanging[6], revolving roulette wheel[7] against[8] the dark night sky. A dazzling[9], monstrous twirling[10] eye that always reminded Fenwick of the pinwheels[11] she loved to blow into as a child.

"This is not happening," she said, starting to walk toward the base of the ride[12].

It was not impossible, of course. All the rides were still connected to the park's electrical source. They had to be turned on when prospective buyers[13] came to pick[14] through what Five Mountains was selling.

The big wheel moved almost noiselessly[15]. With the carriages empty, there was not the usual screaming and laughing of passengers.

Except …

Fenwick stopped dead[16], waited for the Ferris wheel to make another complete rotation. Allowed her eyes to focus on the ride. She thought she saw someone—no, more than one person—sitting in one of the carriages as it did a swing[17] near the bottom, where there were more lights.

The wheel went around again, and this time Fenwick was sure. There looked to be[18] three people in one carriage. All the others were empty.

Goddamn kids, she thought. Snuck onto the grounds[19], figured out[20] how to start the ride, decided to have some fun.

1. volée de marches
2. entrée du parc
3. Tourner à droite
4. grande roue haute de 5 étages
5. éclairée
6. à ras de terre
7. telle le plateau tournant d'une roulette de casino
8. se détachant sur
9. éblouissant
10. tourbillonnant
11. petits moulins à vent
12. bas de l'attraction
13. des acheteurs potentiels
14. faire leur choix
15. sans bruit
16. net
17. passait
18. Il semblait y avoir
19. Se seront faufilés ici
20. ont dû comprendre

Except there had to be someone else. Someone who could stop the ride, or those three would be stuck on there for a very long time.

As she neared the wheel, it was making another loop[1]. She saw the numbers stenciled[2] onto the side of each carriage: 19 … 20 … 21 … 22 …

Here it was. Carriage twenty-three. Three people sitting side by side.

"Hey!" she shouted. "What the hell do you think—"

As the carriage swept past, Fenwick noticed that none of the passengers was moving.

And it didn't look like any of them were wearing clothes, either.

She reached the base of the Ferris wheel, located the controls[3]. She'd never worked as a ride operator, but she'd been around them often enough to know the basics. She grabbed the lever to power back[4] the wheel, to start slowing it gradually. She craned her neck upward[5], watching for carriage twenty-three, hoping she could time it right so that it stopped[6] at the boarding platform[7].

Very nearly did it too.[8] She didn't get the wheel to fully stop until it had gone about three feet too far for the passengers to make a safe exit.

But it didn't matter. Because they weren't passengers.

They were mannequins. All female, all unadorned[9]. Well, nearly.

Gloria Fenwick looked around and began to feel very afraid.

A single word was painted, in bold red, on each of the mute[10] amusement-park-goers.

Read across, the message was[11]:

YOU'LL BE SORRY[12]

---

1. entamait une autre boucle
2. peints au pochoir
3. commandes
4. levier de freinage de
5. se tordit le cou pour regarder en l'air
6. faire en sorte qu'il s'arrête
7. quai d'embarquement
8. Et elle y parvint presque !
9. sans rien sur le dos
10. muets
11. Lues à la suite, elles formaient le message suivant
12. VOUS LE REGRETTEREZ

TWENTY-FIVE

BILL Gaynor had to bring in[1] one of those companies that cleaned up crime scenes. The detective—Duckworth, his name was—had given him the name of a firm. Not local. There weren't enough crimes like this in Promise Falls to justify a service that catered to this exclusive a clientele[2]. But there was one in Albany, and they came up in the late afternoon, once the crime-scene investigators were finished doing whatever it was they did[3] and had cleared out[4].

They did a good job in the kitchen. They'd managed to mop up[5] all the blood in there. The carpet on the stairs and in the second-floor hallway was a different matter. Gaynor had tracked[6] blood through much of the house when he'd gone in search of Matthew. The cleaners had gotten up[7] some of the stains[8], but they'd told Gaynor he'd probably want to have all that carpeting ripped up and replaced[9]. It was a light gray, and there was only so much they could do[10].

Sure, he'd replace the carpet. And then he'd put this house on the market[11]. There was no way he could live in this place, raise his son here.

It hadn't occurred to[12] Gaynor that he'd have to pay for the cleaning. The head of the crew[13]

1. faire venir

2. consacré à une clientèle si limitée

3. de faire ce qu'il avaient à faire

4. étaient partis

5. éponger

6. semé

7. eu raison de

8. taches

9. faire enlever et remplacer toute la moquette

10. ils ne pouvaient pas faire grand-chose

11. en vente

12. n'était pas venu à l'esprit de

13. chef d'équipe

handed him the bill[1] without blinking[2]. "We take Visa," he said. "You might want to check with your insurance company. This might be something they'd reimburse you for."

"I work for an insurance company," Gaynor said.

"Well, there you go," the man said. "Every cloud[3], as they say."

There were so many things one had to do[4], he thought, but he didn't know where to start. As he'd told the detective, neither he nor Rosemary had immediate family[5]. No siblings[6], no living parents. Truth be told[7], neither of them had ever really had many friends. He had the doctor, of course. As far as he knew[8], his wife really had no one. She loved to talk to Sarita, and probably considered her a friend, but really, Gaynor thought, you couldn't be friends with the help[9].

What they had was Matthew.

The strangest random[10] thoughts went through his head. Questions, images. Where would he sleep tonight? In that big empty bed? What would he do with Rosemary's toothbrush? Throw it out[11]? Why'd she have to be killed in the kitchen? Of all the rooms in the house? Why not the garage? Or the basement? He might even have been able to hang on to[12] the house if she'd been killed in a room he didn't have to spend so much time in.

But how could one avoid the kitchen? How could he not, every time he had to go in there, see his wife's body on the floor?

He was going to have to go in there.

He'd retreated to his second-floor office[13] a couple of hours ago after putting Matthew down in his crib[14] for a sleep. He'd informed his employers of the day's events, and soon after took a call from the president of the company, a man named Ben

Corbett. He offered his condolences and told Bill to take as much time as he needed.

"And we have a lot of investigators[1] at our disposal," Corbett said. "I can put one on this if you want. I'm betting the police in a town like that can't find their asses in a snowstorm[2]. Am I right? I know a guy I can call up there. Weaver, his name is. Cal Weaver. Used to work for the local cops but went solo[3]. Lived out around Niagara for a while but I think he moved back."

"I don't think that's going to be necessary, Mr. Corbett, but I thank you," Gaynor said. "The police have a pretty good idea who did it. Some crazy woman. She's got a history[4]."

"Of killing people?"

"No, but from what the detective said—he called me a while ago—she tried to steal a baby out of the hospital a while back. A nutcase[5]."

"Well, the offer stands[6]. You need anything, you call me." A pause. "Oh, and Bill."

"Yes?"

"As much as I would like to expedite matters[7] where your wife's life insurance policy is concerned[8], I have to take a hands-off approach with this[9] and let things go through the usual channels[10]."

"Of course, Mr. Corbett, I understand that."

"Especially considering that the payout[11] in your wife's case ... I don't feel very comfortable discussing this with you at this time, Bill, so I hope you'll forgive me."

"That's okay," Gaynor said.

"As I was saying, the payout in your wife's case is a million dollars. So the firm will be doing its due diligence[12], but you've indicated that the police already have a pretty good idea what's happened."

1. enquêteurs

2. sont pas très démerde

3. s'est mis à son compte

4. passé

5. dingue

6. je maintiens ma proposition

7. Même si j'aimerais que les choses aillent vite

8. en ce qui concerne l'assurance-vie de votre femme

9. ne dois pas intervenir

10. canaux habituels

11. prime

12. va suivre sa procédure

"Yes, they do."

"Okay, then. My thoughts are with you. We'll be in touch."

Gaynor hung up the phone, took a deep breath, and put a hand to his chest. His heart was pounding.

He needed a drink.

He went to the liquor[1] cabinet, poured himself[2] a scotch, and then pulled himself together[3] so that he could send out e-mails to clients he was supposed to meet with[4] over the next week. Family emergency, he said, and offered his apologies. Gave them the name of an associate who could help them.

He was looking mindlessly[5] at his in-box[6] when he heard Matthew stirring in the next room. When the baby woke, he'd be hungry.

Gaynor went into the hallway and down the stairs, careful not to step on the slightly faded red footprints he'd left[7] earlier. As he entered the kitchen he forced himself to look away from where he'd found Rosemary. Focused in[8] on the fridge. Rosemary always prepared two days' worth of bottles of formula[9], and there were still four of them in there. He warmed a bottle, wondering what he would do when these were all gone. He'd never made up bottles[10] for Matthew. Didn't have a clue how to do it[11].

He had a steep learning curve ahead of him[12].

God, where was Sarita when he needed her?

He had some theories in that regard[13]. He had a feeling he wouldn't be seeing Sarita around here anymore. The police could look for her all they wanted. Good luck with that.

But he had to find someone to replace her, soon. Before he went back to work. Someone who could

1. à alcools
2. se versa
3. se reprit
4. qu'il était censé voir
5. distraitement
6. boîte de réception
7. qu'il avait laissées
8. Se concentra
9. assez de biberons pour deux jours
10. de biberons
11. Ne savait pas du tout comment faire
12. allait devoir en apprendre, des choses
13. sur la question

come into the house, or maybe someone he could drop the baby off with[1] in the morning.

God, the things that had to be worked out[2].

And a funeral. He hadn't even thought about a funeral.

He took the warmed bottle back upstairs, entered Matthew's room. He'd already pulled himself up, was standing at the railing[3]. Pretty soon he'd be walking.

"Hey, little man," he said. He lifted Matthew out of the crib, held him in one arm, and handed him the bottle with his other hand. The baby grabbed hold and shoved the rubber nipple[4] into his mouth.

"Yeah, you eat up," he said.

How did you explain to a baby that his mother wasn't coming home? What could you say?

"We're going to be okay," he said softly. "You and me are going to be okay."

Downstairs, the doorbell rang. Police, Gaynor thought. Maybe here to tell him they'd charged that insane woman[5]. Gaynor considered putting Matthew back in the crib, but didn't think he should leave the baby alone while he sucked on the bottle.

Gaynor carried Matthew downstairs and opened the front door. There was a man standing there, but Gaynor knew he wasn't from the police department.

"Bill, I'm so sorry," the man said. "My apologies for not getting here sooner. It's been quite the day[6]."

"Jack," Gaynor said.

"May I come in?"

"Yeah, sure, of course."

1. chez qui il pourrait déposer le bébé

2. qu'il fallait organiser

3. contre les barreaux

4. fourra la tétine

5. mis la folle en examen

6. une sacrée journée

Gaynor closed the door as Jack Sturgess came into the foyer.

"If you want a drink or something," Gaynor said, "you can go into the kitchen and help yourself[1], but I just … I can't go in there. I had to get this for Matthew, but …"

"It's okay," Sturgess said. "I just wanted to drop by[2] and see how you and the baby were."

"Matthew's … okay. I'm … I'm just trying to figure out[3] what I should be doing first. I don't know where to begin. I mean, the priority is Matthew. I've gotta look after him, and I don't know the first thing to do[4]. I've never made up the formula before. Rose did that, and Sarita. I've talked to the office, and I've been in touch with clients, and I had these people here—there're actually companies[5] that do nothing but clean up after … God, I don't know if I can hold it together[6]."

"You'll be okay. You will be. But you're right: The important thing is Matthew."

Gaynor looked misty-eyed[7] at the doctor. "You've always been there for us. Every step of the way[8]. Rose, she was so grateful for everything you did."

The doctor rested[9] a hand on the man's shoulder. "You all deserved happiness[10]. And I really thought you'd found it. You didn't deserve this."

"I thought, when I heard the doorbell, it'd be the police. Telling me they've charged that woman."

"Yes, well, that may very well happen," the doctor said.

"I guess it's been all over the news[11]."

"Pretty much[12]," Sturgess said.

"The detective, he called me a while ago. They know about her history. About trying to steal the baby from the hospital. They'll nail her[13] with this, I just know it."

1. te servir

2. passer

3. décider

4. n'y connais rien

5. il y a carrément des boîtes
6. vais tenir le coup

7. posa un regard embrumé
8. Constamment

9. posa
10. Vous méritiez d'être heureux

11. Je suppose que c'est dans tous les journaux
12. À peu près, oui
13. vont la coincer

"It may never get to that," Sturgess said.

"What are you talking about?"

"She's in the hospital. She tried to kill herself."

Gaynor's mouth dropped. "You're kidding."

The doctor shook his head. "But ... she wasn't successful."

Gaynor said. "That's, I mean, it's an awful thing to say, but it would almost be better if she'd succeeded."

"I don't know how to respond to that, Bill."

"I'm just thinking," Gaynor said slowly, "that if the woman had died, if there was never going to be a trial[1], maybe they wouldn't have to do any autopsy on Rose. They won't have to ... they won't have to do things to her, cut her open[2]. I can't bear the thought of it. And even if this Marla Pickens woman doesn't die, if she does go to trial, I mean, for Christ's sake, it's obvious what[3] happened to Rose. All you had to do was see her lying there to know. Why the hell do they have to cut her open when it's so fucking clear what happened?"

"Bill, I'm sorry, but they've probably already done that. It's standard procedure[4], even in deaths that are pretty straightforward[5]."

Matthew was pushing the bottle away. He'd had enough for now. Gaynor handed the bottle to Sturgess, placed the child on his shoulder, and lightly patted[6] his back. When Gaynor spoke, he whispered, as if the baby were somehow old enough[7] to understand what he might be saying.

"I'm worried about that," Gaynor said.

"About the autopsy?"

Gaynor nodded.

"About what it might show[8]," he said. "What else they might find."

---

1. procès

2. lui ouvrir le corps

3. il n'y a pas de doute sur ce qui

4. la procédure normale

5. semblent des cas très clairs

6. tapota

7. assez grand

8. pourrait révéler

The doctor studied him. "I think you're concerning yourself[1] needlessly[2] there."

"But if they figure out[3]—"

Sturgess held up a cautious hand. "Bill, I think I have an idea[4] what you're talking about, and you're taking several leaps here[5]. As you say, the cause of death in your wife's case is pretty obvious. It's unlikely anyone's going to be looking at anything beyond that. I can't think of any reason why they would."

"You think?" Gaynor asked, still patting Matthew's back.

"I do. You worry about your boy, and—"

"When will they release her[6]? I have to plan a funeral and—"

"Why don't I look into that[7]," Jack Sturgess said.

Matthew burped[8].

"Attaboy[9]," Sturgess said.

1. tu t'inquiètes
2. inutilement
3. comprennent
4. devine
5. t'emballes
6. me rendre le corps
7. Je pourrais me renseigner
8. fit un rot
9. Bravo

TWENTY-SIX

David

DURING dessert, the phone rang. Dad, Ethan, and I were sitting at the kitchen table, finishing up some chocolate ice cream, while Mom stood at the counter rinsing dinner plates. Dad and I had both told her to sit down, that she should stay off[1] her leg, but she wouldn't listen. When the phone rang she was standing right by it[2], and grabbed the receiver from its cradle[3].

I watched her face drain of color[4] while she listened to whoever was on the other end.

"Okay, Gill," she said. So now we knew who it was, and who it was likely about[5]. "Keep us posted[6]." Slowly she hung up the phone.

"What is it?" Dad asked.

Mom looked at Ethan, wondering, I guessed, whether to[7] discuss this in front of him. But the kid didn't miss much[8], and before we'd sat down to eat he'd asked what was going on with my cousin Marla, so I'd told him. I left out the graphic[9] details, including what I'd witnessed in the Gaynors' kitchen, but Ethan knew Marla was in big trouble, and that the police probably viewed her[10] as the

1. épargner

2. juste à côté

3. socle

4. devenir tout pâle

5. de qui il devait s'agir

6. Tiens-nous au courant

7. si elle pouvait

8. avait oublié d'être bête

9. les plus crus

10. la considérait

prime suspect in the death of the mother of the baby I'd found her with.

Although Ethan didn't say it, I think it may have put into perspective the trouble he was in with regard to[1] the pocket watch.

"It's okay," I said to Mom. "I've explained things to Ethan."

Mom took a breath[2] and said, "Marla's in the hospital."

"What's happened?" I asked.

"She ... Agnes and Gill had taken her back to their house. Marla couldn't go home. She was left alone in the kitchen for a second and ..."

"No," I said.

Mom nodded.

"What?" Ethan said. "What happened?"

I looked at him. "Marla tried to kill herself. Is that right, Mom? Is that what happened?"

She nodded again. "I have to get off my feet[3]." I shot up out[4] of my chair and pulled hers out[5] for her. Once she was settled in[6], I sat back down.

"How?" Ethan asked. "Like, with a knife? Did she stab herself? Did she turn on the oven and put her head into it? I saw that on TV once." He might as well have been asking how birds fly. Pure, simple curiosity.

"Jesus, Ethan," Dad said. "What a thing to ask." He looked at Mom and asked, "How *did* she do it?"

"Her wrist," Mom said wearily[7]. "She cut her wrist."

"That's where all the blood comes out," Ethan said, in case we didn't know.

"You know what?" I said to him. "Why don't you go do something?"

1. son pépin avec

2. prit une inspiration

3. reposer ma jambe
4. me levai d'un bond
5. tirai sa chaise
6. bien installée

7. d'un ton las

212

Ethan wiped his mouth[1] with a napkin[2] and dropped it on the table. "Okay." He knew this wasn't the time to push it[3].

Once he'd left the room, Mom asked, and not for the first time today, "What are we going to do?"

Dad said, "There's not really anything we can do. Makes you wonder[4], though, if she really did do it. I mean, why the hell else would she try to kill herself?"

"You," Mom said, looking at me. "You need to help her."

"What would you have me do[5], Mom?"

"Really? You have to ask that? What have you spent your career doing? Asking questions, finding things out. You can't do that for your cousin if you're not getting paid for it?"

"That's low[6]," I said.

"I don't care! Marla's family."

"You want me to go around asking questions? What if I find out something that proves she really did this? What then?"

Mom pondered that[7] for a second. "Then you'd find proof[8] that she had a good reason."

"Excuse me? For stabbing some woman to death?"

"I don't mean it like that. I mean that she wasn't in her right head[9]. That she wasn't responsible for what she did. If she did it, which I don't think she did. Marla's always been a good girl. Not quite like the rest of us[10], I know, but she's not a mean girl[11]. She'd never do anything like that. Not unless something had gone very wrong[12] in her head."

"Mom, honestly—"

"And besides, if it weren't for her[13], you wouldn't be sitting there right now."

I went silent.

1. s'essuya la bouche
2. serviette
3. le moment d'en rajouter
4. C'est à se demander
5. veux-tu que je fasse
6. mesquin
7. réfléchit
8. la preuve
9. dans son état normal
10. Pas tout à fait comme tout le monde
11. méchante
12. se soit vraiment détraqué
13. sans elle

1. Là, elle marque un point

2. radeau

3. d'environ 1,80 m sur 1,80 m

4. des bidons étanches

5. l'avaient amarré

6. à 30 m

7. rive

8. on s'en servait comme plongeoir

9. te jeter en piqué

10. sur le rebord

11. t'es claqué la caboche

12. se trempant les

13. en rêvant à toi

14. un vrai béguin pour toi

15. à pleins poumons

16. comme un boulet de canon

Dad said, "She's got you there[1]."

I looked at him. "What are you talking about?"

"I'm not the only one with a bad memory," Mom said. "You've forgotten what happened that summer at Agnes's cabin?"

Marla had alluded to something when we were in the car.

"Wait a sec," I said. "The raft[2]. This is about the raft." Back then, the Pickenses had built a wooden platform, about six by six[3], floated it on sealed oil drums[4], and anchored it[5] a hundred feet[6] from the shoreline[7]. We'd go out there and dive off it[8].

"We'd told you not to go out there alone," Mom said. "And especially we told you not to do flips off it[9]. We kept telling you one day you'd hit your head on the edge[10]."

"Which, one day, I did," I said, the incident now starting to come back to me.

"You knocked yourself out," Dad said. "You did a flip, whacked your noggin[11] on the edge of the raft, and went into the water unconscious."

"Marla saw me," I said.

"She was sitting on the dock, dangling her[12] feet in the water, mooning after you[13]—she had such a crush on you[14]," Mom said. "She saw you hit your head and go into the water facedown, and you didn't move a muscle. She went running up to the cabin, screaming at the top of her lungs[15] that something had happened. Agnes and I were sitting at the kitchen table playing cards. Agnes ran out of that cabin like she'd been shot out of a cannon[16]. Jumped in the boat and went out there and got you."

"I don't really remember it," I said. "I only remember being told about it, after."

"You lost about a day," Dad said. "Of memory. Agnes saved your life, but she'd never have had a chance if it wasn't for Marla."

"Think about that," Mom said. "And you've got nothing else to do. You might as well be doing[1] something useful." She put her hand to her mouth, then reached out and touched my cheek. "I'm sorry. That was an awful thing to say."

"And it's not exactly true, anyway," Dad said. "The boy got a job offer today."

Forty years old, and still "the boy." Still that boy who fell off that raft and nearly died.

"You did?" Mom said. "What is it?"

I shrugged. "I don't know. I have to think—"

"Randall Finley offered him a job as his right-hand man[2]," Dad said. "How about that?"

Mom looked nearly as horrified as when she'd taken the call from Marla's father. "Finley? That horse's ass[3]? He's offered David a job?"

"What's wrong with Finley?" Dad shot back. "He's a good man."

"What's he want David for?" she asked him.

"I'm right here[4]," I said.

"Gonna help him take another run at the mayor's seat," Dad said. "I bet, with David's help, he could do it, too."

Now she looked at me. "I forbid it[5]."

I sighed. "I haven't given him an answer yet."

"It pays a thousand dollars a week," Dad said.

"I wouldn't care if it paid a hundred thousand dollars a week," she said. I had to admit, for that kind of money[6], right now I'd have done PR[7] for the Taliban.

There was a knock[8] at the door. Mom started to push herself away from the table, but Dad was

1. Autant que tu fasses

2. bras droit

3. sale type

4. Je suis là, dites

5. te l'interdis

6. une telle somme

7. géré les relations publiques

8. On frappa

already on the move. Once he was out of the kitchen, Mom said, "You can't be serious."

"It'd help until something better comes along," I said. "I'm not a fan of the guy, but it's a paycheck[1]."

She put her hand on mine a second time and closed her eyes. "Do what you have to do. I haven't got the energy for this, not with everything else that's going on. But I want you to help Marla. Will you?"

"Yes," I said. "I don't know how. But … okay. I'll … I don't know … I'll ask around. Maybe find something that helps." I smiled sheepishly[2]. "I don't know how I could have forgotten about the raft."

"We nearly lost you," Mom said, and sniffed[3]. "I can still see little Marla, busting into the cabin, looking like she was almost in shock, saying, 'David! David! David's gone!' I'll never forget it." She caught a tear with her finger before it had a chance to run down[4] her cheek.

"Someone for you," Dad said, standing in the doorway, looking at me.

"Who?" I said.

"She didn't say. Just asked for you. I invited her in, but she said she'd wait outside." His eyebrows went up half an inch. "Nice looker[5]."

Mom brightened[6]. "Who is she, David?"

"I have no idea," I said, "but I'm not going to find out sitting here."

There was no one on the porch when I went out the front door. She was standing at the foot of the steps. I couldn't tell who it was right away[7], given[8] the dim[9] porch light, and the fact that she was looking out toward the street, arms crossed over her chest[10].

"Hello?"

---

1. salaire
2. d'un air contrit
3. renifla
4. couler sur
5. Belle nana
6. Le visage de Maman s'éclaira
7. du premier coup
8. à cause de
9. faible
10. les bras croisés sur la poitrine

She turned around. "Hey," Samantha Worthington said.

"Hi," I said. "You're unarmed[1]."

She dug into the front pocket of her jeans. When her hand came back out, it was wrapped around something[2]. I could guess what.

She came halfway up the steps, arm extended. "I believe this is yours. Or your kid's. I don't know. All I know is, it's not Carl's."

I opened my palm to allow her to set[3] the pocket watch on it. Our fingers brushed together[4] lightly. Samantha retreated, ran her fingers through her hair to get it out of her eyes, and said, "Sorry."

"It's okay."

"Not just about the watch."

"You mean the shotgun in my face."

"Yeah," Samantha said. "That." She forced a smile. "You get some fresh shorts[5]?"

"I did."

"I was doing laundry, grabbed Carl's jeans; they felt kind of[6] heavy. Found the watch in his pocket." She shook her head. "You'd figure, if he was going to lie to me, he'd do a better job of covering up after himself[7]."

"His future as a master criminal looks uncertain," I said.

She pointed toward the street, where a small Hyundai sedan sat[8]. "He's in the car. I brought him to apologize to your boy."

I opened the door a crack[9] and called in, "Ethan! Out front[10]!"

Almost instantly I heard stomping[11] on the stairs, and then he emerged. "Yeah?"

Samantha looked at her car and made a waving-in gesture. The door opened and a black-haired boy Ethan's age got out.

1. n'avez pas d'arme

2. tenait quelque chose

3. poser
4. se touchèrent

5. avez changé de short

6. il [le jean] m'a paru trop
7. il se planquerait un peu mieux que ça

8. stationnait

9. entrouvris
10. Viens voir dehors
11. un grand bruit de pas

My son looked at Carl, then at me. I put the watch in his hand and said, "You can give this to Poppa in a minute." He looked at it, stunned[1], like he'd won the lottery. "This is Carl's mom, Ms. Worthington."

"Hi," she said as Carl approached. Once her son was standing next to her, she said to him, "You know what to say."

"Sorry I took the watch," he said, looking more at the ground than at Ethan. "That wasn't right."

"Sorry I punched you and stuff[2]," Ethan said.

Carl shrugged. "Okay."

There was an uncomfortable three seconds of silence. Then Ethan asked, "Do you like trains?"

"What?"

"Do you like trains? My grandpa has some. In the basement. If you want to see them."

Carl, his face blank[3], looked at his mother. "Uh, yeah, I guess[4]," she said. The boy came up the stairs and disappeared into the house with Ethan.

"The Middle East[5] should be so easy," I said, coming down the steps.

"Carl's not a bad kid," Samantha said defensively. "He's just … like his father sometimes. I don't like it when he gets like that. He can be a bit of a bully[6]. But there's a good kid in there[7], I swear. Some days it's just a little harder to find."

"Sure," I said.

"And yet, he's kind of my rock[8], you know? He's there for me. We're there for each other. I guess that's why, when you said he had that watch, I just stood up for him[9]." She raised her hands a moment, a gesture of futility. "Now what do I do? I feel like an idiot standing here. The plan was, Carl says he's sorry and we go[10]. Now he's in there with your kid."

1. stupéfait

2. pour le coup de poing et tout

3. inexpressif
4. si tu veux

5. Moyen-Orient

6. brute
7. ça cache son côté gentil

8. en quelque sorte mon seul soutien

9. l'ai défendu

10. on repart

218

"You want a coffee or something?" I asked. "You're welcome to come in."

She looked at the house. "You got a nice place. Beats[1] the shithole[2] I'm living in."

1. Mieux que
2. trou à rats

"Your place isn't a shithole," I said. "And besides, this my parents' house."

"I thought, when Ethan said the trains were his grandfather's, that maybe they'd been handed down to him[3] or something."

3. il en avait peut-être hérité
4. circuit

"No. My dad built a small layout[4] in the basement for Ethan. At least, he says it was for Ethan."

"When I looked up an address for Harwood, this was the only one that came up. So, that's cool that you live with your folks[5]? You and your wife and Ethan?"

5. parents

"Just Ethan and me."

"Oh," she said. "Divorced?"

I shook my head. "My wife passed away[6] a few years ago."

6. est décédée

She nodded quickly. "Oh, sorry, didn't realize. So, well, whaddaya know[7]. We're both raising boys on our own."

7. çà par exemple

Did I want to know why she was a single parent[8]? The short answer was yes, I was curious. But did I think it was a good idea to ask? Maybe not. I was grateful she'd returned[9] the pocket watch, and it was nice of her to apologize for scaring the shit out of me[10]. Once Ethan finished showing Carl the trains, Samantha Worthington and her son could be on their way[11].

8. mère célibataire
9. rendu
10. de m'avoir fichu la trouille de ma vie
11. s'en aller

So all I said was "It can be a challenge[12]."

12. C'est pas facile tous les jours

"No shit[13]," she said. "Especially when your ex is in jail and his parents think they should have custody[14]."

13. Tu m'étonnes
14. la garde

Well, there it was. No need to ask. Although I now had even more questions. Before I could

1. qui me
trottaient

2. le jour de mon
embauche,

3. ça craint

4. inventé

5. bavasse

6. m'éviter la
honte

7. laverie
automatique

8. machines à
laver

9. prendre toutes
les espèces dans
la centrale de
paiement

10. distributeurs
de lessive

11. Vous rigolez

12. au garage

choose just one of the many bouncing around[1] in my head, she asked, "So what do you do?"

"The last fifteen years or so I've worked for newspapers," I said. "I'd worked at the *Standard*, then went to the Boston *Globe*, then came back here to work for the *Standard* again, and first day on the job[2] they closed the paper."

"Oh, man, that sucks[3]," she said. "I didn't know they'd shut down the *Standard*."

"It's been quite a few weeks now."

She shrugged. "I don't read the papers. Books, mostly. I've got enough shit going on in my own life, I don't need to read about everyone else's. I like escaping into a good story instead, where everything's made up[4]. It doesn't have to be happy. I don't mind bad things happening to good people, so long as they're not real. God, I'm blathering[5]. So that's why you're living with your parents? You're out of work?"

"We're moving out shortly," I said. "I just got something else."

Had I already made up my mind about Finley's offer, or did I reach a decision in that instant to deflect shame[6]?

"Oh, that's great," she said. "Congrats."

"Thanks," I said. "You?"

"Hmm?"

"What do you do?"

"I work in a Laundromat[7]," she said. "It's pretty exciting. Cleaning the washers[8], emptying out the coin holders[9], keeping the detergent dispensers[10] full."

"Sounds good," I said.

"Are you kidding me[11]? Every day I want to kill myself."

"Sorry. My sarcasm detector is in the shop[12]."

"Yeah, well, you should get it fixed[1]. Who the hell would want to work in a Laundromat? The only good thing is, I'm on my own; if things are slow I can read. And I can nip out[2] and do things if I have to, like pick up Carl at school." She rolled her eyes[3]. "And when the school calls in the middle of the day and says he's being suspended for fighting, I can go and get him."

Carl seemed too old to be chauffeured[4] to and from school. Samantha must have been reading my thoughts.

"If I don't watch him, they'll snatch him[5]."

"They?"

"Brandon's—that's my ex—parents, or maybe even friends of his, or theirs. They've got money—his parents, that is—and his friends, like Ed, that asshole[6], are just dumb enough[7] to think grabbing[8] Carl would be a smart thing to do[9]. My former in-laws[10] always hated me, and hate me even more now that I've moved away from Boston to Promise Falls. Once Bran got sentenced[11] for those holdups I was gone[12]."

"Holdups?"

"Bank robberies[13], actually[14]," she said offhandedly[15]. "Armed. He's not even up for parole[16] for ten years. And they think it's *my* fault. Like someone else stuffed all that money in the trunk[17] of his car."

This woman had problems like the *Standard* had typos[18].

"That's who you thought might have been at the door when I came knocking," I said.

"Yeah," Samantha said. "But I wouldn't have shot ya[19]."

"Why's that?"

"You got nice eyes[20]."

TWENTY-SEVEN

WALDEN Fisher was driving through downtown[1] Promise Falls shortly after nine[2], heading home, when he thought he saw Victor Rooney's aging, rusted van parked at the curb[3].

Not parked all that well[4], either. It was a parallel-parking spot[5] that Victor appeared to have gone into nose-first[6]. The van's back end was jutting out[7] a good three feet[8] into the path of traffic[9], about half a block past Knight's, one of Promise Falls' downtown bars.

Walden was betting that was where he'd find Victor, should he choose[10] to go looking for him. He took his foot off the gas pedal[11] of his Honda Odyssey and held a quick debate in his head about what to do.

He found a vacant[12] spot in the next block, pulled up[13] alongside the car ahead, and backed in[14], the way it was supposed to be done[15]. Walden got out and walked back almost two blocks to Knight's and went inside.

It could have been any neighborhood bar in America. Rock music coming out of the speakers, but not loud like a nightclub. Patrons[16] could still carry on a conversation without having to shout at the top of their lungs[17]. Low lighting from Tiffany lamps, a pool table[1] in the back[2], a few tables packed with[3] guys who'd just finished playing together on some team for some sport in some local community[4] center, a handful[5] of guys on stools[6] watching a baseball game on a flat-screen hanging on the wall above the bar.

At the far end, sitting alone, watching the game without really watching it, was Victor, his right hand wrapped around[7] a bottle of Old Milwaukee[8]. Here was the man who'd almost become Walden's son-in-law.

Walden hauled himself up[9] onto the stool next to him. "Hey, there, Victor."

The man looked at Walden, blinked[10] twice, focused[11]. "Jesus, Mr. Fisher, how are you?"

"I'm okay, good. Saw your van out there. Thought I'd pop in and[12] say hello."

"Funny seeing you," he said, raising his bottle to him. "Uh, would you like a beer?"

The bartender[13], a thin, elderly man who looked like a walking twig[14], had approached. Walden glanced at him and said, "Just a Coke."

The bartender nodded, retreated.

"You sure you don't want a beer?" Victor asked. Walden thought Victor sounded as though he'd had a few already, and judging by how he'd parked the van, probably a few before he'd arrived.

"I'm sure," Walden said. "What are you up[15] to these days?"

Victor shrugged. "A bit of this, a bit of that. Odd jobs[16]. Construction. I'm in kind of a lull[17] at the moment."

"I heard you and the fire department came to a parting of the ways[18]."

"Yeah, well, that really wasn't for me. It's a pretty macho environment, you know? I gave it

1. billard
2. à l'arrière
3. bourrées de
4. municipal
5. poignée
6. des tabourets
7. tenant
8. [marque de bière]
9. se hissa
10. cligna des yeux
11. fixa son regard
12. que je passerais
13. barman
14. brindille sur pattes
15. Qu'est-ce que tu deviens
16. Des petits boulots
17. période creuse
18. avez mis un terme à votre collaboration

1. ai tenté le
coup
2. cavalier

3. me démerde

4. à reprendre
mon jeu en main

5. drôle
d'expression
6. une espèce de
spectacle
7. le petit
William
8. théâtre
9. y font les
acteurs
10. qui n'en finit
pas

11. faire votre
boulot

12. est morte

13. pas vous
plaire

a shot[1], but I never felt comfortable there. Too gung ho[2] for my tastes."

"Sure."

"Fuck 'em, I say. I get by[3]. I do."

"If you ever need anything, you know you can give me a call."

"That's very kind of you, Mr. Fisher. It really is. But what I need, I don't think you or anyone else can provide."

"What would that be?"

"I need *someone* who can *help me* get my *act* together[4]," he said, setting the bottle down and miming something with his hands, as though he were assembling something. "You see, my *act* is in pieces. Isn't that a funny saying[5]? Get your *act* together? What's that supposed to mean? That we're all actors? That all of this is some performance[6]? What was it Billy[7] Shakespeare said? That all the world's a stage[8] and men and women merely players[9]. Something like that. I think what we're in is a tragedy without any kind of ending[10]. What do you think, Mr. Fisher?"

"I think you've had a lot to drink, Victor."

"You are correct," he said. "Don't think I'll be jogging tonight. I don't know how you do it."

"Do what?"

"Get up every day and go about your business[11]. How do you and Beth manage that?"

"Beth passed on[12]," Walden said. "Just a while ago."

"Oh, bloody fuck," Victor said, shaking his head, taking a drink. "I had no idea. I'm so sorry." Another head shake. "I almost—this is going to come out wrong[13], and I apologize in advance—but I almost kind of envy her. If I died, I could stop being so sad." He paused. "And angry."

"It's been three years," Walden said.

"Later this month," Victor said, nodding, indicating he was already well aware[1]. "Saturday of the Memorial Day weekend. Isn't that kind of ironic? We shall remember Olivia on Memorial Day. Oh, yes, we shall." He raised his beer in a toast. "To Olivia."

1. parfaitement conscient

"You should probably head home[2]," Walden said.

2. rentrer chez toi

"Like I said, I don't know how you manage. I mean, I was never actually married to her. She was the love of my life—God, what a cliché—but it's true, you know? But I only knew her a couple of years. But she was *your* daughter. That's got to be worse."

"You find ways to manage," Walden said.

"I don't even know if I'm still grieving[3], exactly," Victor said. "But it was like what that writer said in that book. It was a tipping point[4], what happened to Olivia. I went off the deep end[5] then, and I've been trying to climb back up[6] ever since, but once you're down there, all this other shit happens to you that keeps you there. Is this making any sense?"

3. en deuil

4. point de basculement

5. ai sombré

6. remonter à la surface

"Yeah."

"I mean, I've had plenty of time to get over[7] Olivia, right? Lots of time to move on[8]."

7. oublier

8. tourner la page

"You never get over it," Walden said.

"Yeah, I get that. But people have to find a way to move forward, right? I mean, fuck, look at all those people who were in concentration camps. What could be worse than what they went through? Yet they went on with their lives when they got freed and the war was over. I mean, sure, they probably never got over it, but they became

1. loucha vers

2. si je suis bien placé

3. aujourd'hui encore

4. n'y penseront même pas
5. Tout juste

6. beau-père génial

7. parcourut du regard
8. gorgée à

functioning members of society." He squinted at[1] Walden. "Would you call me functioning?"

"I don't know that I'm qualified[2] to judge that," Walden said.

"Well, let me answer it for you. I am not. But I'll tell you what I am, to this day[3]. I'm angry."

"Angry," Walden repeated.

"At myself. And all the others. What do you think they'll do on the third anniversary?"

"I bet they won't give it a thought[4]."

Victor pointed his index finger at Walden. "Right you are[5], Mr. Fisher."

"Walden. You know you can call me Walden." He paused. "What do you mean, angry at yourself?"

Victor looked away. "I was late."

Walden nodded. "I know."

"I was late meeting her. If I'd been on time, none—"

Walden rested a hand on the young man's shoulder. "Don't torture yourself."

The younger man looked at him, smiled. "I think you'd have been a damn fine father-in-law[6]."

Walden was less certain Victor would have been the best son-in-law in the world, but it did not stop him from saying, "And I'd have been proud to be your father-in-law."

The bartender set a Coke on the counter but Walden didn't touch it.

Victor surveyed[7] the room. "You think it was any of them?" he asked, taking another pull off[8] the bottle.

"Any of them what?"

"You think it could have been any of these guys sitting right here? Who did it?"

"I don't know."

"Every time I walk around this town, I look at everybody and wonder, Was it you? Or you?" He finished off the bottle. "These are our neighbors. I was born in this town, grew up with these people. For all I know[1] I'm living next door to a maniac[2]. Maybe hanging out in a bar with one[3]."

Victor raised the bottle, then rammed it straight down[4] onto the bar, shattering it[5], leaving him with nothing in his hand but the neck and shoulder[6].

"Hey!" the bartender said.

But other than that, the place went silent. All the patrons stopped their conversations in midsentence and turned to look down toward the end of the bar, where Victor had come off his stool and was standing, staring at all of them.

"Was it any of you?" he asked, his voice barely above a whisper[7].

"Vick," Walden said quietly. "Stop."

"You need to take your son home," the bartender told Walden.

"He's not—" Walden started to say, then decided not to bother.

"Was it?" Victor Rooney asked again, moving closer to a table where five men were sharing a pitcher. "Was it any of you assholes?"

One of the men, broad of chest and more than six feet tall, kicked his chair back[8] and stood up. "Think maybe you've had enough[9], pal," he said.

Walden tried to take Victor by the arm, but the younger man shook him off.

"Oh, I've had enough[10], that's for sure," Victor said. "I've had enough of the whole lot of you."

Another man stood. Then a third.

"Come on," Walden said, getting a firmer grip on the man's arm. "I'm taking you home."

1. Si ça se trouve,

2. fou

3. que je bois un verre dans un bar avec l'un d'eux

4. l'abattit brutalement

5. l'explosa

6. goulot

7. à peine plus haut qu'un murmure

8. repoussa sa chaise du pied

9. tu as ton compte

10. j'en ai ma dose

This time Victor didn't shake him off. He allowed Walden to lead him toward the door, but not before whirling around[1] for one last shot[2].

"Assholes!" he said. "Every last one of you!"

Walden got him through the door and pushed him out onto the sidewalk.

"You pull a stunt like that again[3]," Walden said, "and you're going to end up in the hospital. Or worse."

Victor was fumbling in his pocket for his keys[4]. Once he had them out, Walden grabbed them.

"Hey."

"I'll drive you home," Walden said. "You can come back for your van tomorrow."

"What if I don't remember where it is?"

"I'll remember."

"I guess."

"And then I think we need to talk," Walden said. "About getting your life back on track[5]."

"I'm going to leave this town," Victor said. "I'm going to get the hell out of here[6]."

"When? Do you have something lined up[7]? A job?"

"I just want out[8]. Everywhere I look, I'm reminded of Olivia."

"How soon are you leaving?" Walden asked, unable to hide the concern[9] in his voice.

"Not sure. Still got a few things to do here; then I'm gone. End of the month, I'd say."

"Hang in[10], at least till then," Walden said. "Maybe something will still work out for you here. I could ask around[11]."

Victor smiled. "Don't waste your time on me."

1. se retourner
2. flèche
3. refais ce genre de numéro
4. chercha fébrilement ses clés dans sa poche
5. te remettre sur les rails
6. me tailler
7. de prévu
8. me casser
9. inquiétude
10. Attends
11. demander autour de moi

TWENTY-EIGHT

BARRY Duckworth had learned less from his search[1] of Sarita Gomez's room than he'd hoped.

The detective already knew the Gaynors' nanny had no phone of her own[2]. But she didn't have a computer, either. At least not one that she'd left behind in the apartment. So there were no e-mails to check, no bookmarked[3] Facebook page. No electric bill[4]. No monthly Visa statement[5]. No invoice[6] from a visit to the dentist. Nor were there any personal letters, or even an address book[7]. Sarita either packed up everything in a hurry, or she led a very simple, off-the-grid[8] kind of existence. No digital trail[9] here.

No bloodstained[10] uniform, either.

Duckworth had asked the nanny's landlord[11], she of the amazing banana bread[12], whether she might have any pictures of Sarita. "On your phone, anything like that?"

No such luck[13]. Duckworth didn't even know what this woman he was searching for looked like.

He was driving back to the station[14] when he realized there was something big[15] he had allowed to slip through the cracks[16].

The Thackeray College predator.

1. fouille

2. à elle

3. ajoutée aux favoris

4. facture

5. relevé de carte

6. facture

7. carnet d'adresses

8. clandestine

9. trace numérique

10. taché de sang

11. propriétaire

12. la reine du cake à la banane

13. Mais non

14. commissariat

15. important

16. qui lui était complètement sorti de la tête

The Gaynor murder had so completely taken over his day that he'd neglected to do anything following his chat[1] with the college's head[2] of security. Clive Duncomb. "Asshole," Duckworth said to himself behind the wheel[3] of his unmarked car. Duckworth had left his business card with Duncomb and told him to e-mail him the names of the three women who'd been attacked. They needed to be interviewed by the Promise Falls police. But the day had gone by[4] and no names, no e-mail at all from Duncomb. Duckworth could just guess what the ex-Boston cop thought of the local police. That they were a bunch of know-nothing rubes[5].

"Asshole," he said again.

Duckworth called the station and asked to be put through to[6] Chief Rhonda Finderman.

"Hey," Finderman said, answering right away. "I was just about to check in with you[7]."

Finderman wanted to know what progress was being made in[8] the Gaynor case, and apologized for not knowing much about it. "I'm on this national association of police chiefs that meets all the time, the mayor's committee on attracting jobs, plus this task force[9] with the state police about co-ordinating data[10]. I'm up to my ass in administrative shit[11]. So, Rosemary Gaynor. Someone killed her and kidnapped her baby?"

Quickly Duckworth brought her up-to-date[12]. Then he told her about how Clive Duncomb, Thackeray's head of security, didn't think he needed to bother letting the Promise Falls police know they might be dealing with a possible rapist[13] on campus.

"That horse's ass," Finderman said. "I've had the pleasure[14]. We had lunch one time; he said he

1. petite conversation
2. chef
3. au volant
4. était passée
5. bande de bouseux bons à rien
6. qu'on lui passe
7. vous appeler
8. comment on avançait sur
9. groupe de travail
10. les données
11. dans les paperasses jusqu'au cou
12. la mit au courant
13. violeur éventuel
14. l'honneur et l'avantage de le croiser

really liked my hair. Take a guess how that went over[1]."

"You know anything about him? Beyond[2] his being a horse's ass, I mean?"

Rhonda Finderman paused. "What I hear is he worked vice[3] in Boston. And that he left. And brought along his new wife, who may have been someone he met in the course of his duties[4], if you get my drift[5]."

"The thing is, I've got my hands full[6], but we need someone out there[7], taking statements from the students[8] who've been attacked, that whole drill[9]. We need to find this guy before he ups his game[10]."

"I'm down[11] two detectives," she said. "I'm going to have to move someone up[12], temporarily at least."

"Okay."

"You know Officer[13] Carlson? Angus Carlson?"

Duckworth paused. "I do."

"Try not to gush[14]."

"It's your call[15], Chief."

"We were all young once, Barry. You telling me you weren't a know-it-all when you started?"

"No comment."

She laughed. "He's not that bad. He presents this front of being a[16] wiseass[17], but I think there's more to him than that[18]. We got him about four years ago, from Ohio."

"It's your call."

"I'll have him call you[19]; you can bring him up to speed."

"Fine." There was still something else on Duckworth's mind. "One other thing. I ran into Randy this morning."

"Finley?"

1. Devinez comment je l'ai pris

2. À part

3. qu'il était dans la police criminelle

4. dans le cadre du travail

5. si vous voyez ce que je veux dire

6. j'ai pas le temps

7. sur place

8. les dépositions des étudiantes

9. et tout le tintouin

10. ne passe à la vitesse supérieure

11. Il me manque

12. faire monter quelqu'un en grade

13. l'agent

14. Cachez votre joie

15. à vous de voir

16. se donne des airs de

17. gros malin

18. il vaut mieux que ça

19. lui dire de vous appeler

"Yeah."

"Jesus, him and Duncomb in one day. It's like an asshole convention[1]."

1. Ça fait un certain nombre de cons au mètre carré

"He called me directly after finding all these squirrels someone had strung up on a fence near the college. He said he's running for mayor[2] again, and he was looking for me to be a department snitch[3], maybe give him something to run on. I'm probably not the only one he's asking."

2. candidat pour la mairie

3. mouchard de service

"He's looking for something on me[4]?"

4. contre moi

"He's looking for anything he can get on anybody. I think you'd be near the top of the list. So would Amanda Croydon."

"The mayor's squeaky-clean[5]," the chief said.

5. irréprochable

"Finley could find a way to make that negative."

"He's a weaselly[6] son of a bitch," the chief said. There was a long pause.

6. sournois

"You there?" he asked.

"Yeah," Rhonda said. "I'm just thinking about how he might go after me[7]." Another pause. "I think I run a clean department. Maybe he'll go after something I did before this job."

7. me coincer

She'd come up through the ranks[8], becoming chief nearly three years ago after several years working as a detective, often alongside Duckworth.

8. monté les échelons

"You did good work," he said. "I wouldn't want it getting back to you[9] that an approach like that had been made, and that I hadn't told you."

9. qu'il revienne à vos oreilles

"Appreciate it, Barry."

Three seconds after he'd ended the call, another one came in.

"Duckworth."

"Hey, it's Wanda." Wanda Therrieult. The medical examiner who would have conducted[10] the autopsy on Rosemary Gaynor.

10. avait dû mener

"Yeah, hey," Duckworth said.

"Where are you?" He told her. "Swing by[1]."

He said he could be there in five minutes.

It was a cold, sterile room, but that was the way it was supposed to be.

The body was laid out on an aluminum table, draped in a light green sheet that matched the walls[2]. Bright fluorescent lights shone down from the ceiling.

Wanda Therrieult, fiftyish[3], short, and round[4], was sitting at a desk in the corner of the room, tapping away at a keyboard[5] and drinking from a Big Hug Mug when Duckworth entered the room.

"You want a coffee or anything?" she asked when she saw him, taking off a pair of reading glasses. "I got one of these single-cup things[6] where you can pick what flavor you want[7]."

She got up and showed him the machine, and a rack[8] filled with various kinds of coffee that came in tiny[9] containers the size of restaurant creamers[10].

"Yeah, sure," he said, examining the labels. "What the hell is Volluto? Or Arpeggio? What's that supposed to be? What do you have that's closest to[11] what I get at Dunkin'?"

"You're hopeless[12]," she said. "I'll just pick you one."

She chose a capsule, put it into the machine, set a mug in place, and hit a button. "Now it'll work its magic."

"You should think about getting a doughnut[13] machine, too. Why hasn't Williams-Sonoma come up with one of those[14]? A gadget you put on your countertop[15] where you touch a button and out pops a fresh chocolate glazed."

1. Passe me voir

2. de la même couleur que les murs

3. la cinquantaine

4. rondouillette

5. tapant joyeusement sur son clavier

6. machines à expresso

7. on peut choisir le parfum qu'on veut

8. compartiment

9. mini

10. dosettes de crème

11. qui se rapproche le plus de

12. un cas désespéré

13. à beignets

14. inventé un truc comme ça

15. plan de cuisine

1. la plus naze

Wanda studied him. "I was about to say that's the dumbest[1] idea I've ever heard, but then thought, I would buy one of those."

"It's twenty years today," he said.

"What's twenty years?"

2. à partir d'aujourd'hui

"I've been with the department two whole decades as of today[2]."

3. Arrête

"Get out[3]."

"Would I lie?"

"So, what, you joined when you were ten?"

4. se fout de ma gueule

"I'm a trained investigator, Wanda. I can tell when someone is bullshitting me[4]."

She smiled. "Congrats. Was there a thing? A little ceremony?"

He shook his head. "No. You're the only one I've told. I didn't even mention it to Maureen. It's no big deal."

"You're one of the good ones, Barry." The machine beeped. She handed him his coffee, raised

5. trinquèrent

her own, and they clinked mugs[5]. "To twenty years of catching bad guys."

"To catching bad guys."

"And you've got a pretty bad one out there now," she said, tipping her head in the direction of the body.

"Show me."

Wanda set her mug down, went over to the examining table, and pulled back the sheet, but only as far as the top of the dead woman's breasts.

"I wanted to show you something first," she

6. marques

said, pointing to Rosemary Gaynor's neck. "You

7. hématome

see these impressions[6] here? This bruising[7]?"

8. regarda de près

Duckworth took a close look[8]. "Thumbprint[9]

9. Une empreinte du pouce

there, on this side of the neck, and four fingers over on this side. He grabbed her around the throat."

"With his left hand," she said. "If she had been grabbed by the front, the thumbprint would be a little more to the front of her neck, not so far down the side."

"So he throttled her[1] from behind. You suggesting he's left-handed[2]?"

"Just the opposite."

Wanda pulled the sheet back further, exposing the woman to her knees. The body had been washed clean of blood, making the gash across her abdomen graphically clear[3]. It ran roughly from hip bone to hip bone[4], dipping[5] slightly en route.

"Our boy put the knife in and basically sliced his way across, going from her left to right side. The cut runs at a fairly consistent depth[6] all the way, about three inches[7]. Now, you'd figure[8], if someone was being attacked that way, they'd try to pull back[9], or fall, something, but that's not the case here." She turned and faced him and held out her arms[10], as though inviting him to dance. "May I?"

She came around behind him. "This won't be quite right because you're taller than I am, and I figure[11] the killer was a good four or five inches taller[12] than the victim in this case, but this will give you the right idea."

Wanda pressed herself up against his backside[13], then, with her left hand, reached over[14] his left shoulder and grabbed his neck, pressing her thumb onto the left side, her fingers digging into the right.

"Once he was holding her tight up[15] against himself," she said, "he reached around[16] like this ..."

And she brought her right arm around his right side, reaching as far as she could, and made the motion of driving a knife[17] into the left side of his abdomen, then moved her arm across to his right.

---

1. l'a étranglée

2. gaucher

3. ce qui rendait encore plus nette l'entaille qui lui traversait l'abdomen

4. allait d'une hanche à l'autre

5. s'affaissant

6. sur une profondeur assez régulière

7. 7,6 cm

8. Bon, on se dit que

9. se dégager

10. lui tendit les bras

11. d'après moi,

12. faisait bien une dizaine de centimètres de plus

13. fesses

14. tendit sa main gauche vers

15. bien serrée

16. a passé le bras par-devant,

17. fit mine de lui enfoncer un couteau

1. a scié en travers

2. Compris

3. de perdre la tête

4. d'un ton neutre

5. vraie ordure

6. blessure

"The knife was in, and while he held her firmly, he just sawed right across[1]."

"Got it[2]," he said.

"I'm gonna let you go now before I lose control[3]," Wanda said flatly[4]. She went around the examination table, across from Duckworth.

"Jesus," he said.

"Yeah. This guy's a nasty piece of work[5]."

Duckworth couldn't take his eyes off the wound[6]. "You know what it looks like?" he said.

Wanda nodded. "Yeah."

"A smile. It looks like a smile."

TWENTY-NINE

David

ETHAN had already returned[1] the watch to his grandfather, even before he and Carl had disappeared into the basement to see the trains. Once Samantha Worthington and her son had left, I went back into the house and found Dad in the kitchen holding the item[2] that had once[3] belonged to his own father.

He looked at me and said, "I'm confused[4]. Was that woman Sam?"

"Yeah," I said.

"Son of a bitch[5]," he said. "Best-looking Sam I ever saw."

I went up to my room, closed the door, and took out my cell phone. I called up[6] Randall Finley's number in my list of "recents," and dialed[7].

"Yeah?" he said.

"I'll do it," I said.

"Good to hear," Finley said.

"But I can't get to it just yet. I've got a family matter to deal with[8]."

"Well, deal with it as fast as you can," Finley said. "We got lots to do."

1. rendu

2. objet
3. autrefois
4. perdu

5. Ben merde

6. recherchai
7. lançai l'appel

8. à régler

237

"And there's something I want to make clear."

"Go right ahead, David."

"I won't do dirty[1]. I won't do underhanded[2]. I see you pulling stunts like you got in trouble for[3] seven years ago, I'm out. That clear?"

"Crystal[4]," Randall Finley said. "I wouldn't have it any other way[5]."

"I'll be in touch tomorrow," I said, and ended the call.

Now it was time to go to the hospital.

Mom and Dad made noises about coming[6] with me, but I suggested it would be better if I went on my own to talk to Marla.

I found her on the third floor of Promise Falls General. I checked in at the nurses' station[7] to confirm which room she was in.

"Who are you?" a nurse asked, almost accusingly.

"I'm her cousin," I said. "I'm Agnes Pickens's nephew."

"Oh," she said, her tone changing instantly. Being a relative of[8] the hospital administrator had bought me some instant respectability. "Ms. Pickens and her husband were just here. I think they've gone to the cafeteria for coffee. If you'd like to wait—"

"No, that's okay, I can head straight down[9]. It's three-oh-nine[10], right?"

"Yes, but—"

I gave her a friendly wave as I continued on down the hallway. I entered Marla's room—a private one, no surprise there—tentatively[11], in case she might be sleeping. I peered[12] around the corner, and there she was, eyes shut, wrist bandaged, the bed propped up[13] at a forty-five-degree angle.

---

1. d'affaires louches
2. de sournoiseries
3. faire le genre de trucs qui vous ont fait plonger
4. Comme de l'eau de roche
5. C'est bien ainsi que je l'entends
6. parlèrent de venir
7. passai par le bureau des infirmières
8. Ma parenté avec
9. y aller directement
10. [la chambre] 309
11. d'un pas hésitant
12. glissai un œil
13. rehaussé

I bumped[1] a chair, which set off[2] the smallest squeak[3], but it was enough to make Marla open her eyes. She looked at me blankly[4] for a second, so I said, "Hi, it's David," remembering her problem with faces, even those you'd figure[5] she would know best.

"Hey," she said groggily.

I came up alongside the bed and took hold of her hand, the one not connected to the bandaged wrist.

"I heard," I said.

"I guess I kind of lost it[6] for a second," she said, glancing at the bandages. "Mom wants them to keep me overnight." She rolled her eyes. "I'm worried they're going to move me to the psych ward[7]. I do *not* need to go to the psych ward."

"Well, what you did, it's got everyone worried."

"I'm fine. Really." She looked at me. "The policeman was very mean to[8] me."

"What policeman?"

"The one asking all the questions. Duck something."

"Duckworth."

"He made a big deal out of what I do. Like just because I make up reviews I'd lie about what's going on with that woman who died."

"He has to ask tough[9] questions," I said. "It's his job."

"Mom says she's going to try and get him fired[10]."

"I'm sure she'd like to," I said, giving her hand a little squeeze. "My mom gave me a little history lesson today."

"About what?"

"About when I hit my head on the raft. How if it hadn't been for you[11], I'd have been a goner[12]."

1. me cognai dans
2. laissa échapper
3. un très léger couinement
4. l'air absent
5. dont on aurait pensé
6. J'ai craqué
7. service psy
8. méchant avec
9. rudes
10. le faire virer
11. si tu n'avais pas été là
12. y serais passé

The corners of her mouth went up a fraction of an inch. "No problem."

"I want to help, Marla. You're in a jam[1]. The baby thing, your having Matthew—"

"I told you, someone came to the door and—"

"I know. What I was going to say was, Matthew being with you, it doesn't look good in connection with what happened to Mrs. Gaynor. You get[2] that, right?"

She nodded.

"So I'm going to start asking around. Find out how Matthew could have ended up with you. Find your angel."

She smiled. "You believe me."

What I had come to believe was that Marla believed it. "Yes," I said. "I want you to answer a few questions so I can get started. You up to that[3]?"

A weary nod[4].

"I know your face blindness makes it hard to describe people, but the woman who came to the door with Matthew, is there anything you can tell me about her? Hair color?"

"Uh, black?" she said, as if she was asking me.

"I wasn't there," I said. "But you think it was black?"

She nodded. Rosemary Gaynor had black hair, but if it had been her at the door it would have meant she'd handed off her own baby to Marla. That didn't make a lot of sense[5].

And plenty of women had black hair.

"I know the smaller details are tough, but how about skin color? Black, white?"

"Kind of … in between[6]."

"Okay. Anything else? Eye color?"

She shook her head.

"Moles[7] or scars[8], anything like that?"

1. dans le pétrin

2. comprends

3. t'en sens capable
4. hochement de tête las

5. n'était pas très logique

6. Disons… entre les deux

7. Des grains de beauté

8. des cicatrices

240

Another shake.

"How about her voice? What did she say to you and what was her voice like?"

"It was pretty[1]. She said, 'I want you to look after this little man. His name is Matthew. I know you'll do a good job.' That was about all. Her voice was kind of singsong[2]? You know what I mean?"

"I think so," I said.

"And she left me the stroller. She said she was sorry she didn't have anything else for me. And then she was gone."

"Did she leave in a car?"

Marla concentrated. "Yeah, there was a car." She sighed[3]. "I'm even worse with those than faces. It was black, I think."

"A pickup truck? An SUV[4]? A van? A convertible[5]?"

She bit her lip. "Well, it wasn't a convertible. A van, maybe. But I wasn't paying much attention because I had Matthew to look after."

"Didn't you think it was kind of strange? Someone just doing that[6]?"

"Sure," she said, looking at me like I was an idiot. "But it was such a wonderful thing, I didn't want to question it. I thought, Maybe this is how the universe is supposed to unfold[7]. I lose a child, but then I'm given one to make up for that[8]."

I thought there was more—or less—to this[9] than the universe trying to make things right[10].

Knowing a reasonable explanation was unlikely to come from Marla, I tried to figure it out[11] myself. If what Marla believed was really what happened, how did one make sense of it[12]?

For someone to be able to take Matthew's baby, Rosemary Gaynor must have already been dead. Otherwise she would have tried to stop it from happening.

1. jolie
2. chantante
3. soupira
4. 4×4
5. décapotable
6. Que quelqu'un fasse ça
7. fonctionne
8. compenser
9. qu'il devait y avoir une explication plus compliquée, ou plus simple
10. arranger les choses
11. l'imaginer
12. l'interpréter

So someone kills Matthew's mother. And there's this baby in the house.

The killer doesn't harm Matthew. Whatever has motivated him—or her—to murder the woman, it's not enough to do in[1] the baby, too.

The killer could have just left[2]. The baby would have been found eventually[3].

But no. The killer—or someone—wants to leave the baby with someone.

Why Marla?

Of all the people in Promise Falls the baby could have been left with, it's Marla. Who lives clear across town[4]. And who has a history[5]—albeit a short one[6]—of trying to steal a baby out of a hospital.

Oh, shit.

It was perfect.

"David?" Marla asked. "Hello?"

"What?"

"You looked all spaced-out there[7] for a second." She smiled. "You look like I feel[8]. Like I'm in dreamland or something. They've got me on something[9]. I kind of go in and out[10]. Last time I felt like this was when I was at the cabin."

"I was just thinking," I said. "That's all."

I asked her a bunch of other things. About this student named Derek she'd told me about earlier in the day who'd gotten her pregnant, and where I might be able to find him. I tried asking again whether there was any chance she might have a connection[11] to the Gaynors. I'd brought along one of my reporter's notebooks[12] and was scribbling down[13] everything Marla said in case something that didn't seem important now would turn out to be later[14].

---

1. ne le pousse pas à tuer
2. partir tout simplement
3. au bout d'un moment
4. à l'autre bout de la ville
5. des antécédents
6. assez maigres, d'accord
7. complètement à l'ouest
8. as l'air de ce que je ressens
9. m'ont fait prendre un truc
10. suis un peu entre deux eaux
11. le moindre lien
12. carnets
13. notais
14. se révèlerait l'être

But the entire time, I was thinking about something else.

About how, if I—let's say—had wanted to kill Rosemary Gaynor, and wanted to pin the crime on[1] someone else, who better than some crazy woman who'd tried to kidnap a baby months earlier? What better way to frame her[2] than to leave the dead woman's baby with her?

Maybe even leave a little blood on the door.

Was that a reach[3]? Was that totally ridiculous?

To pull off something like that[4], someone would have to know what Marla had done. And her escapade had been pretty well hushed up[5] by my aunt. There'd been nothing in the news, no charges laid[6].

For someone to put Rosemary Gaynor's death on[7] Marla, that person would have to be connected somehow[8] to both Marla and the Gaynors. Otherwise there'd be no way that person would know how to exploit Marla's history.

But who—

"Excuse me, who are you?"

I turned and saw a man standing in the hospital room doorway. He was wearing a proper suit[9], was about six feet tall[10], and looked like he thought he owned the place[11].

"I'm David Harwood," I said. "I'm Marla's cousin. And you … ?"

"I'm Marla's doctor," he said. "Dr. Sturgess. I don't believe we've ever met, David."

1. mettre le crime sur le dos de
2. la piéger

3. tiré par les cheveux
4. inventer un truc pareil
5. étouffée
6. aucune plainte déposée

7. sur le dos de
8. d'une façon ou d'une autre

9. beau costume
10. faisait dans les 1,80 m
11. semblait se prendre pour le maître des lieux

THIRTY

"I'VE got a good feeling," Clive Duncomb said. "This is the night we're going to catch this son of a bitch."

The entire Thackeray College security team was crowded[1] into Duncomb's office, including Joyce Pilgrim, the lone female member[2]. Thirty-two[3], five-five[4], one hundred and thirty-nine pounds[5], short brown hair. At Duncomb's request, she had not shown up[6] tonight in anything resembling a security uniform. She was in jeans, a pullover sweater[7], and a light jacket.

Duncomb wasn't happy, but didn't say anything. When he had first suggested to Joyce that she act as a decoy[8], in a bid[9] to draw out the man who'd been attacking young women on campus, he'd wanted her to wear high heels, fishnets[10], and a skintight[11] top. Joyce had pointed out[12] that this sicko[13] was attacking students, not hookers[14], and if she was going to be wandering[15] the campus as bait[16], she wasn't going to be spending her time fending off requests for blow jobs[17]. She suspected Duncomb just wanted to see how she'd look in an outfit like that[18], the pig.

Maybe *he* was the predator, she thought.

Okay, she knew that wasn't true. The description provided by the three women who'd been attacked so far didn't match[1] Duncomb. Not as tall as the security chief. Slighter of build[2]. They knew they were looking for a young man, although they didn't have much of a[3] description. In each attack, he'd been wearing a numbered[4] sports sweater with a hood[5].

When she took a job at the college as a security guard, she couldn't have anticipated that she'd be doing something like this. What Duncomb expected of her sounded more like police work. Which was exciting and distressing[6] at the same time. She liked doing something more important, more challenging[7] than wandering around making sure lecture room[8] doors were locked.

But still, she knew she wasn't adequately trained[9] for this. She had raised the point[10], and not for the first time, at the beginning of this meeting.

"God, you sound like that hick[11] Promise Falls cop," Duncomb said.

"What cop?" Joyce asked.

"He was here this morning, throwing his weight around[12], suggesting we didn't know how to look after our own affairs. I spent eighteen years with the Boston PD[13]. I think I know a thing or two more[14] than some local hot shot[15] who spends most of his time investigating the murders of forest creatures."

"Huh?" Joyce said.

"Never mind. We've got this[16]. And besides, you've got more backup[17] than anyone could ever hope for. You got me, the boys here"—and he pointed to the three other men in the room, not one of them over the age of twenty-five, and all grinning like village idiots—"and most important,

1. ne correspondait pas à
2. Moins costaud
3. n'en avaient pas vraiment la
4. numéroté
5. capuche
6. perturbant
7. stimulant
8. des amphis
9. suffisamment formée
10. émis l'objection
11. on croirait entendre ce plouc de
12. à faire l'important
13. dans la police de Boston
14. m'y connais un peu plus
15. le caïd du coin
16. On gère
17. soutiens

you've got protection in your purse[1], and I'm not talking condoms[2]."

The other three laughed.

Duncomb was speaking, of course, of the hand-gun[3] he had provided Joyce. Not only had he given her a weapon[4], but instruction in its use[5]. Almost three minutes' worth[6].

"And we'll be in constant communication," Duncomb reminded her.

Joyce's cell phone would be on[7] the whole time[8], and tucked[9] into her jacket. She had a Bluetooth earpiece[10] that was hidden by her hair, not that anyone was likely to notice it late at night anyway. She could talk to Duncomb anytime she wanted.

"Okay," she said hesitantly. She hadn't even told her husband, Malcolm, what her security duties had entailed[11] of late[12]. He would have freaked out[13]. But he was between jobs[14], and they needed her income[15]. So she'd kept him in the dark[16].

Joyce hoped Duncomb's instinct was on the money[17]. That they'd get this guy tonight and she could return to checking locked doors and sending drunk kids back to their dorms[18].

"Now," Duncomb said, "Michael, Allan, and Phil here, and me, are all going to be walking the grounds[19], no more than a minute away. Anything fishy[20] happens, you just say the word[21] and we come running. Okay?"

"Yeah," she said.

"Let's roll[22]," the security chief said, Joyce thinking, The guy believes he's in a TV show[23] or something.

Just because it was dark didn't mean the campus had gone to sleep. Far from it. Students were heading to and from evening lectures[24]. Music spilled out[1] of the residences. Two young men were playing Frisbee in the dark.

Very few women were walking alone. Thackeray's president had put out[2] a carefully worded advisory[3] that it made sense[4] for female students to walk in groups after dark. In pairs[5], at least. In an earlier statement he'd suggested women find male students they trusted to escort them from one part of the school to another, but that triggered a social media shitstorm[6] within the college. Many young women were outraged[7] at being told to find a man to protect them. Twitter hashtags like #needaman[8] and #walkmehomeprez[9] and #dontneedadick[10] began to spread. Joyce thought, political correctness aside[11], it made a hell of a lot of sense[12], but she figured students were always just waiting for something to get angry about, and the president had played right into their hands[13].

Duncomb thought the walk between the athletic center and the library was a good location[14]. It was nearly a quarter of a mile[15] long, with a wooded area[16] along one side and, for about half the stretch[17], a road on the other. Even better, it was not as well lit[18] as it could be, which made it a prime spot[19] if you were a would-be rapist[20]. One of the three women who'd reported being grabbed said she'd been attacked along here.

Duncomb wanted Michael and Phil to walk back and forth[21] between the two buildings, one going one way, one the other. He ordered Allan to wander[22] the wooded area. And Duncomb would be in a car parked alongside the path, where he had a reasonably good view of everything. Plus, he'd be on the phone at all times with Joyce.

Once everyone was in position, Joyce entered the athletic center. The plan was that she would

1. s'échappait

2. publié

3. notice formulée avec soin

4. était raisonnable

5. Par deux

6. avait fait un foin du diable sur les réseaux sociaux

7. offusquées

8. #besoin-dunmec

9. #ramène-moichezmoi-president

10. #pasbesoin-dequeue

11. mis à part

12. était une super bonne idée

13. leur avait tendu la perche

14. emplacement

15. 400 m

16. zone boisée

17. la moitié du chemin

18. éclairé

19. endroit idéal

20. violeur en puissance

21. fassent les cent pas

22. parcourir

stay there about five minutes, then come out and start walking in the direction of the library.

"Okay," she said, standing in the center's foyer. "I'm coming out." She had a long-strapped[1] purse slung over her shoulder, one hand planted inside it, resting on the gun.

"Got it," Duncomb said. From his car he saw Joyce come out the front doors and head[2] west, or left, toward the library a quarter of a mile away. "I see ya. You're looking good. You know, you could easily pass for nineteen or twenty. You know that?"

"So you've said[3]," Joyce whispered, her head down, not wanting it to be obvious[4] that she was talking to anyone. An attacker might be deterred[5] if he thought Joyce was already on the phone with a person who could send help.

"I'm just saying, you keep in shape[6]. I bet your husband appreciates it."

She'd thought about going to the college's human relations department and filing a complaint about Duncomb[7]. Thackeray had a sexual harassment policy[8], which was brought in years ago to keep[9] professors from jumping on their students, but it applied across the board[10]. Even though the policy, which was there for everyone to read on the college's Web site, stressed[11] that no individual's employment would be placed in jeopardy[12] by lodging a complaint[13], she knew the real world was very different. Sure, she might be able to keep her job, but would she want it? It was a small department, and everyone in it was male except for her. Whenever Joyce thought of Michael, Allan, and Phil, what came to mind was Larry, Darryl, and Darryl, the backwoods clowns from that old TV show[14]. She'd have a hard time[15] building a case[16] without their support. She'd broached[17] the subject once with Allan, after Duncomb had asked her what she thought about something he called "the lifestyle," which evidently was a fancy[1] name for swapping spouses[2]. Joyce had said, "Not much." She decided to talk to Allan about it, given that he was the only one on the team who seemed to have an IQ higher than a pomegranate's[3]. He'd said Duncomb was just goofing around[4], that she shouldn't take him so seriously.

"You there?" Duncomb said. "You're not saying anything."

"I heard you, Clive," she said.

There was a male student coming from the direction of the library. Black, six-foot-six[5], thin. Wearing jeans and a gray school hoodie[6] that zipped up the front[7]. The hood[8] was down[9] and his head was held high.

"Got someone coming my way[10]," she whispered.

Their paths[11] crossed. He kept on walking toward the athletic center; she continued on to the library. There was another young man headed her way, but it was Phil.

"*Rrruffff*," he whispered as he passed.

She didn't want to make a show of turning around[12], checking behind her, but she couldn't resist. She wanted to make sure Michael was back there somewhere. Joyce did not see him.

"Where's Michael?" she said.

"He's around[13]," Duncomb said.

"Yeah, well, is he around somewhere near *me*?"

"Where are you, anyway? I lost you where the lights are spaced too far apart."

God, Joyce thought.

"I'm almost to the library."

"Oh, yeah, I see you."

1. pompeux
2. l'échangisme

3. ne pas avoir le QI d'une huître
4. ne faisait que blaguer

5. 1,98 m
6. sweat à capuche
7. devant
8. capuche
9. baissée
10. qui marche vers moi
11. chemins

12. se faire remarquer en se retournant

13. dans le coin

"I'm going in for five minutes, then coming back out."

"Got it. Remember, if you have to tinkle[1], I can hear everything." Duncomb chortled[2].

She entered the library, and there was Michael, talking to two girls by the counter.

"I found Michael. He's hitting on[3] a couple of students. You want to give him a call and tell him to do his fucking job?"

"I've got him on walkie-talkie. Who are the girls?"

"How would I know?"

As she passed Michael, she heard the small radio clipped to his jacket squawk[4]. "Gotta go, ladies," he said. "Gonna catch me a rapist[5]."

Joyce took the elevator to the second floor, wandered through the stacks[6] for a few minutes, then took the stairs back down. "Coming out," she said quietly.

"Gotcha[7]," Duncomb said.

Strolling back to the athletic building, she crossed paths with Michael and Phil. Saw three girls walking together, briskly[8], to the library. A boy and girl leaning up against a lamppost[9], making out[10]. She encountered half a dozen male students coming her way, but none tried anything.

Five minutes at the athletic building, then back to the library. Approaching, together, were Michael and Phil. Chatting, glancing back and forth at each other.

"Jesus, Clive, Darryl and Darryl are walking together, *not* split up[11]!"

"They got out of sync[12]," Duncomb said. "We'll get it sorted next time around[13]. Also, just FYI[14], we've lost Allan for a while."

"He's not in the woods?"

---

1. faire pipi
2. ricana
3. drague
4. couiner
5. me faire un violeur
6. entre les rayons
7. Pigé
8. d'un pas vif
9. réverbère
10. à se peloter
11. séparément
12. ont perdu le rythme
13. va régler ça au prochain tour
14. que tu saches

"Call of nature[1]," Duncomb said.

"Are you kidding me?[2]" Joyce said. "He's in the *woods*!"

"First of all, it wasn't the sort of thing you can do standing[3] in the woods, and second, even if it was, you don't exactly want someone to find you with your dick in your hands when there's a sex pervert in the neighborhood[4]."

This was just getting better and better.

She was about halfway along the route when she heard footsteps behind her. Someone had caught up to her[5], but was not passing[6].

"Hey," she said softly.

"Yeah?" Duncomb said.

"I got someone on my tail[7]. Can you see?"

"You're just out of range[8]. … Okay, yeah, I see you. Okay, it's a guy, walking along, head down." A pause. "Wearing a blue hoodie, head covered."

Joyce felt her insides starting to melt[9].

"This could be it," she said.

"He's getting closer. Closer. Hang on, hang on … Nope, stand down[10]. The guy's heading for a car."

Joyce gave herself permission to steal a quick glance[11] over her shoulder. Duncomb was right. The guy had a remote[12] in his hand. Lights flashed[13] on an old van.

"I want to get a closer look at him anyway," Duncomb said. "Back to you in a minute."

"Okay," Joyce said.

She was turning back to eyes front[14] when someone came out of the trees and grabbed her.

He wrapped one arm around her body[15], placed a hand over her mouth, and lifted her off her feet[16]. Joyce guessed he was three or four inches[17] taller than her, putting him at five-eight

---

1. Une envie pressante
2. Tu rigoles ?!

3. debout

4. dans les parages

5. l'avait rejointe
6. ne la dépassait pas

7. sur mes talons
8. portée

9. son ventre se nouer

10. c'est bon

11. glisser un rapide coup d'œil
12. clé
13. Des phares clignotèrent

14. se retournait dans le sens de la marche
15. l'entoura d'un bras
16. la souleva du sol
17. une dizaine de centimètres

1. dans les
1,75 m
2. dans les 63 kg
3. l'emportait
4. l'avait fait
virevolter
5. toilettes

6. plaquée sur
7. appareil

8. l'écouteur
tomber

9. présente un
risque
10. reprendre
contact

11. rien
distinguer de
son visage
12. sans savoir
13. pisser
14. se mit à
califourchon
sur elle
15. cloué au sol

or five-nine[1], maybe a hundred and forty pounds[2]. She could feel the muscle in his arms as he carted her off[3] into the bushes.

In the second that he whirled her around[4], she saw no other person on the path. Allan was off in the bathroom[5] somewhere, Michael and Phil were probably approaching the athletic center about now, and Duncomb had gone to get a better look at the guy who'd just been on her tail.

At least she could still talk to him.

Except she couldn't.

Not because her attacker had his hand clamped over[6] her mouth, but because the Bluetooth device[7] that had been clipped to her ear was gone. When the man lifted her off the ground, she'd felt the earpiece dislodge[8]. It was back there on the path somewhere.

Which meant that she did not hear Duncomb say, "I don't think that guy is up to much[9]. I'm going back to the car. Hang on, think I've lost you. ... Let me just touch base[10] with Mike and Phil and I'll get back to you."

Once the man had her into the trees and beyond the view of anyone else passing along the path, he threw her down onto the ground.

His description matched that provided by the three women. His head was hooded, but even when Joyce looked up and directly into his face, she couldn't make out anything about him[11]. He was wearing a black ski mask.

Duncomb, unaware[12] that he was not being heard, said, "Okay, I got them; they're coming your way. Let me ask you this. If you're a woman, can you take a pee[13] in the woods?"

The man straddled her body[14]. He had her left arm pinned down[15] with his right hand, at the wrist, and his left hand over her mouth. Her right was trapped against her body, held in place with his thigh[1]. But her right hand was still inside her purse.

1. cuisse

Holding the gun.

"Okay, okay," he said to her. She watched his lips move in the circular opening of the mask. "Don't make any noise. It's going to be okay. Just be cool and nothing's going to happen."

She had her fingers around the butt[2] and was working to get her index finger on the trigger[3]. If he'd relax his thighs just a bit …

2. crosse

3. gâchette

"You just stay here for five seconds," he said. "I'm going to take off[4]."

4. me casser

Duncomb said, "You there? Oh, I get it. I crossed a line[5] with the peeing question. Okay, I'm an asshole. But tell me where you are, Joyce. I don't know where the hell you are. Joyce?"

5. ai dépassé les bornes

Joyce wondered what the hell this guy on top of her was talking about. He'd dragged her[6] into the bushes so he could run off? Not that that was[7] bad news, but it didn't make sense.

6. l'avait entraînée

7. Non que ce soit

Maybe he couldn't get it up[8].

8. bander

Whatever. She didn't give a shit[9]. She just wanted to get that gun out of her purse and blow this fucker's head off[10] in case he changed his mind.

9. s'en foutait

10. faire sauter la cervelle de ce connard

"We good[11]? Are we good?" he asked her. "Just nod if we're good."

11. d'accord

His sweaty palm still over her mouth, she forced a nod.

"Okay," he said.

He took his hand off her mouth, released his grip on her wrist, and started to get off her.

Joyce got her right arm free. Brought the gun up fast.

"Jesus!" the man said, bringing his left arm back, then swinging it hard against Joyce's arm.

The gun flew from her hand, landing in the blanket of leaves[1] covering the forest floor.

The man dived for[2] the gun, his legs draped[3] over Joyce's. He got his hand on it, scrambled to his knees[4], and pointed the weapon at Joyce. She'd started getting to her feet, but froze[5].

"Goddamn it," the man said. "I was never going to do anything[6]." He angled the gun away[7], so that if it went off, it wouldn't hit Joyce. "It's all for show, a gig[8], a kind of social experiment, he called it."

"What?" Joyce said.

"No one actually gets hurt[9] or anything, so—"

There was a stirring[10] in the bushes to the left. Then a deafening[11] bang. One side of the attacker's head blew clean off[12].

Joyce screamed.

Clive Duncomb emerged from the brush, gun in hand.

"Got the son of a bitch," he said.

1. tapis de feuilles

2. fondit sur

3. enroulées

4. se remit péniblement à genoux

5. se figea

6. allais rien faire du tout

7. pointa le revolver de biais

8. taf

9. Sans blesser personne

10. mouvement

11. assourdissant

12. sauta net

THIRTY-ONE

David

"**HI,**" I said, extending a hand to Dr. Jack Sturgess in Marla's hospital room.

He took the hand, gave it a firm shake[1], and said, "Marla really needs her rest[2]."

"Sure," I said. "I understand that."

"You were with her this morning," Sturgess said, keeping his voice low, drawing me toward him out of Marla's range of hearing[3]. "You found her with that woman's child."

"That's right."

He raised his index finger, a "give me two seconds" gesture, then stepped around me and approached Marla. "How are you feeling?"

"Okay," she said.

"I'm just going to see your cousin out[4]; then I'll come back and check on you[5]."

I guessed that meant I was leaving. Sturgess led me into the hall, let the oversize[6] door to Marla's room close, and said, "I just wanted to thank you for looking out for her[7] this morning."

"I didn't really do anything. I was just trying to sort out[8] what happened."

1. la serra fermement

2. de se reposer

3. hors de portée de voix de Marla

4. raccompagner ton cousin

5. voir comment tu vas

6. énorme

7. vous être occupé d'elle

8. démêler

1. état très fragile

"All the same, thank you. She's in a very delicate condition[1]."

"Yeah," I said, nodding.

2. a obtenu

"What did Marla tell you about how she got hold of[2] that baby?"

"Same as she's told everyone else, I suppose," I said.

"Yes, yes, the mystery woman who came to her door. A delusion[3], more than likely."

3. hallucination

"You think?"

The doctor nodded. "I'd say yes. But it might be helpful[4], in understanding her state of mind, to know just[5] who she believes it was who delivered this child to her."

4. utile
5. au juste

"I don't know if I'm following you."

"Well, let's say she saw a tall, dark stranger. That might signify something totally different than if she'd seen a six-year-old girl."

"Dr. Sturgess, are you Marla's psychiatrist?"

"No, I'm not."

6. interpréter

"If anyone should be trying to read anything into[6] Marla's fantasies, wouldn't it be her psychiatrist?"

7. s'éclaircit la gorge

Sturgess cleared his throat[7]. "Just because I'm not Marla's psychiatrist doesn't mean I'm not interested in her mental health. A person's mental state is very much related to their physical well-being[8]. For God's sake, I'm treating her for a slit wrist[9]. You think that doesn't have something to do with her state of mind?" He gave me a withering look[10]. "I'm trying to help this girl."

8. bien-être
9. poignet entaillé
10. regard noir

"So am I," I said.

Eyebrows shot up. "How?"

"I don't know. Any way I can."

"Well, coming here, visiting her, letting her know you care, that's good. That's a very good thing to do. She needs that kind of love and support."

"I was thinking of doing more than that," I said.

"I don't understand. What else could you possibly do?"

"I don't know. **Ask around**[1], I guess."

"What does that mean? 'Ask around.' "

"What it sounds like," I said. "Ask around."

"Are you some sort of private detective, David? Because if you are, **it's never come up**[2]. I'm sure someone would have mentioned it."

"No, I'm not."

"**My recollection is**[3] ... didn't I used to see your **byline**[4] in the *Standard*? But that was a long time ago. You were a reporter once?"

"I used to be at the *Standard*. Then I was at the *Globe*, in Boston, for a while. Came back here to write for the *Standard* just as it closed down."

"So, this *asking around*, then, it'd just be something to do to **keep busy**[5]?"

I gave myself a couple of seconds, then asked, "What's your problem with this, exactly?"

"Problem? I didn't say I had a problem with it. But since you've asked, in case you haven't noticed, the police are very much involved in this. They **are doing plenty of**[6] *asking around*. That's **kind of what they do**[7]. So I don't see what purpose there would be in your **going around**[8] **troubling people**[9] at a time like this with a **bunch of**[10] questions. And that would begin with Marla. It's great, your stopping by to say hello, but I don't want you subjecting her to some kind of interrogation."

"Really."

"Really. The last thing *anyone* involved in this horrible business needs is **some amateur sleuth**[11] **poking his nose**[12] into things."

"Amateur sleuth," I said.

---

1. Me renseigner

2. on ne m'en a jamais parlé

3. Dans mon souvenir

4. signature

5. vous occuper

6. n'arrêtent pas une seconde de

7. un peu leur boulot

8. l'intérêt que vous alliez

9. déranger les gens

10. tas de

11. qu'un limier du dimanche

12. aille fourrer son nez

"I mean no offense," Sturgess said. "But Marla's in a delicate condition. As is Mr. Gaynor. The last thing he needs—"

"Wait," I said, raising a hand. "You know Bill Gaynor?"

Sturgess blinked[1]. "I'm sorry?"

"You know the Gaynors?"

"Yes, yes, I do," he said. "I'm their family physician[2]."

"I didn't know that."

"Well, why would you? What business would it be of yours[3] to know who my patients are?"

"It just seems like quite a[4] coincidence," I said.

Sturgess shook his head condescendingly. "Promise Falls is not that big a place. It's hardly shocking[5] that I could end up treating two families with a connection[6]. Oh, look."

Aunt Agnes was striding down the hall, her husband, Gill, a few steps behind her. Her eyes landed[7] on me and she offered up one of her rare smiles.

"David," she said, giving me a quick hug and a peck[8] on the cheek. "Have you been in to see Marla?"

"I have. She seems … good. Tired, but good."

Gill joined his wife at her side, extended a hand[9]. "Dave, good to see you."

I nodded. "Uncle Gill," I said.

Jack Sturgess spoke up. "Your nephew and I were just having a nice chat. David here has expressed his intention to make some inquiries into the circumstances of[10] the day's events, and I suspect he's decided to do this without consulting either of you."

"Is that true?" Gill asked.

"Well, what I was thinking—"

1. cilla

2. médecin de famille

3. En quoi ça vous regarderait

4. une sacrée

5. pas vraiment surprenant

6. liées entre elles

7. Son regard s'arrêta

8. après une embrassade rapide

9. me tendit la main

10. mener sa petite enquête sur

Agnes said, "What do you mean, inquiries?"

I raised a cautious[1] hand. "I just want to do whatever I can to help Marla. The police may already've made up their minds about what happened, but maybe if I ask a few questions, I might be able to turn up[2] something that would make them think twice[3]."

I braced myself for[4] a verbal assault[5]. I figured that even if Agnes accepted that my intentions were honorable, she was such a control freak[6] she wouldn't want anyone doing anything for a member of her family without her direct supervision.

So when she reached for my hand, squeezed it, and said, "Oh, thank you, David, thank you so much," I was caught off guard[7].

"Yes," Gill said, laying a hand on my shoulder. "Anything you can do, we'd be most grateful."

I glanced at Dr. Jack Sturgess. He did not look happy.

1. prudente

2. découvrir

3. réfléchir à deux fois

4. me préparai à

5. confrontation

6. avait un tel besoin de tout régenter,

7. pris de court

THIRTY-TWO

BARRY Duckworth was beginning to think he would never get home.

He was in his car, headed in that direction[1], still trying to get his head around[2] what he'd seen at the coroner's office[3], when he got a call on his cell.

"Duckworth."

"Detective, it's Officer Carlson. Angus Carlson."

"Officer Carlson. I thought I might be hearing from you. You been talking to the chief?"

"I heard from her a few minutes ago. About lending a hand[4] to the detective division."

"Yeah," Duckworth said.

"I'll be reporting to you[5]."

"Yup."

"I'm looking forward to the opportunity."

"Sure. See you in the morning."

"There's another reason why I'm calling," Carlson said.

"Another squirrel joke?"

"No, sir. But it's sort of connected[6]. Well, not connected, really. It's just that I'm at a scene that maybe doesn't warrant[7] your attention, but it's so weird, and to have something this weird[8] happen the same day as that thing with the squirrels this morning, I thought maybe you'd like to—"

1. vers chez lui précisément

2. digérer

3. chez le médecin légiste

4. prêter main-forte

5. serai sous vos ordres

6. en lien

7. ne nécessite pas

8. d'aussi bizarre

"Spit it out[1], Carlson."

Officer Carlson told him where he was, and what he'd found.

"I'll swing by[2]," Duckworth said.

Carlson met Duckworth at the Five Mountains admission gates and led him through the darkened park to the Ferris wheel, which reminded him of a monstrous, illuminated tambourine.

"This is what I thought you'd want to have a look at[3]," the officer said, pointing to the three mannequins with the words YOU'LL BE SORRY painted across them.

Duckworth walked around the scene, inspecting it from all angles.

"Could just be kids," Carlson said.

"Could be," the detective said, but it didn't feel like kids to him. He could see[4] kids wanting to fire up[5] a mothballed[6] Ferris wheel and take it for a joyride[7], as dumb a stunt as that might be[8], considering that it wasn't exactly easy, if security showed up[9], to make a run for it[10] when you were at the top of the wheel.

But there hadn't been any kids on the wheel when it was found in operation. Just these three lifeless passengers. Whoever'd gotten the ride started[11] had plenty of time to get away[12] before anyone else got here.

Still[13]...

"Search the park," Duckworth said. "See if there's anyone hanging around[14] to watch the show[15]. Maybe somebody left something behind[16]. Dropped a backpack[17], something." Some other uniformed Promise Falls police had arrived, and Carlson told them to fan out[18].

1. Accouche	
2. Je passe voir	
3. qu'il fallait vous faire voir	
4. imaginer	
5. démarrer	
6. au rebut	
7. faire un tour avec	
8. même si ce ne serait pas malin	
9. des vigiles survenaient	
10. prendre la fuite	
11. Ceux qui avaient fait démarrer	
12. avait eu tout le temps de partir	
13. Tout de même	
14. est resté	
15. observer la scène	
16. a laissé traîner quelque chose	
17. Laissé tomber un sac à dos	
18. se déployer	

"Who'll be sorry?" Duckworth asked aloud, although he wasn't directing the question to anyone in particular. "And for what?"

"Sorry they're going out of business?" Carlson offered. "The park's gone under[1], you know."

Duckworth knew. "Where's the woman?"

Carlson said Gloria Fenwick was waiting in the admin offices for a detective to speak with her. Before going to find her, Duckworth told one of the other officers not to touch the mannequins. Not before they'd been fingerprinted[2].

"They're not real fingers," the officer said, perplexed.

"The mannequins," Duckworth said. "Have them dusted for fingerprints[3]."

"Oh, yeah," the officer said.

A lifelong traffic cop[4], Duckworth thought.

He had to press an intercom buzzer[5] at the door to the building where Fenwick worked. "Who is it?" she asked nervously. When he told her, she buzzed him in[6]. She was waiting for him at the top of a flight of stairs[7], a blanket wrapped around her shoulders. She led him into the main office area filled with cubicles and computers[8].

Every overhead light was on[9].

"I'm freezing," she said. "Ever since I saw those … those dummies[10], I can't stop shivering."

They found some comfortable couches[11] to sit on in a lounge by reception.

"It's nice to see you again," Duckworth said.

Fenwick studied him[12]. "I'm sorry. Have we met[13]?"

"It was a few years ago. The woman who disappeared here at Five Mountains."

---

1. a fait faillite
2. qu'on ait relevé les empreintes
3. Faites relever les empreintes dessus
4. Celui-là resterait à la circulation
5. Interphone
6. lui ouvrit
7. volée de marches
8. grand open space avec plein de box et d'ordinateurs
9. Tous les plafonniers étaient allumés
10. mannequins
11. canapés
12. le dévisagea
13. On se connaît

"Oh!" she said. "I remember you. You're the one who wanted to search[1] every single car leaving the park."

"Tell me what happened here tonight."

She told him: seeing the light outside the office window, discovering the Ferris wheel in full rotation, the painted mannequins.

"You didn't see anyone?" he asked.

She shook her head.

"I'd like to have a look at your surveillance footage[2]," he said.

Another shake of the head. "There is none. The cameras are all off." Fenwick shrugged[3]. "This time of year, even if the park wasn't closing for good[4], the cameras would be off. We wouldn't normally open until next week. There'd be no one here to monitor them[5]. We have a security guard sweep through[6] a couple of times a day, but this was before his next scheduled[7] stop."

Duckworth asked, "How many people lost their jobs because of the park going under[8]?"

"Everyone," she said. "Me, too, eventually[9]."

"How many is that?"

"About two hundred people directly employed by Five Mountains. And then, some of the concessions[10], they hired their own people[11]. The ripple effect[12]. Plus, there were plenty of local businesses we patronized[13]. Cleaning services, gardening, things like that."

"Anyone seem particularly hostile about being let go[14]?"

Fenwick leaned back into the couch[15] and stared at the ceiling[16]. "It happens. It's business. People were upset[17]. Some people cried. But it wasn't like anyone said, 'I'll get you for this[18].' No one who said anything like what was written on those

1. fouiller

2. vos vidéos de surveillance

3. haussa les épaules
4. définitivement

5. les regarder
6. qui fait une ronde
7. prévu

8. le parc a fermé

9. en dernier

10. certains forains

11. personnel

12. effet boule de neige

13. chez qui on sous-traitait

14. mis au chômage

15. se radossa au canapé

16. fixa le plafond

17. le prenaient mal

18. Vous me paierez ça

1. Je ne veux
plus rester seule
ici le soir

2. une bonne
idée

3. s'est donné
beaucoup de mal

4. monter cette
mascarade

5. se coltiner

6. jusqu'ici

7. Est-ce qu'il est
difficile

8. Faire marcher
le manège

9. en particulier

dummies." She paused. "I will never be alone here at night again[1]."

"That's smart[2]."

She stopped looking at the ceiling. Fixing her eyes on his, she asked, "You think it's a serious threat?"

"I don't know," Duckworth said. "But someone went to a lot of trouble[3] to stage all that[4]. Had to drag[5] three dummies out here[6], paint them, get them into that car, start up that ride. How hard would it be[7] for someone to do that? Get the ride going[8]?"

"If you've got any experience with machinery or electronics, I mean, I guess anyone like that could figure it out."

"Kids?"

She thought a moment. "I doubt it. Unless it was some kid we hired last summer."

"Can you find me the names of the employees who ran that specific[9] ride?"

"I could probably do that," she said. "But not now. I don't want to spend another minute here tonight."

Duckworth smiled. "Tomorrow's good." He gave her one of his cards. "I can get one of the officers to escort you to your car."

"Thank you," she said.

Duckworth was going back down the stairs when his cell phone rang once again.

"Yeah."

"This Detective Duckworth?"

"It is."

"Yeah, well, it's Clive Duncomb over at Thackeray."

"You were supposed to send me the names of the women who'd been assaulted."

"Yeah, well, about that," Duncomb said. "There's been a development[1]."

"It was a righteous shoot[2]," the Thackeray College security chief said, standing over the body of the man who had attacked Joyce Pilgrim. Their light sources were[3] a half-moon, the stars, and five flashlights[4] that were being wielded[5] by Duncomb, the three male members of his team, and Duckworth.

"Well, I guess that settles it, then[6]," Duckworth said. He gazed down at what remained of the man's head, then let his eye trail down the rest of the body[7]. The man was in a fleecy[8] dark blue or black hoodie—it wasn't easy to tell in this light—with a large white 2 stitched[9] onto the left of the zipper, and an equally large 3 to the right.

"I saw him with a gun in his hand, kneeling[10] over Joyce. I was coming into the trees here, trying to find her, and that's the situation I encountered."

"You can make a full statement[11] at the station," Duckworth said.

"Come on. It's all pretty cut-and-dried[12]. Like I said, it was righteous[13]."

Duckworth shone his light directly into Duncomb's face. "Don't say that word again."

"It's justified, is all I'm saying. I saved Joyce's life."

"After putting her at risk[14]. Right now this is a homicide. And I'm in charge[15]. You'll be coming in for a full statement. The whole lot of you[16]."

The only member of the security team not there was Joyce Pilgrim. She was at the athletic building, being babysat[17] by a Promise Falls officer until Duckworth was finished here.

1. Il y a du nouveau

2. de la légitime défense

3. L'éclairage était fourni par

4. torches

5. brandies

6. dans ce cas, c'est réglé

7. glisser le long du corps

8. polaire

9. cousu

10. à genoux

11. déposition

12. clair comme de l'eau de roche

13. légitime

14. l'avoir mise en danger

15. c'est moi qui commande

16. Tous autant que vous êtes

17. gardée

1. des armes
2. de toute façon
3. lui prendre son flingue
4. ont un permis de port d'arme
5. officiellement
6. vu que
7. n'en aurez plus besoin
8. c'est pas trop demander
9. la moutarde lui monter au nez
10. vous obéir
11. on me l'avait pas dit
12. fiche de paie
13. à la surveillance du passage piéton devant la maternelle
14. bouclé plus d'affaires
15. dans la police de Boston
16. n'en voit passer
17. en dix ans
18. vous mets les menottes
19. vous colle au trou
20. quel merdier
21. prit la parole
22. portefeuille
23. on venait de lui poser

"Many of the students around here carry weapons[1]?" Duckworth asked, shining the light back onto the body.

"Sure hope not, but that's not his anyway[2]. Joyce let this clown get her gun off her[3]."

"Your security people all licensed to carry[4]?"

"Well, not technically[5]. But seeing as how[6] Joyce was the bait, I made a decision to give her one of my—"

"Wait, so that's *your* gun this guy had?"

"Yeah. And when you're done with it[7], if it's not too much fucking trouble[8], I'd like to have it back."

Duckworth felt blood rushing through his neck[9].

"What did I say to you this morning? About sending someone with her experience to act as a decoy?"

"If I'm supposed to report to you[10], it's news to me[11]," Duncomb countered. "You don't sign my paycheck[12]."

"No, but the college president does, and if he's got any sense, you'll be a nursery school crossing guard[13] before the end of the week."

"I closed more cases[14] working the Boston PD[15] than this town sees[16] in a decade[17]. You can't talk to me like—"

"I just did. If you say one more thing I'll cuff you[18] and lock you up[19] for the night. God, what a clusterfuck[20]. Does anyone know who this kid is?"

A member of the security team spoke up[21]. "I'm Phil. Phil Mercer? Uh, I've got his wallet[22] here." He held it up, shined a light on it. "He's a student here. Well, was. His name is—"

"You've touched the body?" Duckworth asked.

"I couldn't have gotten at his wallet otherwise," he said, as if he'd just been asked[23] the stupidest question he'd ever heard.

266

The detective sighed. "Who is he?"

"Hang on; let me look at this license[1] again. Okay, Mason Helt. His student card is here and everything. Here you go[2]."

And he tossed[3] the wallet in Duckworth's direction.

The detective, stunned[4], managed to catch the wallet and still hang on to[5] the flashlight.

He looked at Duncomb. "You must be so proud," he said.

Duckworth found Joyce Pilgrim sitting on a wooden bench[6] in an empty gymnasium. He dismissed[7] the officer who was standing near her, then parked himself[8] next to her on the bench.

"How are you doing?" he asked after identifying himself[9].

"I'm okay," she said, her legs pressed tightly together, her fingers knitted[10] into tight double fist[11]. She was hunched over[12], her shoulders tight, as if she were trying to close in on herself.

"I'm sorry about what you went through[13]. Have you been seen by the paramedics[14]?"

"I'm not hurt[15]," Joyce said. She shook her head slowly. "I can't work for that asshole anymore."

Duckworth did not have to ask.

"I don't blame you."

"I'm not trained[16] for this. I can't do this kind of thing. I can't."

"Duncomb shouldn't have put you in this position. That was wrong."

"I have to call my husband. I don't think I can drive home on my own[17]."

"Sure."

"I still can't believe what he said to me," Joyce said.

"What did he say to you?"

---

1. permis de conduire

2. Tenez

3. jeta

4. ébahi

5. tout en gardant

6. banc

7. congédia

8. s'installa

9. s'être présenté

10. entrelacés

11. un double poing serré

12. repliée sur elle-même

13. ce que vous venez de vivre

14. les secours

15. blessée

16. formée

17. toute seule

"Clive didn't tell you?"

"Why don't you tell me," Duckworth said gently.

"When that kid got my gun, he pointed it away[1] from me. Said he was sorry, that he'd never have actually, you know, that he wouldn't have raped me."

"Go on[2]."

"He said it was … what was the word? He said it was a gig[3]. That he was, like, conducting a social experiment[4]."

"A gig?"

"That was the word. He said that was what 'he' wanted. Like another person. Like he was asked[5] to do it, or hired. Does that make any sense?"

It didn't. It was an entire day of things that hadn't made sense. The hanging[6] of twenty-three squirrels, three mannequins in a Ferris wheel carriage, a—

Wait a second.

Duckworth closed his eyes for second. Thought back[7] to only an hour ago, as he walked around the base of the Ferris wheel.

All of the carriages were numbered.

The carriage holding those three mannequins had a number stenciled[8] on the side of it. Duckworth closed his eyes, trying to picture it[9].

The number painted on the side was 23.

The hoodie worn by Mason Helt was emblazoned[10] with the number 23.

And how many squirrels had been found hanging by their necks that morning in the park?

Twenty-three.

It probably meant nothing. But …

"That is one hell of a coincidence," he said aloud[11].

"You talking to me?" Joyce Pilgrim asked.

1. l'a éloigné

2. Continuez

3. un taf

4. c'était une expérience sociologique

5. Comme si on lui avait demandé

6. pendaison

7. Repensa

8. inscrit

9. le revoir dans sa tête

10. orné

11. tout haut

THIRTY-THREE

David

SINCE the first person Jack Sturgess had cautioned me against visiting[1] was Bill Gaynor, I decided to see him first. I didn't know what I'd ask him, but maybe now, some twelve hours[2] after our first encounter, we'd be able to have something approaching[3] a civil conversation.

Maybe, given that I was the one who'd shown up with Matthew, he'd even want to talk to me. Ask questions about how it all happened.

So I parked Mom's Taurus out front of his Breckonwood house, and made the trip to the front door. You wouldn't know[4] anything had happened here earlier in the day. No police cruisers, no yellow crime-scene tape, no news vans[5]. Everyone had been and gone[6].

The street was quiet, and most of the houses were dark, including this one, save for[7] the light over the front door. At the house next door, however, several lights were still on.

I rang the bell.

I could sense steps within the house, someone approaching the door from the other side. The

---

1. m'avait déconseillé d'aller voir

2. une douzaine d'heures

3. qui ressemble à

4. On ne se serait pas douté

5. de camionnettes de la presse

6. était parti

7. hormis

1. juste à gauche

2. me jeter
un coup d'œil
rapide

3. s'éteignit

4. ce fut tout

5. venait de
vivre

6. où je pourrais
passer

7. à cette heure
tardive

8. à laquelle je
pensais

9. que j'aie
atteint ma
voiture

10. qui devait
avoir dans les
80 ans

11. faisant son
âge

12. robe de
chambre à
carreaux

13. d'humeur

14. loucha

curtain at the window immediately left[1] of the door opened, and I saw Bill Gaynor take a quick peek at me[2].

"Go away," he said. Not shouting, but just loud enough for me to hear through the glass.

"Please," I said.

The light over my head went out[3].

And that was that[4]. I wasn't going to ring that bell a second time. Not after what this man had been through[5].

I could think of only one other place I might drive by[6] this late at night[7] before I went home to bed. A place I'd been thinking about[8] for a while now.

But before I made it back to the car[9], I heard the door open on the neighboring house that was still lit up. A man I guessed to be in his eighties[10], thin and elderly[11], wearing a plaid housecoat[12], had taken a step outside.

"Something going on out here?" he asked.

I said, "I'd come by to see Mr. Gaynor, but he's not in the mood[13] for visitors right now."

"His wife got killed today," the man said.

"I know. I was here when he found her."

The man took another step out of his house, squinted[14] in my direction. "I saw you this morning. I was watching from the window. There was a fight on the lawn, a woman with their baby."

"Yeah," I said.

"What the hell's been going on? I asked the police but they didn't tell me a damn thing. They had plenty of questions, but weren't interested in answering mine."

I cut across the lawn and met him at his front step. "What do you want to know?" I asked him. "My name is David, by the way."

"I'm Terrence," he said, nodding[1]. "Terrence Rodd. I've lived here twenty years. My wife, Hillary, passed away[2] four years ago, so it's just me here. But I'm not moving out[3] unless I have to. Guess how old I am."

"I'm not good at ages," I said. "Sixty-eight."

"Don't mess with me[4]," Terrence said. "Really, how old do you think I am?"

I pondered[5]. "Seventy-nine," I said. I really thought eighty, but it was like when you put a four-dollar item on sale for three ninety-nine. It looks better.

"Eighty-eight," Terrence said. He tapped his temple with the tip of his index finger. "But I'm still as sharp up here as I ever was[6]. So you tell me, what happened there?"

"Someone stabbed Rosemary Gaynor to death," I said. "It was pretty horrible."

"Who did it?"

I shook my head. "Far as I know, there hasn't been an arrest."

"So it wasn't Bill, then," he said, nodding.

That threw me[7]. "If it had been, would you have been surprised?" I asked.

"Well, yes and no. Yes, because he sure doesn't strike me[8] as the kind of guy who'd do it, but no, because isn't it usually the husband who does it when a wife gets killed? I spent a lifetime analyzing statistics, so you kind of look at what's most likely to happen. What's your interest in this?"

"Like I said, I was here when Mr. Gaynor found her."

That seemed to be enough for him. He nodded. "Nice couple. Hell of a thing[9]. Everybody on the street's probably making damn sure their doors are locked tonight, but most of these things, it's

1. en hochant la tête

2. est décédée

3. ne veux pas déménager

4. Vous moquez pas de moi

5. réfléchis

6. y en a toujours autant là-dedans

7. me surprit

8. ne me fait pas l'effet

9. Sacrée histoire

271

somebody you know that does it. Even if it wasn't Bill, which I'm not saying I think it is."

"I get that."

"Cute little baby, too. Baby's okay, right?"

"Yes," I said.

"Thank God. I'm freezing out here in my bathrobe. Nice talking to ya."

"You mind if I ask you a couple of questions?"

He hesitated. He'd have to invite me in if he wanted to warm up. "You didn't do it[1], did you?"

"No," I said.

"Hang on one second." He went back into the house, closed the door. It reopened in ten seconds. Now he had a phone in his hand.

He held it up in front of me. "Smile."

I smiled. There was a flash. He turned his attention to the phone, tapped away[2].

"I'm just gonna e-mail this to my daughter in Des Moines. If I end up dead, they'll have your picture."

"Fair enough[3]," I said.

There was a *whoosh* as the e-mail was sent. "Come on in[4]," he said.

I followed him into the house. He said, "I keep a lot of lights on until I go to bed. I don't sleep too well, wander[5] the house a lot. Don't usually go to bed till about one in the morning. Try watching one of those classic movies on Turner[6], then I go to bed, but I wake up early."

"Oh, yeah."

"Usually can't sleep in[7] past six. Used to read the paper in the morning, but the goddamn assholes shut the *Standard* down."

"I heard," I said.

"Come into the kitchen. Want some hot chocolate? I usually make some hot chocolate at night."

1. C'est pas vous qu'avez fait ça

2. tapota rapidement

3. D'accord

4. Entrez donc

5. me promène dans

6. [chaîne TV américaine]

7. ne peux plus dormir

"That'd be nice."

The place was done in lots of wood: wood cabinets, wood floor, even wood panels over the fridge and other appliances[1]. Not one thing out of place, either[2]. Nothing in the sink[3], no piles of bills[4] and envelopes by the phone. A real estate[5] photographer could have walked in and not had to do a moment's prep[6].

"Beautiful home," I said.

He filled two mugs with milk from the fridge and put them into the microwave. Set it for ninety seconds. "I'll give it a stir[7] halfway through," he said.

"Did you know the Gaynors well?"

Terrence shrugged. "Said hi coming in and out, that kind of thing. And they have a nanny, too, comes by most days. Name of Sarita. She was the nicest of the bunch[8], really."

"Yeah?"

"Sweet girl. I know you're not supposed to call them girls anymore. She was a woman. Tough little thing[9]. Went from one job to the other. I think she was sending money back to family in Mexico. Don't think she was here legally, but hey, people do what they have to do."

"Do you know what her other job was?"

"Nursing home[10]. I was trying to remember the name of it earlier, when the cops were here asking questions, couldn't think of it. There's only about fifty of them in the area. Reason I know she worked at one is, I asked her what it was like there[11], in case I get to the point I can't look after myself here on my own, and it sounds like an okay joint[12], but truth is, I hope one day, when it's my time[13], I just go." He snapped[14] his fingers. "Just

1. appareils ménagers

2. Et rien qui dépassait

3. évier

4. factures

5. d'agence immobilière

6. faire ses photos sans toucher à rien

7. remuerai

8. du lot

9. Une dure à cuire

10. Dans une maison de retraite

11. comment c'était là-bas

12. pas trop mal

13. mon heure sonnera

14. claqua

1. prévois
2. abattu
3. juge assesseur

4. gloussa

5. ont
emménagé

6. n'étaient pas
souvent là

7. grossesse

8. d'en boire une
gorgée
9. d'un ton
d'excuse
10. de temps en
temps
11. La conversa-
tion dévia
12. de ce dont
j'étais venu
parler

like that. I go to bed one night and just don't wake up the next day. What do you think about that?"

"Who was it who said, 'I expect[1] to die at one hundred and ten, shot[2] by a jealous husband'?"

"Thurgood Marshall, associate justice[3] of the United States Supreme Court," Terrence said, and chuckled[4]. "That sounds good, too." The microwave beeped. He took out the mugs, gave each a stir, and put them back into the oven for another minute and a half.

"I think I had more conversations with Sarita in the last ten months she's been coming over than I've had with the Gaynors since they moved in[5]. Although, a year back or so, they weren't around much[6] anyway."

"Where were they?"

"Boston. Bill, he works for some insurance company based there, and he had to be away for several months, so Rosemary went and lived with him. Did the last few months of her pregnancy[7] there; first time I saw them after they came back, she had the baby."

The oven beeped again. He took out the mugs, handed one to me. I blew on it before taking a sip[8]. It was good hot chocolate.

"I don't have any marshmallows," he said apologetically[9]. "Used to buy them once in a while[10], would forget I had them; I'd open up the bag and they were hard as golf balls."

We ended up straying off topic[11], at least from the topic I'd come to discuss[12]. Terrence used to own horses, and he wanted to tell me all about it. I didn't pay much attention, but he was a nice man, and the time passed pleasantly.

I thanked him for the hot chocolate and the conversation, and as I was heading back to the Taurus he said, "Davidson."

"Sorry?"

"Davidson Place. It just came back to me. That's where Sarita works."

I headed back in the direction of my parents' house, not sure I really knew anything more than when I'd set off from there[1]. At least, not anything useful. But the following morning I'd do the same again. Ask questions.

I'd go to Davidson Place. I would look for Sarita.

I didn't drive straight home. Made a couple of turns along the way that took me into a neighborhood[2] I'd visited earlier in the day.

I pulled the car over to the curb and killed[3] the engine. Left the key in the ignition[4]. Sat behind the wheel[5], watching a house. There were no lights on.

Probably everyone had gone to bed.

Carl, as well as his mother, Samantha.

I stared at the house for about a minute, feeling hungry all over[6], before I turned the key and continued on my way.

1. j'en étais parti

2. quartier

3. coupai
4. contact
5. Restai assis au volant

6. plein de désir

275

THE SECOND DAY

THIRTY-FOUR

THE naked[1] woman was sitting on the edge[2] of the bed, weeping[3].

The man who remained under the covers on the other side of the bed stirred[4], rolled over. He reached out[5] and touched the tips of his fingers to[6] the woman's back.

"Hey, babe," he said.

She continued to cry. Her face was in her hands, her elbows[7] on her knees.

The man threw off[8] the covers and huddled[9] behind her on the mattress, on his knees, pressed his naked body up against hers and wrapped his arms around her[10]. "It's okay, it's okay. It's going to be okay."

"How can it be okay?" she asked. "How can it ever be okay?"

"It just ... I don't know. But we'll find a way."

She shook her head and sobbed[11]. "They'll find me, Marshall. I know they'll find me."

"I'm going to look after you," he said comfortingly[12]. "I will. I'll keep them[13] from finding you."

She broke free[14] of him and walked to the bathroom of his small apartment, closed the door. He put his ear to it, said, "You okay in there, Sarita?"

"Yes," she said. "I just need a minute."

1. nue
2. au bord
3. en larmes
4. remua
5. étendit le bras
6. du bout des doigts
7. coudes
8. rejeta
9. se blottit
10. l'enlaça
11. sanglota
12. d'un ton rassurant
13. les empêcherai
14. se dégagea

1. à se demander

2. parcourut des yeux son appartement

3. plaque chauffante

4. qu'il avait ramassées

5. le jour des encombrants

6. On tira la chasse

7. ouvrit le robinet

8. et je recommence à zéro

9. gagner ma vie

10. puisque tu parles de sous

11. sous-vêtements

12. enfila

13. culotte

14. mit son soutien-gorge

15. écouter ce que j'ai à dire

Marshall stood outside the door, wondering[1] what he should do. He looked about his place[2], which consisted of a single room, not counting the bathroom. A small fridge, hot plate[3], and sink over in one corner, a bed, a couple of cushioned chairs he'd scored[4] on junk day[5] when people were putting things out on the street.

A toilet flushed[6], a tap ran[7], and then the door opened. Sarita stood in front of him, head down, and said, "I'm going to have to go home. I'm going to have to go back to Monclova."

"No, you're not going back to Mexico," he said, taking her into his arms again. "You've got a life here. You've got me."

"No, I have no life here. I go home, or I just disappear somewhere, get a job, start doing the whole thing all over again[8]." She sniffed. "I need to make a living[9]. I have people counting on me. I can make more money here."

"I can lend you some," he said. "Shit, I can give you some money. I don't have a lot, but I got two, three hundred I could give you."

Sarita laughed. "Seriously? How long would that last me?"

"I know, I know. It's not like I'm a fucking millionaire, you know? But now that you mention money[10], I was kind of thinking about something in the night."

She pushed past him and found her underwear[11] on the floor at the foot of the bed. She stepped into[12] her panties[13], then slipped on her bra[14] while Marshall stood and watched her.

"Whatever it is, I don't want to know," Sarita said.

"Come on, you have to at least hear me out[15]. It could be the answer to your problems. For *both* of us, really. If you need to get away, that's cool[1]; I get that[2]. But I could come with you."

"I don't know," she said. "I don't want to get you in trouble."

"Come on," he said. "We're in this together."

"No," Sarita said. "We're *not*. You haven't done anything wrong. Except for hiding me. When they find out you've been keeping me here, you could be in all kinds of trouble[3], and not just because I'm not supposed to be here."

She pulled on her jeans, then put on a blouse[4] and began to button it up. Marshall glanced around, saw his boxers[5] on the floor, and stepped into them. "I'm gonna call in sick[6]," he said. "We'll figure out something[7]."

He picked up a cell phone on his side of the bed. "Yeah, hey, Manny, I've got some kind of bug[8], been puking my guts up[9] all night. Can't afford to give something like that to the geezers[10]. Yeah, okay, thanks."

He put the phone back down.

"That's disrespectful," Sarita said. "They're nice old people."

"I don't mean anything by it[11]," he said. "Anyway, I don't have to go in[12]. So now we can talk about my idea."

She shook her head. "My only idea is to get as far away from here as fast as I can. Maybe you could drive me to Albany or something? And then I can catch a train."

"Where are you going to go?"

"New York? I got a cousin there. I just have to find her."

"Sit down," he said.

"I don't—"

"Just sit down and hear me out, okay?"

---

1. pas un problème
2. comprends

3. risques d'avoir un tas d'ennuis
4. chemisier

5. caleçon
6. me faire porter pâle
7. On va trouver une solution
8. virus
9. dégueulé
10. vioques

11. dis pas ça méchamment
12. aller bosser

She dropped onto the end of the bed and looked up at him. "What?"

"There's stuff this Gaynor guy isn't going to want to come out[1], right?"

"Maybe it's already out there[2]," she said.

"Yeah, but maybe it isn't. Maybe it's not going to come out. Maybe they'll pin his wife's murder on someone right away[3] and they won't find out about the other stuff[4]. You put in a call[5]; you tell him you can keep that from ever happening. For, you know, a price."

"That's the stupidest thing I've ever heard," Sarita said. "It's all going to come out."

"'Cause of what you did," Marshall said. "You shouldn't have done that."

"I *had*[6] to do it," she said.

"But maybe it won't matter. Maybe it won't come out."

"You're crazy," she said. "I have to get out of here. You think the police aren't looking for me? I guarantee it."

"You won't be easy to find. How do they trace you? You got no phone, no license, no credit cards. You've bailed[7] from your apartment. You're, like, totally off the grid[8]. It's like you don't even exist." He smiled, tickled[9] the underside of her chin with his index finger. She turned her head away. "Come on; it's like you're a spy[10] or something."

"I am no spy. I feed old people and babies and then clean up their piss and shit. That's what I do."

"Okay, okay," he said. "Listen, you hide out here[11] while I go empty out[12] what I got at the ATM[13]. You take it, get on a train to New York. But you have to promise you'll get in touch when you get there. I need to know you're okay. I love you.

---

1. des trucs que ce Gaynor va vouloir garder cachés

2. que ça se sait déjà

3. tout de suite

4. n'apprendront pas le reste

5. l'appelles

6. étais obligée

7. as quitté

8. as disparu de la circulation

9. chatouilla

10. comme si tu étais une espionne

11. reste planquée là

12. retirer

13. distributeur

282

You know that, right? I love you more than anything in the whole world."

Sarita was tearing up again[1]. She put her hands over her face.

"I can't get it out of my mind," she said.

Marshall hugged her again[2]. "I know, I know."

"Seeing Ms. Gaynor like that. It was so awful, how she looked."

"I'm tellin' ya," he said. "It's an opportunity. He's got money. Fancy house, nice car. Guy like that has to have[3] money. I mean, shit, you worked for them. You ever see financial statements[4], that kind of thing?"

She brought her hands down, thought a moment. "Sometimes," she said quietly. "But I never really looked at them. I didn't bring in the mail[5] or anything. I just helped with the house and the baby. Ms. Gaynor, she was so upset[6]. She thought having a baby would make her happy, but it just made it worse[7]."

"Yeah, well, raising kids is no joke[8]," Marshall said. "I think I'd get pretty depressed if I had to look after a baby."

Sarita shot him[9] a look.

"Unless it was with you," he said quickly.

"I think her husband knew all along[10] what was going on, but when Ms. Gaynor found out[11] …"

"You have to stop thinking about it," Marshall said. "You just have to move on, you know?"

"It's my fault," Sarita said. "If it hadn't been for me[12] she never would have started putting it together[13]."

"Yeah, but it doesn't mean it has anything to do[14] with what happened to her," Marshall said. "Unless[15] you think it was him. The husband."

1. refondait en larmes

2. la serra à nouveau dans ses bras

3. a forcément
4. des relevés bancaires

5. n'allais pas chercher le courrier
6. malheureuse
7. n'a fait qu'empirer les choses
8. c'est pas de la tarte

9. lui décocha

10. savait bien
11. a appris

12. Sans moi,
13. ne serait jamais doutée de rien
14. que ça ait un rapport
15. Sauf si

She shook her head. "He loved her. I mean, he was away a lot[1], and he hardly ever talked to me, but I think he loved her."

"Yeah, but sometimes, even people who were in love once[2], they do bad shit[3] to each other. All the more reason to give him a call, tell him what you know. He'll come across[4]; I guarantee it. You'll have enough money to get settled in someplace else[5], and have some left over[6] to send to your folks."

"No," she said firmly. "No."

He put up his hands. "Okay. You say no, then it's no."

"All I ever wanted to do," she whispered, "was the right thing. I'm not a bad person, you know?"

"Of course not."

"I've always tried to be good. But sometimes it doesn't matter what you do, it's wrong."

Marshall gave her a kiss on the forehead. "You wait here while I get you some money. And I'll pick up something to eat, too. Maybe an Egg McMuffin and some coffee."

Sarita said nothing as Marshall finished getting dressed. Before he left, he double-checked[7] that the slip[8] of paper where he'd written Bill Gaynor's phone number was still in his pocket.

---

1. souvent absent
2. qui se sont aimés
3. des sales coups
4. paiera
5. t'installer ailleurs
6. il t'en restera
7. revérifia
8. bout

THIRTY-FIVE

BARRY Duckworth was up at six.

He hadn't gotten in until nearly midnight. As he'd pulled into the drive he'd noticed a white van parked at the curb opposite his house, but didn't give it much thought[1]. He hadn't noticed the writing on the side.

He struggled up the stairs, stripped down to his boxers[2], and collapsed into bed next to Maureen. She mumbled[3], "Hmmm," and went back to sleep.

He was worried he'd lie awake all night. Haunted by the sight of that student with half his head blown off. Rosemary Gaynor on the autopsy table, the ghoulish[4] smile cut across her abdomen. Those three mannequins on the Ferris wheel.

Even those goddamned[5] squirrels.

But he didn't dream about any of those things. He went into a six-hour coma. He'd set his mental alarm for[6] six thirty a.m., but his eyes opened at five fifty-nine. He glanced over at the clock, decided it wasn't worth[7] trying to get back to sleep when he'd be getting up so soon. He swung his thick legs from under the covers, planted his feet on the carpeted[8] bedroom floor.

Maureen rolled over. "That was late last night."

1. ne s'en était guère préoccupé

2. s'était mis en caleçon

3. avait marmonné

4. macabre

5. satanés

6. s'était programmé pour un réveil à

7. que ça ne valait pas la peine

8. couvert de moquette

"Yeah," he said, rubbing his eyes, then reaching for his phone to see whether he had any messages. There was nothing that needed his immediate attention.

"I tried to wait up for you," she said.

"Why?"

"To celebrate."

"Huh?"

"Twenty years. On the job. I didn't forget."

Now, with light coming through the window, he saw two tall fluted glasses[1] on the dresser[2]. An ice bucket[3], a bottle of champagne. By now, the bucket would be full of water.

"I didn't see that when I came in," he said.

"My detective," Maureen said. "Nothing gets past you[4]."

"I'm sorry," he said.

"Shh," she said. "I should have said something[5]. But we can have a little celebration now."

She reached down[6] under the covers, found him.

When they were finished, he said, "I have to get moving."

Maureen threw back the rumpled sheets[7]. "Go. I'll put on the coffee."

He padded down[8] the hallway to the bathroom, reached into the shower and turned on the water, stuck in[9] his hand to test whether the hot water had traveled two floors up from the old heater[10] yet. He caught a brief glimpse of himself[11] in the mirror before stepping in[12].

It always depressed Duckworth to see himself naked. *What the hell happened?* How could Maureen enjoy making love with someone who looked the way he did? He hadn't been this heavy[13] when he was in college[14], and he was certainly

1. flûtes à champagne
2. la commode
3. seau à glace
4. ne t'échappe
5. J'aurais dû te prévenir
6. tendit le bras
7. draps froissés
8. descendit à petits pas
9. tendit
10. chaudière
11. aperçut son reflet
12. d'entrer dans la douche
13. aussi gros
14. à la fac

in better shape[1] when he joined the Promise Falls police. He blamed, in part, all those hours he sat in a cruiser as a uniformed officer. He hated that the cliché, at least where he was concerned[2], was true: Barry Duckworth liked to stop at doughnut shops. It wasn't just that he liked doughnuts, which he did, very much. It was a way of breaking the boredom[3]. You went in, you had a coffee, you ate a doughnut, you talked to the people behind the counter, took a seat and shot the breeze[4] with a few of the customers.

He liked to think of it at the time[5] as public relations.

And when he made[6] detective, well, it wasn't like the movies, where you were running down alleys and jumping over fences[7]. You spent your time talking to witnesses[8] and making notes and sitting at a desk and writing reports and phoning people.

Every year, he got just a little bit heavier.

And now, he figured, he was at least eighty pounds over[9] what he should be[10]. All these thoughts ran through his head[11] in the seconds before he stepped under the hot water. That, and one other thing.

The number 23.

Three times in one day that number had reared its head[12]. Twenty-three dead squirrels. The number on the Ferris wheel carriage holding the three painted mannequins. That student's hoodie.

Maybe it was nothing, he thought, as he soaped[13] his considerable belly. There were numbers surrounding us[14] all the time. There were probably numerical coincidences everywhere if you knew where to look[15]. License plates[16], dates of birth, home addresses, Social Security numbers.

1. en meilleure forme

2. dans son cas

3. rompre l'ennui

4. tapait la discute
5. à l'époque

6. était passé

7. des barrières
8. des témoins

9. dépassait d'au moins une trentaine de kilos
10. son poids normal
11. lui passèrent par la tête
12. s'était manifesté

13. savonnait
14. autour de nous
15. en cherchant bien
16. Plaques minéralogiques

And yet …

He'd keep his eyes open. Have that number in the back of his mind[1] as he continued with his investigation. Make that[2] *investigations*.

Now that Angus Carlson was going to be assisting[3], Duckworth hoped he could hand off some[4] of his workload. Assuming[5] Carlson would be starting in the detective division today, Duckworth was going to give him a list of things to look into[6]. Those strung-up squirrels for starters[7]. See if he thought they were so funny then. And Duckworth still wanted the other Thackeray College students, the three who'd been attacked before last night, interviewed. Maybe Joyce wasn't the only one who'd heard some very strange comments from Mason Helt. Finally, he wanted Carlson to go back out[8] to Five Mountains and find out who fired up[9] the Ferris wheel.

Duckworth could concentrate his efforts on the Rosemary Gaynor investigation, and finding the missing nanny, Sarita Gomez. The old guy who lived next door said she worked shifts[10] at a nursing home, but didn't know which one. There were several in the Promise Falls area, so it might be better to go to the station[11] and work the phones[12] than drive from facility[13] to facility.

He cranked the taps shut[14], reached for the towel[15], stepped out onto the mat[16]. He was holding the towel around his waist—there wasn't quite enough material[17] to allow him to tuck it into place[18]— and glanced out the bathroom window, which looked out onto[19] the street.

That white van from the night before[20] was still there. Even though the sun wasn't quite up yet[21], Barry could make out[22] the words written on the side.

Finley Springs Water.

He blinked[1] a couple of times to be sure he was reading that correctly. What the hell was Randall Finley's van doing parked out front of[2] his house? Was that actually the same van that had been there the night before?

Had Randy been waiting to talk to him last night and returned this morning?

He skipped shaving[3]. Duckworth ran his fingers through his hair, dressed hurriedly[4], not bothering with a tie[5], which he could do after breakfast, and followed the smell of brewing[6] coffee to the kitchen below.

"It's ready," Maureen said when he came into the room.

"What's Randall Finley doing here?"

"What?" she said.

"Finley, you know—first-class asshole, former mayor? That Finley?"

"I know who you mean. He's here?"

"His van's parked across the street. I think it's been there all night. Was he hiding under our bed?"

"You got me[7]. We've been having an affair for the last[8] six months."

Duckworth stared at her and waited.

Maureen smiled, let out a short laugh. "That's not Finley's van. I mean, yes, it belongs to his company[9], but Trevor's got it."

"Why would our son have Finley's van?"

"I'm sure it's not the only van Finley owns," Maureen said. "The man probably has a small fleet of them[10]. You could hardly[11] run a bottled-water company with just one van."

"That's not the question," Duckworth said, growing more impatient[12] with each passing second.

1. cilla

2. juste devant

3. ne prit pas le temps de se raser

4. à la hâte

5. sans mettre de cravate

6. frais

7. m'as eue

8. C'est mon amant depuis

9. entreprise

10. toute une série

11. difficilement

12. qui s'impatientait davantage

"Why is *our* son driving *that* man's truck?" He paused. "And why is it *here*?"

"Trevor paid me[1] a little surprise visit last night," Maureen said. "I mean, he was coming to visit both of us, but you ended up[2] working late. He's upstairs, asleep, although he'll probably be down any minute[3]. He has to be at work at seven thirty."

"Our son is working for Finley?"

Maureen nodded enthusiastically. "I know! Isn't it wonderful? He's been going through such a bad patch[4]. The breakup[5] with Trish, trying to find work. Now he's got this job and I think it's doing wonders for him[6]. I could see a real change in him. It's taken him forever[7] to move past losing that girl, and add to that being out of work, and—"

4. en a tellement
bavé récemment
5. rupture
6. lui fait un
bien fou
7. tellement
longtemps

"He can't work for that man," Duckworth said, taking a seat at the kitchen table.

"Now you're talking like a crazy person," his wife said, filling a cup with coffee and putting it in front of him. "Our son gets a job and you want him to quit[8]?"

"What's he doing for him?" he asked.

Maureen put a fist on her hip[9]. "You're the detective. There's a truck on the street, filled with cases of bottled water. Trevor has the key, which allows him to take this truck anywhere he pleases. I'll wait while you put it together[10]."

There was noise on the floor above them. Trevor's old bedroom, where he hadn't lived for a couple of years. He was getting up.

"He was sorry to have missed you last night," she said.

"I'll just bet he was[11]."

"But at least you get a chance to see him this morning." When Duckworth said nothing, she continued. "Don't you be negative about this. Don't go bursting his bubble[1]."

"I'm not going to be negative. I just want to know how he ended up working for that asshole."

"That's the spirit[2]," she said.

"He should go back to school, learn a trade[3]. Not drive a truck around for some blowhard[4]."

Trevor showed up a minute later, his hair suggestive of some sort of electrocution. He had on a pair of sweatpants[5] and a T-shirt. He gave his mother a kiss. "Thought I'd grab some breakfast[6] before I get dressed," he said to her. He looked at his father and smiled as he ran his[7] fingers through his hair.

"What's going on with you and Finley?" Duckworth asked.

"Good morning to you, too, Dad," he said.

"When'd you start working for him?"

"A week ago," he said.

"How'd that come about[8]?"

"I saw an ad[9] online. He was looking for drivers; I applied[10]; I got it. Is that a problem?"

"Your father and I are delighted," Maureen said. "Is it part-time, full-time?"

"Full-time," Trevor said. "It's not a ton of money, but it's better than what I was making before, which was a big fat zilch[11]."

"Does he know who you are?" his father asked.

"Uh, well, I filled out the application form[12] with my name on it, so I would say that yes, he knows who I am."

"That's not what I mean. Does he know you're my son?"

"*Our* son," Maureen said. "I don't remember you making him alone."

1. gâcher son plaisir

2. Bien, continue

3. métier

4. flambeur

5. pantalon de jogging

6. mangerais un truc

7. en se passant les

8. ça s'est fait

9. annonce

10. ai postulé

11. zéro

12. formulaire de candidature

"Shit, I don't know, probably," Trevor said. "I mean, he probably told me at some point[1] to say hello. So, hello."

Duckworth shook his head.

"I don't need this," Trevor said. "I'll get something on the way[2]."

"Trev," his mother said, but he didn't stop. Maureen looked at her husband and said, "You can be a real horse's ass[3] at times. It's not always about you[4]."

She set a bowl in front of him. He looked down at it.

"What is this?" he asked.

"That," she said, "is fruit."

When Barry heard the front door open and close, and looked out the window and saw Trevor Duckworth heading for the Finley Springs truck, he chased after him[5]. Trevor was about to close the door when Duckworth, winded[6], caught up.

"Hey," he said.

"What?" Trevor said.

"Just give me a second." He took four deep breaths, then said, "I'm sorry."

"Sure, whatever[7]."

"Listen to me. I'm glad you've got a job. It's great. We're glad to see you get something."

Trevor, perched on the edge of the driver's seat, said, "But?"

Duckworth couldn't help but[8] smile. "Yeah, there's always a *but*. Look, I'm not going to tell you to quit this job."

"Like I'd have to if you did[9]."

"Yeah, I get that. You're a grown man[10]. You don't have to do what your parents tell you. All I want to say is, watch your step around[11] Finley."

1. à un moment

2. en route

3. un vrai chieur
4. Tout ne tourne pas autour de toi

5. lui court après
6. essoufflé

7. peu importe

8. ne put réprimer un

9. Comme si tu pouvais m'obliger

10. adulte

11. méfie-toi de

"It's just a job, Dad. I'm delivering water."

"Sure, that's the job. But a guy like Finley … he always has an agenda[1]. I had a run-in[2] with him yesterday. He wanted something from me I wasn't prepared[3] to give."

"What?" Trevor asked.

"An advantage. He wanted to use me to further[4] his ambitions. Wanted me to snitch on[5] others in the department. And I can't help but wonder if he'd find an angle using you."

"I just drive, Dad."

"Okay. I've got one last thing I'll say, and then I'll shut up about it. Don't ever compromise yourself[6] with him. Keep your nose clean[7] and don't make mistakes. Because if he's got something on you, I promise you, sooner or later, that son of a bitch will use it."

Trevor's eyelid fluttered[8].

"What?" Duckworth asked.

"Nothing," Trevor said. "I hear ya[9]. I gotta go or I'm going to be late."

Duckworth stepped back, allowing Trevor to close the door. He started up the van, turned it around in their driveway, and took off up[10] the street.

1. arrière-pensée
2. des mots
3. disposé

4. servir
5. que je lui donne des infos sur

6. Ne te compromets jamais
7. les mains propres

8. La paupière de Trevor frémit

9. Message reçu

10. partit dans

THIRTY-SIX

David

1. passai voir
2. se lève

3. de chauffeur

I popped in to see[1] Ethan before he was out of bed[2], told him I had a lot of things to do today, and that he'd have to get himself to school. No ride[3].

"Okay," he said.

"You feel better?" I asked. It was meant as a general question. Did he feel better about Carl, after their meeting the night before? After showing him Dad's model railroad? And after getting the pocket watch back?

"My tummy's okay this morning," he said. So he'd taken the question more literally, but in a way, answered the question I thought I'd asked. If he wasn't feigning illness, and wasn't anxious about attending[4] school, then maybe he did feel better about things generally.

4. d'aller à

I hadn't planned to have breakfast, but Mom had already put a cup of coffee at my place at the table. I grabbed it without sitting down, took a sip[5], set it on the counter.

5. gorgée
6. se battait
7. et la tapait du doigt

"I have to go," I said. To Dad, who was struggling[6] as usual with the tablet, jabbing it[7] like he was Moe poking Curly's eyes out[1], I said, "Ethan can walk today. Scoot him out[2] in plenty of time[3] to get to school."

"Sure. He gonna have any more trouble with that boy?"

"I hope not."

Dad nodded. "That's good."

There was something different about him today. Actually, I'd noticed it first late yesterday. He was more pensive. When he'd put his arms around me in the garage and intimated[4] he wasn't the good man I'd always thought he was, I'd wondered[5] what he was beating himself up about[6]. Maybe it had something to do with Mom. I could tell something was going on with her[7]. That she was becoming more forgetful, that Dad was covering up[8] her mistakes. I could see that getting him down[9], but if Dad was being any less attentive, less supportive, the evidence wasn't there[10]. He seemed as devoted[11] to her as always.

"I saw that girl," Mom said, sitting down with her own coffee.

"What girl?"

"The one who came over last night with her boy. She seemed nice."

"You didn't even talk to her, Mom. I didn't even know you'd seen her."

"I was looking out the window," she said.

Ethan and I had to get out of this house[12].

"Yes, she seemed nice," I said. "But she's got plenty of baggage[13]."

"Who doesn't?" Mom asked. "You think we didn't have baggage when we met each other?"

Dad looked up from the tablet. "David doesn't need to take on another woman with a checkered past[14]," he said. "What did that detective say?"

1. comme dans un numéro des *Three Stooges* [artistes burlesques américains]

2. Poussez-le dehors

3. assez tôt

4. laissé entendre

5. m'étais demandé

6. ce qu'il avait à se reprocher

7. que quelque chose n'allait pas chez elle

8. masquait

9. comprenais que ça le déprime

10. ça ne se voyait pas

11. dévoué

12. Il était temps que nous déménagions, Ethan et moi

13. un sacré passif

14. au passé sulfureux

"What detective?" I asked. "What are you talking about?"

"In the books. There were a whole bunch of them[1]." Dad had read a lot of crime fiction over the years. "This one had 'money' in the title, I think. The detective says something like, 'Never go to bed with a girl who's got more troubles[2] than you do.' "

"Donald!" Mom said.

The thing was, Dad, or the detective he was quoting, was right. I didn't need more problems. I had something of a history[3] trying to rescue[4] damsels in distress and it had not gone well. Sam Worthington sounded like another one. An ex-husband serving time[5] for bank robbery and nasty in-laws[6] who wanted custody[7] of Carl.

That wasn't a checkered past. That was a shitstorm[8].

And despite that, I hadn't stopped thinking about Sam all night.

I needed to get her out of my head. I had more than enough to worry about. I had a new job working for Randall Finley, and was committed to[9] looking into Marla's situation, hoping I might find something that would help her.

I'd start with that.

"I really have to go," I said. I took one more sip of the coffee and poured[10] the rest into the sink.

When I opened the door, I nearly ran down[11] my aunt, but managed to stop short[12].

She was just about to ring the bell. "Aunt Agnes," I said.

"David," she said. "I apologize for coming by unannounced[13]."

"No, that's okay. Come in."

---

1. toute une série

2. de problèmes

3. eu tendance par le passé à
4. sauver

5. en prison
6. de méchants beaux-parents
7. la garde
8. la panade générale

9. m'étais engagé à

10. versai
11. faillis bousculer
12. de justesse

13. à l'improviste

As she stepped inside she said, "Your mother's been calling about Marla, and I thought I'd drop by and bring everyone up-to-date[1]."

I called into the house. "Mom! Agnes is here!"

I heard a chair scraping across[2] the floor. A second later Mom appeared and hobbled[3] toward her sister. Her leg was still hurting. The two of them threw their arms around each other. Despite my aunt's reputation for coldness, and the strain[4] that sometimes existed between her and my mother, I guessed that deep down[5], they still cared for each other[6]. Aunt Agnes just wasn't very good at showing it sometimes.

"How is she?" Mom asked. "How is Marla doing?"

"She's okay," Agnes said. "Hello, Don." Dad had made his way out[7] of the kitchen to see what was going on. "I know you've been phoning and I thought I'd just stop by and tell you she's probably going to come home today, although frankly, having her at the hospital is great, because I can wander up there[8] anytime I want to see her. But it's the wrong place for her. She needs to be home. Gill and I are going to spell each other[9] so there's always someone there."

"What about ..." Dad started to ask. "You know, the baby, and the woman ..."

Agnes smiled, clearly understanding what he was trying to ask, but didn't want to put into words. "The police are doing what they have to do, and we're doing what we have to do. I've got Natalie Bondurant on it."

"Do you really think Marla should be going home this soon[10]?" Mom asked. "I mean, considering[11] what she tried to do, wouldn't it be better—"

"I think I know what I'm doing where my own daughter is concerned," Agnes said.

---

1. vous tenir tous au courant
2. traverser en raclant
3. boitilla
4. tensions
5. au fond
6. s'aimaient quand même
7. était sorti
8. faire un saut
9. se relayer
10. aussi vite
11. quand on pense à

"Of course," Mom said. "Of course you do. All I'm saying is, if something did happen again, if there was another ... incident ... it might be better if she was already at the hospital and—"

"Arlene, *please*," Agnes said.

Mom said nothing, at least for a couple of beats[1]. I guessed she'd gotten the message. *Back off*[2].

"I know what you're thinking," Mom said. "You think I don't know anything."

"I didn't say that," Agnes said. "I'm just making the point[3] that Marla is my daughter, not yours, and I resent[4] that you would suggest that I don't have her best interests at heart."

"My God, I never said such a thing," Mom said. "You're putting words into my mouth[5]."

"For Christ's sake, stop it," Dad said. "Both of you. Arlene, your sister's going to know what's best for her own daughter."

Mom glared[6] at my father for what she surely saw as treason[7]. She took a second to compose herself[8], underwent[9] an emotional reboot[10], and said to Agnes, "I'm very sorry if you thought that was what I meant. Anything you need, you just ask. You know we think the world of[11] Marla and would do anything to help her." She reached out and took her sister's hand in hers. Agnes didn't do anything to stop her.

"Thank you," my aunt said, her voice still slightly frosty[12].

"And David's going to help, you know."

Agnes shot a smile at me that seemed genuine[13]. "I know. And I appreciate that. I truly do. Listen, I must get to the hospital, for more reasons than I can count[14]. David, I seem to have caught you as you were leaving. I'll head out[15] with you."

Marginal glossary:

1. deux secondes
2. T'en mêle pas
3. te rappelle seulement
4. prends mal
5. me fais dire ce que je n'ai pas dit
6. jeta un regard noir
7. une trahison
8. se maîtriser
9. effectua
10. redémarrage
11. avons énormément d'affection pour
12. glacée
13. sincère
14. tout un tas de raisons
15. repars

Agnes allowed Mom to give her a half hug and kiss, and Dad offered the same gesture. Heading down the steps, she said to me, "I'm glad I caught you."

"Yeah," I said. "This is good."

"I know the kind of signals I send off[1]. That I don't need anyone's help. That I know everything. That I'm too proud to accept assistance[2]." Maybe she was waiting for me to contradict her. When I didn't, she smiled. "I know yesterday, when I found you and Marla at the Gaynors' house, I may not have seemed very appreciative of what you'd done. Trying to get to the bottom of things[3]. And for that I apologize."

"It was a stressful time," I offered.

"Indeed." We had reached her car, a silver Infiniti sedan. "But I have to put my ego aside[4]. This is about Marla. I know she may not always speak highly of me[5], but she's the most important thing in the world to me, and all I want is for her to get through this[6]."

She placed a hand on my wrist, and I could feel it tremble.

"She's my baby," she said. "My one and only[7]. I'll do anything to help her with this." Agnes kept a grip on my wrist. "I have one request, however."

Slowly, I said, "Okay."

"This is very difficult for me." She swallowed[8], looked up the street for a second to avoid eye contact[9]. "It's about your uncle Gill."

"What about him?"

"What I would ask is, anything you might learn about Gill, would you be discreet?"

"What are we talking about here, Agnes?"

She released her grip, managed to look me in the eye. "Your uncle and I have ... we've had some

---

1. quelle impression je donne

2. de l'aide

3. comprendre ce qui se passait

4. de côté

5. ne dit pas que du bien de moi

6. qu'elle s'en sorte

7. seul et unique enfant

8. avala sa salive

9. mon regard

1. problèmes
2. prends ta mère de haut

issues[1]. I know sometimes I lord it over your mother[2] about how I chose a career and she chose to make her career in the home ... and I'm sorry about that. I know there are times you must all think I'm a total ..."

Agnes almost smiled. "I was about to say control freak, but I can't help but wonder[3] what word you thought I was going to say."

3. m'empêcher de me demander
4. n'avais aucune intention
5. de le lui dire
6. quels qu'aient été mes succès
7. me bat à plate couture

I wasn't about[4] to share[5].

"Anyway, what I'm saying is, for all I may have achieved[6] in the working world, your mother has it all over me[7] in the marriage department. What I'd give for a man like Don. Someone who's there for you, who you can trust."

"What are you trying to say, Agnes?"

"I don't know any other way to say this." She let out[8] a long breath. "Gill doesn't always come home at night, if you get my understanding. And when you start asking questions, maybe someone's going to tell you that. If they do, I'd be grateful[9] if you could keep it to yourself."

8. poussa

9. reconnaissante

"Whatever's going on between you and Gill is none of my business," I said. "I'm sorry you two are having problems."

She grimaced. "It is what it is. Let me know what you find out[10]. Not just about Gill, but anything else. Good or bad. I'm wondering whether I need to hire[11] a private detective for this. That's not to diminish what you'll be able to do, but if you think I need to bring someone else in[12], you tell me."

10. apprendras

11. engager

12. associer quelqu'un d'autre

"I will. There is something I'd like to ask you right now." Agnes blinked[13], surprised, maybe, that I was already at this stage[14].

13. sourcilla
14. que j'en sois déjà là

"Go ahead."

"Tell me about Dr. Sturgess," I said.

"Jack?" Agnes said. "What about him[1]?"

"I just … What's your take[2] on him?"

Agnes shrugged. "On a personal level, he's been our GP[3] for years. For the last ten, I think. And professionally, I have the utmost confidence[4] in him. He's on the board at[5] the hospital. He's someone whose opinion I value[6] in a number of areas." She eyed me with concern[7]. "This is about what happened when Marla was having the baby."

"Well—"

"David, I was *there*. That man—that man and I—did everything we could to save that baby. It was the worst moment of my entire life, let me tell you. There's not a minute of any day since then that I haven't thought about what happened. If there's anyone to blame for what happened, it's me. I should never have insisted Marla give birth anywhere but[8] the hospital. We were in the midst of[9] that outbreak[10] and—"

"I'm not talking about that," I said.

She was taken aback[11]. "What, then?"

"At the hospital last night, when I said I was going to help Marla by asking around, he tried to talk me out of it[12]. Belittled[13] the effort."

"He had no business doing that[14]," Agnes said. "Why would he try to stop you?"

"I don't know. There's another thing."

Agnes waited.

"He's also the GP for the Gaynor family."

Agnes's mouth opened half an inch in what clearly looked like astonishment[15]. "Are you sure about that?"

I nodded. "He told me. He was cautioning me against[16] talking to Bill Gaynor. Said the man wouldn't be up to it[17]. So he must have known Rosemary Gaynor. Has he mentioned that to you?"

---

1. Que veux-tu savoir
2. avis
3. médecin traitant
4. une confiance absolue
5. au conseil d'administration de
6. dont je respecte l'opinion
7. inquiétude
8. ailleurs qu'à
9. en plein dans
10. épidémie
11. prise de court
12. m'en dissuader
13. Minimisé
14. n'avait pas à faire ça
15. semblait de la stupéfaction
16. me déconseillait de
17. n'en aurait pas la force

"I don't … I'm not sure."

"You'd think[1], in the last twenty-four hours, that it might have come up[2]," I said.

Agnes considered this. "You would, wouldn't you?"

"Yeah. Regardless of what[3] Marla did or didn't do, there has to be some kind of connection[4] between her and the Gaynors. There may be several out there[5] we don't know about, but one that we know for certain is, their family doctor is Jack Sturgess."

"Thank you for this, David," she said quietly. "Thank you very much." Her face hardened[6]. "If that son of a bitch has been anything less than honest[7] with me, I'll haul him[8] into the operating room and cut his nuts off[9] myself."

1. Il paraîtrait normal
2. vienne sur le tapis
3. Quoi que
4. un lien
5. plusieurs autres
6. se durcit
7. a manqué d'honnêteté
8. le traînerai
9. lui couperai les couilles

THIRTY-SEVEN

MARSHALL did not go to the ATM for money[1] for Sarita Gomez.

Once he was a few blocks from his home, he pulled into the lot[2] of a McDonald's and got out his phone. He entered a number, put the phone to his ear, and waited.

There were four rings. Then a pickup[3].

"Hello?"

"Is this Mr. Gaynor?"

"Who is this? If you're some goddamn reporter I have nothing to say."

"Is this Bill Gaynor or not? Because I'm telling you right now, you better not fuck around with me. Because if you do, you're going to be pretty goddamn sorry[4]."

Dead air[5]. Then: "Yes, this is Bill Gaynor."

"That's good. Now we're starting off on a good foot here[6]."

"Who is this?" Gaynor asked. "Tell me who this is or I'm hanging up right now[7]."

"Now we're starting off bad again. I'm going to talk, and you're going to listen. Okay? Trust me; it's in your interests."

"What do you want?"

---

1. tirer de l'argent au distributeur

2. se gara sur le parking

3. on décrocha

4. vraiment le regretter

5. Silence

6. on repart du bon pied

7. raccroche immédiatement

"What do I want? I want to do you a favor[1], that's what I want. I'm trying to be a good citizen here by keeping quiet about[2] things I know. Things that if they came out[3] could cause you a fucking boatload of trouble[4]."

"I don't have any idea what you're talking about," Gaynor said, but his voice lacked confidence[5].

"Oh, I think you do."

"Look, I don't know what kind of crazy shakedown[6] you're trying to pull, but it's not going to work. I don't know who you are, so fuck you. Something horrible happens to someone, and every nut comes out of the woodwork[7]. Jesus, what the hell's wrong with people[8]? For God's sake, I've just lost my wife. Have you no sense of decency?"

Marshall pressed on[9]. "I'm trying to do the decent thing here, Mr. Gaynor, if you'd only shut up and listen. And yeah, I know about your wife. And I'm betting you know a lot more than you're letting on[10]. Am I right? I'm guessing there's a whole lot[11] you haven't mentioned to the cops about your perfect little family. The sort of thing I could mention if I wanted to."

The other end of the line went quiet[12]. Marshall figured Gaynor was thinking it through[13]. Finally the man said, "What is it you want?"

"Fifty thousand."

"What?"

"You heard me. Fifty thousand dollars. You get that to me, and I won't breathe a word about what I know."

"I don't have that kind of money."

"Give me a break.[14] Guy like you? Nice house? Flashy car?" The truth was, Marshall had no idea what kind of car Bill Gaynor drove, but he was betting it was a nice one. A whole lot nicer than his shitbox van[1], that was for sure.

"I'm telling you, I don't have fifty thousand just lying around[2]," Gaynor insisted. "You think I keep that kind of money under my mattress?"

"What if I gave you till noon to get it? Would that help?"

"Goddamn it, who are you?"

"You already asked me that."

"Does this have something to do with Sarita?" Gaynor asked. "Did she put you up to[3] this? Are you working with her?"

Marshall found that more than a little troubling, that the man put it together that fast[4]. But it made sense. How many people other than Sarita could know what was really going on in the Gaynor household[5]?

Marshall told himself to stay cool[6]. He could do this. He could squeeze enough money out of[7] this guy to give Sarita a fresh start somewhere else. In fact, if he could really get fifty thou[8] out of the guy, it would be enough for both of them. They could run off[9] together. They could both kiss their shit-ass jobs good-bye[10]. Fifty grand[11], that would be more than enough to set themselves up somewhere else. More than enough to stay off society's radar[12] for months.

"I don't know who this Sarita person is and I don't care," Marshall said. "You pay up, or you're fucked. I make an anonymous call to the cops. If that's what you want, I can do it."

"Okay, okay, let me think," Gaynor said. "I can probably raise most of it. I'd have to cash in some investments[13], go to the bank when they open[14]."

1. camionnette merdique
2. qui traînent
3. a demandé de faire
4. ait pigé si vite
5. chez les Gaynor
6. garder la tête froide
7. faire cracher assez de tune à
8. [thousand]
9. partir
10. dire adieu à leurs boulots merdiques
11. briques
12. planqués
13. toucher des placements
14. à l'ouverture

"You do what you have to do," Marshall said. "Bank opens at what? Ten? So you should have the money by eleven?"

"I'm going to have to call you back."

Marshall was about to say, *Yeah, right, like I'm going to give you my number*, then realized Gaynor would already have it on his phone now. "Okay," he agreed. "If I don't hear from you by ten thirty, I call the cops."

1. vous rappelle

"I get it. I'll be in touch[1]."

Gaynor ended the call. Marshall smiled to himself. This was going to work. He was sure this was going to work.

2. fâchée contre

Sarita, she'd be upset with[2] him at first when she found out what he'd done. But when she realized it was enough for them to have a life together, she'd come around[3]. He knew it.

3. changerait d'avis

Love would conquer[4] all.

4. aurait raison de

THIRTY-EIGHT

David

I decided Davidson Place would be my first stop.

The nursing home[1] was on the west side of Promise Falls. A low-rise building in that netherworld[2] between the suburbs[3] and industrial land. I remembered from when I was a reporter how neighbors banded together[4] to fight just about anything[5] they believed would impact[6] the quality of their domesticity[7]. Group homes[8] for mentally challenged[9] kids. Halfway houses[10]. Shopping malls. Homes too big for the lot[11].

But for the life of me[12], I had a hard time[13] getting my head around[14] why someone would object to[15] a nursing home in their community. Were they worried about being kept awake at night by the sounds of shuffling feet[16]?

I parked in the visitors' lot and looked for reception. That took me to the lobby[17], where I saw several old souls[18] sitting in wheelchairs[19], fast asleep[20]. A woman behind the counter asked whether she could help me, and I said I was looking for Sarita.

"Sarita Gomez?" she asked.

1. maison de retraite

2. zone mal définie

3. banlieues pavillonnaires

4. faisaient front

5. pratiquement tout

6. mettrait à mal

7. vie quotidienne

8. Centres d'hébergement

9. handicapés mentaux

10. Centres de réinsertion

11. quartier

12. j'avais beau essayer

13. bien du mal

14. à comprendre

15. s'opposerait à

16. des bruits de pas traînants

17. hall d'entrée

18. vieilles personnes

19. fauteuils roulants

20. profondément endormis

I didn't know, but I said, "Yes."

"I haven't seen her today, but I can check whether she's in[1]. Can I ask what it's concerning[2]?"

That was when it occurred to me[3] that the police had not already been here. If Barry Duckworth had been asking for[4] Sarita, it would be all over the building[5]. Was it possible I had the jump[6] on him? The Gaynors' elderly neighbor had said something about not being able to remember the name of this place when he'd been talking to the police.

"It's a personal matter," I said, then added, in an attempt[7] to make my inquiry sound work related[8], "It has to do with someone's care[9]."

The woman figured out[10] I was telling her it was none of her business[11]. She picked up the phone, entered an extension[12], and said, "Gail, you seen Sarita around? Okay, uh-huh, got it."

She hung up[13] and looked at me. "Sarita didn't come in for her shift yesterday and she's not in today. I'm sorry."

"Did she call in sick?" I asked.

The woman shrugged. "Probably. I didn't get the details."

"Would I be able to talk to her supervisor[14]?" I leaned over the counter and said in a voice just above a whisper, "It's very important. It's the kind of thing I think Davidson Place would like to sort out quietly[15]."

The woman could read into that whatever[16] she wanted. Maybe I had a loved one[17] here. Maybe I had a complaint about the care of my ailing[18] grandmother. Maybe there was a theft allegation[19].

"What's your name?" she asked. I told her. "Just a minute." She picked up the phone again. I turned away, only half listening. Then she said to

---

1. si elle est là

2. C'est à quel sujet

3. je me rendis compte

4. avait demandé à voir

5. tout le bâtiment en parlerait

6. un cran d'avance

7. pour tenter

8. donner à ma question un caractère professionnel

9. quelqu'un dont elle s'occupe

10. comprit

11. que ça ne la regardait pas

12. composa un numéro de poste

13. raccrocha

14. responsable

15. régler discrètement

16. interpréter ça comme

17. être cher

18. souffrante

19. accusation de vol

me, "Mrs. Delaney will be down to see you short-ly[1], Mr. Harwood. Have a seat over there."

I dropped into a nearby vinyl chair. Across from me[2] sat a man who I guessed was in his late eighties or early nineties, dressed in a shirt and pants[3] that he'd probably acquired when he was forty pounds heavier[4]. His neck stuck out[5] of the collar like a flagpole[6] in a golf-green hole[7]. He was holding an Ed McBain paperback mystery[8], open to about the midpoint[9], staring at the page, and in the five minutes I waited for Mrs. Delaney to show up, I never saw his eyes move once, and the page was never turned.

"Mr. Harwood?"

I glanced up[10]. "Yes. Mrs. Delaney?"

She nodded. "You were asking about Sarita Gomez?"

"I was hoping to speak with her," I said, standing.

"I'd like to speak with her myself," the woman said. "I'm afraid she isn't here, and attempts to reach her[11] have been unsuccessful."

"Oh," I said. "She hasn't shown up for work?"

"May I ask what this is concerning? Do you have someone here at Davidson?"

"I don't. This concerns work Sarita does outside of this facility."

"Then why are you asking me about it?"

"I'm trying to locate her. I thought, since she works here, I might be able to talk to her, ask her a few questions."

"I'm afraid I can't help you," Mrs. Delaney said. "Sarita did not show up this morning. She's a good worker[12], and the residents here like her very much, but as I'm sure you can imagine, some kinds of employees are more reliable[13] than others."

"I'm sorry?"

1. sous peu

2. En face de moi

3. pantalon

4. faisait 20 kg de plus

5. dépassait

6. petit drapeau

7. trou de terrain de golf

8. polar de poche

9. environ à la moitié

10. levai les yeux

11. la joindre

12. employée

13. fiables

1. s'interrompit

2. tentai ma chance
3. sans papiers

4. ce que vous lui voulez
5. frapper un grand coup
6. vous dit quelque chose
7. infos

8. ils ne devraient pas tarder

9. sèchement
10. pour le compte d'une des parties

"That fact that she's—" The woman cut herself off[1].

"The fact that she's what?" I thought, then took a shot[2]. "Undocumented[3]? Is Sarita working here illegally?"

"I'm sure that's not the case," Mrs. Delaney said.

"Do you have an address for her?" I asked.

"Just a number where she can be reached. I spoke to the person at that number and she tells me Sarita's gone away. I couldn't tell you whether she'll be coming back or not. And you still haven't told me what business you have with her[4]."

Time to hit her between the eyes[5]. "She worked as a nanny for the Gaynors. That name mean anything to you[6]?"

Mrs. Delaney shook her head. "Should it?"

"Did you watch the news[7] last night? That woman who was fatally stabbed in her home over on Breckonwood?"

A flash of recognition. She had heard the story.

"That was horrible. But what does it have to do with Sarita?"

"She was their nanny."

Her hands flew to her mouth. "Oh, my God," she said.

"I'm surprised the police haven't been here already, but I think you should be expecting them[8]."

"This is unimaginable. Are you saying Sarita had something to do with that?"

I hesitated. "I'm saying she may know something about it."

"Who are you, if you're not with the police?" she asked pointedly[9].

"I'm investigating on behalf of an interested party[10]," I said, which was as artful a dodge as

310

I could think of on the spot[1]. "When was the last time you saw her?"

"It would have been yesterday morning sometime, I think. She probably had the six-to-one shift[2]. She does four shifts a week here, mostly early mornings. I don't know about these other people she works for, but I think she works there before she comes here. And she can work any shift[3] on weekends. This is terrible. She couldn't have had anything to do with this. Everyone likes Sarita."

"You say you tried to call her?"

"She doesn't have a phone. I called her landlady. She said she's taken off[4]." She leaned in[5]. "That sounds bad, doesn't it?"

"Does she have friends here? Anyone who might know where I might be able to find her?"

She went mute[6]. I knew she'd thought of someone instantly, but was debating whether to tell me. Finally she said, "There's someone here I think she's been seeing[7]. You know, in a relationship[8]."

"Who?"

"Marshall Kemper. He's one of our custodians[9]."

"I need to talk to him."

She hesitated. "Follow me."

She led me out of the lobby, down a hallway, then down a flight of stairs to the basement[10], and then through another hallway of pipes and ductwork[11] and the industrial sounds of air conditioners[12] and pumps. When she got to a door marked OPERATIONS MANAGER, she knocked, and a second later a short, stout[13] black man answered.

"Yeah?"

"Manny," Mrs. Delaney said, "we're looking for Marshall. Where would he be this time of day?"

1. l'esquive la plus futée qui me vînt à l'esprit

2. a dû travailler de 6 h à 13 h

3. à n'importe quelle heure

4. est partie

5. se pencha vers moi

6. se tut

7. qu'elle fréquente

8. avec qui elle a une liaison

9. concierges [et agents d'entretien]

10. sous-sol

11. tuyaux et canalisations

12. climatiseurs

13. trapu

"Normally he'd be getting the trash pickup ready[1], but this turns out not to be a normal day. Marshall phoned in sick a while ago."

Mrs. Delaney looked at me.

"I need an address," I said.

THIRTY-NINE

"THERE'S a problem," Bill Gaynor said, speaking into the kitchen phone while Matthew, in his high chair, stuffed[1] dry Cheerios[2] into his mouth.

"What kind of problem?" Dr. Jack Sturgess said.

"I got a call. Someone wanting money. Blackmail[3]. The guy was a goddamn blackmailer."

Gaynor turned his back to his son and kept his voice down[4]. He didn't want Matthew to hear foul language[5]. He worried the kid would be spouting expletives[6] before he could say "Daddy." A word, Gaynor thought sadly, his son was likely to utter[7] before "Mommy."

"Who was it?"

"It's not like he said, 'Hi, I'm Joe Smith, your neighborhood extortionist[8].' He didn't identify himself[9]. But he must be someone who knows Sarita."

"Why?" Sturgess asked.

"I've been thinking about this. Rose had been funny[10] these last few weeks. I think she knew the truth somehow. I think it was weighing on her[11]. I can't say for sure, but it was little things she said, the way she was acting[12]. And I've been trying to figure out, if she did know, who might she have

1. fourrait

2. [céréales pour enfants]

3. Du chantage

4. parlait à voix basse

5. des gros mots

6. ne débite des insanités

7. prononcerait sans doute

8. l'extorqueur du quartier

9. ne s'est pas présenté

10. bizarre

11. la contrariait

12. comment elle se comportait

313

found out from[1]? Who might have helped her put it together?"

"Sarita?" the doctor said.

"Yeah. I'm wondering if she could have been in a position[2] to know something."

Sturgess thought about that. "It's possible."

"It would explain a lot. The way things have gone down[3]. This guy who called me, it sounds like maybe he's got it figured out[4]."

"What's he want?" Sturgess asked.

"Fifty thousand."

"Jesus."

"I haven't got it," Gaynor said. "After I came up with[5] a hundred grand for you, I've got nothing left. I'm going to have to put Rose's funeral on my line of credit[6]."

"Let me think," Sturgess said.

"Give me half of what I paid you," Gaynor said. "A loan[7]. I'll pay it back. There'll be insurance money coming in."

"Rosemary's million-dollar policy[8]," the doctor said. "Clearly your blackmailer doesn't know about that or he'd be asking for a lot more than fifty thousand."

"So you know I'll be able to reimburse you once my company makes good on the policy[9]. So help me now with the fifty."

"That's … going to be difficult," Sturgess said. "I don't have it to give[10]."

"What the fuck are you talking about?" Gaynor said, whispering angrily, glancing back[11] at Matthew to make sure he wasn't choking on[12] a Cheerio. "How could someone blow through[13] a hundred thousand dollars that fast[14]?"

"My financial needs are none of your business[15], Bill. Sounds to me like if anyone is to blame here,

---

1. par qui elle aurait pu l'apprendre

2. en mesure

3. se sont passées
4. est au courant

5. Depuis que j'ai sorti
6. marge de crédit

7. emprunt

8. assurance

9. m'aura réglé la prime prévue dans le contrat
10. ne les ai plus
11. en jetant un coup d'œil par-dessus son épaule
12. ne s'étouffait pas avec
13. claquer
14. aussi vite
15. ne vous regardent pas

it's at your end[1]. You need to fix this[2], and you need to fix it fast."

"I'm telling you I don't have the money. Maybe I should just not pay him, let him say whatever the hell he wants to say, to whoever he wants to tell it to. The police'd be pretty goddamn interested."

"Don't joke, Bill."

"Who said I'm joking? If this gets out, all I have to say is I knew nothing about it. Not at the time[3]. That I thought everything was aboveboard[4]. You know who they'll come after[5]? You, that's who. Is it the gambling[6], Jack? Is that where the money went? Did even a dime[7] of that money go to where you said it was going to go? You kept it all, didn't you, to pay off[8] your debts? How do you think that'll look[9] when it comes out? What you did for the money, and what you did with it when you got it?"

"Just shut up!" Sturgess said. "I'm trying to work this out[10]."

"You'd better work it out fast. The call is set for ten thirty. I'm supposed to be at the bank when it opens. And what if when I get there the accounts are frozen[11] or something, because of Rose's death? Then there won't be a damn thing I can do about this."

"Tell him you have the money," the doctor said. "When he calls you, tell him you've got it."

"But I won't."

"That's okay. This guy, do you think he knows you to see you[12]?"

"How would I know that?"

"You didn't recognize the voice?"

"I'm telling you[13], Jack, I don't know who it is."

1. vous
2. régler ça

3. à l'époque
4. officiel
5. iront chercher
6. tes dettes de jeu
7. centime
8. liquider
9. De quoi ça aura l'air à ton avis

10. trouver une solution

11. bloqués

12. te connaît de vue

13. Puisque je te le dis

"We have to assume[1] he knows what you look like, so you're going to have to be the one who meets him. Has he said where he wants to meet?"

"No. He'll probably do that when we talk at ten thirty."

"We need to think about that. We need to know how he wants to do the handoff[2]. It needs to be in a very public—no, not a public place. Not a place with cameras. Someplace isolated. That'd be better. Soon as you know what he wants to do, you call me. Don't commit to anything[3]. Tell him you've got the funeral home[4] on the other line and you have to deal with it; you'll call him back. Then we'll talk, figure out how we're going to do this."

"What are you talking about, Jack?" Gaynor asked. "What are you going to do?"

"You won't pay him, but you'll make him think he's going to be paid."

"What? A briefcase[5] full of cut-up paper? I'm not fucking James Bond, Jack. And what about Matthew? I'm supposed to bring along a baby to pay off a blackmailer?"

"Get a grip[6], Bill. Listen to me. There's two things we have to do. One, we have to shut this asshole down[7], make it clear to him that he can't pull something like this[8]. And two, we have to find out[9] how he knows what he knows." The doctor paused. "If he found this out from Sarita, then we have to find her."

"The police have to be[10] looking for her," Gaynor said. "I'm betting she's gone to ground[11]. She's in hiding."

"But the police still might find her," Sturgess said. "We need to find her first."

FORTY

AGNES Pickens, breezing into[1] the administrative offices of Promise Falls General, shouted into the office of her assistant, Carol Osgoode, as she strode down the hall to her own[2].

"Yes, Ms. Pickens?" Carol said, getting out from behind her computer and running to the door.

"In my office!" Agnes said.

Agnes was already seated behind her desk, her eyes on the doorway[3] as Carol appeared. She wasn't out of her twenties[4], this girl, and there were times when Agnes wondered whether she needed someone older to assist her, but what Carol lacked in life experience[5] she more than made up in[6] dedication[7]. She did what she was told[8], and she did it quickly.

"What happened after I left yesterday?" Agnes asked, her chin angled slightly up[9] so she could look Carol, whom she had not invited to take a seat, directly in the eye.

"At the board meeting?"

"Yes, of course the board meeting. Did anything happen?"

"Everyone just left. I mean, you were running[10] the meeting, and so they all went off and did whatever it is they do," Carol said.

---

1. débarquant avec assurance dans

2. en passant à pas vifs dans le couloir vers son propre bureau

3. seuil

4. n'avait pas trente ans

5. la grande jeunesse de Carol

6. était largement compensée par son

7. dévouement

8. ce qu'on lui disait

9. légèrement levé

10. dirigiez

Agnes nodded. "That's exactly what I wanted to hear. I was worried they might have tried to carry on without me[1]."

Carol shook her head. "I don't think anyone would dare[2]," she said.

Agnes's eyes narrowed. "What do you mean by that?"

Carol looked panicked. "I didn't mean anything negative. It's just … everyone knows you're in charge[3] here, and no one would try to do anything without your knowledge[4]. I told them I figured you would want to reschedule[5] as soon as possible, but of course, that was before anyone had any idea what sorts of things you were dealing with."

"I suppose my troubles are the talk of the place[6]," Agnes said.

"Everyone's concerned[7]," Carol said. "For you and Marla. And I just … I just can't …"

"Carol?"

Agnes's assistant put her hands over her face and began to weep[8].

"Good heavens, Carol?"

"I'm sorry," she said. "I'm really sorry. I'll go now and—"

Agnes came around the desk, put her arm around the woman's shoulder, and steered her[9] into a leather chair. "Let me get you a tissue[10]," she said, and snatched several[11] from a box on a shelf[12] behind her desk. She handed them[13] to Carol, who dabbed her[14] eyes and then blew her nose[15]. She wadded[16] the tissue into a ball and surrounded it with her hands.

"What's going on, Carol?"

"Nothing, nothing," she said. "I just feel … I feel so terrible for you and what you're going through.

318

---

1. continuer sans moi
2. oserait
3. aux commandes
4. à votre insu
5. fixer une nouvelle date
6. ont fait le tour de l'hôpital
7. inquiet
8. pleurer
9. la mena
10. mouchoir [en papier]
11. en tira plusieurs
12. étagère
13. les tendit
14. se tapota les
15. se moucha
16. roula

I mean, I know there's no end of tragedies[1] in this building every day, but when something happens to someone you know, someone you work for ..."

"It's okay," Agnes said.

"You're dealing with it so well, and I really admire that. I just don't know how you do it."

Agnes pulled over another chair so she could sit knee-to-knee with her assistant. "Believe me, Carol, inside, I'm a basket case[2]." She put a hand on Carol's knee. "I can't believe you'd be this upset[3] about something happening to me."

Carol looked at her with red eyes. "Why would you say that?"

"Because, my dear, I can be a first-class bitch[4]." Agnes smiled. "In case you hadn't noticed."

Carol allowed herself a short laugh that sounded more like a clearing of the throat[5]. "I wouldn't say that."

"Not to my face, you wouldn't," Agnes said. "I know what I am, I know how I come across[6]. You can't run[7] a place like this and be a nice person. And when you're a woman you have to be even tougher[8], and you can't worry about what they think of you[9]. But it doesn't mean you don't feel, or that you're not hurting inside."

"I know."

"You take a lot of abuse[10] from me and you keep on going[11], and I respect that about you. And I'm touched that you'd be so worried about my situation. But you don't have to worry about me. I'll sort things out. We'll get through this[12]. Gill and I and Marla, we'll do whatever it takes. That's the way I've always been. Maybe sometimes I come across like I don't care[13], but that's not true."

Carol nodded.

1. ce ne sont pas les tragédies qui manquent

2. dans tous mes états

3. aussi secouée

4. vraie garce

5. raclement de gorge

6. pour quoi je passe

7. diriger

8. encore plus dure

9. comment on est perçue

10. en vois de toutes les couleurs

11. t'accroches

12. allons nous en sortir

13. passe pour indifférente

"Are you going to be okay?" Agnes asked. "Do you want to take the day[1]?"

She shook her head violently. "No, I'm certainly not going to leave you, not when you have this much to deal with[2]. I mean, how would it look[3]? *You* can come to work, but *I* have to go home?"

Agnes patted her[4] hand. "Okay, then. I want you to reschedule that board meeting for tomorrow, first thing[5]. And let everyone know[6] there's a chance I might have to cancel again. My—our—situation is a bit unpredictable[7] at the moment."

"Of course."

"And now I'm going to go up and see how Marla is doing. I think I'll have her sent home today."

"I couldn't believe it when I heard."

"Well, everything about this is pretty unbelievable. Gill's going to take some time off[8], or at least conduct all his business from the house, so there'll be someone there with Marla at all times. He's there now. We'll spell each other."

"That sounds like a good idea," Carol said. She stood. "Thank you for this. And there's just one other thing I'd like to say."

"Okay," Agnes said, and waited.

"I just know Marla didn't do anything bad."

"Well, that's nice of you, Carol."

"I've met her lots of times, and I don't think she has a mean bone in her body[9]. She's a good person."

Agnes smiled. "Let everyone know about the rescheduled meeting. I'll be back in a while."

Agnes left her office, heading for the elevators[10]. Carol returned to her own desk, tossed her tissue into the wastebasket[11] tucked[12] under it, then took a small makeup mirror from her purse[13] to make sure she looked presentable. When she was finished with that, she took out her cell phone. She found the number she was looking for, then put the phone to her ear and listened to the rings[1].

After five, someone picked up.

Carol said, "Hey, it's me. ... I just had the most amazing conversation with, you know, my *boss*. ... She was so nice to me. I've been a total wreck about[2] what's going on, and I kind of lost it[3] and she was really comforting. I've never really seen her like that before. ... Yeah, kind of weird ... And it got me thinking[4] about us, you know, that maybe it's time to, you know. I mean, there's just no future. ... I know, I know. ... I just don't think I can keep[5] doing this. ... I kind of figured you'd be thinking along the same lines[6]. ... I know. ... I hear ya[7]. ... Look, I have to go; there's a lot going on here. ... Don't say that. ... You're going to make me cry. ... I love you, too, Gill."

1. sonneries

2. complètement foutue en l'air par

3. ai un peu craqué

4. m'a fait penser

5. continuer à

6. la même chose

7. suis d'accord

FORTY-ONE

WALDEN Fisher ended up taking Victor Rooney back to his house after escorting the man out of that bar. Walden wasn't certain that, if he'd dropped Victor off at his own house[1], he wouldn't just head back out[2] and get himself into more trouble.

So he put Victor in the spare room[3], the one that had once been his daughter Olivia's bedroom, and where, Walden suspected, Victor had probably slept on more than one occasion when he was seeing Olivia, when Walden and his wife had been out to dinner[4] or out of town[5].

It was a long time since anything like that had bothered[6] Walden. Back then, he'd suspected his daughter and Victor were having sex[7], and he couldn't say he was happy about it at the time, but he and Beth had been young once, too, and it wasn't as if they'd waited for their wedding night[8].

You couldn't run your kids' lives[9], he told himself. It was hard enough when they were in their teens[10], but once they were adults, all bets were off[11]. You could let them know[12] you were there for them, but if you tried to tell them what to do, well, you might as well try teaching a goat[13] how to drive a tractor.

Walden was in the garage out back of the house, tending[1] to a few things, when he saw movement in the kitchen window. He returned to the house to find that Victor was up, hair tousled[2], eyes dark and heavy lidded[3].

"I wondered where the hell I was," he said, his voice sounding as if it were coming through a can of gravel[4]. "When I opened my eyes I knew I wasn't home. I don't even remember you bringing me here last night."

"You were pretty out of it[5]," Walden said.

"I know where you found me. I remember that. But not a lot else[6]."

"You were about to get yourself beat up good[7]."

"What was I doing?"

Walden shook his head. "It doesn't matter. There's still coffee. Should be hot. You should have some."

"Yeah, I guess," he mumbled[8], and disappeared back into the house. Walden went in after him, poured him some coffee.

"Just black," Victor said, taking the mug from Walden. "I feel kinda like shit."

"You look kinda like shit."

Victor grinned, took a sip.

"Victor, I know this is none of my business, but I'm gonna put my oar in anyway[9]."

"Yeah, sure, whatever," he said.

"You're a bright[10] guy. I mean, you always were. Good at school. You picked up stuff fast[11]. Good with[12] your hands, as I recall[13]. Mechanically inclined[14], but book-smart[15], too."

"A real whiz kid[16]," he said, nodding.

"What I'm saying is, you've got something to offer. You have skills[17]. There's got to be someone in

323

1. à s'occuper

2. en vrac

3. la paupière lourde

4. seau de gravier

5. passablement bourré

6. pas grand-chose d'autre

7. te faire casser la gueule

8. marmonna

9. m'en mêler quand même
10. intelligent
11. apprenais vite
12. Doué de
13. si je me souviens bien
14. Branché mécanique
15. intello
16. petit génie
17. des compétences

1. en aurait besoin
2. de te torcher

town here who could use those[1]. But you have to stop getting wasted[2] every night."

"You been spying on me?"

"No, I'm just—I'm making an assumption[3]. But tell me I'm wrong."

3. fais une hypothèse

Victor set his coffee on the counter. "Why aren't you upset?"

"Excuse me?"

4. bousillé

"I don't get it. Why aren't you a mess[4] like I am? She was *your* fucking daughter."

5. boulet de canon
6. saisit
7. l'approcha brutalement de
8. bascula en arrière
9. secoua les assiettes
10. saisit
11. de toutes ses forces

Walden came at him like a cannonball[5]. He grabbed[6] the man by his jacket, yanked him close to[7] his face, then threw him up against the counter. Victor's head flung back[8], hit the upper cupboards, rattled dishes[9]. But Walden wasn't finished. He grabbed hold of[10] Victor again with everything he had[11], and this time threw him down onto the floor.

He was some three decades older than Victor, but Walden had no trouble throwing the man around. Maybe it helped that he was angry, and Victor was hungover[12].

12. avait la gueule de bois

"Never!" Walden shouted. "Never say that!" He brought back a leg and kicked Victor in the thigh. The younger man pulled in on himself[13], put his hands up over his head in case Walden's shoe connected with him there next.

13. se recroquevilla

"I'm sorry! Jesus! I'm sorry!"

14. souffre

"You think you're the only one who grieves[14]?" Walden said, still shouting. "Goddamn your arrogance, you little shit."

15. l'ai dit sans y penser

"Okay! I didn't mean it[15]!"

16. s'efforça de

Walden collapsed into a kitchen chair, rested his arms on the table, and worked on[16] catching his breath. Slowly Victor got to his feet, pulled out a chair on the other side of the table, and sat down.

"I was out of line[1]," he said.

Walden's hands were shaking.

"Really. That was wrong. I should never have said anything like that. You're a good man. I know you miss her. You've always been good to me. What you did for me last night, bringing me here, I appreciate that. That was real decent of you[2]."

Walden looked at his hands, put one over the other to stop the trembling. Slowly he spoke.

"I had Beth," he said. Victor looked at him, not sure what he meant by that[3], so he waited. Walden continued. "I had Beth, so I had to hold it together[4]. She went to pieces[5]. She was never really able to move on. What would have happened to her; who would have looked after her[6] if I went to the bar every night to feel sorry for[7] myself? Where would she have been then?"

He lifted his hand and pointed an accusing finger at Victor. "I couldn't be as selfish as you. I couldn't drown my sorrows[8] the way you have. I had responsibilities, and I met them[9]."

"I had nobody to be responsible for," Victor said. "So what difference did it make what I did?"

"What difference?" Walden asked. "Are you asking what's the point[10]?"

"Is there one? What about you? Now that your wife is gone? Now that you've lost the person—the people—who were most important to you, what's the fucking point?"

"We honor them," Walden said.

"What the hell is that supposed to mean?"

"When you do what you do, you shame[11] Olivia."

"What? I don't get that. I don't get that at all."

"People see you and they think, What kind of man is he? Can't make anything of himself. Full of self-pity. They wonder, What was Olivia thinking,

1. ai dépassé le bornes

2. vraiment chouette de votre part

3. entendait par là

4. tenir le coup

5. s'est écroulée

6. se serait occupé d'elle

7. m'apitoyer sur

8. noyer mon chagrin

9. ai été à la hauteur

10. à quoi bon

11. faites honte à

that she'd spend the rest of her life with this man? What you do, the way you act[1], it diminishes Olivia. Makes people think less of her[2]."

"That's horseshit[3]. People aren't entitled[4] to grieve?"

"Of course they are. For a period. But then you have to show people what you're made of[5]. Show people what Olivia saw in you in the first place. So people know she was a good judge of character. It's all about character."

Victor appeared to be thinking about that. "I don't know. What about you? How do you honor her? How do you honor Olivia? And Beth?"

"I'm finding my own way to do that," Walden said. He looked away, out the window. "You should go," he said.

"Okay," Victor said, pushing back his chair.

"Of all the things you said last night, you were right about one thing."

"What was that?"

"You shouldn't have been late[6]," Walden said. He turned away, looked down at his right hand, spotted[7] a rough[8] fingernail, brought it to his mouth and bit it.

.. votre manière d'agir

2. Ça la fait baisser dans l'estime des gens

3. de la connerie

4. n'ont pas le droit

5. de quel bois tu es fait

6. n'aurais pas dû arriver en retard

7. remarqua

8. mal limé

326

FORTY-TWO

David

I was planning to head straight[1] to the address I had for Marshall Kemper, the Davidson Place custodian who'd booked off sick[2] who, I hoped, might know where I could find Sarita Gomez.

I felt an urgency to get there, but I realized my route would take me to within a block of[3] where Marla'd told me Derek Cutter, the young man who'd gotten her pregnant[4], lived. He was someone I wanted to talk to, and this might be my best chance at catching him.

So I hung a left[5] and pulled up[6] in front of a brick duplex, a simple box of a building[7], constructed without a single nod[8] to any kind of architectural style. One apartment on the first floor, another on the second. Marla had said Derek shared the upper apartment with some other students. I parked at the curb, then went up and rang the bell for the top unit[9].

I heard someone running downstairs, and then the door opened. It was a young woman, maybe twenty, in a tracksuit[10], her hair pulled back into a ponytail[11].

1. me rendre directement

2. s'était fait porter pâle et

3. juste à côté de là

4. l'avait mise enceinte

5. fis un détour à gauche

6. m'arrêtai

7. bâtiment carré tout simple

8. la moindre référence

9. de l'étage

10. en jogging

11. queue-de-cheval

"Yeah?" she said.

"Hi," I said. "I was looking for Derek."

Her mouth made a big "O." "Oh, yeah, right, he said he called you late last night, after all the shit that went down[1]. He'll be glad to see you."

"Wait, I think—"

But she was already heading back up[2], taking the steps two at a time[3], shouting, "Derek! Your dad's here!" She must have turned right around when she got to the top, because a second later she was flying past me[4]. "Just go on up[5]. I gotta do my run."

I climbed the stairs, and as I reached the door to the second-floor[6] apartment it opened, and a man I guessed was Derek looked startled[7] to see me.

"You're not my dad," he said. He looked thin in his T-shirt and boxers[8], his legs coming out of them like two white sticks. He had a patchy beard[9], and black hair hanging over his eyes.

"No, I'm sorry, your girlfriend, she just assumed[10]. I didn't have a chance to set her straight[11]."

"She's not my girlfriend; she's a roommate[12], and, like, who are you?"

"Marla's cousin," I said. "I'm David Harwood."

"Marla?" he said. "You're Marla Pickens's cousin?"

"You got a minute?"

"Uh, sure, yeah, come on in[13]."

He created a space on the couch by clearing away[14] several books and a laptop[15]. I sat down and he perched himself on the end of a coffee table[16] that was littered with[17] half a dozen empty beer cans.

"Why are you here about Marla?" he asked.

When his roommate mentioned something about "all the shit that went down," I'd assumed

---

1. le bordel d'hier soir

2. remontait déjà

3. les marches deux à deux

4. me dépassait en trombe

5. Montez

6. du premier étage

7. parut surpris

8. son caleçon

9. barbe clairsemée

10. c'est ce qu'elle a cru

11. rectifier son erreur

12. colloc

13. entrez donc

14. dégageant

15. ordinateur portable

16. table basse

17. encombrée de

it had to do with the Gaynor murder, and Marla's possible involvement[1]. It had made the news[2].

"You haven't heard?"

"I've heard about what went down on campus last night, but that hasn't got anything to do with Marla, does it?"

Now it appeared neither of us was up to speed[3], but on totally different events. "What happened at Thackeray?" I asked.

"Fucking security killed one of my friends, that's what happened," Derek said. "Shot him in the goddamn head."

"I don't know anything about this," I admitted. "Who was your friend?"

"Mason. They're saying he was the guy[4]."

"What guy?"

"Who was attacking girls at the college. There's no fucking way[5]. He wasn't like that."

"What's his last name[6]?"

"Helt. Mason Helt. He was a really good guy. He was in the drama program with me. He was really good. They say he was attacking one of the security guards, who was, like, bait[7] or something, and then he got shot. It's nuts[8]."

"I'm sorry about your friend," I said. "That's why you called your dad?"

Derek nodded. "Yeah, just because, you know, I kind of freaked out[9] and I just needed to talk. I was surprised when Patsy said it was my dad at the door, because I didn't tell him to come out or anything." He fixed his eyes on me more closely. "You look familiar to me[10]."

I had a feeling why that might be, but I didn't want to lead the witness[11]. No sense in Derek's taking a dislike to me[12] if it didn't have to happen[13].

"I don't think we've ever met," I said honestly.

---

1. éventuelle implication

2. était passé aux informations

3. n'était au courant

4. que c'était lui le mec

5. Même pas en rêve

6. nom de famille

7. un appât

8. dingue

9. ai un peu flippé

10. me dites quelque chose

11. influencer le témoin

12. Pas la peine que Derek me prenne en grippe

13. on pouvait l'éviter

1. hurliez avec
les loups

2. m'ont fait
vivre un enfer

3. Sans doute

4. numéro un

5. innocenté

6. traumatisante

7. d'un drôle
d'air

8. d'y avoir joué
un rôle

9. des trucs

10. s'en prendre
à lui

11. là où elle
nous menait

12. participer
au cirque
médiatique

13. si éphémère
fût-il

14. se retrouvent
mêlés

15. à l'actualité

16. se sont
séparés

17. arriveraient à
s'en remettre

18. recoller les
morceaux

"You were one of the pack[1]," he said. "One of the ones who made my life hell[2]. I recognize you."

"Yeah," I said. "I'd have been one of them[3]."

It was a long time ago. Seven, eight years? The Langley murders. Father, mother, son, all killed in their home one night. Derek and his parents lived next door, and for a period of a day or two, Derek was a prime[4] suspect. The real killer was found and Derek completely exonerated[5], but it had to be a scarring[6] experience.

"Every once in a while," he said, "people still look at me funny[7]. Like they think, Maybe it wasn't that other guy. Maybe it really was him. Thanks for being a part of that[8]. For putting my picture in the paper. For writing stuff[9] that wasn't true."

I could have told him I'd been doing my job. That it wasn't the press that arrested him, but the police. That the media didn't just decide one day to pick on him[10], but that we were following the story where it led[11]. That the *Standard* wouldn't have been doing its duty if it had decided not to be part of the media frenzy[12], no matter how short-lived it was[13]. That sometimes innocent people get caught up[14] in current events[15], and they get hurt, and that's just the way it is.

I didn't think he'd be interested in hearing any of that.

"It's why my parents split up[16]," Derek said.

"I didn't know about that," I said, although Marla had mentioned something about it.

"Yeah, like, for a while, it looked like maybe they could ride it out[17]. But that didn't happen. My parents, they couldn't patch it all together[18]. So my mom moved away, and they had to sell the house, and everything pretty much went to complete shit, thanks very much. If I could have gone to college someplace other than Promise Falls, I would have, but I couldn't afford it[1]."

For what it was worth[2], I said, "I'm not here as a reporter. I don't even work as one anymore. And the *Standard* doesn't even exist."

"So, what then? Why are you here? What's going on with Marla?"

I told him.

"Jesus," he said. "That's totally fucked-up[3]. So they think she killed this woman and ran off with her kid?"

"That's not what Marla says happened, but I'd bet it's what the police think."

"So what are you doing?"

"Trying to help. Asking around. Hoping I'll find out something that makes it clear she didn't have anything to do with it."

Derek shrugged. "I don't know what to tell you. We've talked maybe half a dozen times since she lost the baby, ran into her[4] a couple of times, but that's it[5]."

"Did you know about the earlier incident, when she tried to smuggle a baby out[6] of the hospital?"

He nodded. "She told me about it. She said she just kind of lost her mind for a second. But that was pretty crazy of her[7]."

"How'd you meet?"

His story matched[8] Marla's. They'd struck up[9] a conversation in a Promise Falls bar, hooked up[10]. Saw each other pretty seriously for a while.

"She was one of the weirdest[11] girls I ever went out with," he said.

"How so?"

"Well, first of all, she has this thing? Where she doesn't exactly recognize you?"

"Face blindness," I said.

---

1. n'avais pas les moyens
2. À tout hasard
3. tordu
4. on s'est croisés
5. c'est tout
6. enlever un bébé
7. de sa part
8. était la même que
9. avaient engagé
10. étaient sortis ensemble
11. les plus bizarres

1. affabulait

2. [magazine d'information américain]

3. que je retrouvais

4. me coiffer

5. les peignais en arrière

6. ce serait plus dur pour elle de

7. chemise à carreaux

8. signaux

9. avez appris

10. n'avait pas eu ses règles

11. m'a fait l'effet d'une bombe

12. gerbé comme un malade

13. ce que j'avais à faire

14. où tout ça nous menait

"Yeah. I thought she was making it up[1] at first, but then I Googled it and found out it was a real thing. And then I saw an episode of *60 Minutes*[2] where they talked all about it. More people have it than you might think. Brad Pitt even says he thinks he's got it. Every time I'd meet[3] Marla, I'd walk up to her, and she'd be looking at me, like she thought it was me but she wasn't quite sure, and then I'd say, 'Hey, it's me,' and she'd hear my voice, and then she'd be sure. It was really strange. She told me to always wear my hair[4] the same way. Like, hanging like this, you know? That if I combed it back[5] or something, which I would never do, because I don't really do anything at all with my hair, she'd have a harder time[6] recognizing me. Or, like, wear a plaid shirt[7]. I wear a lot of plaid shirts. She said those kinds of visual cues[8] really worked for her."

"I know," I said. "The family started noticing it when she was a teenager. Tell me about when you found out[9] she was pregnant."

"She told me she'd missed her period[10]. It was like a bombshell[11], you know?"

"How'd you take the news?"

"Honestly? I got off the phone—she didn't tell me in person—and I barfed my guts out[12]. I used, you know, protection and everything, almost every time."

"Almost," I said.

He rolled his eyes. "Yeah, I know."

"How'd your parents take it?"

"I didn't tell my mom. Just my dad. He's kind of a traditional guy. He said I had to accept responsibility, and do whatever I had to do[13], and he'd be there to support me. And once we kind of knew where this was all going[14], he'd bring my mom

332

into the loop[1]. So, you know, I told Marla I would stand by her[2], help her any way I could. That it was her decision to make, whatever she did."

"And she decided to have the baby."

"Yeah, which, if I'm telling the truth, was not exactly what I was hoping she would do. But like my dad said, it was her call[3]. She said she wanted to have the kid; she really wanted to have a baby, said it would give her a focus[4], that it would really help her get her life together[5], right? And she said it was up to me[6] how involved[7] I wanted to be[8], but I was never sure whether she meant that[9], or if she was trying to guilt-trip me[10] into stepping up[11] and asking her to marry me or something like that, which I did not want to do. Marry her. I just wasn't ready for anything like that."

"Sure," I said. "You're still in school and all."

"This is my last year. I graduate[12] later this month. I didn't even realize for a long time how much older than me she was. I thought she was maybe a year or two, but she was, like, seven or something. It's like I've got this thing[13] for older women."

"What?" I said.

"Mrs. Langley?"

Right. The neighbor who'd been murdered years ago. Derek had been rumored to have had a sexual relationship with her. It was one of the things that had made him, briefly, a suspect.

He shook his head. "We don't have to get into that[14], do we?"

"No."

"Anyway, I started thinking maybe it wasn't a guilt trip, that Marla really didn't want me that involved[15], and part of that may be that her mom didn't like me."

1. mettrait ma mère au courant

2. que je la soutiendrais

3. à elle de décider

4. un but dans la vie

5. prendre sa vie en main

6. à moi de voir

7. quel genre de rôle

8. avoir

9. était sincère

10. me faire culpabiliser

11. pour que je prenne mes responsabilités

12. passe mon diplôme

13. un truc

14. n'est pas obligés de parler de ça

15. que je sois si présent que ça

"You met Agnes?"

"I never actually did, but Marla told me she wasn't pleased. She runs the hospital, right? I mean, you'd know[1], if Marla's your cousin. Her mom would be your aunt, right? She's a bigwig[2] around town. And I'm the son of a guy who runs a landscaping company. You could just guess how much she loved that."

I felt as though I'd been dipped[3] into a bucket of shame. Derek had my aunt pretty much nailed[4].

"And then," I said, "Marla had the baby."

The young man nodded, and then began to tear up[5]. "It was so weird. I was really sorry I got her pregnant, and didn't want her to have the kid, and didn't want to have the responsibility, right? But when I found out the baby—it was a little girl, but you probably know that—died when it was, like, coming out, it kind of hit me[6]. I never expected that to happen. But it hit me real hard."

He sniffed, used the back of his hand to wipe away[7] a tear. "All of a sudden I was thinking about what she might have grown up to be[8], what she'd have been like[9], whether she'd have looked like me and all that kind of shit[10], and I was so shook up[11] about it that I kind of, you know, went to pieces[12]."

"What happened?"

"I moved back in with[13] my dad. We're pretty close[14]. It was a good thing we hadn't told Mom anything. I mean, it would have killed her to think she had a granddaughter, and that she died right away[15]." He swallowed[16]. "Marla told me about holding her. Holding the baby when she was dead. She said she was in kind of a daze[17], but she looked at all her little fingers and her nose and all and said she was really beautiful, even though she

---

1. devez le savoir

2. gros bonnet

3. trempé
4. bien cerné ma tante

5. fondit en larmes

6. m'a fait un choc

7. essuyer
8. aurait pu devenir
9. quelle genre de personne elle aurait été
10. toutes ces conneries
11. secoué
12. me suis écroulé
13. suis retourné habiter chez
14. assez proches
15. aussitôt
16. avala sa salive
17. dans le coaltar

334

wasn't breathing. She even had a name chosen[1] for her. Agatha Beatrice Pickens. Agatha sounded sort of like her mother's name, but was different, she said."

He wiped his eyes again.

"I'm sorry," I said. "These things can affect you in ways you never expect[2]."

Derek Cutter nodded. "I guess[3]."

We both heard the sound of a car door closing. Derek got off[4] the table and looked out the window.

"Oh, shit," he said. "I know that guy."

I joined him at the window. I knew that guy, too.

"Detective Duckworth," I said.

"Yeah. He was the one who thought I'd done it[5] when our neighbors got killed. What's he doing here?"

I could think of two possible reasons: Duckworth wanted to talk to him about Marla Pickens for the same reasons I had. Or maybe he wanted to ask him about his dead friend Mason Helt.

"I hate that guy," Derek said. "Can you tell him I'm not here?"

"I can't do that, Derek."

"Great."

"I want to ask you one last quick question."

"Fine, whatever[6]."

"I want your gut feeling about[7] Marla."

"Gut feeling?"

"Can you imagine her killing Rosemary Gaynor?"

He thought a moment. "My gut?"

"Yeah."

"One night we were at this thing[8] at the college—this was before she got pregnant, I think. And there's a whole bunch[9] of kids around, and

---

1. avait même choisi un nom

2. auxquelles on ne s'attend pas

3. Possible

4. se leva de

5. que j'étais coupable

6. si vous voulez

7. savoir ce que votre instinct vous dit sur

8. soirée

9. tout un groupe

1. faisait vraiment chier

2. je sais pas quelle connerie

3. a fait mine de lever la main sur

4. l'aurait vraiment frappée

5. attrape

6. la jette en plein sur

7. à deux mètres

8. en visant mal

9. s'est mis à saigner comme un dingue

10. se jeter sur elle

11. le mettait au défi

this guy was really giving shit to[1] this girl about her talking to some other guy or some shit like that[2], and you could see she was really intimidated, looking real scared, and he went to raise his hand to[3] her—I don't know if he'd have actually hit her[4], but you never know—and Marla, who's been watching all of this, grabs[5] this beer bottle and throws it right at[6] this asshole's head. We were only like six feet away[7], so even if her aim hadn't been great[8], she had a good chance of hitting him. And she does, right on his fucking nose. Lucky thing the bottle didn't break or the guy might have lost an eye, but his nose started bleeding like crazy[9]. And the guy looks at Marla, like maybe he's going to come at her[10], and she shouts, 'Yeah, I'm right here!' Like she was just daring him[11] to try something. Swear to God, you had to see it to believe it."

"Jesus," I said.

Downstairs, the doorbell rang.

"So when you ask me what my gut thinks about Marla, I don't know if there's anything she could do that would surprise me," he said.

FORTY-THREE

DUCKWORTH thought, *I'm an idiot.*

He'd just pulled up[1] in front of the house where he'd been told by the Thackeray College registration office[2] that he could find Derek Cutter, when he realized what he should have asked[3] Sarita Gomez's landlord, Mrs. Selfridge, she[4] of the magnificent banana bread.

When Duckworth had left the station that morning he'd dragooned[5] a female officer[6] and put her on the phones to call nursing homes in and around Promise Falls to try to find where Sarita worked. It had occurred to him[7] that, even if they were to[8] call the right place, someone might deny[9] employing a person here illegally.

It was on the way to interview Derek that it hit him[10].

"Stupid, stupid, stupid," he said to himself.

He pulled right over to the curb, a couple of blocks away from Derek's address, and got out his notebook and phone. He found Mrs. Selfridge's number and dialed[11].

She answered on the third ring. He identified himself.

"Oh, hello, Detective," she said. "If you're wondering if Sarita's come back, she hasn't. She's paid

1. venait de se garer
2. bureau des inscriptions
3. comprit ce qu'il aurait dû demander à
4. celle
5. harponné
6. policière

7. Il s'était dit
8. même s'ils parvenaient à
9. nier
10. qu'il percuta

11. le composa

up to[1] the end of the month, but I'm thinking I should start looking for a new tenant[2]. I got a feeling she's flown the coop[3] for good[4]."

"You might be right," Duckworth said. "I wanted to thank you again for that banana bread. I was wondering, would you be willing to part with the recipe[5]? And if you say no, I'm pretty sure I can get a subpoena[6]."

That made her laugh. "I don't even have it written down. I just do it out of my head[7]. But I guess I could come up with something[8]."

"And there's another thing," he said. "I can't believe I didn't think of this yesterday. Your phone, that Sarita used?"

"Yes?"

"I'd like you to go through[9] the call history[10]. Calls in and out[11]."

"I could do that," she said. "You want me to do that before or after I get you the recipe?"

"Before," Duckworth said, with some regret. "Sarita probably made, and received, calls from the nursing home where she worked. Once we have that number, we'll know her employer. And there may be other numbers, too, that might help me find her." He paused. "And when I do, I can ask her whether she's going to keep the room."

"Oh, I'd really appreciate that."

"You have the card I left with you?" he asked. She said yes. "Okay, if you'd take down[12] those numbers and e-mail them to me, I sure would appreciate it."

Mrs. Selfridge said she would get right on it[13], and Duckworth said good-bye.

Idiot, he thought again. He wanted to plead overwork[14]. Juggling too many cases at once[15]. A murder, a fatal shooting[16] at Thackeray, strange goings-on[1] in the night at Five Mountains. Dead squirrels, for God's sake.

And then there was the home front[2]. How the hell did his son end up working for that asshole Randall Finley? That son of a bitch couldn't be trusted[3]. There had to be a reason he'd hired[4] his son. Sure, Trevor would be a good hire for any company, but you didn't have to be a rocket scientist[5] to drive a truck. Finley could have hired anyone[6] for a job like that. Why Trevor?

While he waited for Sarita's landlady to get those numbers, he'd continue on to Derek Cutter's residence. The young man's name had surfaced[7] twice in the last day, in two separate investigations. Not only had he been identified as the man who'd gotten Marla Pickens pregnant, he was also reported to be a friend of Mason Helt, the student Clive Duncomb had shot in the head.

Duckworth had much to discuss[8] with Derek.

He was about to put the car in drive[9] when his cell rang.

"Duckworth."

"Hey, Barry. Cal Weaver."

There was a voice from the past.

"Son of a bitch. I knew you were back[10]. I've been meaning to call[11]."

"Everyone's busy," Weaver said.

"Where you living?"

"You know that used bookstore downtown[12]? Naman's?"

"Yeah."

"Above it."

"Okay."

"I was living at my sister's for a while," Weaver said. "But that was temporary till I got my own place."

---

1. d'étranges événements

2. la situation chez lui

3. n'était pas quelqu'un de confiance

4. pour qu'il ait embauché

5. fallait pas sortir de Saint-Cyr

6. n'importe qui

7. été évoqué

8. de nombreux sujets de conversation

9. s'apprêtait à redémarrer la voiture

10. de retour

11. Je comptais t'appeler

12. bouquiniste du centre-ville

"I knew you'd moved back from Griffon," Duckworth said. "I heard about[1] what happened there. I'm sorry."

"Thanks," Weaver said. "Listen, you're working the Rosemary Gaynor murder."

"I am."

"Neponset Insurance has asked me to look into it. Bill Gaynor works for them, and all their insurance is with them[2] as well."

"Okay," Duckworth said.

"There was a million-dollar policy on Ms. Gaynor. Before there's a payout[3] to Mr. Gaynor, there's the usual due diligence[4]."

"Of course," Duckworth said.

"But from what I understand[5], this one may be a bit of a slam dunk[6]," Weaver said.

"I'm in the middle of my investigation[7], Cal. No charges yet[8]."

"But this Marla Pickens is looking good for it[9]."

"She's a suspect."

"She had their baby," Weaver said. "And it wasn't the first time she pulled a stunt like that[10]. Am I right?"

"You are."

"Look, I don't want to get in your way on this[11], and I'm not doing an active investigation of my own[12], not at this stage[13]. I'm hanging back[14], monitoring developments[15], waiting to see if there's an arrest. I wanted to give you a heads-up[16], is all."

"Appreciate it," Duckworth said. "Listen, we should have a beer sometime, get caught up[17]."

"Sure," Weaver said noncommittally[18], and ended the call.

Duckworth was thinking he should have reached out[19] to his old friend before now, but even more than that, he was thinking Bill Gaynor wasn't

---

1. ai appris
2. chez eux
3. le paiement de la prime
4. on suit la procédure habituelle
5. si je comprends bien
6. sans surprise
7. enquête
8. Pas de mise en examen pour l'instant
9. va certainement plonger
10. faisait un coup pareil
11. m'en mêler
12. de mon côté
13. pour l'instant
14. attends
15. je surveille l'évolution
16. te prévenir
17. se raconter le bon vieux temps
18. évasif
19. faire signe

going to have any trouble[1] paying for a new nanny to look after Matthew.

A million bucks[2].

When Duckworth bumped into[3] David Harwood coming out of Derek Cutter's place, he asked him what he was doing there. "Trying to find out what happened, same as you," the former reporter said on his way to an old Taurus parked on the street.

Duckworth found Derek waiting for him at the door to his apartment.

"Hey, Derek," Duckworth said. "How you been[4]?"

"Okay."

"How's your dad?"

"Okay."

Once upstairs, Duckworth asked about Marla Pickens. Derek said, "I'll tell you what I just told the other guy."

Which he did.

Then Duckworth turned to[5] Mason Helt. "I hear you guys were friends."

"They fuckin' executed him; that's what I hear," Derek said.

"Did you know Mason was stalking[6] women on campus, attacking them?"

"You think if I knew something like that I wouldn't say something about it?"

"So you had no idea[7]."

"No. I still don't believe it. I've got some experience with being accused of something I didn't do."

Duckworth felt[8] he'd apologized enough years ago for all of that. "When was the last time you talked to him?"

341

---

1. n'aurait aucun mal à

2. de dollars

3. tomba sur

4. Comment va

5. passa au cas

6. suivait

7. n'en savais rien

8. trouvait

"Maybe two weeks ago? We ran into each other and he invited me to his place for a couple of beers." Derek moved his lips in an out[1]. "He said he got this weird kind of job. Sort of an acting thing[2]. We'd been taking some theater classes together."

"What kind of acting thing?"

"I asked him. I said, 'Like in amateur theater? Something on campus or off[3]?' I even wondered if he'd tried out for some kind of commercial[4] or something like that."

"Which was it?"

"Well, none of those. Mason said it was a private thing. I thought, Maybe it's got to do with[5] sex, you know? Like maybe some old guy'd hired him to come to his house and dance or strip or do some kinky kind of role-play[6]."

"Why would something like that come to mind[7]?" Duckworth asked. "Have you ever been asked to do something like that?"

"Geez[8], no. It's just because he was so secretive about it[9], it made me wonder. But I kept asking him about it, and what he would say was, it was kind of like, you know when they hire actors to pretend they're sick[10] and medical students have to figure out[11] what they've got?"

"I've heard of that."

"Like[12] what he was doing was part of a study or something. But he also implied[13] it was a bit risky." He shook his head. "He sure turned out to be right about that[14]."

"Did Mason say who hired him?"

"No, but he said he'd be able to buy me a few rounds[15] for the next few weeks on what he was getting paid[16]."

Margin notes:

1. fit la moue
2. truc d'acteur
3. à la fac ou en dehors
4. avait fait un bout d'essai pour une pub
5. une histoire de
6. des jeux de rôle un peu cochons
7. te viendrait en tête
8. Ouh là
9. en faisait un tel secret
10. simuler une maladie
11. deviner
12. Comme si
13. a aussi laissé entendre
14. La suite lui a bien donné raison
15. tournées
16. avec sa paie

It fit with[1] what Joyce Pilgrim had told him. Mason, just before Clive Duncomb shot him, had said he wouldn't hurt her. That the attack was some kind of gig[2].

"Mason was wearing a hoodie when he was shot," Duckworth said. "With the number twenty-three on it. You ever see him wearing that?"

"That's weird that you should bring that up[3]," Derek said.

"Why?"

"That time I ran into him, he'd been to some sports store[4] in Promise Falls. Where you can buy stitch-on[5] letters for varsity[6] jackets, that kind of thing. He had this white plastic bag, and I asked him what was in it, and he said it was for the gig, but he wouldn't show it to me. But he had to leave the room for a second to take a leak[7], and I peeked[8] inside, and it was two numbers. The way they were in the bag, they made a thirty-two, but yeah, could just as easy[9] be twenty-three."

"So whoever hired him, for whatever it was he was supposed to do, he had to be wearing[10] that number."

"I guess[11]," Derek said. "Why would someone do that?"

"I don't know."

"What's the significance of twenty-three?"

"I don't know."

"Maybe it's a reference to Psalm Twenty-three," Derek offered[12].

"You're going to have to help me there," the detective said. "I sleep in[13] on Sunday mornings if I'm not on duty[14]."

"Well, I haven't been to church in years either, but my parents used to send me to Sunday school[15] when I was really little. Psalm Twenty-three is the

---

1. correspondait à

2. boulot

3. parliez de ça

4. dans une boutique de sport
5. à coudre
6. d'équipes universitaires

7. aller pisser
8. ai jeté un coup d'œil

9. tout aussi bien

10. il fallait qu'il porte

11. suppose

12. suggéra

13. fais la grasse mat'

14. d'astreinte

15. au catéchisme [le dimanche]

1. qui dit
2. berger
3. vallée de l'ombre de la mort
4. sans craindre aucun mal
5. me dit quelque chose

one that goes[1] 'The Lord is my shepherd[2].' And there's that part that talks about walking through the valley of the shadow of death[3], but not fearing any evil[4]. You know?"

"It rings a bell[5]," Duckworth said.

FORTY-FOUR

TREVOR Duckworth had rarely driven a van with so few windows. There was the front windshield[1], of course, and the roll-down ones[2] on the driver and passenger doors. But that was it[3]. The cargo area[4] was totally closed in[5]. There wasn't even any glass on the two rear[6] floor-to-ceiling doors.

Visibility was a bitch[7].

A couple of times over the years, he'd found himself[8] behind the wheel of a rental[9], helping someone move[10], and he hated having to back the damn thing up[11]. Couldn't see where you were going. He'd adopted a style of backing up very slowly and hoping that if and when he hit something—or somebody—he'd hear it and stop before he did too much damage[12].

But after a few days of working for Finley Springs Water, he was getting the hang of it[13]. He could back this sucker[14] up pretty nicely using only the mirrors that were bolted[15] to the two doors. He'd dropped off[16] about a hundred cases of water at several convenience stores[17] around Promise Falls, and had now returned to the plant[18] with an empty truck. He drove up in front of the loading docks[19], put the column shift into reverse[20], spun the wheel around[21], and guided the truck

---

right up to the platform. Stopped an inch short[1], never touched the bumper[2].

Hot damn[3].

He grabbed a clipboard from the other seat that listed the places he'd been and how much had been delivered, and headed to the office with the paperwork[4].

God, his dad could be such a dick[5] sometimes.

Giving him a hard time[6] about working for Randall Finley. Who cared[7]? A job was a job, and Trevor'd been out of work too long. How long had his parents been at him[8] about getting a weekly paycheck[9]? And then he finally gets one, and his dad's not happy about it. At least his mother seemed pleased. It was funny about her. She could be such a huge worrier[10]. Like when he was going around Europe with Trish, and was out of touch with[11] his parents for days or weeks at a time. It drove[12] his mother crazy. And yet now that he was back in Promise Falls, she was okay. She was the one he could go to[13] when he had a problem. His dad was another story. Maybe it was the whole thing about being a cop[14]. You got all hard-ass[15] about everything.

And then all this shit about how Finley might have hired him to get some sort of leverage over[16] his father. Sometimes, Trevor thought, his dad believed the whole world revolved[17] around him.

Just as well he lied to him[18] about how he got the job at Finley Springs.

Trevor had said he'd found the job online. That wasn't exactly the truth. Yes, the water-bottling company had placed ads on the Internet looking for drivers, but Trevor had been offered the job in person. He was at Walgreens, buying half a dozen microwavable[19] frozen dinners, which was about

---

1. à trois centimètres

2. pare-chocs

3. Putain

4. paperasse

5. si pénible

6. Le faire chier

7. Qu'est-ce que ça pouvait faire

8. sur son dos

9. salaire hebdomadaire

10. se rendre malade d'inquiétude

11. ne contactait pas

12. rendait

13. qu'il pouvait allait trouver

14. ça le problème quand on était flic

15. On se prenait la tête

16. pour avoir prise sur

17. tournait

18. Il avait bien fait de lui mentir

19. à mettre au micro-ondes

the only thing[1] he ever ate these days at his apartment, when this guy coming down the aisle[2] the other way caught his eye and said, "Hey, aren't you Barry's boy[3]?"

"Yeah," Trevor said.

The man extended a hand. "Randy Finley. I think we may have met a few years ago, when you were just a kid. Your dad and I worked together some[4] when I was mayor. How you doing? Did I hear you were touring around Europe at some point? With the Vandenburgs' girl? Trisha?"

"Trish," Trevor said.

They made some small talk[5]. Finley asked after[6] Trevor's father. Said they didn't cross paths that much anymore[7], not since Finley left politics and started up a new business. Had Trevor heard of his water-bottling operation?

Trevor said he had not.

Finley said, "If you know any guys looking for work, point them in my direction[8]. Rest of this town is going to shit[9], but we're hiring. Like I say, if you know anyone."

"What kind of work?" Trevor asked.

"Well, drivers for a start[10]."

"I'm kind of looking for a job," Barry Duckworth's son said.

"Well, shit, you got a driver's license?" Trevor nodded. "Come on up and see me[11], then."

Trevor got the job. If he'd told his father how it had happened, you could just bet he'd have read something sinister into it[12]. Like maybe Finley hadn't just bumped into him[13]. That he'd somehow arranged it. And Trevor didn't even give much thought to the fact[14] that Randy knew all about him being in Europe with Trish Vandenburg.

---

1. à peu près tout
2. allée
3. le fils de Barry
4. un peu
5. avaient papoté
6. avait demandé des nouvelles de
7. n'avaient plus tellement l'occasion de se croiser
8. envoie-les-moi
9. part en couilles
10. pour commencer
11. Passe me voir
12. y aurait vu un plan malveillant
13. ne l'avait pas croisé par hasard
14. n'avait pas vraiment relevé

Promise Falls was still a small town in many ways, even if there were more than thirty thousand people living here.

Trish.

He didn't think about her quite as often. Hell, she crossed his mind only every ten minutes now, instead of every five. How many times had he apologized to her[1]? Said he was sorry? That what he'd done, he really wasn't like that[2]? He'd just lost his head for a second. She'd actually told him once that she'd forgiven him. But that didn't mean she was coming back.

Stupid, stupid, stupid.

Trevor wished he could turn back the clock[3], start over[4]. You make one stupid mistake, and you never stop paying for it.

He was slipping[5] into the office to drop off[6] the clipboard when he felt a hand slap him atop[7] the shoulder.

"How's it hanging?[8]" Finley asked.

Trevor Duckworth spun around[9]. "Hey, good, Mr. Finley. Things are good."

"I told you before, you call me Randy."

"Randy, yeah. Just did a run[10], left the truck at the dock so they can load it up again. Think I'm doing a run to Syracuse today."

"Sounds good, sounds good." Finley's smile was wide enough to show off his crooked[11] teeth. "I was gonna get myself some horrible coffee. Want a cup?"

Trevor didn't, but it didn't seem like a good idea to say no. Finley went over to the coffee machine sitting[12] on a table in the corner of the room, glanced[13] into two empty mugs to see whether they were relatively clean, and filled them.

---

1. s'était-il excusé auprès d'elle
2. ça ne lui ressemblait vraiment pas
3. remonter le temps
4. reprendre à zéro
5. se faufilait
6. déposer
7. une claque sur
8. Ça roule ?
9. fit volte-face
10. Je reviens d'une tournée
11. de travers
12. posée
13. jeta un coup d'œil

"You know, I make this coffee with our own springwater, and it still tastes like shit[1]. What do you take?"

"Some milk, if you've got it."

"That all?"

"Yeah?"

"Because I usually add something a bit stronger." He went over to his desk, opened a drawer, and took out a bottle of whiskey. He poured a shot[2] into the coffee, held out[3] the bottle to Trevor, and said, "You?"

"No, sir. I mean, no, thanks, Randy. I'm heading back out[4] soon."

"Of course you are," he said, and tucked the bottle back into his drawer. He came around the desk and parked his butt[5] on the edge[6], took a sip[7]. "It does make bad coffee better. There's not much it doesn't make better."

Trevor smiled as he took a sip out of his mug. The boss was right. It was bad.

"You're working out real good[8]," Finley said. "I've been asking around, and everyone's happy with you. I mean, you're new, and you still got time to fuck up[9], but so far, so good[10]." Finley laughed.

"I'm glad to have a job," Trevor said. "I like driving around. It gives you time to think."

"Sure, it would[11]. You got a lot on your mind[12]?"

"Not really."

"When I was your age, what I had on my mind most was pussy[13]." He laughed. "Not that anything has really changed. But I am, for the purposes of the official record[14], a happily married man."

"Yeah, well, you know."

"And I don't mean to brag[15], but I got my fair share of it[16]," he said. Patting his belly[17], he said, "Hard to believe, but at one time I cut a slightly

1. le goût est dégueulasse

2. versa une rasade
3. tendit

4. repars

5. posa ses fesses
6. bord
7. gorgée

8. bosses bien
9. as encore le temps de merder
10. jusque-là, ça va

11. forcément
12. des soucis

13. les gonzesses
14. officielle-ment

15. me vanter
16. ne me suis pas privé
17. En se flattant la panse

349

1. il fut un temps où j'avais plus d'allure

2. quand je regarde vers le bas

3. je me vois même pas la queue

4. au garde-à-vous

5. grand sourire

6. passe peut-être

7. Entre hommes

8. faire une remarque, comme ça,

9. bien

10. dont tu auras peut-être entendu parler

11. la remarque pouvait paraître sévère

12. faiblesses

13. bien décrites

14. ai bel et bien frappé

15. instinctive

16. un geste maladroit

17. m'a mordu la queue

18. comme toi

19. se sentit flancher

more dashing figure[1]. These days, looking down[2], I can't even find my cock[3]. Even when it's standing at attention[4]." Another grin[5]. "But as long as *some-one* can find it, then all's right with the world."

"Sure," Trevor said.

Finley pointed a friendly finger toward him. "But I'll tell you this. I may come across[6] some-times as a bit of a pig, but—"

"Not at all."

"But I always treat women with respect. When men get together[7], sure, we may say the odd com-ment[8] a woman might interpret as disrespectful, but we don't mean it that way, do we?"

"No," Trevor said.

"But when we're with them, we treat them right[9]. That's what I do. I admit, there was an incident a few years ago you may have heard about[10]. I acci-dentally hurt a young woman—"

"I remember something about that," Trevor said. "Wasn't she fifteen?" He hadn't meant anything by it, then realized he might be coming off as judg-mental[11]. So he quickly added, "But I could be wrong about that."

"No, no, you're right. My weaknesses[12] have been well documented[13]. I did end up striking[14] this woman, but it was a reflexive[15] action caused by some carelessness[16] on her part during a mo-ment of intimacy."

Trevor looked at him, not comprehending.

Finley said, "She bit my dick[17]." When Trevor had nothing to say, the former mayor continued. "So I can understand when even a well-intentioned man such as yourself[18] can have a moment when he makes an error in judgment."

Trevor felt his insides weaken[19].

"You probably don't know this, but the Vandenburgs have been friends of mine going way back[1]. Did you know that?"

Trevor shook his head.

"I've known Patricia—*Trish*—since she was a little girl. An adorable child, and a lovely young woman. It was a shame[2], what happened between you two."

Trevor Duckworth said, "I ... I don't see ... I should go."

"No, you stay right here[3]. In fact, why don't you close[4] the door. Yeah, that's good. It's better to be able to talk in private." He took another sip of his spiked coffee[5]. "I believe, every once in a while, people deserve a break[6]. The benefit of the doubt. I'm betting you never, ever meant[7] to hurt that girl."

3. reste là
4. si tu fermais
5. café arrangé
6. il faut laisser leur chance aux gens
7. n'as *jamais* eu l'intention de

"It was ..."

"An accident? Well, I'm not sure you'd call it that[8]. It's not like you ran into the back of her with a shopping cart[9] at the grocery store, is it?"

Trevor's face flushed[10]. "I never ... I mean, I told her I was sorry."

"Have you considered how lucky you were?" Finley asked. "That she didn't have you charged[11]? Because I can tell you, she did think about it." He paused. "I guess you didn't know that hiring you was the *second* favor I had done for you[12]."

"I don't understand."

"Trish is kind of like a niece to me. I'm her unofficial uncle."

"You talked to Trish?"

"I told you, we lived next door to the Vandenburgs for years. When you punched her in the face[13]—"

"I didn't punch her; I—"

"When you *punched* her in the face, she came to me. She was afraid to go to Duffy and Mildred—you know, her parents—for fear Duffy would grab a gun and blow your fucking head off[1]. She said to me, 'No man will ever hit me twice.' Trish is a strong woman. She was done with you at that moment, and there was never a snowball's chance in hell[2] she'd ever go back with you. Her question was whether to file a complaint[3]."

Trevor tried to find his voice. "It was all so stupid. It was a dumb argument[4]; that's all it was. I wanted to go back to Germany, maybe find a job there, and she said it was time to settle down[5] here and do something with our lives, you know? And she started attacking me, criticizing me, saying I couldn't figure out what to do with my life[6], and she was waving her hands at me[7], and I thought she was actually going to swat me[8] or something, and I came at her backhanded[9], but I ended up hitting her in the side of the head. It was a fucking accident. I swear to God."

"Trish told me she stayed in her apartment for three days till the bruising went down[10]," Finley said.

Trevor could think of nothing to say to that.

"So, she asked me what I thought she should do. I told her she was fully within her rights[11] to charge you. That you had assaulted her[12]. I even offered to go to the Promise Falls police with her. They got a woman chief now, as you'd well know, and I can't imagine she'd have liked the sounds of what you did. But I also spelled out for her the pitfalls[13]. That, first of all, your father is a detective with the force[14], and there would be a lot of attention surrounding the case[15] because of that. Her parents would learn details about her life she

---

1. ne te fasse sauter la cervelle

2. la moindre chance

3. de savoir si elle devait porter plainte

4. dispute idiote

5. nous installer

6. ne savais pas quoi faire de ma vie

7. m'agitait les mains sous le nez

8. me gifler

9. ai paré en revers

10. le bleu disparaisse

11. avait tout à fait le droit

12. l'avais attaquée

13. lui ai expliqué les risques

14. inspecteur dans la police

15. l'affaire susciterait beaucoup d'intérêt

might rather they not know[1]. There was no telling[2] what might come out about her own background. Not that there was anything that salacious, but in a trial[3], the most innocent things can be made to sound sordid. No one knows better than me about that."

He patted the tops of his thighs[4] and pushed himself off the desk. "So there you have it[5]."

"Why'd you hire me?" Trevor asked.

"Why?" Finley's face was a mask of innocence. "Because you're a decent young man in need of employment. And you're doing a very good job. What other possible motive[6] could I have?"

"What about my dad?"

"What about him?"

"He said … he said you might have hired me to get at him somehow[7]."

Finley shook his head. "Nothing could be farther from the truth. I don't have it in for[8] your father. He's a good man. Quite the contrary. I don't want to get at him, as you say. In fact, just yesterday I offered to help him. You see, I'm going to be running for mayor again, and I think your dad would make a good chief[9]. All I might ever want from him is to keep his ears open. About things in the department. Issues I might want to address[10] in my campaign."

"What did he say?"

Finley smiled. "Not a lot[11]. But maybe one day you'll want to tell your father about our little chat[12] here today, and maybe he'd be more inclined[13] to be in my corner[14]. What do you think? Or failing that[15], I'm guessing that when you go home for Sunday dinner, you hear things. About your dad's work. Stuff that maybe isn't part of the public discussion. If you're ever interested in sharing

1. dont elle préférait peut-être qu'ils ne sachent rien

2. On ne pouvait pas prédire

3. procès

4. se claqua les cuisses

5. tu sais tout

6. motif

7. chercher à lui nuire

8. n'ai rien contre

9. chef de la police municipale

10. Des problèmes que je pourrais avoir à régler

11. Pas grand-chose

12. conversation

13. enclin

14. de mon côté

15. à défaut

anything like that, I can tell you right now, I would be an attentive listener."

Trevor Duckworth swallowed hard. His mouth was dry. He needed a drink, but the last thing he wanted was a mouthful[1] of Finley Springs Water.

1. gorgée

"I think," he said, "I'd better do my run to Syracuse."

2. déontologie

"Good lad," Finley said. "I like your work ethic[2]."

FORTY-FIVE

SOMEONE was knocking lightly on the door of Marshall Kemper's apartment.

Sarita Gomez was standing in front of the bathroom sink[1], staring at[2] her reflection[3] in the mirror, when she heard it.

She froze[4].

The police had found her. They must have discovered where she worked. Maybe someone had told them she'd been seeing[5] Kemper. So now they were here. She knew she was stupid to think she could hide out[6] for long. She had to get out of Promise Falls. She had to get as far away from here as she could, as quickly as possible.

Sarita stepped out[7] of the bathroom and approached the apartment door in bare feet[8], trying to step lightly[9] so as not to make any of the floorboards creak[10]. She stood three feet from the door, held her breath.

Another knock.

Then, "Babe! It's me!" An urgent whisper.

She went to the door, unlocked it, removed the chain. Marshall entered the room with a McDonald's bag.

"I got breakfast," he said, setting the bag on the counter of the kitchen nook[11]. He pulled out two

1. lavabo
2. fixant
3. reflet
4. se figea

5. sortait avec

6. rester cachée

7. sortit
8. pieds nus
9. d'un pas léger
10. pour ne pas faire craquer le plancher

11. coin cuisine

355

coffees, five breakfast sandwiches, and five hash browns[1]. "I was starving[2] and figured you would be, too."

He unwrapped[3] a sandwich and bit into it, stuffing nearly a third of it into his mouth at once.

Sarita said, "Did you get some cash?"

Marshall said, "Mmphh nth."

"I don't feel safe here. I want to get a train to New York."

Marshall got enough food down his throat[4] to talk. "I didn't go to the cash machine. I did something else. Somethin' that'll give you way more money[5]. Both of us."

He held out a sandwich to her, but she didn't take it.

"What did you do?"

"You gotta listen to me, babe. I know you were worried about this, but I've got the ball rolling[6]. This is going to work. This is going to set us up good[7]."

"Tell me you didn't call Mr. Gaynor."

"Look, just hear me out[8]."

"You idiot!"

"No, listen!" He reached out to her with the hand that wasn't holding a breakfast sandwich, but Sarita stepped back[9]. He took a quick bite of biscuit, egg, and sausage. "This is going to work out. He's going to give us fifty thousand dollars."

"Oh, my God. You mentioned me[10]? You told him I was part of this[11]?"

"No, no. I'm not an idiot. When I say us, I mean we get the money. But as far as Gaynor knows, he's just dealing with one guy[12], and he has no idea who that guy is."

"I told you not to do this."

"Come on, you're not thinking straight[1] because you're so directly involved. I'm taking a step back[2]. I can see the whole picture[3]. You have to trust me on this." He glanced at his watch. "Guy's going to be calling me very soon. If I haven't heard from him by ten thirty, so far as he knows, I go to the cops with everything I know[4]. Everything you've told me."

"You can't do that. You can't go to the police."

Marshall rolled his eyes. "Of course I'm not going to the cops! But he doesn't know that! That's the beauty of it[5]. That's why he's going to come up with fifty thou[6]. A guy like that, he won't even miss that kind of money[7]. But for us, it's a chance to start our lives over[8]."

"You're making things worse. Things are already bad and you're making them worse."

"Come on, babe. How is this worse? This is a *solution*. This is a way out of the mess."

"You told me you wouldn't do this," Sarita said. "I have to go. I have to get out of here[9]."

"Hold on. Just for a little while. Maybe another hour? Gaynor's gonna call me any second[10]. I go get the money; I come back; we go. Anything we need, we can buy it on the way."

She walked to the window, looked out at the street, walked back. She paced[11].

"All I ever wanted was to do the right thing[12]," she said. "When I saw her there in the kitchen, I had to do something[13] and—"

"And you *did* a good thing. It wasn't like you could leave the little fucker there[14]. But that part's over. Now we're—"

The cell phone in the front pocket of Marshall's jeans rang.

---

1. as du mal à réfléchir

2. un peu de recul

3. ai une vision d'ensemble

4. dis tout aux flics

5. C'est ça qu'est bath

6. trouver cinquante briques

7. c'est rien pour lui

8. recommencer à zéro

9. me tirer d'ici

10. d'une seconde à l'autre

11. fit les cent pas

12. Je voulais juste bien agir

13. il fallait que je fasse quelque chose

14. Tu pouvais quand même pas laisser le morveux là-bas

He tossed his sandwich onto the counter and dug in his pocket for the phone, put it to his ear.

"Right on time, Mr. Gaynor," Marshall said. Sarita watched him, slowly shaking her head.

1. prononçait silencieusement

She was mouthing[1], *No, no, no,* as Marshall put a finger to his lips.

"It wasn't easy," Bill Gaynor said.

"But you did it."

"I got the money."

"That's excellent," Marshall Kemper said. "Now, here's what I want you to do. You know the Promise Falls Mall?"

"Of course," he said.

Marshall said, "Okay, so I want you to put the money in one of those eco bags[2]. You got one of them?"

2. sacs recyclables

"Yes."

"You can get it all in there, right?" he asked. "Will it fit[3]?"

3. Tout va tenir dedans

"It'll fit," Gaynor said.

"Okay, so you put the money in the eco bag. There's a hot-dog place over on the left side, and right near the end of it there's a garbage can[4]. Just put the bag in there and walk away."

4. poubelle

"Leave the money in the garbage?"

5. sans tarder

"I'll collect it soon enough[5]. But here's the thing. I'll be watching. I'll know what you look like, but you won't know me. And I'll be watching to see if anybody's watching you. You understand?"

"I understand."

6. faire le malin

"Because if you try to pull something[6], then I go to the cops. You get that?"

"I told you, I understand."

7. déposez le sac

"Okay. You make the drop[7]; you get out. Simple as that. You did the right thing, Gaynor. You're not going to hear from me again after this. I'm not one of those guys who's going to come back again and again and hit you up for money[1]. I got ethics[2]."

"Whatever[3]," Gaynor said. "When do you want to do this?"

Marshall looked at his watch again. Sarita could see him thinking, timing things.

"One hour," Marshall said. "Don't be late."

"I won't."

Gaynor ended the call[4]. Marshall looked at Sarita and smiled. "We're going to be rich, babe."

"Fifty thousand is not rich," she said. "Even someone as poor as me knows fifty thousand is not rich. You're a fool."

"I'm gonna finish my sandwich and then I gotta go," he said. He put a hand behind her neck and pulled her toward him. Kissed her. "You just wait. I'm going to take care of you."

Marshall got a seat in the far corner of the food court[5]. It wasn't as busy as he'd hoped, eleven o'clock on a weekday morning. There were a few seniors[6] sitting around drinking coffee, some of them clustered together[7], shooting the shit[8]. What they did, Marshall knew, was arrive here before the shops opened, do their mall walk[9], traipsing[10] from one end of the place to the other twenty or thirty times in their goofy-looking running shoes[11]; then they bought some coffee and doughnuts and sat around and talked for three hours because they had nothing else in the world to do. This was their last stop[12] before they hit[13] Davidson Place[14].

Marshall bought himself a newspaper and a Coke and sat at a table that gave him an unobstructed[15] view of the hot-dog stand and the nearby garbage receptacle. It was one of those units with one opening for trash[16], another for recyclables,

1. vous demander de la thune
2. une morale
3. C'est ça
4. raccrocha
5. patio des fast-foods
6. vieilles personnes
7. assis en groupes
8. à bavasser
9. petit tour dans la galerie
10. flânant
11. baskets ringardes
12. étape
13. avant de finir à
14. l'hospice
15. dégagée
16. les déchets

and a place on top to leave your plastic tray. The food court was at the end of a broad hall[1], which meant there was only one direction Bill Gaynor could come from.

Ten minutes after Marshall had settled in, he saw a man approaching.

The man was carrying a baby up against his chest with one arm, and an eco bag hung from the end of his other arm. At first Marshall thought, Who brings a baby to pay off a blackmailer[2]? Then he thought, Oh, yeah, his nanny didn't show up for work[3] today.

Duh[4].

Marshall tried to keep his focus[5] on the sports pages of the *Times Union*, the closest thing you could get to a local paper[6] these days. Every few seconds he'd steal a quick glance[7] at the man.

He strolled past where Marshall was sitting, heading in the direction of the garbage.

Marshall felt a tingling all over[8]. So close to so much money. When Gaynor had his back to him[9], Marshall could not take his eyes off the bag.

Gaynor reached the trash, took a quick look around, pushed open the hinged door[10], and shoved the bag inside. Baby still in his arm, he turned and walked back in the direction he'd come from. Marshall waited until he was out of sight.

"All right," Marshall said, getting up, leaving his paper and Coke behind. He began walking briskly[11] toward the trash.

At a table just a few steps away from it, an elderly man cut short[12] his discussion with three other seniors and jumped to his feet. He moved—a lot faster than Marshall thought he should have been able to at his age—toward the trash bin.

---

1. au bout d'une grande galerie
2. payer un maître chanteur
3. sa nounou n'est pas venue bosser
4. Peuh
5. rester concentré
6. ce qui s'apparentait le plus à un journal local
7. lançait un coup d'œil
8. se sentit parcouru d'un frisson
9. lui tourna le dos
10. couvercle à bascule
11. rapidement
12. interrompit brusquement

"Get out of my way, old man," Marshall said under his breath[1].

The old man had nothing in his hands to throw away[2]. Once he'd reached the trash, he opened the door with one hand and reached in with the other.

"Hey!" Marshall shouted from thirty feet away[3]. "Hey!"

He closed the distance in a second, put his hand on the man's arm and started to pull it out[4].

"Get your paws off me[5]," the old man said.

"What the hell are you doing?" Marshall asked.

The man said, "Guy just threw away a perfectly good bag[6]." He'd found it and was pulling it through the opening[7]. "See? That's a good bag. No good reason to throw away that—"

"Give that to me," Marshall said. "That's mine."

"I found it!" the man said. Then, seeing that it had paper stuffed in it, he added, "There's something in here."

"It's mine. Let go of it. He left it there for me, you dumb bastard[8]."

The man was no match for[9] Marshall, who ripped it from his hands[10]. The man yelped in pain[11]. "You twisted my arm, you motherfucker!"

"I'm sorry! I'm sorry! But it's mine!"

Marshall ran.

Behind him, the old guy shouted, "Hey! He broke my arm!"

Just keep moving. Don't look back.

Marshall nearly ran into the glass doors on the way to the parking lot, they were so slow to retract[12]. He had his keys out, unlocked the van from fifty feet away, jumped in behind the wheel, and keyed the ignition. He tossed the bag onto the seat next to him, threw the van into drive[13], and tore out of the lot[14] as fast as he could.

1. à mi-voix
2. à mettre à la poubelle
3. à dix mètres de lui
4. entreprit de tirer dessus
5. Me touchez pas avec vos sales pattes
6. sac en bon état
7. le faisait sortir
8. espèce de connard
9. ne faisait pas le poids contre
10. le lui arracha des mains
11. glapit de douleur
12. à s'ouvrir
13. mit en marche [conduite automatique]
14. quitta le parking en trombe

A mile down the road, he pulled into a Walmart lot, stopped the car, and reached over for the bag.

His heart was pounding[1] and his shirt was soaked with sweat[2]. What the hell was that old guy doing, rooting around[3] in the trash? Who needed a used eco bag that badly[4]?

Marshall thought the bag should have been a little heavier than it was. But then again[5], when was the last time he'd carried fifty grand[6]? How much was that supposed to weigh[7]?

Gaynor had placed some newspapers over the top of the bag. Marshall tossed them into the foot well in front of the passenger seat[8], expecting to see bundles of cash[9] with rubber bands around them[10].

There was an envelope. A business envelope. A very thin business envelope.

"Jesus, the guy didn't write a check, did he?"

He tore it open, found a single sheet of paper inside. Gaynor had written the following:

Didn't feel safe leaving money in trash[11].
Have different plan for delivery. Call me.

---

1. battait à tout rompre
2. trempée de sueur
3. à fouiller
4. à ce point
5. d'un autre côté
6. cinquante patates
7. peser
8. par terre devant le siège passager
9. des liasses de billets
10. entourées d'élastiques
11. une poubelle

FORTY-SIX

AGNES tapped lightly on the hospital room door before entering. She found Marla sitting up in bed, sipping some tea from her breakfast tray[1].

"Haven't they taken that away yet?" Agnes asked.

"They came by[2], but I told them I was still working on it[3]," Marla said. "The tea is cold, but that's okay."

"I'll call down, tell them to bring you some hot."

"No, please, Mom. I know that whatever you ask them to do, they'll jump[4], but I just want to be treated like any other patient."

Agnes smiled. "You're not just any other patient. You're my daughter. And if there was ever a time when I was willing to throw my weight around[5], it's now." She rested a hand on her daughter's bare arm, inches above her bandaged wrist. "But the truth is, I'm getting you out of here. You're better off[6] at home than here. It's a good hospital—no, it's a great hospital, no matter how some sons of bitches want to rank it[7]—but you're better off with us."

"I'd like that," Marla said weakly.

"How are you feeling?"

1. plateau

2. sont passés
3. n'avais pas fini

4. se précipiteront

5. veux user de mon influence

6. seras mieux

7. l'évaluer

"Okay. The doctor—not Dr. Sturgess, but the psychiatrist?—was in to see me a while ago, and he's going to give me something."

1. arrangé ça

"I know. I already have that sorted[1]. Do you feel like you're going to do anything like that again?"

Marla shook her head. "No, I don't. I just felt,

2. accablée
3. ordonnance

you know, overwhelmed[2] by everything that was happening at the moment. But the prescription[3], it's supposed to help with that." She put a hand on top of her mother's. "Really, I won't do it again."

"Promise?"

"I promise."

4. prudemment
5. me suffit

"Okay, then," Agnes said cautiously[4]. "That's good enough for me[5]."

"Carol was in to see me," Marla said. "I really like her."

"I'm lucky to have her. She told me this morning that she's very worried about you."

Marla nodded. "That's what she said. Even though I've only met her a few times, she really seems to like me."

"What about Dr. Sturgess? Has he been in to

6. prendre de tes
nouvelles

check on you[6]?"

Marla shook her head. "I haven't seen him all day."

7. ne t'étais pas
assoupie

"No? Are you sure you hadn't just nodded off[7] or something?"

"I'm pretty sure. I mean, I've been sleepy, but I don't think he was here."

8. trouva

Agnes took out her cell phone, called up[8] a contact, tapped. She put the phone to her ear.

"I always thought you weren't supposed to use a

9. je fais ce qui
me chante

cell phone in the hospital," Marla said.

"In my hospital, I can do whatever I damn well

10. ça tombe sur
un répondeur

please[9]. You—Damn, it's gone to message[10]." She

chose not to leave one and put the phone away. "Just a second."

Agnes left the room and walked up to the nurses' station[1]. "Has Dr. Sturgess been by?" she asked.

No one had seen him.

Agnes returned to Marla's bedside. "Okay, why don't we get you dressed[2]."

"Tell me about it[3] again," Marla said dreamily.

"Oh, sweetheart, no."

"Please. It's so hard for me to remember; it helps when you tell me about it."

"But, darling, it's too sad. I just can't." Agnes's eyes began to moisten[4].

Marla, still sitting up, rested her head on the pillow and looked off[5] in the direction of the ceiling, her eyes not focused on anything in[6] particular.

"It is sad, I know that. But the thing is, I still had a child. A beautiful little girl. And she lived inside me for nine months, and I loved her, and I believe she loved me back. And I mourn her[7] every day. I *want* to remember her, those few moments I got to hold her. But it's a memory I have a hard time holding on to[8]."

"Marla, sweetheart—"

"Please, Mom? I know sometimes it's even harder for you to talk about than it is for me, but believe me, I like to hear this."

Agnes took a deep breath[9] through her nose. "I'll do it, but I don't think it's a good idea."

Marla waited for her mother to begin.

"After the baby came out, the doctor and I ... even though we knew its condition[10], we—"

"Her."

"I'm sorry?"

"*Her* condition. Agatha Beatrice Pickens was never an *it*."

---

1. salle des infirmières

2. si je t'aidais à t'habiller

3. Raconte-moi

4. briller de larmes

5. détourna le regard

6. sans rien fixer de

7. porte son deuil

8. du mal à garder

9. inspira profondément

10. état

1. serra
2. l'avons enveloppée
3. couverture

Agnes squeezed[1] her daughter's hand. "Of course she wasn't. We cleaned Agatha up, wrapped her up tight[2] in a blanket[3], and we propped some pillows behind your back so you could sit up, and then Dr. Sturgess put Agatha in your arms so you could hold her for a few moments."

"And tell me what I did," Marla said.

"You ..."

4. détourna la tête
5. calme

Agnes stopped a moment and turned away[4], but didn't take her hand off her daughter. She took another breath and, once composed[5], continued.

"You looked into Agatha's face and you said she was beautiful."

"I bet she was."

"You said she was the most beautiful child you had ever seen."

"And then what? I kissed her, didn't I?"

6. à peine
7. murmure haletant

Agnes closed her eyes. She could barely[6] say the words. They came out in a halting whisper[7]. "Yes, you did."

"On the forehead?" Marla asked.

"Yes," Agnes said, opening her eyes.

8. très fort
9. sentir son goût
10. son contact
11. l'emporter
12. t'ai laissée te reposer

It was Marla's turn to close hers. "When I think hard[8], I think I can taste her[9]. I can remember the feel of her[10] on my lips. And the smell of her. I'm sure I can. And what happened after that?"

"We had to take her away[11]," Agnes said. "The doctor took her away. And I let you rest[12]."

"I was very tired. I think I slept for a long time."

"You did."

13. des soucis que je te donne
14. bien dans ma tête

"But you were there when I woke up," Marla said, and smiled. "I'm sorry about all the trouble I've been[13] since then. I know I'm not quite right[14], that I've gone a little crazy."

"Don't say that. You're fine. You're strong. You're a good girl and I'm very proud of you. You're getting your life back on track[1]."

Marla looked into her mother's face. "I hope so. I don't think I've given you much[2] to be proud of."

Agnes leaned over the bed and took her daughter into her arms. "Don't ever say that. Don't think that for a minute."

"But I know," Marla said, her voice muffled[3] by her mother's shoulder, "you've always been worried about what people think. I know I haven't lived up to your expectations[4]."

"Stop it," Agnes said. "Just stop it." She took a deep breath. "I've told you about my friend. When I was in my teens. My best friend, Vera."

"Yes, Mom."

Agnes smiled. "I know. I've told you about her many times. About how, when she was twenty-three, and six months from graduating[5] at the University of Connecticut, she got pregnant."

"I know."

"I want you to listen. You need to hear this, even if I've told you before. It was actually her professor who got her pregnant[6]. Those kinds of things happened back then[7], professors having affairs[8] with their students. This was before that was seen as inappropriate[9], before sexual harassment policies[10]. Vera was going to go to medical school after college; she wanted to be a surgeon[11], but when she got pregnant, everything changed. It was a difficult pregnancy, and she had to withdraw from[12] her courses. And, of course, this professor was hardly going to[13] leave his wife and marry Vera. He tried to get her to end the pregnancy[14], but her faith[15] wouldn't permit that. And so she had this child, and was on her own to raise it—her

1. reprends le cours de ta vie

2. tellement de raisons

3. étouffée

4. ne suis pas à la hauteur de tes attentes

5. passer son diplôme

6. l'avait mise enceinte

7. à l'époque

8. des liaisons

9. déplacé

10. règles contre le harcèlement sexuel

11. chirurgienne

12. abandonner

13. n'allait pas

14. avorter

15. religion

1. l'avaient
pratiquement
reniée

2. ne se sont
jamais réalisés

3. saigne

parents pretty much disowned her[1]—and none of her dreams … none of them ever came true[2]. Of course, she wanted to have a baby one day, but this child, it came at the wrong time for her. Her life could have been very different, and my heart aches[3] for her every time I think about her. That baby came at the wrong time for her."

"Mom, I know. …"

"What I'm saying is, I know how sad you must be, how devastating this has been for you. But maybe, I don't know, maybe this is the way it's supposed to be for you. It wasn't the right time. Look at you. These Internet reviews, they might lead to something better, more rewarding[4]. You're moving forward[5]. What happened last night"—and Agnes glanced at her daughter's bandaged wrist— "is a bump in the road[6]. A big bump, sure, but a bump in the road. You're going to be okay. You're moving ahead."

4. enrichissant

5. avances

6. accident de
parcours

Marla's eyes closed briefly. She was drifting off[7].

Agnes released her daughter and said, "You start getting ready. I'm going to step out into the hall and call Dr. Sturgess to let him know I'm discharging you[8] on my own[9]."

7. s'endormait

8. te laisse sortir

9. de mon propre
chef

"Okay." Marla paused. "I say bad things about you sometimes, Mom. But I love you."

Agnes forced a smile, stepped out into the hall, walked past the nurses' station, giving the staff a curt nod[10], and continued on down the hall until she reached a supply room full of linens[11].

10. bref
hochement
de tête

11. draps

12. ne la
surprenne

13. pleura

She stepped in, closed the door, leaned her back up against it to make certain no one would walk in on her[12], placed her hand over her mouth, and wept[13].

FORTY-SEVEN

David

FROM Derek's, I went to the address for Marshall Kemper that I'd gotten from Mrs. Delaney at Davidson House.

It was, as it turned out[1], around the corner from[2] Samantha Worthington's place, and was little more[3] than a low white box of a house[4] that had been divided into two. There were two doors fronting the street[5], pushed to the far ends[6] of the house, and two identical windows set beside them.

Kemper's apartment was 36A Groveland Street, the other 36B.

I got out of the car, walked up to 36A, and, finding no doorbell[7], knocked. There was no response, so I knocked again, louder this time.

Still nothing.

I got my face up close to the door and called out, "Mr. Kemper? Are you in? My name's David Harwood! I need to talk to you!"

Stopped yelling[8] and listened. Not a sound from inside.

I walked over to 36B and knocked. I could hear a TV, so when no one came after the first knock, I

1. en fait

2. à deux pas de

3. guère plus

4. maisonnette blanche rectangulaire

5. côté rue

6. aux extrémités

7. sonnette

8. de crier

369

decided to try again. A few seconds later, an elderly[1] woman slowly opened the door.

"Yes?" she said.

"Hi," I said. "I was looking for Marshall Kemper."

She tilted her[2] head. "That's the man who lives next door. You got the wrong place."

"I know that. He's not home. I wondered whether you'd seen him around."

"Whatcha want him for[3]?"

"He's an old friend," I said. "I was passing by and thought I'd drop in on him[4]. Haven't seen him in a while."

The woman shrugged. "I don't keep track of his comings and goings[5]. But I don't see his van out there, so I guess he's not home. I'm missing[6] *The Price Is Right*[7]."

"Sure, sorry," I said. "Thanks for your time."

She was starting to close the door, then stopped, as if something had occurred to her[8]. "Maybe him and that girl went off on a holiday together or something."

"Girl?" I said. "You mean Sarita?"

Another shrug. "Maybe. Nice little thing[9]. Always says hi to me. Oh, it's the showcase[10]. Gotta go." She started to close the door but I put my hand up to stop it.

"When's the last time you saw her?" I asked.

"What?"

"When did you last see Sarita?"

Third shrug. "Last night[11], maybe? I don't know. I get the days mixed up[12] sometimes."

This time, when she went to close the door, I didn't try to stop her.

So Sarita, if it was Sarita, had been here recently. Since Rosemary Gaynor had been murdered. Maybe Kemper had taken her in[13], was hiding her.

Marginal notes:

1. âgée
2. pencha la
3. Qu'est-ce que vous lui voulez
4. ai eu envie de passer le voir
5. ne suis pas ses allées et venues
6. suis en train de rater
7. [émission télévisée]
8. une idée lui était venue
9. Gentille cocotte
10. ça commence
11. Hier soir
12. mélange les dates
13. l'avait recueillie

Maybe the two of them had taken off[1] together. Which strongly suggested they had something to do[2] with the woman's murder. The harder it was to find Sarita, the more likely it seemed to me[3] that Marla really hadn't killed that woman.

Not[4] that I'd found out anything useful so far[5] that might help my cousin. Even Derek wasn't willing to dismiss outright[6] the idea that she could be a killer. Nothing she did would surprise him, he'd said. Not the sort of thing you wanted to hear someone say on the stand[7] in front of a jury[8].

I went back to 36A and banged on the door once more.

"Sarita?" I called out. "Sarita Gomez? Are you there? If you are, I really need to talk to you. I'm not the police. I have nothing to do with them. I'm trying to help out a friend. If you're in there, please open the door and talk to me."

I waited.

After thirty seconds, I used my hand as a visor[9] and peered[10] through the window. I could make out[11] a bed and a kitchen area, a couple of chairs. But I didn't see any movement.

"Nuts[12]," I said under my breath.

As I walked back to my car, my phone rang. I looked at it, saw that it was Finley.

"How's it going?" he asked.

"Fine."

"So how long I gotta wait[13] before you start helping me out?"

"I don't know. Another day or so, maybe."

"Because this job isn't going to sit around[14] forever," Finley said. "Plenty of others who'd like to take it."

"Then maybe you should hire[15] one of them," I said.

---

1. pris la tangente
2. à voir
3. plus il me semblait probable
4. Ça ne voulait pas dire
5. jusqu'ici
6. hésitait à éliminer
7. à la barre
8. des jurés
9. visière
10. regardai
11. distinguer
12. Dingue
13. faut que je poireaute
14. vous attendre
15. embaucher

"Fuck it, you're the one I want. Just get done doing whatever the hell it is you're doing. I'm hearing things through the grapevines[1], that there's something weird[2] going on in town. A bunch of dead squirrels—I found those myself—and the Ferris wheel out at Five Mountains starting up on its own with some mannequins in it with some creepy threat[3] written on them, and last night at Thackeray—"

"Save it[4]," I said. "I haven't started yet. When I have, you can tell me all about it."

"This is serious shit[5], Harwood. If I didn't know better[6], I'd say someone was going around trying to rattle the good folks[7] of Promise Falls."

"What, are you saying these things are connected?"

"Who knows? And even if they aren't, this is the sort of thing I can use. Telling people they deserve to[8] feel safe in their homes, that—"

"I meant what I said. Save it. Soon as I can devote all my attention to your needs I'll let you know."

Finley grunted[9]. The call ended. We all have our ways[10] of saying good-bye.

Getting behind the wheel[11], I wasn't sure what to do next.

When in doubt[12], head home[13]. I figured I could come back here later in the day, see if Kemper or Sarita had turned up[14].

It wasn't my subconscious at work[15] that took me past[16] Samantha Worthington's on my way home. It really was the most direct route. But as I approached her address, I found myself taking my foot off the gas[17] so I could look at her place[18] as I drove by.

It wasn't as if I'd been thinking of her every single moment since she'd been to the house to return the pocket watch. But she'd been in the back of my mind[1]. Like a head tune[2] that's been playing for hours without your realizing it, and then suddenly you say, "How the hell did I get the theme[3] from *The Rockford Files*[4] in there?"

But Samantha's lurking[5] presence in my thoughts was a bit different from a tune from a seventies TV show.

She'd be at her job now, I figured. Managing the Laundromat. I didn't know which one, which was probably just as well[6]. If I had, I might have found myself concocting some lame[7] excuse to drop by.

I could just imagine what my mother would say if I headed out the door with a basket of dirty laundry[8]. "What are you thinking?" she'd say. "You are not taking that out to be done! You leave that with me right now!"

Add it to the list of reasons I needed to move out[9].

What I didn't expect, as I rolled past Samantha's place, was that she would walk out the front door[10].

And look right at me.

Shit.

I had an instant to decide how to handle it[11]. I could speed off[12], pretend I hadn't seen her. Except it was pretty clear[13] I had. I could still speed off, but she'd be left with the impression that I was up to something[14], that I had something to hide, that I was stalking her[15].

Which I was not.

Okay, maybe driving by here the night before was a little suspect, but this was legit[16]. I was just passing by going from point A to point B.

1. je l'avais dans un coin de la tête
2. air entêtant
3. air du générique
4. [feuilleton policier]
5. en toile de fond
6. pas plus mal
7. bidon
8. linge sale
9. déménager
10. apparaîtrait à la porte
11. réagir
12. partir fissa
13. assez évident
14. comploterais quelque chose
15. la suivais
16. réglo

I could wave and keep on going.

But that would look stupid.

I hit the brakes[1]. Not too hard. Not hard enough to squeal the tires[2]. But a nice, even[3] slowdown. I brought the car to a halt[4] at the opposite curb[5] and powered down[6] the window.

I said, "Hey, I thought that was you."

She walked to the sidewalk, talked to me across two lanes. She grinned. "You got me[7] under surveillance?"

"Yeah," I said. "Right here in broad daylight. Just heading back to my folks' house from a job thing." Kind of a lie, although I had just been talking to Finley. "You off[8] today?"

Samantha shook her head. "No. But like I said, I can leave the place unattended for short periods of time. I came home for some lunch[9]. Heading back now."

"Thanks again," I said.

"For what? The watch, or not shooting you?"

I smiled. "Take your pick[10]." I still had my foot on the brake. "I should let you go."

"Listen," she said, "do you have two seconds?"

I moved the gearshift[11] into park[12], but the engine was still running[13]. "What is it?"

"My wifi is out, and I think it's the modem, but I never know how to reset the thing[14], and when Carl gets home he'll want to go online and won't be able to."

I nodded, put the window up, killed[15] the engine, and locked the car. I waited for a blue pickup truck with tinted windows to pass, then ran across the street.

"You sure you don't mind?" she asked. "I could call someone."

---

1. freinai
2. faire grincer les pneus
3. souple
4. arrêtai la voiture
5. trottoir d'en face
6. fis descendre
7. m'avez placée
8. Vous bossez pas
9. manger un morceau
10. Au choix
11. levier de vitesses
12. en position parking
13. tournait encore
14. redémarrer le machin
15. éteignis

"No, you don't want to do that[1]," I said. "Usually all you have to do is unplug it[2], wait a few seconds, plug it back in, and wait a couple of minutes. You bring a cable guy[3] out to the house and he'll charge you a hundred bucks[4]."

"I really appreciate it," she said, leading me back to her front door. She had her keys out, unlocked the door and swung it open.

"Where's the modem, Samantha?"

"Sam," she said. "Call me Sam. It's right there, under the TV, with the DVD player and the Nintendo and all that stuff[5]."

I was in a small living room the moment I stepped into the place[6], with the entertainment unit[7] on the side wall. I got out my phone and went to the settings to see whether I could detect any wifi signal[8]. I wasn't getting anything.

I got down on my knees, took hold[9] of the modem, pulled out the wire[10] on the back that led to a power bar[11].

"Can I get you anything[12]?" Sam asked. "A Coke, a beer?"

"I'm okay," I said. I was counting to ten in my head. When I got there, I pushed the wire back into the jack[13]. "Okay, let's see what happens here."

The row of lights[14] on the modem started to dance[15].

"That looks promising," Sam said.

"See if you can get on[16]."

She had a laptop[17] on a table in an L off the living room[18]. She sat down, tapped away[19]. "Hang on[20]. Okay, yeah, it's connected. Oh, that's great. Thanks for that."

I stood, positioning myself on the opposite side of the table. "No problem."

---

1. pas la peine
2. le débrancher
3. électricien
4. vous prendra cent balles
5. et tout ça
6. dès l'entrée
7. tous les éléments vidéo
8. réseau
9. m'emparai
10. tirai le câble
11. multiprise
12. Vous voulez boire quelque chose
13. prise
14. rangée de voyants
15. clignoter
16. vous connecter
17. ordinateur portable
18. renfoncement en L du salon
19. se mit à pianoter
20. Attendez

1. vous ai cherché sur Google

2. cochon

3. s'évanouit

4. fâché

5. signées de vous

6. sur

7. ne m'attendais pas à trouver ça

8. n'est pas au courant

9. Vous avez dû en baver

10. On fait avec ce que la vie nous amène

11. comprends

12. passé

13. Que ça nous plaise ou non

"I Googled you[1]," she said, glancing down at the computer. She laughed. "That almost sounds dirty[2], doesn't it?"

But her smile faded[3] when I said, "Why'd you do that?"

"Don't be mad[4]. I mean, mostly what I found were lots of stories with your byline on them[5], that you wrote for the *Standard*."

I guessed they hadn't shut down the Web site yet.

"But there were also stories *about*[6] you," she said.

"Yeah," I said.

"I do that with people I meet all the time. Google them, I mean. I just, you know, was just curious." Her face became more serious. "I had no idea what I'd find[7]. I'm really sorry."

I said nothing.

"Your wife, Jan?"

I nodded.

"That was terrible. Really tragic. It wasn't like I was expecting to find anything like that. Mostly I was just checking to see that you weren't a serial killer or anything."

"I'm not," I said.

"Yeah, well, if you are, the Internet doesn't know about it[8]. It has to have been hard[9] these past few years."

I shrugged. "You deal with what life hands you[10], I guess. There's not really much else you can do."

"I get that[11]. I mean, really, I do. We've all got a history[12], don't we?"

"I guess we do," I said. "And we have to live with it."

She forced a grin. "Whether we like it or not[13]."

376

"Ain't that the truth[1]," I said.

I felt like we were spinning our wheels[2]. We stared at each other, neither of us moving, neither of us heading toward the door.

Sam touched her fingers to[3] the hollow[4] at the base of her neck, rubbed lightly. The top of her chest swelled[5] with each breath. "How long has it been[6]?"

I waited several seconds before answering, wanting to be sure I understood what she was asking[7].

"A while," I said. "In Boston. Couple of times. Didn't mean anything. I've been … reluctant[8]. I'm just worried about Ethan. I've been trying to limit my complications."

Sam nodded. "Same." A pause. "I wouldn't want to add to those[9]. But … it wouldn't have to mean anything[10]."

I came around the table as she pushed her chair back and stood. It just happened. My mouth was on hers. We were two people who'd walked in from the desert and hadn't had water in weeks[11].

She twisted[12] in my arms, presented her back to me, and pressed herself up against me. Hard[13]. I slipped my arms under hers and took a breast in each hand. Found her nipples[14] beneath blouse and bra[15].

Sam tipped forward[16], put her palms flat on the table.

"Here," she breathed[17]. "Right here."

And for a while, I let my own needs come[18] before Marla's or Randy's or anyone else's. Maybe even Sam's.

When I left an hour later, I happened to notice a blue pickup truck parked up the street, windows

1. Vous pouvez le dire
2. faisions du surplace
3. toucha du doigt
4. creux
5. se gonflait
6. Ça fait combien de temps
7. sa question
8. réticent
9. vous en rajouter
10. ça pourrait être juste comme ça
11. depuis des semaines
12. se retourna
13. Fort
14. le bout de ses seins
15. le soutien-gorge
16. se pencha en avant
17. souffla-t-elle
18. fis passer mes propres besoins

1. teintées
2. n'y prêtai aucune attention

too tinted[1] to tell whether anyone was inside, but didn't give it another thought[2].

FORTY-EIGHT

"**WHAT** the hell[1]!" Marshall shouted in the co-coon of his black van, looking at the note[2] that Bill Gaynor had left for him in the bag. "You prick[3]!"

So Gaynor just decided he'd change the location of the drop[4], did he? Who the hell did he think he was[5]? Did he think he was running this operation[6]?

"Son of a bitch," Marshall said to himself.

Was the guy setting him up[7]? Leading him into some kind of trap? Hard to know, when Marshall hadn't called him yet to find out where he wanted to hand over the money. But it was fishy[8], no doubt about it.

Then again, Marshall told himself, maybe the guy had a point[9]. Look at that old guy at the mall who tried to get to the bag before Marshall could. Could you blame[10] someone for not wanting to put fifty thousand dollars in a garbage bin?

So then maybe it *wasn't* a trap. Gaynor was just being cautious[11]. He didn't want to take any chances[12] that the money would go to the wrong person. It probably wasn't like he could go out and get another fifty grand just like that. Suppose it was the other way around[13], Marshall thought.

1. Putain de merde
2. message
3. Espèce de connard
4. lieu du dépôt
5. Non mais, pour qui il se prenait
6. le boss
7. Est-ce que le mec lui montait un sale coup
8. louche
9. n'avait pas tort
10. en vouloir à
11. prudent
12. le moindre risque
13. l'inverse

Would he want to dump that kind of cash[1] where any asshole might grab it? Probably not.

The thing was, Marshall was so close to the money he could taste it. He and Sarita were ready to hit the road[2], to make new lives for themselves. So he wanted to believe Gaynor's motives[3] were genuine[4]. It wasn't as though Marshall was really going to call the cops now, and miss out on[5] getting that money.

He'd have to do what Gaynor asked—call him. He reached into his pocket for his cell[6], and the instant he touched it, it rang, causing him to jump[7]. He looked at the name on the screen—D. STEMPLE—and did not recognize it. No, wait. Wasn't that the name of the woman who lived in the other side of the house? Mrs. Stemple?

He accepted the call, put the phone to his ear. "Hello?" He could hear a television in the background.

"Marshall?"

It was Sarita. Made sense[8] that if she had to call him, she would ask to use the phone next door. He didn't have a landline[9] in his apartment, and Sarita had never owned a cell phone.

He could hear a television blaring[10] in the background, and Mrs. Stemple saying, "It's not long-distance, is it?"

"No," Sarita told her. Then, to him: "A man was here."

"What?"

"I have to get out of here. I can't stay here any longer."

"What man?"

"First he knocked on the door, asking for you. I hid behind the bed; I didn't move. He called for you and then I heard him go next door. Where I am now. The lady who lives next to you."

"Yeah, yeah, I know. I saw her name on the phone."

"Then he came back, and this time he started calling out for me."

"Jesus. Was it a cop?"

"I don't know. He said he wasn't."

"That's just what a cop might say[1]."

1. Ça veut rien dire, au contraire

"He said his name was David Harwood, that he needed to talk to me, that he was trying to help out a friend."

"So what happened then?"

"He gave up[2]," Sarita said. "I didn't go to the door. He must have figured no one was here. I heard a car start up, and when I peeked outside, there was no one there. The man was gone, no car."

2. a laissé tomber

"Okay, then. We're good."

"I have to get out of here. If that man could figure out[3] I might be here, who else will figure it out? The next time it might really be the police."

3. a pu piger

"Just ... okay, okay. I get[4] that you're scared; I get that. But just hang in[5]. In another hour or so, everything is going to be okay. You'll see."

4. vois bien
5. attends encore

"You got the money?"

"Not yet. But it's going to happen."

"Forget the money. What you're doing is wrong[6]. You have to—"

6. mal

"Please just let me do this for you. For us. Trust me. I have to go. I won't be long."

Marshall ended the call. He had to get back to Gaynor, find out where he wanted to leave the money. Gaynor answered on the first ring.

"You shouldn't have done that," Marshall said. "You shouldn't have changed the plan. I told you, I'll go to the police. I will!"

"I'm sorry, I'm sorry, honestly, I am. I just—"

"I'm in charge, okay? I'm the one calling the shots on this[1]." Marshall tried to keep[2] his voice from shaking.

"I know, I know," Gaynor said, sounding respectful. "I get that. But I just couldn't do it. I didn't think it was safe. I thought, What if someone else is watching and tries to get the money before you do? The mall's such a public place. A lot of people could see me do that."

"Okay, fine," Marshall said. "Let me think of another place where—"

"You don't have to," he said. "It's already taken care of[3]."

"What?"

"I've left it somewhere. Somewhere a lot safer."

"Whoa, whoa, hang on. *You* don't decide where the money goes. *I* do that. That's the way it works[4]."

Had this guy never seen a movie? Did the parents of the kidnapped kid choose where to drop off the money? This was not the way these things were done.

"I've never been involved in anything like this before," Gaynor said. "Is there a fucking playbook[5] I'm supposed to follow? You want the money or not?"

That was the question, wasn't it? And Marshall knew the answer.

"Okay, fine, where is it?"

"It's in a mailbox[6]," Gaynor said.

Marshall thought, Hey, maybe that's not that bad an idea. Putting the money in a locked box in a post office. There might be video cameras, but

---

1. C'est moi qui commande
2. empêcher
3. réglé
4. comme ça que ça marche
5. manuel
6. boîte aux lettres

he could wear a broad-brimmed[1] hat or something so no one would get a good look at[2] his face. But how did Gaynor plan to get the key to him[3]?

So Marshall Kemp asked.

And Gaynor said, "Not that kind of mailbox. One out in the country, along the side of the road."

"What?"

"It's perfect," Gaynor said. "It's out in the middle of nowhere. No one's going to see you pick it up. The mailman doesn't even go by[4] until the middle of the afternoon."

"You saying the money is right there, now?"

"It's there. I put it there myself. Let me give you directions."

What was he supposed to do? Tell him to forget it? Tell Gaynor to go back and get the money and deliver it someplace else[5]?

No, that'd take too long. If the money was in the mailbox now, Kemper could go get it, race home[6], grab[7] Sarita's stuff[8], throw it in the van, and take off[9]. If he insisted on a third delivery point, he'd be looking at[10] another hour, hour and a half.

"Okay, where's this mailbox?" Marshall asked.

A country road about five miles[11] out of Promise Falls, Gaynor explained. Out in the middle of farmland[12] and woods. Not even visible, Gaynor said, from any houses. The mailbox was at the end of a small private road that led into forest.

"You know those stick-on[13], slanted[14] letters you can get at Home Depot[15]?" Gaynor asked. "It says 'Boone' on the side, in those letters. The little metal flag[16] will be down. If it's up, someone *might* think something was in there."

"If that money's not there," Marshall warned, "I go to the police. I'm not kidding around here[17]." Trying to sound tough[18].

1. à large bord
2. ne pourrait voir clairement
3. lui filer la clef

4. ne passe même pas

5. ailleurs

6. foncer chez lui
7. choper
8. les affaires
9. filer
10. ça lui prendrait encore
11. à env. 8 km

12. terres agricoles

13. autocollantes
14. penchées
15. [boutique de bricolage]
16. fanion

17. ne blague pas, là
18. un ton de dur à cuire

1. démarra
2. en vue
3. aérer la voiture
4. un tour de reconnaissance
5. ralentit à peine
6. voitures de police
7. dans les deux sens
8. pas débile
9. s'arrêta
10. menait bel et bien
11. abri de chasse
12. poussaient carrément au bord de
13. à 6 m
14. rouillé
15. de 25 cm de haut
16. 60 cm de profondeur
17. hangar
18. arrondi
19. grinçante
20. extirpa

He tossed the phone onto the seat next to him and hit the gas[1].

Marshall had no problem finding the mailbox, and it was as Gaynor had described it: well isolated, no residence in sight[2]. And hardly any cars on the road. He'd put down the front windows to let the fresh country air blow through[3].

The first thing Marshall did was some recon[4]. He barely slowed[5] when he saw the mailbox with BOONE on the side. He kept on going to the next road. He figured, if Gaynor had called the cops, there'd be a few cruisers[6] posted nearby. But there were no cop cars within two miles, either way[7], of the mailbox.

No helicopters in the air, either.

Maybe he hadn't done anything like this before, but Marshall Kemper was no fool[8].

He turned the van around and returned to the Boone lane, pulled in[9]. It did indeed lead[10] into thick forest. Someone must have had a home deep in there somewhere. A hunting cabin[11], maybe.

The trees came right up close to[12] the road.

He stopped with the driver's door about twenty feet[13] from the mailbox, a rusted[14] aluminum container about ten inches high[15], two feet deep[16]. Shaped like a barn[17] with a rounded[18] roof. He walked around to the front of it, pulled down the squeaky[19] door, and there, just like Gaynor promised, was a package.

Not an eco bag, but something the size of a shoe box, wrapped in brown paper, with string tied around it. He worked[20] the package out of the box, closed the door, and went back to his truck.

As he was getting in, he felt something sharp[1] jab him[2] in the neck.

"Jesus!" he shouted, the package falling out of his hands and hitting the gravel road.

For a split second[3], he wondered whether he'd been stung by a bee[4]. But as soon as he turned his head, he saw that there was someone in the passenger seat.

A man, late fifties[5], nice suit.

With a syringe[6] in his hand.

"What the— What the fuck did you do?" Marshall said. He slapped his hand on his neck where the needle[7] had gone in.

The man pointed the business end[8] of the syringe at Marshall, using it like a gun to keep him from attacking him.

"Listen to me," the man said. "You don't have much time. You're probably already starting to feel the effects. It works fast."

The guy was right about that. Marshall felt his arms getting heavy. His head was turning into[9] a bowling ball.

"What did you do?"

"Listen to me," he said again. "I have a second syringe. It'll counteract[10] what I just injected into you. Because it's going to kill you."

"Like, an anecdote[11]?"

"Yeah, like that. But there isn't much time."

"Then get the thecond thyringe[12]!" Christ, it really was fast. His tongue was expanding[13] like a sponge.

"Just as soon as you answer my questions. How did you find out[14] what you know about Gaynor?"

"I justht did, thass all."

"Was it Sarita?"

Marshall shook his head.

1. de pointu
2. le piquer
3. fraction de seconde
4. piqué par une abeille
5. la cinquantaine bien avancée
6. seringue
7. aiguille
8. bout pointu
9. se changeait en
10. neutraliser
11. [il pense "antidote"]
12. [second syringe]
13. gonflait
14. appris

"Clock's ticking[1]," the man said.

Marshall nodded. "Yeah."

"Where is she?"

He tried to shake his head, but it was getting harder and harder to move it. "I'm not delling[2]. ..."

2. [telling]

"Tick-tock."

3. [She's at my place]

"Sheeth at my plathe[3]."

"Is she there now?"

Another feeble nod.

"Where do you live?"

4. prononcer

5. du mal

6. fouilla

Marshall tried to form[4] the words, but he was having a hard time[5] getting them out. The man opened the van's glove box, rooted around[6] until he found the ownership and insurance papers[7].

7. la carte grise et les papiers d'assurance

"Is this up-to-date[8]?" the man asked. "Groveland Street? Apartment 36A?"

8. à jour

Another nod.

"Good, that's good. That's all I wanted to know."

9. de toutes ses forces

Struggling with everything he had[9], Marshall said, "Other thyrinth."

"There is no other syringe."

10. suffoquer à grand bruit

Marshall started to make choking noises[10], leaned forward, put his head on the top of the steering wheel.

Another man approached the van on the passenger side.

"Did he tell you, Jack?" the second man asked.

"Yeah, he did. I know where Sarita is. How's the hole coming[11], Bill?"

11. Comment avance le trou

Bill Gaynor raised his dirty hands. "I've got three fucking blisters[12]."

12. ampoules

13. C'est pas à lui qu'il faut t'en plaindre

Jack Sturgess, tipping his head in Marshall Kemper's direction, said, "Don't complain to him[13]."

FORTY-NINE

MRS. Selfridge came through for[1] Barry Duckworth. An e-mail, which included phone numbers related to[2] Sarita's use of Mrs. Selfridge's landline[3], dropped into[4] his cell shortly after he left Derek Cutter's place. He tapped on an already highlighted[5] number, hopeful that whoever picked up would prove to be helpful[6].

He got lucky.

"Davidson House," a woman said. "How may I connect you[7]?"

"Sorry, wrong number," he said, and headed straight there[8].

Shortly after he arrived, he was introduced to a Mrs. Delaney, who told him that yes, Sarita Gomez had worked for them, and no, she was not in today.

"I told all this to the other gentleman," she said.

"What other gentleman?"

Mrs. Delaney pondered[9]. "I don't think he ever told me his name. But he said he was conducting an investigation[10]."

"What did he look like?"

The man Mrs. Delaney described could be David Harwood. It also could have been a number of other people.

"What did you tell him?"

----

1. avait tenu sa promesse envers
2. liés à
3. téléphone fixe
4. arriva sur
5. déjà en surbrillance
6. se révèlerait en mesure de l'aider
7. À qui souhaitez-vous parler
8. s'y rendit directement
9. réfléchit
10. menait une enquête

"Well, I told him about Mr. Kemper."

"Who's that?"

Mrs. Delaney told him, and provided an address to the detective, just as she had[1] for the other man. Duckworth left.

He parked out front of the Kemper address and went to the door. Banged on it good and hard[2].

"Mr. Kemper! Marshall Kemper! This is the police!"

Duckworth peered through the window, saw no life. He went around to the back of the house and looked through a window there, too. Except for maybe the bathroom, he could see into pretty much[3] all of the apartment.

He went to the front door and banged again, just in case he was being ignored. "If there's anyone inside, you need to open the door! My name's Barry Duckworth and I'm a detective with the Promise Falls police!"

Nothing.

He marched over to the other door, banged just as loud[4]. About half a minute later, an elderly woman slowly opened it. The moment he saw her, Duckworth was sorry for hitting[5] the door with quite so much force.

"What's all the racket[6]?" she asked, a television blaring in the background. It was one of those court shows[7]. That lady judge who tore a strip off everybody[8].

"I'm with the police, ma'am. Sorry for the noise."

Duckworth took out his identification and displayed it for the woman. Didn't flash it[9], gave her plenty of time to look it over.

"Okay," she said. "You passed the test."

"What's your name, ma'am?"

1. tout comme elle l'avait fait

2. Frappa fort à la porte

3. pratiquement

4. tout aussi fort

5. regretta d'avoir frappé

6. ce raffut

7. procès télévisés

8. remonte les bretelles à tout le monde

9. Ne se contenta pas de l'agiter sous son nez

"Doris Stemple."

"Are you the landlord[1], by any chance? Do you rent out[2] the unit[3] next to you here?"

She shook her head. "Landlord's name is Byron Hinkley. Lives in Albany. Comes by once a week, if I'm lucky[4], to cut the grass. But if you've got a leaky tap[5] or something, don't hold your breath[6]."

"I'm looking for Marshall Kemper."

"Yeah, well, he don't live here. That's his place next door."

"Have you seen him?"

"He in some kind of trouble?"

"I just need to talk to him, Ms. Stemple."

"Don't give me that Ms. shit[7]. It's Mrs[8]. My husband, Arnie Stemple, died fifteen years ago."

"Mrs. Stemple, have you seen Mr. Kemper lately?"

"Saw him head out[9] early today, I think. At least, I heard his truck take off[10]."

"Have you seen a woman? Her name would be Sarita. Sarita Gomez. I think she might be with him."

"The Mexican girl, yeah, I seen her. I think she took off with him."

"And when was this?"

"Like I said, not long ago. They took off in kind of a hurry[11]."

"Did they say anything to you?"

"I was only watching from the door here. I doubt they even noticed me."

"Have you noticed anything unusual next door the last day or so? Odd comings and goings[12]? Strange people dropping by?"

Doris Stemple shook her head. "I won't lie. I kind of watch what's going on. But I haven't seen anything weird lately[13]. There's a kid up the street, he's about nine, likes to walk around with

---

1. propriétaire

2. louez

3. partie

4. et encore

5. robinet qui fuit

6. faut pas compter sur lui

7. Lâchez-moi avec vos madame ou mademoiselle

8. Je suis une femme mariée

9. sortir

10. démarrer

11. avaient l'air pressés

12. De drôles d'allées et venues

13. ces derniers temps

his privates hanging out[1]—he's not right in the head[2]—but other than that, not that much goes on around here."

Duckworth handed her[3] one of his business cards. "If you see Mr. Kemper, or his girlfriend, would you please call me? And if you see them, don't tell them I was asking around for them[4]. I'd like them to be here when I get back."

She waved the card in the air with her bony[5] hands. "Okeydokey," she said. "I'm gonna go back and watch TV, if that's all right with you[6]."

"Sure," Duckworth said. "Thanks very much for your time."

He got back behind the wheel of his car and decided to return to the station[7]. He was still waiting to hear back from the hotel in Boston where Bill Gaynor had been staying[8]. He wanted to know whether the man had left for home when he'd said he had.

Doris Stemple closed the door of her apartment, locked the door, and called out in the direction of the bathroom, "You can come out now."

Sarita Gomez emerged slowly. "He's gone?"

"He's gone."

"He was police?"

"He sure was," the woman said, backing into an overstuffed[9] chair that was, curiously, in a nearly upright position[10]. She settled herself against the cushioning, gripped a small black remote control[11] that was tethered[12] to the chair with a black cord, touched a button, and the piece of furniture[13] slowly descended into its original position, its motor softly whirring[14] the entire time. When it was finished, her eyes were perfectly level with[15] the television.

---

1. les parties à l'air
2. pas bien dans sa tête
3. lui tendit
4. que je les cherchais
5. osseuses
6. si ça vous gêne pas
7. commissariat
8. avait séjourné
9. trop rembourré
10. presque à la verticale
11. télécommande
12. connectée
13. siège
14. ronronnant
15. en face de

"Can I use your phone again?" Sarita asked.

"Still trying to raise[1] that boyfriend of yours?"

"That's right."

"Okay, that's fine. Just don't be putting[2] any calls to Mexico on there."

"I won't do that."

She used the landline, entered the same number she'd been trying for the last fifteen minutes. Marshall was not answering. It kept going to message[3].

"Marshall, when you get this, call Mrs. Stemple. *Please.*"

Sarita hung up, slowly crossed the room, and sat down in the chair next to the old woman. She reached over and patted[4] the young girl's hand.

"Still no luck?"

Sarita shook her head. "Something's gone wrong."

"What's he off doing[5]?"

"Something really, really stupid."

"Well, that's men for you[6]. Anytime they do something smart[7] it should show up[8] on that little ticker runs[9] across the bottom of the screen on CNN[10]. That'd be news[11]."

Sarita took a tissue[12] from the box on the small table next to Mrs. Stemple and dabbed[13] her eyes, blew her nose.

"Must be bad, the police coming around, looking for both of you," the old woman said.

Sarita said, "Yeah. But I'm not a bad person. All I wanted to do was the right thing. But now that I did it, I have to get away."

"You don't seem like a bad person to me. You seem like a nice girl. And thank you for helping me make my bed and warming up my soup."

Margin glosses:
1. contacter
2. ne va pas passer
3. Elle tombait toujours sur le répondeur
4. tapota
5. parti faire
6. c'est bien les hommes
7. malin
8. s'afficher
9. bulletin qui défile
10. la chaîne d'info
11. nouveau
12. mouchoir
13. s'essuya

1. m'occuper
2. mon métier
3. parie
4. faire ma valise
5. encore un peu
6. Pas que ça me regarde
7. ai appris
8. qui m'employait
9. qu'elle n'aurait pas dû savoir
10. déglutit péniblement
11. Seigneur
12. Pas avec certitude
13. qui cloche chez lui

"I needed to keep busy doing something[1]. And it's what I do[2]. I look after people at Davidson House."

"Well, I'll bet[3] you're one of their favorites," Mrs. Stemple said. "What do you think you'll do?"

"I can't wait much longer for Marshall. I'm going to pack my stuff[4] and get out of here in a little while, but if it's okay with you, I'm going to hang out here awhile[5]. In case Marshall calls, and to make sure that policeman isn't going back to his place."

"Okay by me. Don't get much company," she said.

"I'm going to try calling him again."

"It's only been a minute."

But Sarita left the chair and tried anyway. Fifteen seconds later, she was back sitting down.

She used another tissue to dab at her eyes. "I think something bad has happened. Maybe he's been arrested."

Doris said, "None of my business[6], but you want to tell me what kind of trouble you're in?"

"I ... figured out[7] something. I heard some things, and I told someone. I told Mrs. Gaynor. She was the lady I worked for[8]. I thought it was the right thing to do. I told her something she wasn't supposed to know[9], I guess." She swallowed hard[10]. "And now she's dead."

"Good Lord[11]," said Mrs. Stemple. "You know who killed that woman? I saw that on the news."

Sarita shook her head. "Not for certain[12]. But Mr. Gaynor ... I never liked him. I've never trusted him. There's something not right about him[13]. When I found her ..." She had to stop. Her eyes opened wider, as if seeing something that, in her

392

memory, was more vivid[1] than what was actually around her.

"When I found her, I tried to set things straight[2]."

"And what was that, darlin'?"

Sarita didn't hear the question. "But I didn't do enough. I should have explained." She turned and looked at the old woman. "I … I hate to ask this, but would you have any money?"

"Money?"

Sarita nodded. "I need to get to New York. Maybe a bus, or on the train. I have to get to Albany first. I'd tell you[3] I'd pay you back[4], but I'm not sure I'll be able to do it. Not anytime soon[5]. If you had anything you could spare[6]—I have to tell you the truth—you'll probably never see it again."

The old woman smiled. "You wait here." She grabbed the remote button for the chair and slowly, almost magically, she was elevated into a standing position. She walked slowly into her bedroom, where she could be heard[7] opening and closing several drawers. When she returned, she had several bills[8] in her hand, which she handed to Sarita.

"There's four hundred and twenty-five dollars there," she said.

Sarita appeared ready to weep[9]. "I can't thank you enough."

"I bet no one ever gave you a tip[10] at Davidson Place for all the work you done, did they?"

Sarita shook her head.

"Well, then, you take that, and you get out of here[11]."

"Thank you," Sarita said. "Thank you so much. For that, and for not giving me away[12] when the policeman came to the door."

"No problem."

"I wouldn't ever want to get you into trouble."

---

1. paraissait plus réel
2. arranger les choses
3. J'aimerais vous dire
4. que je vous rembourserai
5. de sitôt
6. en trop
7. on l'entendit
8. billets
9. parut au bord des larmes
10. pourboire
11. file
12. ne pas m'avoir trahie

1. eu affaire aux

2. faisais le tapin

3. je m'en cogne

Mrs. Stemple shrugged. "I've dealt with[1] cops before. Back when I was your age, when I was a working girl[2], I had to deal with those assholes all the time. I don't know what you and your boyfriend did, darling, but I don't give a rat's ass[3]."

FIFTY

WALDEN Fisher trekked up[1] to the Promise Falls cemetery almost every day. He liked to go up after he'd had breakfast, but once he'd taken Victor Rooney back to his van, he'd decided to run a few errands[2], and his visit to the cemetery got pushed back to midday.

Just so long as he got there[3].

He'd only started making this a daily trip[4] since Beth had died. He had wanted to come up here more often to kneel[5] at his daughter Olivia's headstone[6] and say a few words, but Beth would not accompany him. It was too upsetting[7] for her. Even when they were just driving around town, both of them in the car, Walden had to make sure their travels[8] did not take them past the cemetery.

All Beth had to see was the gates of the place to be overcome[9].

Sometimes in the evenings, and on weekends when he wasn't working, Walden would tell Beth he was off to Home Depot, and come up here instead to visit his daughter. But one[10] couldn't justify a daily visit to the hardware giant[11]. No home needed that much maintenance[12]. So he got up here only once a week or so.

1. faisait l'effort d'aller

2. faire quelques courses

3. Du moment qu'il y allait

4. à y aller tous les jours

5. s'agenouiller

6. tombe

7. bouleversant

8. trajets

9. submergée par l'émotion

10. on

11. géant du bricolage

12. autant de réparations

1. caveau

But now, with Beth gone, with his wife and daughter both here sharing a plot[1], there was nothing to stop him from coming as often as he wanted.

2. était passé chez

He didn't always bring flowers, but today he did. He'd popped into[2] a florist on Richmond, at the foot of Proctor, for a bouquet of spring flowers. It was only after he'd gotten back into his car that he realized the woman behind the counter had shortchanged him[3], giving him a five instead of a ten.

3. ne lui avait pas rendu assez

There were some things you couldn't worry about[4].

4. moins importantes que d'autres

5. allée de gravier

6. Bientôt

He parked his van on the gravel lane[5] that led through the cemetery and walked slowly over to the Fisher family plot. There was a headstone for Olivia, one for Beth, space for a third.

"Soon enough[6]," he said, setting a bouquet in front of each stone. He went down on one knee, positioning himself midway between the stones so he could address them both.

"It's a beautiful day," Walden said. "Sun's shining. Everyone's hoping we have nice weather for the Memorial Day weekend. Still a couple of weeks away. No sense[7] listening to what the weathermen[8] have to say. They can't get what it's going to be like tomorrow right[9], so who knows what the long weekend's going to be like. I'm not going anywhere, of course. I'll be right here."

7. Inutile

8. les gens de la météo

9. n'arrivent pas à prédire le temps qu'il fera demain

He paused, focused on the words "Elizabeth Fisher" carved[10] into granite.

10. gravés

11. fiches de recettes

12. que tu gardais

13. l'idée m'est venue

"The other day, I couldn't stop thinking about that paprika chicken dish you always used to make. I went all through your box of recipe cards[11] and through all those cooking books you saved[12], and I couldn't find it anywhere. And then it hit me[13] that you probably never even had the recipe written down anywhere, that it was all in your head, so I thought, I'm going to give it a try. Because I almost never really bother when it comes to dinner[1]. Lots of frozen dinners, microwave stuff, the kind of food you'd never let into the house. So I thought, I'll make something. How hard could it be[2], right? Some chicken, some paprika, you throw it in the oven. Right. So I got some chicken and gave it a try, and did you ever stop to notice how much paprika looks like cayenne[3]?" He shook his head. "Darn near killed myself[4] with the first bite[5]. Went into a coughing fit[6]. Had to drink a glass of water real fast[7]. You would have laughed your head off[8]. It was a sight to see[9], I'm telling you. So I had to throw the whole mess out, and went and got myself some KFC and brought it home."

Walden went quiet[10] for a moment. Then: "I miss you both so much. You were my whole world; that's what you two were."

He turned to OLIVIA FISHER. "You had your whole life ahead of you. Just finishing up school, ready to fly on your own[11]. Whoever did this to you, he didn't just take you away from me. He killed your mother, too. It just took longer where she was concerned[12]. It was a broken heart that caused her cancer. I know it. And I guess, if a broken heart can kill ya, he'll get me eventually, too[13]. Of course, it wasn't just him that broke my heart. There's plenty of blame to go around[14]. Truth is, I'm guessing it won't be all that long before I'm joining you. Soon we'll all be together again, and you know, it takes away the fear of dying. It really does. I'm almost to the point where I can[15] get up in the morning and say, If it happens today, that's okay. I'm ready."

1. prends rarement la peine de me faire à dîner
2. Ça peut pas être si compliqué

3. piment de Cayenne
4. Failli me tuer
5. à la première bouchée
6. quinte de toux
7. à toute vitesse
8. aurais bien rigolé
9. quelque chose
10. se tut

11. de tes propres ailes

12. pour elle

13. finira par m'avoir aussi
14. Ce ne sont pas les coupables qui manquent

15. J'en viens presque à pouvoir

Walden Fisher put both hands on his raised knee, pushed himself back into a standing position.

1. continuer à

"I'm gonna keep[1] coming to visit," he told them. "Long as I'm still breathin', I'll be up here."

2. bout

He put the tips[2] of his fingers to his lips, then touched his wife's headstone. Repeated the pro-

3. Fit la même chose

cess[3] for his daughter.

Walden turned and walked slowly back to his van.

FIFTY-ONE

SEEING no cars in the distance in either direction, and confident[1] that there would be none for the next couple of minutes, Jack Sturgess and Bill Gaynor dragged[2] Marshall Kemper's body out of his van and into the forest. He weighed about two hundred pounds[3], but he felt like a lot more than that to the two men, who were, at this stage of their lives, unaccustomed[4] to what amounted to manual labor[5].

"My hands are killing me[6]," Gaynor said. "I haven't dug a hole since I was in my teens[7]."

"You should have brought gloves," Sturgess said. "I would have[8], if you'd told me before we left what it was you had planned for me to do[9]."

"Maybe when I asked you to bring a shovel[10], that should have been a clue[11]."

Once they had Kemper into the woods, and out of sight in case anyone drove by, they dropped him and caught their breath[12]. The grave[13] Gaynor had dug[14] was another twenty yards in[15].

"I want to know who this son of a bitch is," Sturgess said, and knelt down, careful not to touch[16] the knees of his pants to the forest floor, and worked[17] the dead man's wallet[18] out of his back

1. certains
2. traînèrent
3. une centaine de kilos
4. peu habitués
5. ce qui revenait à du travail manuel
6. me font un mal de chien
7. l'adolescence
8. C'est ce que j'aurais fait
9. prévu de me faire faire
10. pelle
11. aurait dû te mettre la puce à l'oreille
12. reprirent leur souffle
13. tombe
14. creusée
15. 20 mètres plus loin
16. poser
17. retira
18. portefeuille

1. carte grise

2. correspond à

3. prénom

4. mit la main
5. appareil

6. ne vois pas
bien ce qu'il y a
de drôle

7. éteignit le
téléphone

8. le rangea

9. ne le localise

10. je le jetterai

11. avec lui

12. ne reste
pas là

13. cadavre

pocket. "It said Kemper on the ownership[1]. But if that isn't his van, he could have been lying."

He examined a driver's license. "Okay, that's good. Marshall Kemper. Address matches[2] the ownership. You ever heard of this guy?"

"What was the first name[3] again?"

"Marshall."

Gaynor thought a moment. "I think I may have heard Sarita talk about him. To Rose. A boyfriend or something."

For the third time since Sturgess had stuck the needle into the man's neck, the dead man's cell phone rang. Sturgess dug[4] into his pocket, found the device[5], studied it.

"Stemple," he said.

"What?" said Gaynor.

"That's who's trying to call him. Stemple."

"It could be Sarita," Gaynor said. "She doesn't own a cell phone. She uses other people's phones."

The phone continued to ring in Sturgess's hand. "Maybe I should answer it, ask her if she's where Kemper said she is."

"I guess you could. …"

"A joke," Sturgess said.

"I don't see much very funny about this[6]."

Sturgess powered the phone off[7], tucked it[8] into his own pocket. "We don't want anyone doing any triangulating[9]," he said. "I'll turn it back on later, far from here, then ditch it[10]."

"With the van?" Gaynor asked.

That had been why Sturgess needed someone else along[11]. He couldn't have done this alone. He needed another driver, so Kemper's van wouldn't be left sitting here[12] and lead the police to his body[13].

"Whose property is this?" Gaynor asked. "Who's Boone?"

"Patient of mine[1]," he said. "Taylor Boone. Rich old guy, got a nice house way up that lane[2], up top[3] of a hill. Beautiful view."

"How the hell do you know he's not going to turn in that drive any second now[4]?"

"I picked this spot[5] because I know Taylor's off[6] in Europe right now, and because this is as good a place as any[7] to get rid of him[8]."

Gaynor looked down at the dead man. "What the hell did you inject him with?"

"Are you writing a report?" Sturgess said. "It did the job[9]. Come on; we have to get this done, then go find your nanny."

"I'm gonna be sick[10]," he said. And then he was, violently.

"That's great," Sturgess said. "Litter the scene with your DNA[11]. Cover that mess up[12] with some dirt[13]."

"I don't know if I can do this. I just don't know."

"You need me to remind you what we'd have been facing[14] if everything came out[15]? Disgrace would be the least of it. Jail time[16], more than likely. And now, well, we'd hardly get off with a slap on the wrist[17] now, would we?"

"I'm not the one who gave him a fatal injection."

"That's right," Sturgess said. "You're an innocent bystander[18]. Grab his legs."

The doctor got Kemper under the arms. The man was heavy, and they couldn't help dragging his butt across[19] the forest floor. When they reached the hole, they heaved the body in[20]. A shovel was sticking out[21] of the dirt pile next to it.

"Okay, fill it in," Sturgess said.

"You," he said. "I told you, my hands are raw[22]."

1.	à moi
2.	au bout de cette allée
3.	en haut
4.	d'une seconde à l'autre
5.	ai choisi ce coin
6.	en voyage
7.	pas pire qu'ailleurs
8.	nous débarrasser de lui
9.	a marché
10.	vomir
11.	Répands bien ton ADN partout
12.	Cache-moi ça
13.	terre
14.	ce qui nous attendait
15.	le scandale avait éclaté
16.	De la prison
17.	on n'en serait pas quitte pour une réprimande
18.	simple spectateur
19.	éviter de traîner ses fesses sur
20.	y déposèrent difficilement le corps
21.	dépassait
22.	à vif

Sturgess took two handkerchiefs[1] from his suit jacket, wrapped them around his hands, and took a turn with the shovel.

"We can't do this to Sarita," said Gaynor.

"No one said we had to," Sturgess said. "I'm sure we can talk some sense into her[2]."

"Like you tried with this guy?"

"He was blackmailing you[3]. Some people can't be reasoned with[4]."

"I can't believe Sarita put him up to this[5]. She's a decent person[6]."

Sturgess stopped shoveling to catch his breath. "Really? And look at the shitstorm she's brought down on you[7]. On us."

"We don't know for sure it was her," Gaynor said.

"Who else could it be? Who else could have known? More than once, when you and I were having a conversation at your house, I'd come out a door and there she was. She's all ears[8], that woman. She's a sneak[9]."

Sturgess shook his head tiredly, and tossed the shovel at Gaynor, who fumbled the catch[10]. The tool landed in the dirt. Sturgess offered the two handkerchiefs.

"These'll help."

Gaynor wrapped them around his palms. "How does a guy like you become a doctor?"

"I help people," he said. "I've always helped people. I helped you and Rosemary. I've dedicated[11] my life to helping people."

Gaynor continued to throw dirt onto Marshall Kemper. Once the body was fully covered, he patted down[12] the earth with the back of the shovel. Sturgess walked across the grave, compressing the dirt.

---

1. mouchoirs

2. lui faire entendre raison

3. te faisait chanter

4. ne veulent pas entendre raison

5. l'ait poussé à faire ça

6. quelqu'un de bien

7. dans quelle merde elle t'a foutu

8. a toujours une oreille qui traîne

9. moucharde

10. la manqua

11. consacré

12. tassa

"We need to pull some brush[1] over this, too," he said.

Both of them worked at that.

Gaynor suddenly stopped, raised his head, like a deer[2] sensing an approaching hunter. "Wait, I think I heard something."

Sturgess held his breath, listened. In the distance, the sound of a baby crying.

"It's Matthew," Gaynor said. "He must have woke up."

They'd driven out here in Gaynor's Audi. Since he still had no one to look after[3] his son, he'd brought him along, and Sturgess didn't have a child safety seat[4] in the back of his Cadillac. The car was parked a hundred feet[5] farther up the driveway, where it bore[6] left and disappeared behind the trees.

"He's probably hungry," the father said.

Sturgess sighed. "Go—go look after your boy. Take the shovel, throw it in the trunk[7]. I'll catch up[8]."

It had crossed his mind[9] earlier to take the shovel himself and hit Gaynor across the head with it. He could have tossed him[10] into the grave along with Kemper. But then he'd have had the problem of how to get the Audi, and the van, away from here.

Not to mention the problem of what to do with the baby.

That goddamn baby.

He would have to watch[11] Bill Gaynor closely. See if he came to present[12] the same level of risk that this dead-and-buried asshole[13] had. Yes, they'd been friends a very long time, but when it came to saving your own neck[14], you did what you had to do.

And it wasn't just his neck, either[15].

1. des broussailles

2. cerf

3. s'occuper de

4. siège auto
5. à 30 m
6. bifurquait

7. coffre

8. te rejoins

9. Il avait caressé l'idée

10. aurait pu le jeter

11. surveiller

12. venait à représenter

13. ce petit con dans sa tombe

14. quand il s'agissait de sauver sa propre peau

15. pas que la sienne, de peau, d'ailleurs

But the more immediate problem was Sarita. Once she'd been dealt with[1], Sturgess could decide what to do about the poor grieving[2] husband.

1. Une fois son compte réglé
2. en deuil

FIFTY-TWO

David

AS I drove away from Sam's place, I decided to try again to find Marshall Kemper or, even better, Sarita Gomez. Maybe someone would come to the door of his place[1] this time.

On the way, I couldn't stop thinking about what had just happened, about what I might be getting myself into[2]. I didn't need my life to be any more complicated, and Sam Worthington was definitely a complication.

Any other man who'd just had impulsive, spontaneous sex with a woman he barely knew—and at her kitchen table, no less[3]—might be feeling pretty full of himself[4]. *Ain't I somethin'?*[5] And who knew? Maybe this was the start of something. Maybe this rough, animalistic act was the beginning of an actual relationship[6]. Maybe, out of this what some might call sordid encounter, something pretty decent[7] might emerge. Granted[8], it might not be the sort of story you'd share with your grandkids[9] one day, but hey, it was the kind of memory, when you called it up[10], someone might ask why you had that stupid grin all over your face[11].

1. ouvrirait la porte de chez lui

2. dans quoi je risquais de m'engager

3. rien que ça

4. gonflé d'orgueil

5. T'assures, mon gars !

6. vraie relation

7. de pas mal

8. D'accord

9. à raconter à ses petits-enfants

10. on y repensait

11. ce grand sourire idiot jusqu'aux oreilles

405

Except it wasn't in my nature to see the glass as half-full[1]. Not after the kinds of things I'd been through[2] in recent years. I had more than enough to deal with at the moment: raising Ethan on my own, starting a new job, living with my parents. I was hoping that working for Finley, even if it didn't last forever—God forbid[3]—would allow me to rent a place[4] for Ethan and myself. It'd be an interim step to[5] finding us another house.

The one thing I didn't need to bring into the mix[6] was a relationship. Especially not one with a woman who had as many problems going on in her life as I did. Arguably[7] more.

And yet, sometimes we do stupid things. Some needs blind us to[8] reason.

Maybe Sam had been thinking the same thing. As I was leaving, she'd said, "That was nice. We might do that again sometime."

Not, *Call me.* Not, *What are you doing this weekend?* Not, *Would you like to come over for dinner tonight?*

Maybe she figured getting involved with me would screw up her life[9], too. I was reminded of what my father had said. What, exactly, did I have to offer, anyway?

And yet, as I headed for Kemper's address, I found myself wondering[10] when the wifi at Sam's house might kick out[11] again.

I decided this time not to park right out front[12]. I pulled over and stopped the car three houses this side of Kemper's apartment. I had a good view, although I couldn't see in the windows to tell[13] whether anyone was walking around in there.

There was still no other car parked out front, so Kemper was probably out somewhere. I could sit here in my mother's Taurus awhile and hope he showed up.

Do some thinking[1].

It had been half a decade[2] since Jan had died, and yet there wasn't a day I did not think about her. To say my emotions were mixed[3] was to put it lightly[4]. I'd loved Jan once. A love so great it ached[5]. But those aches had eventually mutated[6] into something very different, something bordering on poisonous[7]. Jan had never been who she claimed to be[8], and it made everything I'd once felt for[9] her false[10] in retrospect[11].

I was a different man now. More cautious[12], less foolish. Or so I'd thought. Maybe the way to handle things[13] with Sam was—

I'd have to put that thought on hold[14].

A door was opening. But wait, it wasn't Kemper's apartment; it was the place where the old woman lived.

Someone was stepping outside. Maybe the old woman was coming out for a breath of fresh air[15].

Except it wasn't her.

It was a much younger woman. Late twenties, early thirties, I guessed. Slim, about five-four[16], with black hair. Dressed in jeans and a green pullover top. A friend of the old woman's, I figured. A care worker of some kind[17], maybe.

I thought she'd start walking down to the road, but instead she took a few steps over to the door of Marshall Kemper's apartment. She used a key to open it and disappeared inside.

I'd never seen a picture of Sarita Gomez, but I was betting I'd found her.

I had my hand on the door handle, preparing to get out, when a cab[18] drove past me and stopped out front of Kemper's place. Seconds

---

1. Réfléchir un peu
2. cinq ans
3. mitigées
4. un euphémisme
5. faisait mal
6. s'étaient finalement muées
7. à la limite du toxique
8. celle qu'elle prétendait être
9. tout ce que j'avais pu ressentir pour elle
10. factice
11. avec le recul
12. prudent
13. le mieux à faire
14. de côté
15. prendre un peu l'air
16. env. 1,65 m
17. aide à domicile quelconque
18. taxi

later, the apartment door opened and Sarita reappeared, pulling behind her a medium-size suitcase on wheels[1]. The cabdriver popped[2] the trunk, put the bag in for her, but let Sarita handle[3] the rear passenger door[4] herself. The man got back behind the wheel, and the tires kicked up gravel[5] as he sped off[6].

"Shit," I said, and turned the key.

The cab was heading back into downtown Promise Falls and came to a stop outside the bus terminal[7]. I pulled to the curb and watched as Sarita got out, handed the driver some cash, then waited for him to haul[8] her bag out of the trunk. Dragging it behind her, she entered the terminal.

I got out of the car and ran.

The Promise Falls bus terminal is hardly[9] Grand Central[10]. Inside, it's about the size of a school classroom, with two ticket windows[11] at one end and an electronic schedule board[12] overhead[13]. The rest is filled with the kind of chairs you'd find in a hospital emergency room.

The woman I'd followed was at the ticket booth[14]. I went and stood behind her, looking like the next in line[15], close enough[16] to hear the conversation.

"I want to buy a ticket to New York," she said.

The man behind the glass said she could buy the entire ticket now, but she would have to change buses in Albany.

"Okay," she said. "When does the bus leave for Albany?"

The man glanced at a computer monitor[17] angled off to one side[18]. "Thirty-five minutes," he told her.

She handed over some more cash, took her ticket. When she turned around she jumped[19], evidently unaware[20] someone was behind her.

"Excuse me," she said.

---

1. valise à roulettes
2. débloqua
3. ouvrir
4. portière arrière
5. projetèrent des gravillons
6. démarrait en trombe
7. gare routière
8. sortir
9. pas exactement
10. la grande gare de New York
11. guichets
12. indicateur
13. au-dessus
14. guichet
15. comme si je faisais la queue
16. assez près
17. écran
18. placé de biais
19. sursauta
20. surprise que

"Sorry," I said. I let her wheel[1] her bag past my toes, then stepped up to the window.

"Help ya?" the ticket agent said.

I paused, then said, "Never mind."

I turned around and spotted[2] the woman, sitting in the far corner of the room, as if trying to make herself invisible, which was not easy, since there were only half a dozen people here waiting to catch a bus.

I walked over and took a seat two over[3] from her, leaving the one between us empty. I took out my phone, leaned over, my elbows rested on my knees, and opened up an app at random[4].

Without looking in her direction, I said, "You must be Sarita."

I sensed her stir[5] suddenly. "What did you say?"

This time I turned, sitting up at the same time[6]. I could see fear in her eyes. "I said, you must be Sarita. Sarita Gomez."

Her eyes darted about[7] the room. I could guess what she was thinking. Who was I? Was I alone? Was I a cop? Should she try to run?

I said, "I'm not with the police. My name's David. David Harwood."

"You are wrong," she said. "I am not whoever you said. My name is Carla."

"I don't think so. I think you're Sarita. I think you worked for the Gaynors. And I think you've been hiding out with Marshall Kemper the last couple of days, and are now looking to get out of Dodge[8]."

"Dodge?" she said.

"You want to disappear."

"I told you, I am not that person."

"I'm Marla Pickens's cousin. I don't know if that name means anything to you, but the Gaynors'

---

1. rouler

2. repérai

3. à deux sièges

4. au hasard

5. s'agiter

6. tout en me redressant

7. parcoururent vivement

8. que vous essayez de filer à l'anglaise

baby was left on her doorstep two days ago. The police think she stole the baby, and probably killed Rosemary Gaynor in the process[1]."

"She did it before[2]," the woman whispered.

I leaned in. "She never killed anyone."

"But she took a baby," she said quietly[3]. "At the hospital."

"You know about that[4]."

The woman nodded. She was glancing at the door.

"You *are* Sarita."

Her eyes landed[5] on mine. "I am Sarita," she said.

"Would you like to tell me what you know, or would you like me to call the police?"

"Please do not call the police. They'll either send me home, or find a reason to put me in jail."

"Then why don't we talk," I said. "I've got a feeling[6] you may be able to explain a lot of things."

"Quickly," she said. "I will tell you quickly, so I do not[7] miss my bus."

I shook my head sadly. "You're not making[8] that bus, Sarita. It's just not going to happen."

---

1. par la même occasion
2. l'a déjà fait
3. doucement
4. êtes au courant
5. se posèrent
6. l'impression
7. pour ne pas
8. n'allez pas le prendre,

FIFTY-THREE

ARLENE Harwood had decided on pork chops[1] for dinner and wondered whether Don would like rice or mashed potatoes[2] with them. She even had some sweet potatoes in the fridge, which Don was not all that crazy about[3], but would tolerate once in a while, just so long as she put enough butter on them, and maybe even a sprinkling[4] of brown sugar. She was pretty sure Ethan didn't like sweet potatoes, but she could do up a baked potato[5] for him, or throw some frozen french fries into the oven.

It was nice having all these men around. She knew David wanted to move out as soon as he could, and take Ethan with him, of course. It was the right thing to do. But she was enjoying having them here in the meantime[6].

She went into the living room, thinking her husband might have fallen asleep in the recliner[7], but he wasn't there. Her leg was really hurting today after her stumble[8] on the stairs the day before, so she didn't want to have to trek up[9] to the second floor to search for him. So she went to the foot of the stairs and shouted his name, speculating that he was in the bathroom, extending his stay

1. qu'elle ferait des côtelettes

2. de la purée de pommes de terre

3. même si Don n'adorait pas

4. soupçon

5. pomme de terre en robe de chambre

6. en attendant

7. fauteuil inclinable

8. chute

9. se traîner

because he'd found something interesting to read in *National Geographic*.

No answer.

Then Arlene went to the top of the stairs that led down to the basement. "Don? You there?"

When she didn't get a reply, she figured there was only one place left[1] to check. She went out the back door and limped[2] across the yard to their garage. The main door was closed, but that didn't mean he wasn't there. She tried the side[3] entrance, found it unlocked, and entered.

And there was Don. Standing in front of his workbench[4], clutching[5] a bottle of beer. There were two empties[6] standing in front of him.

"I've been looking all over[7] for you," she said.

"I was right here," he said.

"Well, I had to look in all the other places first before I found that out, didn't I? Me with a bad leg and all[8]."

"You should have looked here first."

"What are you doing drinking beer in the middle of the afternoon?" she asked. "In the middle of the summer, maybe, but now?"

"Is that why you were looking for me? To find out if I was having a beer?"

"I didn't know you were having a beer until I found you."

"Then what the hell do you want[9]?"

She did not answer him. She crossed her arms and looked sternly[10] at him. "What's going on with you?"

He grunted. "There's nothing going on with me."

"How many years have I been married to you? Whatever the number is, double it[11], and that's

1. ne restait qu'un endroit où
2. boitilla
3. latérale
4. établi
5. tenant
6. bouteilles vides
7. partout
8. Et moi qui ai mal à la jambe
9. qu'est-ce que tu me veux, bordel
10. sévèrement
11. multiplie-le par deux

what it feels like," Arlene said. "I can tell[1] when something's eating at you[2]. You started acting funny[3] yesterday."

"I told you, I'm fine. What did you want?"

"I wanted to ask you ..." She stopped herself. "Damn it[4]."

"What?"

"What the hell did I want to ask you?" She shook her head. "This is driving me crazy[5]."

"Where were you when you decided you just had to find me?" Don asked. "They say[6] if you think[7] where you were when—"

"Rice or potatoes?" she asked him.

"What?"

"With pork chops. Rice or potatoes, or sweet potatoes? Oh, and I've got a box of that Stove Top stuffing[8] that Ethan likes."

"I don't care," Don said. "Make whatever you want."

She put a hand on his arm. "Talk to me."

He pressed his lips together, as though keeping[9] the words he wanted to say from escaping. He shook his head.

"Is it David? And Ethan? Is it getting you down[10], having them here? He just needs time to get his life back together. It would have been better if he'd just stayed in Boston, hadn't quit that job at—"

"It's not that," Don said. "I ... I like having them around. I like having my grandson here."

The corner of her mouth went up. "Me, too." She paused, then said, "You'd better spill[11] what it is that's on your mind fast, because I need to head upstairs and lie down[12] with some ice on this goddamn leg. Talk."

Don opened his mouth to speak, then closed it. The fourth time he tried, words came out.

1. sais
2. te sape le moral
3. te comporter bizarrement
4. Merde alors
5. me rend folle
6. On dit que
7. te rappelles
8. farce
9. comme pour empêcher
10. Est-ce que ça te déprime
11. cracher
12. m'allonger

"I have regrets," he said.

Arlene nodded. "Sure. We all do." She hesitated. "I hope I'm not one of them[1]."

He shook his head, put a hand on her shoulder. "No."

"Well, that's something[2], I guess," she said.

"There are times when I could have been a better man."

"Better for whom?" she asked.

"Just … better."

Arlene had always thought, even with all his faults[3]—and there was no question[4] Don had a few—he was as good a man as any woman could hope to find. It was difficult for her to imagine that this was a man who harbored[5] deep[6] secrets, that there could be anything he'd done that would make her think less of him[7].

She'd never had any reason to believe he'd been unfaithful to her[8], even though there would be the occasional fleeting thought[9]. But that had more to do with her own insecurities than with suspicions about Don's behavior.

"There's times," he said, "when you wish you acted differently, but you can't go back and do things again. The moment is gone; there's nothing you can do. And the thing is, even if you tried to do the right thing, there's no guarantee you might have been able to make a difference[10]. But it haunts you just the same[11]. You feel like less of a person[12]."

"Okay," Arlene said slowly.

"Like, for instance," he said, "you remember that time you were backing into[13] that spot[14] at the Walmart, and you—"

"Oh, please don't bring that up."

1. que je n'en suis pas un

2. c'est déjà ça

3. défauts
4. indubitablement,
5. abritait
6. de mystérieux
7. le ferait baisser dans son estime
8. l'ait trompée
9. l'idée lui avait déjà traversé l'esprit

10. changer le cours des choses
11. quand même
12. méprisable
13. faisais une marche arrière
14. place de parking

"You dinged[1] that car, and you got out and had a look, and it was a little dent[2], and you thought about leaving a note[3], but finally you decided to get back in the car and drive off and go shop[4] somewhere else instead that day?"

Now she was annoyed. "Why would you bring that up[5]? That was years ago. I felt so guilty about that. I never should have told you. To this day[6] I feel bad I didn't leave a note. You remember two years ago I was using that machine at the drug-store[7] where you can check your blood pressure[8]? And I thought I broke it? And I told them about it and offered to pay? And lucky for me, they said it had broken down before[9] and it wasn't my fault, but it could have been. I was prepared to do the right thing, so why you'd dredge up[10] that other matter I don't—"

"I only mention it because it was nothing," Don said. "It was nothing compared to what I did—or didn't do."

"What on earth are you talking about?"

Those lips were pressed together again. Arlene sensed he was getting to the hardest part. He said nothing for more than a minute, but finally said, "I was one of them[11]."

"One of what?"

"One of the people who did nothing," Don Harwood said.

1. a cogné
2. bosse
3. petit mot
4. faire tes courses

5. tu reparles de ça
6. Même maintenant,
7. pharmacie
8. tension

9. était déjà tombée en panne
10. ressors

11. l'un d'entre eux

FIFTY-FOUR

ANGUS Carlson phoned his wife, Gale, at the dental clinic where she worked as a hygienist[1]. She was with a patient, doing a cleaning[2], but Carlson told the woman at the desk that it was an emergency.

Several seconds later, Gale came on the line. "What is it? What's happened? Are you okay?"

"It's not that kind of emergency," he told her. "It's something good[3]."

"Oh, God, you gave me a heart attack. You're a cop! Someone says it's an emergency and my mind goes to the worst possible place!"

"Sorry, I didn't think."

"I've got someone in the chair. What's happened?"

"I got a promotion."

"What?" Excited now, no longer annoyed. "What kind of promotion?"

"It's temporary," he said. "But if I do a good job[4], they might make it permanent."

"Tell me."

"Detective[5]," he said. "They've got me working as a detective."

"That's fantastic! That's wonderful! I'm so proud of you."

1. technicienne en hygiène dentaire
2. détartrage
3. une bonne nouvelle
4. fais bien mon boulot
5. Inspecteur

"I just wanted you to know. I wanted you to be the first call."

"Does this mean you'll get more money?"

"I'll probably get a bump up[1] while I'm doing it."

"Because," Gale said gently, "if you get a raise[2], this could be a good time—"

"Only thing I'm a bit worried about is this guy I have to work with. Duckworth. I don't think he likes me. There was this thing with squirrels, and I was just making a joke and—"

"Squirrels?"

"It doesn't matter. I'll just have to work it out[3] with him. Prove to him I'm not an idiot."

"You're not," Gale said. "You're going to do great. But what I was going to say was, if you're going to be making[4] more money, maybe this would be a good time to think about starting a—"

"Please, Gale, don't go there[5]," Angus Carlson said.

"You don't even know what I'm going to say."

"I know what you're going to say. That's not why I'm calling you. I don't want to get into that[6]."

"I'm sorry," Gale said. "I just thought—"

"You know how I feel about this."

"I know, but we've had this discussion. I'm not like her. I'd be a *good* mother. Just because—"

"That reminds me. I'm going to let her know[7]."

"Let who know?"

"My mother. I'm going to let her know."

"Angus."

"I am. She never thought I'd amount to anything[8]. I'm going to tell her."

"Angus, please," Gale said. "Don't say that. Let it go. We left that behind. We came here to get away from all that[9]."

---

1. rallonge
2. augmentation
3. trouver comment bien m'entendre
4. te mets à gagner
5. ne commence pas
6. en parler
7. la mettre au courant
8. n'a jamais cru en moi
9. tourner la page

He didn't say anything for a moment. Finally, his voice somewhat[1] distant: "Okay, okay. You're right. I don't have to do that."

"We should ... celebrate," Gale said, her voice starting to break[2]. A sniff, then: "When you get home."

"Are you crying?"

"I'm not crying."

"You sound like you're crying. This is a big thing for me, Gale. Don't ruin it by crying."

"I said I wasn't crying. I have to go. I have to get back to Mr. Ormin."

"Okay," he said. "We'll go out. You want to do that?"

"You pick[3]," Gale said. "I have to go."

1. un peu

2. chancelante

3. décides

FIFTY-FIVE

THE first thing Sturgess and Gaynor had to do was get rid of Marshall Kemper's van. The doctor drove; Gaynor followed in the Audi. Sturgess was mindful[1] that he didn't want to take any route, or leave the van, anyplace where there might be video cameras. He did not want to be showing up[2] on any surveillance video driving a vehicle owned by a man who would soon be on a missing-persons[3] list. That left out[4] the parking lots of major department stores, fast-food outlets, or getting onto a toll[5] road like the New York State Thruway[6].

Nor did Sturgess want to take a lot of time disposing[7] of the van. He needed to return to Kemper's place, where he believed Sarita was waiting for the man. And then it hit him[8]—the solution was simple: Leave the van at Kemper's house.

He phoned Gaynor in the Audi, told him where he was going. The doctor could hear a baby making gurgling noises[9] in the background. "Hang back a block or so[10]," Sturgess said. "We don't want anyone seeing your car, noticing your license plate[11], out front of Kemper's place[12]."

"What do you want me to do?" he asked.

"You just take care of your kid," Sturgess said. "I'll handle this[13]."

1. gardait à l'esprit

2. apparaître

3. de personnes disparues

4. éliminait d'office

5. à péage

6. autoroute

7. pour se débarrasser

8. l'idée lui vint

9. gazouiller

10. Reste une rue plus loin

11. plaque minéralogique

12. devant chez Kemper

13. m'occupe de tout

He opened the map program[1] on his smartphone—the van did not have GPS in it—and looked up Kemper's Groveland Street address. As soon as he saw it on the screen, he realized he knew roughly[2] where it was, and wouldn't need directions[3].

He kept glancing in the mirror, saw the large mouth of the Audi grille trailing him right up[4] until he turned onto Groveland, at which point Gaynor hung back[5]. Sturgess pulled into the driveway[6] at 36A and 36B. Kemper's place was on the left.

He turned off the engine and sat for a moment before getting out. If Sarita was inside, she might have heard the van pull up and, thinking it was her boyfriend, run outside to greet him[7].

When she didn't, the doctor got out and went to the door. Knocked. When no one answered, he knocked harder. Finally he tried turning the knob[8] and, finding the door unlocked, stepped inside.

"Hello?" he said. "Sarita, are you here?"

It was a small apartment. He walked to the middle of it, surveyed[9] the unmade[10] bed, the dirty dishes[11] in the sink, an untouched[12] breakfast sandwich, men's clothes scattered[13] across the floor. The bathroom door was open. He poked[14] his head in, pulled back the bathtub curtain[15]. Not only did he not see Sarita, he saw no signs that a woman was living here. Which meant either Kemper had been lying, or that he'd been telling the truth, and Sarita had skipped[16].

He had a feeling it was the latter[17].

But if she had been here, she must have left recently. Kemper, desperate for[18] a second needle that would save his life, had said she was here. Maybe she'd been trying to reach him[19] on his phone, and when she couldn't, panicked. She

---

1. itinéraire
2. à peu près
3. d'indications
4. le suivre de près
5. prit ses distances
6. se gara sur l'allée
7. l'accueillir
8. poignée
9. parcourut des yeux
10. défait
11. vaisselle sale
12. intact
13. éparpillés
14. passa
15. rideau de douche
16. filé
17. la seconde option
18. attendant désespérément
19. le joindre

had to know[1] he'd been trying to blackmail Bill Gaynor, so she might be thinking the police had picked him up[2], and this was going to be their next stop[3].

And then he remembered that when Kemper's phone had rung, it had shown STEMPLE as the caller.

Sturgess got out his phone again, opened the app for phone numbers and addresses, and typed in "Stemple."

"Son of a bitch," he said under his breath[4]. The address attached to that name was the apartment next door.

Sturgess walked out, made the short journey to the other apartment, and rapped on[5] the door. He could hear a television. He knocked again, at which point someone hollered[6], "Hold your horses[7]!"

Finally, an elderly woman opened the door. She looked him up and down, at[8] the doctor's expensive suit, and said, "I ain't dead yet[9]."

"Excuse me?"

"You look like an undertaker[10]."

"I'm not," Sturgess said. "You must be Mrs. Stemple?"

"Who wants to know?"

"I'm looking for Sarita. Is she here?"

"Sarita?" the woman said. "Who the hell is that[11]?"

Sturgess put his palm flat on the door, pushed it wide-open[12], and walked in.

"Hey," she said. "You can't do that."

The apartment was slightly larger than Kemper's, with a bedroom attached to the living area. He explored the two rooms, peered into the bathroom.

"I know she was here," Sturgess said. "She made several calls from your phone. Recently. You going to deny that[13]?"

1. devait savoir
2. l'avait coffré
3. étape suivante
4. à voix basse
5. toqua à
6. brailla
7. Du calme là-bas
8. le toisa, regardant
9. suis pas encore morte
10. croque-mort
11. C'est qui, ça, encore
12. l'ouvrit en grand
13. allez pas dire le contraire

"Maybe I was sleeping," Mrs. Stemple said. "Someone could have come in and used the phone while I was having a nap[1] in front of the TV."

"Where is she?" Sturgess said, keeping his voice level[2]. "If you don't tell me, half an hour from now you'll be downtown getting charged with[3] ..." He had to think. "Harboring[4] a fugitive. That's what you'll be charged with."

"You *another* cop?" she said.

Sturgess thought, *Shit*. The police had already been here? Did they already have Sarita?

"I was sent back here to talk to you again," Sturgess said, improvising. "We don't think you were very forthcoming[5] with our other officer."

"Well, I don't know anything about that," she said. "I want you to get out of my house. I want to watch my shows[6]."

Sturgess looked at the high-tech chair in its elevated position. On the small table next to it, a remote[7], a book of crossword puzzles[8], an open box of chocolates, a Danielle Steel[9] novel. That was her whole world there, a command center[10], sitting in front of the television.

Sturgess walked over there, found where the TV cord[11] led to a power bar[12], and yanked it out[13]. The TV went black.

"Hey!" Mrs. Stemple said.

The doctor knelt down, started fiddling with[14] the cables.

"What are you doing?" she asked.

"I'm going to take your DVR[15], your cables, all this shit," he said.

"What the hell for?"

"Because you won't cooperate," he said.

"She went to the bus station."

He stopped. "What?"

Sidebar glossary:

1. faisais une sieste
2. un ton calme
3. mise en examen pour
4. Avoir abrité
5. franche
6. émissions
7. télécommande
8. mots croisés
9. [auteur de romans à l'eau de rose]
10. poste de contrôle
11. câble
12. menait à une prise
13. l'arracha
14. jouer avec
15. magnétoscope [numérique]

"Sarita. She took a taxi to the bus station. She's going to New York. Now turn my TV back on."

"How long ago was this?"

The woman shrugged. "Ten minutes? I don't know. Hook that back up[1]."

Sturgess plugged the TV back in, and the screen came to life[2]. He stood up and said, "There you go."

"Now get out," Mrs. Stemple said.

"Let me help you into your chair," he said.

"My chair helps me get into my chair," she said, and positioned herself in front of it. She settled in, grabbed the remote, and powered the chair back down[3].

"I'll let myself out[4]," Sturgess said.

"Whatever," the woman said.

He exited the apartment, but hesitated before getting out his phone to ask Gaynor to come down the street to pick him up[5]. He stood outside Mrs. Stemple's door, thinking.

Sooner or later, after Kemper was reported missing, someone was going to come back here and interview[6] Mrs. Stemple.

And maybe she'd mention that officer who came to see her, the one who unplugged[7] her TV.

And the police would realize that someone else had been here to see her. Not a cop. Asking about Sarita Gomez.

Who, by that time[8], might be as hard to find as Marshall Kemper.

He hadn't given the woman his name, but would she be able to recognize him? If it ever came to that[9]? If the police put enough of this together[10] to place him in a lineup[11]?

Sturgess felt a pounding[12] in his chest. His mouth was dry.

---

1. Rebranchez-moi ça
2. se ralluma
3. rebaissa le siège
4. connais la sortie
5. venir le chercher
6. interroger
7. avait débranché
8. d'ici là
9. les choses en venaient là
10. découvraient assez d'éléments
11. séance d'identification
12. battement violent

Giving Kemper that fatal injection hadn't been an easy thing to do. But it had been necessary. There were times when you had to do things that were beyond your normal experience.

It was possible that there were other things he was going to have to do that were necessary.

But the doctor wanted a second opinion[1].

He got out his phone, entered a number, waited for the pickup.

"Hey," Sturgess said.

The doctor explained the situation. That Kemper was dead. That he had a lead on Sarita Gomez. But this old lady presented a possible loose end[2].

He was thinking one of the oversize pillows[3] he'd seen in the bedroom would do the trick[4]. Wouldn't leave a needle mark. Would anyone really consider an old woman who'd stopped breathing all that suspicious[5]?

"So, what do you think?" Dr. Jack Sturgess asked.

"Dear God," Agnes Pickens said. "Do what you have to do."

1. l'avis d'un tiers

2. risque éventuel

3. énormes oreillers

4. ferait l'affaire

5. si suspect que ça

FIFTY-SIX

AGNES set her phone down on the kitchen island[1].

"Who was that?" Marla asked. She was sitting on the other side, dipping a spoon tentatively[2] into the bowl of tomato soup her mother had just prepared for her.

"Just the hospital," Agnes said. "Even with all that's going on, they won't leave me alone[3]." She looked out the window, holding her gaze[4] as though staring at[5] something.

They heard Gill coming down the stairs. He slipped an arm around his daughter, gave her a kiss on the cheek, and took the stool[6] beside her.

"Got any more of that soup?" he asked his wife.

Agnes said nothing.

"Agnes?"

She stopped looking out the window, faced him. "What?"

"Is there any more soup?"

"Hang on[7]," she said, and reached for another bowl in the cupboard.

"I put your bag in your old room[8]," Gill said to Marla. "I think you'll be staying with us for a while. Don't you think, Agnes?"

1. plan central de la cuisine

2. avec méfiance

3. ne peuvent pas me laisser tranquille
4. le regard fixe
5. elle observait

6. tabouret

7. Attends

8. ancienne chambre

"Hmm? Yes, of course. Even … even when the police let you go back into your house, you should stay with us. For as long as you like."

"Are you okay, Mom?"

"Yes, I'm fine."

"You just seemed a little weird there for a second."

"I told you, I'm fine."

1. n'ai pas besoin

Marla said, "You know, I don't have[1] to go home anyway. I can do my work anywhere. As long as I have a computer. Dad, could I borrow your laptop? Mine's still in the house."

"Sure, I don't see why—"

2. dit sèchement
3. vive

"I don't know about that," Agnes snapped[2]. Suddenly alert[3], as though she'd just woken up. "Natalie told me how that detective reacted to what you were doing for a living. He was not impressed. You need to find something else to do."

"But, Mom, I—"

4. mentir
5. fait mauvaise impression
6. se décomposa

"No, you listen to me. Going on the Internet and making up reviews—*lying*[4]—about companies you've never had anything to do with, that makes you look bad[5]. Don't you understand that?"

Marla's face fell[6]. "I was really good at it. And I like writing."

7. nouvelle
8. roman
9. gagner ta vie

"That's not *writing*," Agnes said. "Writing is a short story[7], or a novel[8], or poems. If you want to write, write that kind of thing. But you need to make a living[9] some other way."

10. qu'elle en a assez enduré comme ça

"Jesus, Agnes," Gill said. "You don't think she's been through enough[10] in the last couple of days? You really think this is the time for career counseling?"

11. a lancé le sujet

"She was the one who brought it up[11]," Agnes said. "I didn't. All I'm saying is, when you're feeling better, and you want to get back to work, you

426

need to direct your talents in another direction. You can do that. I know you can. You have lots of talent, lots of natural ability."

"What kind of talents do I have?" Marla asked. "I don't really know how to do anything."

"That's not true," her father said. "You're good at lots of things."

"Like what?"

"Well, let's start with the writing. There's lot of other ways you could do that without making up Internet reviews. Like maybe advertising[1]? And think of all the companies that need people to write reports[2] for them. And newspapers. You could—"

"Newspapers are dying, Dad. Look what happened to David."

"You're right, you're right, but—"

The cell phone tucked into the pocket of his sports jacket started to ring. He reached for the phone, saw who it was, accepted the call.

"Hey, Martin, how are you. I'm sorry I haven't gotten back to you[3]. I've been dealing with some issues[4] on the home front[5] and I'm not going to be able to look at your proposal anytime soon[6]. Yeah, sorry about that. Take care."

Gill ended the call, set the phone onto the countertop[7], and made a show of pushing it away from him[8]. It slid across the granite and bumped into Agnes's phone, an identical model, nudging it[9] like a curling stone[10].

"They're a curse[11], those things," he said. "We think they're these great gadgets but we can never get away from[12] everyone who wants us."

"You could turn it off," Agnes said, ladling[13] soup into a bowl.

1. la publicité

2. rédiger des rapports

3. de ne pas t'avoir rappelé

4. des soucis

5. chez moi

6. dans un avenir proche

7. comptoir

8. le repoussa ostensiblement

9. le repoussant

10. palet de curling

11. malédiction

12. échapper à

13. versant une louchée de

"I know, I know; I'm guilty. I could turn it off, but I don't, because I'm afraid I'll miss something. I could say the same thing to you, you know. You've got a phone practically glued[1] to your palm."

Agnes leaned across the island, handed Gill some soup.

"This looks good," he said. "Where's this from?"

"Marla and I stopped at the deli[2] on the way home and picked it up," Agnes said, then shook her head sadly. "It never even occurred to you that I might have made it[3]."

"If it had, I can see I'd have been wrong."

"Stop," Marla said. "Even when you guys kid each other[4], it sounds like fighting[5]."

"We're not fighting," Agnes said. "Gill, have you heard from Natalie today?"

He shook his head. "No. I think maybe she's waiting to see what the cops do next. If they think they have a case, and they file a charge[6], you know, if they decide to—"

"Take me away in handcuffs[7]," Marla said.

Gill sighed. "If they think they have a case against[8] Marla, and arrest her, things go into overdrive[9]. She said they're doing a rush[10] on those bloodstains that were found on the door at Marla's house."

"I'll bet the angel left them," Marla said. "She must have gotten blood on her hands when she took Matthew from that woman's house after someone killed her."

Agnes turned away, removing from the burner[11] the pot[12] she'd used to reheat the soup.

"Can you tell us *anything* more about this angel?" Gill asked.

"I don't know what else to say," Marla said.

---

1. collé
2. épicerie fine
3. Tu n'as même pas envisagé que j'aie pu la faire moi-même
4. vous vous taquinez
5. une dispute
6. retiennent un chef d'accusation
7. menottée
8. assez contre
9. on passera à la vitesse supérieure
10. analysent
11. gazinière
12. casserole

"I think," Agnes said, her back to them, "that we have to be proactive here[1]. I'll call Natalie and tell her we want to know what her game plan[2] is, should we need it[3]." She shook her head in frustration. "I think the fact that there've been no charges up to now[4] is a good sign. They just don't have the evidence[5]. I know things are going to be okay. They only charge someone when they think they've got a strong case[6]."

"You're rambling[7], Mom," Marla said.

"I'm just trying to make a point[8], that's all. I'm calling Natalie right now."

She spun around[9], swept up[10] the phone in one quick movement, and left the kitchen. She went into the living room, sat down on the couch, and glanced at the list of recent calls. She immediately spotted[11] a number she knew, and said, just loud enough that[12] Gill heard her in the kitchen, "How did I miss this from Carol?"

Agnes tapped on the number to return the call[13].

In the kitchen, Gill dropped his spoon in his soup, splattered[14] some tomato on his crisp[15] white shirt, and looked at the other phone resting a couple of feet away[16] from him.

Agnes held the phone to her ear. Her assistant answered after the third ring. "Hey," Carol said in a whisper[17]. "I thought we were going to take a break[18]. Where are you, Gill? Are you at home?"

"Carol?" Agnes said.

A second of silence. Then: "Ms. Pickens?"

Again Agnes said, "Carol?" A pause, and then: "Why did—"

She cut herself off[19], ended the call. Tossed[20] the phone onto the cushion. Took a moment to consider[21] what she'd just learned.

---

1. prendre les devants, là

2. ligne de conduite

3. le cas échéant

4. jusqu'à présent

5. de preuves

6. assez d'éléments

7. radotes

8. faire valoir mon point de vue

9. fit volte-face

10. saisit

11. repéra

12. pour que

13. la rappeler

14. fit gicler

15. impeccable

16. à 60 cm

17. dans un murmure

18. faire une pause

19. s'interrompit

20. Jeta

21. prendre la mesure de

Gill came into the room with the other phone. Smiling innocently. "I think this one is yours." He extended his hand, but Agnes ignored it.

"It was going on right under my nose," she said. "My own assistant."

Gill shook his head. "I don't know what you're thinking[1], Agnes, but whatever it is, you're wrong. Carol just happened to call me[2]; I guess she couldn't reach you[3] at the time, and—"

Agnes raised a hand, picked up Gill's phone again. "She called you while I was still in my office. I was right there." She studied the screen more intently[4], looking at the call history[5]. "She called you yesterday. And three days ago. And two times on Monday."

Agnes stood, then suddenly pitched[6] the phone at her husband, catching him on the temple[7]. It hit the floor hard, skidded along the marble[8].

"Jesus!" Gill said, putting his hand on his head. "I'm telling you, she—"

"Shut up!" she screamed. "Shut up! Shut up! Shut up! Shut up!"

Marla appeared at the edge of the room, rubbing her bandaged left wrist with her right hand. "What's going on?" she asked.

"It's okay," Gill said. "Just a misunderstanding[9]."

The doorbell rang.

"A misunderstanding?" Agnes said. "Is that what you call fucking my assistant[10]? A misunderstanding?"

"There's someone at the door," Marla said shakily[11].

"You're jumping to conclusions[12]," Gill said, raising his voice. "A few phone calls, that's proof of nothing! For God's sake, Agnes, you're absolutely paranoid about this."

1. ce que tu as en tête
2. m'a appelé par hasard
3. n'arrivait pas à te joindre
4. attentivement
5. historique des appels
6. lança
7. à la tempe
8. glissa sur le marbre
9. malentendu
10. Sauter mon assistante, t'appelles ça comme ça
11. d'une voix tremblante
12. tires des conclusions hâtives

"You know what she said? Just now? Before she realized it was me? She said she thought you two were going to take a break. What do you suppose she meant by that?"

The doorbell rang a second time.

"Who *knows* what the hell she meant?" Gill said. "I always thought she was a bit off her nut[1]. I don't know how she's lasted as long as she has[2] working for you. She's a total incompetent, you ask me[3]."

"I hate you," Agnes said. "If you'd fucked around with anyone else[4], I'd still hate you, but maybe not quite so much. This ... this is just rubbing my nose in it[5]."

"Enough!" Marla screamed.

Now someone was pounding on the door. And shouting, "Ms. Pickens! Mr. Pickens!"

Agnes's finger was in her husband's face. "I'll ruin you[6]. I will. I'll ruin you."

"I'm glad it was her," Gill said. "I really am."

Marla went to the front door, threw it open. Detective Barry Duckworth was standing there with two uniformed officers.

Agnes and Gill Pickens turned and stared, dumbfounded[7].

Duckworth waved[8] a piece of paper. "I have a warrant for the arrest of[9] Marla Pickens."

Marla's arms hung limply[10] at her sides. She looked numb[11].

Agnes glanced at her husband, took the phone he was holding, and said, "I'll call Natalie."

1. maboule
2. tenu aussi longtemps que ça
3. à mon avis
4. t'étais tapé n'importe qui d'autre
5. pour me faire encore plus mal
6. vais te démolir
7. bouche bée
8. agita
9. mandat d'arrêt contre
10. pendaient mollement
11. apathique

FIFTY-SEVEN

ACTING[1] Promise Falls detective Angus Carlson's first day out of uniform[2] wasn't going to be anything to brag about[3] to his wife when he took her out for dinner that evening. Barry Duckworth had left him a note of things he wanted him to follow up on[4].

First up, the squirrels.

Carlson figured this was Duckworth's way of getting even[5]. Okay, so maybe he cracked[6] a couple of stupid jokes. Just trying to break the tension[7] was all. Where was the harm in that? Carlson had always been looking for ways to lighten the mood[8]. What had his mother always said? *Turn up the corners of your mouth.*

But Duckworth's list of to-dos[9] didn't end with squirrels. He wanted Carlson to head back out[10] to Thackeray to interview three young women who'd been attacked, presumably[11] by some guy named Mason Helt, who'd been shot in the head by campus security chief Clive Duncomb.

Finally, Duckworth wanted Carlson to go back out to Five Mountains and learn more about those three naked mannequins—"You'll Be Sorry" painted across their chests—that had gone for a spin[12] on the Ferris wheel.

1. à titre temporaire
2. sans uniforme
3. ne mériterait pas qu'il s'en vante
4. qu'il suive
5. prendre sa revanche
6. avait fait
7. détendre l'atmosphère
8. alléger l'ambiance
9. choses à faire
10. que Carlson retourne
11. probablement
12. fait un tour

432

Duckworth had added some cryptic notes[1] about the number 23. How that number was a common element in all three incidents. How it might mean something[2].

"Hmm," Carlson had said under his breath[3] as he read the detective's notes. Duckworth wanted him to be on the alert for[4] any recurrence of that number.

He began his day at the park where the squirrels had been found. Walked carefully through the adjoining[5] wooded area. Talked to anyone who happened to pass by, asked whether they'd noticed anything odd the night before last. Knocked on the doors of nearby houses to ask the same. Came up with a big fat zero[6].

At one door, an elderly man grinned[7] and said, "This case'll be a tough nut to crack!"

Okay, so maybe it wasn't that funny.

He didn't do much better at Thackeray. None of the women he wanted to interview was available[8]. Two had gone home for a couple of days. The third, who apparently was going to be spending the summer at the college taking extra courses[9], couldn't be found[10]. Another student who lived across the hall from her[11] said she could be at the library, or in town doing some shopping, or just out for a long walk.

Carlson wasn't going to waste his entire day out there.

Next stop: Five Mountains.

He went straight to the administration offices, where he found Fenwick. According to Duckworth's exhaustive[12] note, she was going to draw up[13] a list of people who had operated[14] the Ferris wheel during the months the park was open. While it was possible anyone with some

1. remarques énigmatiques

2. Comme quoi il avait peut-être une signification

3. dans sa barbe

4. qu'il guette

5. attenante

6. Résultat : rien de rien

7. sourit largement

8. disponible

9. pour suivre des cours supplémentaires

10. resta introuvable

11. en face, dans le même couloir qu'elle

12. complète

13. dresser

14. fait tourner

mechanical smarts[1] might have been able to get the ride going[2], someone who'd actually run the thing would have an edge[3].

"I'm still freaked out about this[4]," Fenwick said, sitting at her computer, tapping away.

"Sure," Carlson said. "That's totally understandable, you being here alone and all[5], late at night."

"I thought I was going to have a list for you this afternoon, but I haven't heard from our former facilities supervisor[6]. He'd know who ran each ride[7], but of course, head office fired him[8], and it's not like he's in any rush to do me a favor[9]. If I don't hear from him by the end of today I'll call him. Weren't you in uniform last night?"

"I was," he said.

"You look pretty good out of uniform," Gloria Fenwick said, smiling.

"That's the nicest thing anyone's said to me today."

"I think maybe it came out wrong[10]."

"I think it came out just right[11]," Carlson said.

He asked her about how someone would gain access to[12] the park. The admin offices were behind a locked gate[13], and a fence ran around the perimeter of[14] the property. Who had keys? he wanted to know.

Fenwick explained that once most of the Five Mountains staff had been fired, the locks were changed. Fenwick and a couple of other office staff who were tasked with winding the place down[15] had keys, as did the security firm that checked on the property several times a day. That was it[16].

"You seem to be taking this very seriously," she said. "I mean, as unsettling as it was[17], there was no real damage done."

"Detective Duckworth takes everything *very* seriously," Carlson said.

He thanked her, said good-bye, and checked out the Ferris wheel first. In the light of day, things looked a lot less sinister. Of course, the mannequins had been taken away[1], which helped. There was nothing to suggest anything out of the ordinary had gone on[2] here the night before.

Carlson left the Ferris wheel and headed for the closest fence that surrounded the property. If whoever brought in the mannequins didn't have a key, and there was no indication[3] the locks had been broken or tampered with[4], the fence had to have been breached somewhere[5].

It was a wire fence[6], about nine feet tall[7]. A single strand[8] of barbed wire[9] ran along the top of it to discourage intruders[10]. Not that effective[11], but then again, Five Mountains probably didn't want to run several strands. They wouldn't want to be sending off a prison vibe[12].

Rides and exhibits backed up to[13] the fence, where the grass grew taller and was untended[14]. Carlson figured someone could put a ladder[15] up against the fence. It was rigid enough. Drag three mannequins up, toss them over. But then the intruder would have to get over[16], too.

A lot of work.

The park property, a rough[17] rectangle, was about fifteen acres[18], so it was a long, slow trek[19] along the fence. Carlson didn't notice anything until he'd rounded[20] the second corner.

The fence had been cut.

Someone would have needed something like bolt cutters[21], he figured. The chain link[22] had been cut along a post[23], starting at ground level

1. retirés

2. ne s'était passé

3. si rien n'indiquait que

4. ni crochetées

5. on avait dû casser la clôture

6. grillage

7. dans les 2,75 m de haut

8. fil

9. barbelé

10. les intrus

11. ultra-efficace

12. faire prison

13. tournaient le dos à

14. n'était pas entretenue

15. échelle

16. passer de l'autre côté

17. approximatif

18. faisait environ 6 hectares

19. marche

20. eut passé

21. coupe-boulons

22. maille

23. poteau

and going up about five feet[1]. Several links had also been severed[2] along the bottom, creating a simple doorway[3].

The grass, Carlson noted, was matted down[4] on both sides of the fence. About twenty yards[5] beyond it was a two-lane road[6] that ran along[7] the back of the amusement park property.

He could see where someone had worn down a path[8] in the grass between the fence and the road. He thought about what must have been involved. Someone drives up in a truck or van, has to unload[9] three mannequins. Probably has to drag them one at a time to the fence, push them through[10]. Maybe then he moves or hides the truck, returns, carries the mannequins one by one to the Ferris wheel, because that's going to take some time.

Gets the three dummies—which probably had their message painted on them before being brought out here—positioned into one of the carriages. Which, Duckworth had noted, was numbered 23.

As if that really mattered.

The Ferris wheel gets turned on[11], and the intruder takes off[12]. Gets through the opening in the fence, hops behind the wheel[13] of his truck or van, and speeds away.

Carlson wondered why anyone would go to that much trouble[14]. It was backbreaking[15] work. This didn't strike him as something a few teenagers would do for a lark[16].

This was someone who really wanted to send a message.

YOU'LL BE SORRY.

Who was it meant for? Why did the person sending it feel aggrieved[1]? And if this was a real threat[2], what was coming next?

"Beats me[3]," Angus Carlson said to himself.

1. mécontente

2. menace

3. Ça me dépasse

FIFTY-EIGHT

JACK Sturgess came back out of Doris Stemple's apartment for the second time, got out his phone, and called Bill Gaynor.

"Pick me up," he said.

Seconds later, the Audi whisked down[1] the street, came to an abrupt stop[2] long enough for Sturgess to get in on the passenger side, then sped off.

Matthew, in back, strapped[3] into his car seat, was crying. More like shrieking[4].

"Jesus, can't you shut him up[5]?" Sturgess said.

"He's a baby, Jack. That's what they do. Where are we going?"

"Bus terminal. Christ, I can't hear myself think."

Gaynor turned his head around every three seconds to catch Matthew's eye. "Hey, sport[6], come on! It's okay! Have some Cheerios."

The tiny round "O"s of cereal were littered across[7] the backseat. Matthew showed no interest in them beyond batting them about[8] with his tiny hands.

"I need to get him home," Gaynor said. "He's been out all morning and he needs a good sleep."

"Soon enough," Sturgess said.

"Who's at the bus terminal? Sarita? Is it her?"

1. descendit à toute allure
2. s'arrêta brutalement
3. bien attaché
4. un cri strident
5. lui fermer sa gueule
6. bonhomme
7. couvraient
8. à part les jeter en tous sens

438

"Yes."

"How did you find out?"

"From her neighbor. Where she was calling from. She said a cab picked her up a little while ago to take her there. She's getting a bus to New York."

Matthew's shrieking persisted.

"Goddamn it!" Sturgess said. "I can't think with all that screaming!"

Gaynor made a fist[1] and struck it against the top of the steering wheel.

"Shut up! What the fuck would you like me to do? Rosemary is *dead*! Do you remember? My wife is fucking dead! Sarita took off[2]! I'm his fucking father! What would you like me to do?" He raised his eyebrows, as if inviting a response. "Chuck him out[3] the window? Leave him on a church doorstep[4]? If you've got an idea I'd like to hear it!"

Sturgess said nothing, stared straight ahead. Matthew continued to wail[5].

"Nothing? Maybe you've got another needle? Want to stick it in him? Is that what's going on in your head?"

"Just get us to the bus station," Sturgess said. "The sooner we find Sarita the sooner you can go home and look after your son."

Gaynor, slowly depressurizing[6], said, "I never should have listened to you."

"What?"

"I never … never should have gone along with you[7] on this."

Sturgess sighed[8]. It was not the first time Gaynor had made such a complaint. "Well, Bill, there's no turning back the clock[9]. You did what you did. We made a deal[10]. Now we're dealing with the fallout[11]."

1. serra le poing

2. s'est barrée

3. Le jeter par
4. seuil d'une église

5. hurler

6. se calmant lentement

7. te suivre

8. soupira

9. on ne remontera pas le temps

10. avons conclu un marché

11. les retombées

"Fallout?" Gaynor shot the doctor a look. "Is that what you call my wife getting killed[1]?"

Sturgess returned the look[2]. "We don't really know what happened there."

Gaynor's chin quivered[3]. "I got a call, before you asked me to pick you up. They arrested her."

"Marla?"

Gaynor nodded. "They're picking her up right about now."

"Must have happened after I spoke to Agnes," the doctor said. "She'll be devastated. Marla, too, of course."

"Everything points to her[4]," Gaynor said.

"I suppose it does."

"But we know she didn't do it," Gaynor said. "I mean, we know she didn't take Matthew. Right?"

"There are things we know, and things we *don't* know. But what we *do* know is where[5] we're vulnerable, and that's where we have to act. Take this turn[6]; it'll get us there faster."

Matthew's shrieking began to subside[7].

"I think he's crying himself to sleep[8]," Gaynor said.

"At last, something to be thankful for. Okay, it's just up here. We go in; we split up[9]; we try to find her. Any buses waiting to go, we poke our heads in[10], see if she's on one of them."

"I can't leave Matthew in the car. Not here. It was okay in the woods, but not here."

Sturgess closed his eyes briefly, let out a long breath[11]. Maybe an injection was the way to go[12]. For both of them. There might be enough in the other syringe.

"There's no place to park."

"For Christ's sake, park anywhere. I'll go into the terminal while you get the kid out[13]."

1. le meurtre de ma femme
2. soutint son regard
3. trembla
4. Tous les éléments l'accablent
5. quand
6. Tourne ici
7. diminuer
8. va s'endormir à force de pleurer
9. chacun de son côté
10. on jette un coup d'œil
11. poussa un long soupir
12. solution
13. sors le gosse

440

"Okay, but— Hey!"

"What?"

"They just went the other way!"

"What? In a car?"

"Sarita was in it!"

"What?"

"I'm sure of it. I caught a glimpse of her[1] in the front seat. I'm sure it was her."

Gaynor hit the brakes[2], looked for an opening in the traffic so he could do a U-turn[3]. "An old Taurus. I'm sure it was her."

"Who was driving?"

"I think it was that guy."

"What guy?"

"Harwood. The one who was at the house with the woman and Matthew."

"Shit," Sturgess said. "Turn around[4]. Go. Go."

"There's cars com—"

"Cut the fuck in[5]!"

Matthew resumed[6] crying.

Gaynor cut off someone in an Explorer, endured a blaring horn[7] and an extended middle finger[8]. He hit the gas[9]. The Taurus was two cars ahead.

"If I catch up to them, then what?" Gaynor asked.

"Follow them for a while. It's too busy[10] here. Too many people."

"Too many people for what?"

"Just stay on them[11], see where they go."

"What if they're headed[12] to the police?" Gaynor asked.

The doctor didn't have an immediate response to that. Instead he reached down toward the floor, where a small leather bag sat[13] between his feet. He opened it, took out a syringe and a small glass vial[14].

"Jack," Gaynor said warily[15].

1. l'ai aperçue
2. freina violemment
3. demi-tour
4. Fais demi-tour
5. Force le passage, bordel
6. se remit à
7. beuglement de Klaxon
8. majeur dressé
9. mit les gaz
10. Il y a trop de monde
11. Les lâche pas
12. vont
13. était posé
14. fiole
15. d'un ton inquiet

"We'll have to get very close to them, of course. Engage them in conversation. I need to bring him down[1] first. Once he's been done, it'll be easier to do the nanny."

1. l'abattre

"Christ, Jack, what's happened to you? You already killed one man."

The doctor shot him[2] a look. "I seem to remember[3] you were there. I seem to remember you digging a hole for his body. I seem to remember us putting him in there together and covering him up. Do you remember those events differently?"

2. lui décocha
3. Pour autant que je me rappelle,

"This is crazy. We're not ... we're not these kinds of people."

"Maybe we weren't," Sturgess said. "But we are now. If we want to survive." He turned away, looked out the passenger window.

"This has to end[4]," the doctor said.

4. Il faut en finir

442

FIFTY-NINE

David

"LET'S go," I said to Sarita, sitting next to me in the bus terminal. "The police might come looking for you here."

"Where are we going?"

"I don't know. Why don't we just drive. And talk."

I wondered whether she would try to run[1]. Hoping she wouldn't want to take off[2] without her luggage, I stood and grabbed[3] the handle of her bag. "I'll take this for you," I said. "I'm just parked outside."

Slowly, resignedly, she stood. We walked in measured paces[4] toward the door. I didn't want her to fall behind[5], didn't want her out of my sight[6] for a second. Once we were outside, I pointed to my mother's car. "I'm just up here."

I opened the front passenger door, got her settled in, watched her do up[7] her seat belt, then dropped her bag into the trunk. I got in next to her, started the engine, and headed off.

"You said we would just drive, right?"

I nodded.

1. si elle essaierait de prendre la fuite
2. partir
3. saisit

4. à pas lents
5. qu'elle reste à la traîne
6. la perdre de vue

7. attacher

1. Pas question
d'aller

2. pris la fuite

3. s'élargirent de
surprise

4. me parut
révélatrice

5. C'est vous qui
l'avez trouvée

6. ai dû arriver

7. service du
matin

8. sonnette

"No going[1] to the police station."

Another nod.

"I want you to tell me what happened. I want you to tell me why you've been on the run[2], why you've disappeared."

Sarita said nothing.

I decided to start with the big question. "Did you kill Rosemary Gaynor?"

Her eyes went wide with shock[3]. "Is that what people think? Is that what the *police* think?"

"They think Marla did it," I said. "But I don't. So I'm asking you if you did it."

"No!" she said. "I did not kill Ms. Gaynor! I loved her! She was good to me. She was a very good lady. I loved working for her. It's a horrible thing what happened to her."

"Do you know who did kill her?"

Sarita hesitated. "I don't."

"But do you have an idea?"

She shook her head. "I don't know. It was just … it was so awful."

The way she said it told me something[4]. "You found her[5]. You were there."

"I found her," she said, nodding. "But I wasn't there when it happened. I must have gotten there[6] right after."

"Tell me."

"I got there in the afternoon. I had done an early morning shift[7] at Davidson Place. I have two jobs. Many days I work a shift at one and a shift at the other, although at the Gaynors', I do not call it a shift. A shift is when you work for a company, but they're a family, so it is different. But I did my shift at Davidson, then took the bus to the Gaynors'. I have a key, but I always ring the bell[8]. It is courtesy. You do not walk straight into

444

a person's house[1]. But I rang the bell and no one answered. I thought maybe Ms. Gaynor was out. Maybe she was shopping or something like that. Or maybe she was in the bathroom[2], or changing Matthew's diaper[3] and could not come to the door right away[4]. So in a case like that, I use my key to open the door."

"So you went inside."

"Yes, but it turns out[5] the door was open. I come in, and I call for her. I figure she must be home because the door is not locked. I call a few times, and she does not answer, and then I go into …"

She turned her head down and toward the window. Her shoulders shook. While I waited, I took a left, followed by a right, taking a route that would lead us out of downtown[6].

Sarita lifted her head, but did not glance my way[7] as she continued. "I go into the kitchen and she is there, and there is blood everywhere, and even though I am afraid to, I touch her, just in case maybe she is not dead, maybe she is breathing, maybe there is a pulse[8], but she is dead."

"What did you do then?"

"I … I …"

"You did not call the police."

She shook her head. "I did not. I could not do that. I am in this country illegally and no one knows about me[9]. Not officially. Someone like me, the police don't care what happens to me. They would find a way to charge me with[10] something, maybe even think that I did it, that I killed Ms. Gaynor, because that is what they will do. But I called Marshall so he could come get me." She paused, caught her breath. "You asked me if I had any idea who did it."

"That's right."

1. On n'entre pas comme ça chez les gens

2. aux toilettes

3. la couche

4. tout de suite

5. en fait

6. hors du centre-ville

7. ne tourna pas les yeux vers moi

8. que je sentirai son pouls

9. que j'existe

10. m'accuser de

1. me suis demandé

2. comprendre ce qui se passait

3. quand même

4. aurais dû me taire

5. moins de circulation

6. avais du mal

7. à comprendre

8. avait perdu la tête

"I had to wonder[1] ... I had to wonder if it was Mr. Gaynor."

"Why?"

"I wondered if he knew that his wife was start-ing to figure things out[2]. That he'd never been honest with her about everything. I wondered if maybe she had confronted him and he'd gotten angry with her. But even so[3], I mean, I didn't like him; I never liked him, but he didn't seem like a man who would do something like that."

"Sarita, what are you talking about?"

"It's all my fault," she said, and started to cry. "If that's what happened, it's all my fault. I should have kept quiet[4]. I shouldn't have said anything."

We were heading north out of Promise Falls. With lighter traffic[5], it was easier to concentrate on what Sarita was saying. Although I was hav-ing a hard time[6] figuring out[7] what she was talk-ing about.

"Said anything about what?"

"I knew about Marla," she said. "I knew about your cousin. I knew what had happened at the hospital."

"About her trying to take a baby?"

Sarita nodded. "I have friends who work at the hospital who also work at Davidson, and every-one was talking about the girl who tried to steal a baby. That she was out of her head[8] because her own baby had died a few months earlier. And I heard that it was Dr. Sturgess who was the crazy lady's doctor."

"You know Dr. Sturgess," I said.

Sarita nodded. "He is the Gaynors' doctor. And he and Mr. Gaynor are old friends, from a long time ago."

I glanced[1] in my mirror. There was a car there, a black sedan that looked a lot like a car I'd seen in my mirror a few minutes ago. It did not look like a police car.

"They talk a lot," Sarita said.

"What do you mean?"

"The doctor would come over, and they would go into Mr. Gaynor's office. He has an office in the home. They would close the door and they would talk many times."

"About what?"

She shrugged. "I don't know. I hear bits and pieces[2]. Usually about money. I think Mr. Gaynor had a problem. And maybe the doctor, too."

"What kind of problem?"

"Gambling[3], I think. They both had troubles like that[4]. Ms. Gaynor, sometimes she would talk to me, tell me her husband made good money[5] working for the insurance company, but there were times when they still had money problems because Mr. Gaynor liked to bet on things[6]. Dr. Sturgess, too. He was way worse[7]."

While I believed some of what Sarita was telling me, I felt she was holding back[8]. I couldn't help but think she was more involved[9] in this than she was letting on[10]. I kept coming back to my earlier theory.

That Marla'd been set up[11].

Maybe Dr. Sturgess and Bill Gaynor had planned[12] the murder and needed someone to pin it on[13]. Marla was a perfect patsy[14]. Sturgess knew her history and how to exploit it.

But how did Marla end up[15] with the baby?

Then it hit me.

"What do you wear[16]?" I asked Sarita.

"Excuse me?"

1. jetai un coup d'œil

2. des bribes

3. Les jeux d'argent

4. ce genre de problèmes

5. gagnait bien sa vie

6. parier

7. bien pire

8. ne me disait pas tout

9. impliquée

10. n'y laissait paraître

11. piégée

12. prémédité

13. à qui faire porter le chapeau

14. bouc émissaire

15. Marla s'était-elle retrouvée

16. portez comme vêtements

"When you work at Davidson House. What do you wear? Do you wear a uniform?"

"Yes," she said.

"Would you show up for work[1] sometimes at the Gaynors' in your uniform?"

"Yes," she said again. "A lot of times I would get changed at their house, get back into my regular clothes[2]."

"Describe it," I said.

"What?"

"Describe your uniform."

She shook her head, not understanding the question, or at least not what I was getting at[3] by asking. "Pants[4], a top. Simple."

"White pants? A white top?"

Sarita blinked[5]. "Yes. All white."

An angel.

"You delivered[6] Matthew to Marla," I said.

"Yes," she said. "When I found Matthew, found he was alive upstairs in his nursery, I wanted to get him out of the house. I grabbed him, a few of his things, the stroller, left the house, and locked it."

"You left that smudge[7] on the door. At Marla's house. You left some of Rosemary Gaynor's blood on the door."

Slowly she nodded. "I don't know. I guess that is possible. There might have been blood on my hand; I might have touched something. I don't exactly remember. But I think … when I got there, I felt like I was going to pass out[8] from what I had seen, and I put my hand up so I would not fall down."

I believed I'd just saved my cousin from a life-time in prison.

But there was more I needed to know.

Marginal glossary notes:

1. Est-ce qu'il vous arrivait d'arriver au travail
2. habits normaux
3. où je voulais en venir
4. Un pantalon
5. cilla
6. avez amené
7. tache
8. m'évanouir

"There's more you haven't told me," I said. "You were in on it[1] with them."

"I don't know what you're talking about. I had nothing to do with Ms. Gaynor getting killed. I didn't do anything with her husband or her doctor. But … my boyfriend, that's a different story."

"What?"

"Marshall is being very, very stupid. He's been trying to get money out of[2] Mr. Gaynor, and it's very wrong what he's doing, but he wouldn't listen to me. And I don't know what's happened to him. He was supposed to come back to the house, but he hasn't been answering his phone. I haven't been able to get in touch with him."

Jesus, there was more going on here[3] than I could have imagined. But I moved ahead with my argument[4].

"Come on, Sarita. They—Sturgess and Gaynor, or maybe just one of them, I don't know—decided Rosemary was better off dead[5]." She'd just told me Gaynor needed money. Maybe there was a hefty life insurance policy[6] on his wife.

I continued. "So they set out[7] to frame Marla for it. And you made the delivery. You took the baby to her and knew eventually the police would find out[8]. You're the connection."

"No," Sarita said. "You have it all wrong. I was trying to do a good thing."

"A good thing. What the hell—"

That was when I started hearing a horn[9].

The black car that had been trailing behind us[10] was on our bumper[11]. The driver was leaning on the horn[12] and flashing his lights[13].

SIXTY

WHILE Marla was being booked and finger-printed[1], Barry Duckworth went over to his desk and sat down.

Exhausted.

He wasn't sure about Marla, but when the lab reported back that the blood on the door of her house did indeed match up with Rosemary Gaynor's, the chief and the district attorney[2] made the decision: Bring her in[3].

And so he did.

She hadn't said a word the entire way to the station. Just sat in the back of the cruiser as if in some kind of trance. Duckworth had to admit he felt sorry[4] for this girl, even if she had done it. The things that had happened to her had left their mark. The girl was damaged[5]. And her parents weren't making her life any better[6]. He'd heard them screaming at each other while he waited for someone to open the door.

You met a lot of fucked-up people[7] in this line of work[8].

He moved his computer mouse and the screen came to life[9]. He had two new e-mails. He'd heard his phone ding[10] a couple of times in the last hour, but hadn't had a moment to look at it.

The first one was from a[1] Sandra Bottsford, manager of the Boston hotel where Bill Gaynor had been staying[2] when his wife had been murdered. She wrote that she had information for him, and asked him to call her.

The second e-mail was from Wanda Therrieult, the coroner. It was short. *Call me*, it said.

Duckworth decided to call the hotel manager first. He got bounced around some[3]. Bottsford was somewhere in the building, so they transferred him to her cell[4] when he explained who he was.

Finally she answered. "Bottsford."

"It's Detective Duckworth, in Promise Falls. I just got your e-mail. Thanks for getting back to me."

"No problem. I could have explained it in the e-mail, but I thought you might have extra[5] questions, so I figured we should just talk[6]."

"Great. So, I was trying to confirm whether Mr. Gaynor was at the hotel Saturday midday through Monday morning."

"Yeah. Terrible thing, what happened to his wife. Anyway, he checked out of[7] the hotel at six in the morning on Monday. I even checked the security footage[8], and he was there at the front desk[9] bright and early[10] yesterday morning."

A six a.m. checkout sounded about right[11]. If he'd stopped once or twice to get a coffee or hit the bathroom[12], that departure would have seen him getting home at the very time he did[13].

But that didn't nail it down[14] for Duckworth. It was conceivable Gaynor could have left the hotel sometime during the previous forty-eight hours, driven home, killed his wife, then returned to Boston. His wife had clearly been dead at least a day[15] when her body was discovered. Which meant who-

---

1. une certaine
2. séjournait
3. On le passa d'un interlocuteur à un autre
4. le basculèrent sur son portable
5. supplémentaires
6. ferions mieux de parler de vive voix
7. a quitté
8. vidéos des caméras de sécurité
9. réception
10. de bonne heure
11. semblait correspondre
12. faire une pause toilettes
13. exactement à l'heure où il était arrivé
14. ne prouvait rien
15. depuis au moins une journée

ever had killed her had done it more than twenty-four hours earlier. Duckworth was still waiting to hear back from[1] the Mass Pike[2] authorities to see whether Gaynor's car's license plate had been picked up[3] entering or exiting the toll road[4] in the two days before he'd officially returned home.

A round trip[5] would have taken him the better part[6] of five to six hours, but it could be done if he used the interstate highway[7]. His attendance[8] at the hotel conference could serve as his alibi.

Duckworth pressed on. "I'd asked you, I think, if you had anything else that would confirm Mr. Gaynor's presence at the hotel for most of the weekend."

"Yes," said Bottsford, "you'd mentioned that. There were seminars most of Saturday and Sunday, and the conference dinner at five on Sunday, and he was seen at that[9]. There was a charge[10] from the bar at ten p.m., Sunday, and he's visible on the security camera again, crossing the lobby[11] at around eleven. Around midnight there was a call from his room down to the desk[12] to ask for a wake-up call[13] at five, which was done. The call was answered."

That covered Sunday. But Rosemary Gaynor was already dead then.

"What about Saturday, and into Sunday morning[14]?"

"The thing is, Detective, Mr. Gaynor is a regular[15] here. He has stayed here for weeks, sometimes months at a time[16]. Last year his wife was even with him for a very long stay[17]. Everyone here knows the Gaynors. I asked around in the bar and the restaurant, and they saw him quite regularly all through the weekend. And his car did not leave the hotel. I talked to the valet[18], and he remembers

---

1. des infos de
2. [Réseau routier local]
3. repérée
4. autoroute à péage
5. aller-retour
6. pas loin
7. autoroute fédérale
8. présence
9. on l'y a vu
10. consommation
11. hall d'entrée
12. réception
13. qu'on le réveille par téléphone
14. la nuit de samedi à dimanche
15. client régulier
16. d'affilée
17. séjour
18. voiturier

bringing his car up for him at six, and it was the only time the car was asked for in the preceding forty-eight hours."

Duckworth said, "Thanks very much for getting back to me."

"Mr. Gaynor's always been very kind and courteous to everyone here," the manager added. "We feel very bad for his loss[1]."

"Of course. Good-bye."

Duckworth hung up the phone. Just as well[2] to scratch[3] Gaynor from the list of suspects, he guessed, considering that they'd made an arrest[4]. But he'd had to be sure[5].

He picked up the phone and called Wanda.

"How's it going," she said.

"I got your e-mail. What's up?"

"I finished the autopsy on Rosemary Gaynor."

"Okay."

"Not that much to add about the cause of death. And there was no sign of sexual assault[6]. Things are pretty much the way I laid them out for you[7] yesterday. But there was one thing, and it may not be important, but I figured I should let you know[8]. I mean, you'll get the full report, but I wanted to give you a heads-up[9]."

"Go on."

"I was thinking about her baby, what's his name?"

"Matthew," Duckworth said.

"I was thinking about how lucky it was whoever killed[10] the Gaynor woman didn't kill the kid, too. Not because he'd be a witness[11], but because people who do things like this are just out of their heads[12]. Right?"

"Often."

1. sommes de tout cœur avec lui

2. C'était pas plus mal

3. rayer

4. vu qu'ils venaient d'arrêter quelqu'un

5. eu besoin d'en avoir le cœur net

6. agression

7. te les ai présentées

8. t'en informer

9. longueur d'avance

10. la personne qui avait tué

11. témoin

12. tarés

"Well," Wanda continued, "that was on my mind when I stumbled upon[1] some curious scar formation[2] in the woman's pelvis. These scars were whitish in color[3] and had shrunk[4] over time[5], which indicated to me that a procedure she underwent[6] was more than[7] a year ago, maybe a couple of years. It's called maturing[8], when the scars go like that."

"I don't understand."

"Just bear with me[9]. Also, it struck me as kind of funny[10] that there was no sign of fibrous bands[11] in this woman's breasts[12]. Considering[13]."

"Considering what?"

"When a woman is pregnant, because of the hormonal enlargement[14] that takes place in the breasts, you see these fibrous bands. So now I was even more curious, so I took a gander[15] at the back side of the pubic ramus[16]."

"The who?"

"The bone in front of the pelvis near the urinary bladder[17]. You'd expect to see scarring[18] from the growth of the uterus, and—"

"Stop," Duckworth said. "What are you telling me?"

"Rosemary Gaynor had a hysterectomy a few years ago. Everything I know tells me this woman has never been pregnant."

"Say that again."

"She's never had a kid, Barry."

SIXTY-ONE

AGNES Pickens had just finished talking to Natalie Bondurant on her home phone[1] in the kitchen when her cell—definitely hers[2], not Gill's—rang. She snatched it off the countertop, saw who it was, and took the call.

"What?" she said. "Wait, hang on a second."

Gill had gone upstairs, but she didn't want to take a chance[3] he might hear any of this conversation, so she went over to the sliding[4] glass doors that led to the backyard deck[5]. Once outside, she closed the door behind her.

"Okay, what is it?"

"We have a problem," Jack Sturgess said. There was road noise[6] in the background.

"So do I. They just arrested Marla."

"Well," he said.

"Yeah. So I've got problems, too. Huge problems. I don't need any more from you. You just called me with one. Are you telling me you didn't solve it[7]?"

"The old lady's dealt with[8], but yeah, there's a new problem. I've found Sarita."

"That doesn't sound like a problem. That sounds good."

1. téléphone fixe
2. oui, le sien

3. prendre le risque
4. coulissantes
5. terrasse de derrière

6. des bruits de circulation

7. que tu ne l'as pas résolu
8. a eu son compte

"She's with your nephew," Sturgess said. When Agnes said nothing for several seconds, he said, "Did you hear me?"

"I heard you. She's with David? Where? Where are they?"

"They're in a car ahead of us. Just driving around. We're following them. Sarita was ready to hop[1] a bus out of[2] town. David must have found her there. We saw him driving away with her in the car."

Agnes said, "I told him … I gave him my blessing[3] to ask around[4] on Marla's behalf. What else could I say? I didn't want him to think I didn't want to know what might have happened. … I just … I just didn't expect him to make any real progress." Panic was rising in her voice. "How the hell did he find her?"

"How the fuck should I know?" the doctor fired back[5]. "Maybe you should talk to him."

"Talk to him?"

"I don't know. Call him; tell him to back off[6]. Leave this alone. You're his goddamn aunt, for Christ's sake. Talk some kind of sense into him."

"I'm thinking[7]," she said.

"Well, you'd better think fast, because it looks like they're having a real gabfest[8]."

Another silence from Agnes.

"If you don't want to give me any direction," Sturgess said, "I'm just going to have to deal with this as best I can."

"Don't you see the problem here?" Agnes asked. "We know it had to be[9] Sarita who took the baby to Marla's house. So she had to have figured out what really happened. To save ourselves[10] we'd have to … we'd have to keep[11] Sarita from ever talking to anyone."

1. prendre
2. pour quitter
3. l'ai encouragé
4. poser des questions
5. rétorqua, furieux
6. ne pas s'en mêler
7. réfléchis
8. se font un beau brin de causette
9. que c'est forcément
10. sauver notre peau
11. empêcher

456

"Yeah," Sturgess said.

"But ... I need Sarita."

"What?"

"I need Sarita to save Marla. If they've got enough to arrest her, they may have enough to send her away[1]. They're going to send my girl to jail, Jack. Sarita can clear her[2]. When they hear what she has to say, they'll have to drop[3] the charges[4] against Marla."

"Agnes," Sturgess said slowly. "You need to think about what you're saying."

"That's all I'm doing is thinking! My daughter's not going to prison."

"Would *you* like to go there?" the doctor asked. "I know *I* don't want to go there. Because that's where this conversation is going. Think about this, Agnes. Even if Marla were convicted, you could mount a pretty convincing insanity[5] defense. Diminished capacity[6], something like that. Out of her head[7] as a result[8] of a traumatic incident. Odds are[9], if she went to jail, it wouldn't be for long. They might even just commit her for psychiatric care[10] until such time as they deemed her cured[11]. But—"

"You son of a bitch."

"*But* if they come after us, if they find out what we did—Agnes, if they find out what I've done just today, with your blessing[12]—we'll be going away *forever*. Are you hearing me? If you let Marla take the blame, she's out in a year or two and you can look after her[13]. But if you go to jail, you'll *never* be able to look after Marla. You'll see her once a month on visiting day and that'll be it. Is that what you want?"

"Jack, just shut up."

1. l'envoyer en prison

2. la disculper

3. abandonner

4. accusations

5. basée sur sa démence

6. Jugement affecté

7. Folle

8. des suites

9. Il y a toutes les chances pour que

10. l'envoyer en soins psychiatriques

11. le temps qu'ils la jugent guérie

12. bénédiction

13. t'occuper d'elle

"You want to be a good mother, Agnes? Let Marla go to jail. Let them treat her[1]. And when she gets out, you'll be there for her. Let me take care of Sarita."

1. la soigner

"I … I can't … I don't know what—"

"And, Agnes, forgive me, but Marla's not the same kind of issue[2] for me as she is for you. She's your daughter, not mine. I know what I have to do to save myself."

2. ne représente pas la même chose

"God, why did I ever go along with you on[3]—"

3. ai-je marché dans ta

"You sound like[4] Bill. We're in this together, Agnes. You got something out of this and so did I."

4. On croirait entendre

"It was all about money for you," she said. "It was never about money for me."

"Motivations mean fuck-all now[5]. Just don't try coming back at me[6] like you had nothing to do with this[7]."

5. ne veulent plus rien dire

6. te la jouer

7. « je n'ai rien à voir là-dedans »

Agnes was quiet for another moment. Finally she asked, "Where are you?"

"David's driving north out of town. I can see the Five Mountains Ferris wheel in the distance."

"How much do you think she's told him?"

"Who knows? We don't even know how much she knows."

In the background, the sound of an infant[8] crying.

8. bébé

"What's that?" Agnes asked. "Who's that?"

"It's Matthew. He's been screaming almost the whole time."

"You have the baby with you?" Agnes asked.

"I'm with Bill. I've already been through this with him[9]. I thought it was a bad idea, too, bringing the kid, but like he says, what the hell's he going to do? He needs a new nanny."

9. ai déjà parlé de tout ça avec lui

"Jack, seriously, we need to think about this. What about—just give me a second—what about if there's a way to pin it on[1] Sarita, but … silence her[2] at the same time?"

"Go on."

"She … she confesses to you what she did, but then she attacks you, and you have to act in self-defense. Maybe something like that?"

"You're grasping at straws[3], Agnes. And besides, what if she's already told David everything? Have you thought about that? He may already know the whole story."

Before Agnes could respond, the doctor said to Bill Gaynor, "It's pretty isolated here. Flash your lights; hit the horn; get them to pull over[4]."

"Jack?" Agnes said.

"I have to go," he said. "I'll check in with you later. Think about what I said, Agnes. Think about being a good mother."

"Don't you[5] hurt my nephew," she warned. And then, "Or my grandson[6]."

"Oh," said the doctor. "*Now* he's your grandson."

1. faire porter le chapeau à

2. la faire taire

3. te raccroches à du vent

4. force-les à s'arrêter

5. Ne t'avise pas de

6. petit-fils

SIXTY-TWO

David

"**A** good thing," Sarita Gomez repeated, sitting in the car next to me. "I wanted to do what was right."

The black car behind us was still honking[1] and flashing its lights.

"Explain that," I said, holding my speed[2], debating whether to pull over.

"I wanted to return[3] Matthew to his real mother," she said.

I glanced over at her. Not once, but twice. "Marla's baby didn't die."

Sarita nodded. "I'm pretty sure. I knew Ms. Gaynor had never been pregnant, that they had adopted Matthew. She couldn't breast-feed[4]; she never went through all the things a woman goes through. But she didn't want people to know. She wanted them to think she'd been pregnant. The last couple of months before they got Matthew she spent[5] in Boston so the neighbors wouldn't think something funny[6] was going on. They'd never see that she was never actually pregnant[7]."

"Rosemary told you all this?"

1. à klaxonner

2. sans ralentir

3. rendre

4. allaiter

5. les a passés
6. de bizarre
7. n'avait pas été
enceinte

"Not exactly. Bits and pieces came out. I was there so much[1], I figured out what had happened. Dr. Sturgess, he'd come over a lot[2] and talk to Mr. Gaynor and I heard things. And I knew from my friends at the hospital that your cousin ... her baby died around the same time[3] that the Gaynors had Matthew. One time—they didn't know I was there—I heard them talking about when she tried to steal the baby from the hospital, the doctor saying he couldn't have predicted[4] something like that happening. That's when I knew what they'd done. That Ms. Gaynor's baby was really your cousin's baby."

"But ..." I was trying to get my head around this. "But Marla didn't have a son. She had a girl."

"They lied to her[5]," Sarita said. "You wrap up[6] a baby, how are you going to know one way or the other[7]? I think they told her it was a girl just to make everything very different. Does that make sense?"

"*None* of this makes any sense. I mean, Marla told me she held the baby. That it was dead."

Sarita looked at me blankly[8]. "I can't explain that."

The car was still honking. Sarita shifted[9] in her seat, looked back. "That is Mr. Gaynor. That is his car. And I'm pretty sure that's the doctor next to him."

"Why the hell are they following us?"

"They must be looking for me[10]."

When had they spotted us? At the bus station?

"I've got a few questions for both of them," I said, putting on my blinker[11], easing my foot off the gas[12].

"Wait," Sarita said.

1. tellement souvent
2. venait tout le temps
3. vers le moment où
4. anticiper
5. lui ont menti
6. On enveloppe [dans des langes]
7. si c'est une fille ou un garçon
8. d'un regard vide
9. gigota
10. doivent me chercher
11. clignotant
12. relâchant l'accélérateur

"What?" I hadn't put my foot on the brake yet, but as the car slowed, Gaynor stopped honking his horn.

"Where is Marshall?"

"Your boyfriend?"

"He was going to meet Mr. Gaynor. He was going to get him to pay money. And there is Mr. Gaynor, but I don't know what has happened to Marshall."

"What are you saying?" I asked.

"I don't know. But I have a bad feeling[1]."

"Sarita, nothing's going to happen[2]. We're right out in the open[3] here. With what you've told me, I've got a few questions for both of those assholes. I want answers."

Now I put my foot on the brake, steered[4] the car over to the shoulder[5]. It was then that I realized we were on the back side of the decommissioned[6] Five Mountains amusement park. Alongside the road was about sixty feet of tall grass, then a perimeter fence. I noticed that just up from where we were, a section of fence had been cut, the chain link pried back[7].

I shifted my eyes to[8] the mirror, watched Gaynor steer his black Audi over to the shoulder and park a couple of car lengths[9] behind me. I felt like I was getting a speeding ticket[10].

The passenger door opened.

Sarita was right. It was Dr. Sturgess getting out.

"I don't get it[11]," I said to Sarita. "How would they pull it off[12]? I mean, the paperwork alone[13]. How do you—"

Sarita cut me off. "He is a doctor. And rich, and white. He could fake it all[14]. Death certificates, birth certificates, all of it. Who is going to question him?" She shook her head angrily. "It is why I took the baby to your cousin. When I found out

1. pressentiment
2. tout va bien se passer
3. visibles de partout
4. tournai
5. bande d'arrêt d'urgence
6. désaffecté
7. arrachée
8. regardai de nouveau dans
9. l'espace de deux voitures
10. amende pour excès de vitesse
11. ne comprends pas
12. auraient-ils pu réussir un coup pareil
13. rien que la paperasse
14. tout falsifier

what they'd done, I looked up[1] her address, drove by[2] her house many times, wondering if I should tell her. But I never did. Not until Matthew had no one to care for him."

The doctor was coming up to my side of the car. I saw his image looming larger by the second[3] in the driver's-door mirror[4].

He seemed to be holding one arm pressed close to his side.

I powered down[5] the window.

"Dr. Sturgess," I said, once he was even with[6] the door.

He smiled. "Mr. Harwood. I was pretty sure that was you." He leaned over slightly so he could see my passenger. "Hello, Sarita. How are you doing?"

Sarita said nothing.

"I wondered if we could have a talk[7]," Sturgess asked.

"That's Mr. Gaynor back there, isn't it?" I said.

"It is."

"We all going to have a chat together?"

"That would be ideal," the doctor said.

"Where would you like to do that?"

"If you two would like to get out, I think we could have it right here[8]."

I hadn't yet killed the engine[9], and was reaching for[10] the key when my cell rang.

"One sec[11]," I said to Sturgess, holding up a finger[12].

"We really need to talk *now*," he said.

I waved that finger again, went into my pocket for the phone with my other hand. Pulled it out.

Saw who it was.

"Hello?" I said.

Aunt Agnes screamed, "*Run!*"

---

1. ai cherché
2. suis passée devant
3. grossir très vite
4. rétroviseur
5. fis descendre
6. à hauteur de
7. discuter
8. ici même
9. éteint le moteur
10. tendais le bras vers
11. seconde
12. un doigt levé

SIXTY-THREE

BARRY Duckworth made a call back to Boston. The hotel patched him through[1] for a second time to manager Sandra Bottsford.

"You were telling me," he said, "that Mr. Gaynor's wife, Rosemary, spent a couple of months with him at your hotel. When was this?"

The woman thought a moment. "Well, it would have been[2] a year ago. I can check the records, but I'm pretty sure she came about thirteen months ago, and they were here for a three-month stay[3] together."

"Okay. I don't imagine this is something you could have missed[4], but do you remember whether Ms. Gaynor was pregnant?"

Bottsford laughed. "Yes, I think I'd have remembered something like that, and no, she was not pregnant." A pause. "There was something on the news[5] about that. That Ms. Gaynor leaves a child? I hadn't given it much thought until you mentioned it now. I guess they must have adopted. She wasn't pregnant when she was here, and she wasn't looking after an infant[6]."

"Thanks again," Duckworth said. He ended the call, then sat and stared at his computer monitor.

It just had never come up[7].

1. lui passa

2. devait être

3. séjour de trois mois

4. qui aurait pu vous échapper

5. aux infos

6. tout-petit

7. jamais été évoqué

464

Duckworth had never asked Bill Gaynor whether Matthew was adopted. There was no reason to, really. And suppose the baby *was* adopted? What difference would it have made, one way or another?

And yet now he had what he would call a "confluence of events[1]."

Marla Pickens's baby died around the same time Rosemary Gaynor had hers. And now Duckworth knew that the Gaynor woman had not given birth to a child.

Marla ends up with the Gaynors' baby.

Somehow[2].

She'd said it was her baby, although she'd backed away from that[3] pretty quickly. Marla had never seriously argued that she'd given birth to Matthew. Matthew was, in effect[4], a substitute.

And besides, hadn't Marla lost a girl?

Still[5] …

He pushed himself back from his desk and went looking for Marla. She was being booked[6], and Natalie Bondurant was waiting for her to be finished[7].

"I need to talk to Ms. Pickens," Duckworth said to the officer dealing with Marla. "Right now."

"What's going on?" Natalie asked. "You're not talking to her without me there."

"That's fine," Duckworth said. "Let's go in here."

He led them into an interrogation room, waved his arm at two empty chairs on one side of the table. "Please," he said.

The two women sat down.

"You don't have enough to charge[8] my client," Natalie said, "and even if you did, you couldn't have picked a worse time[9]. Ms. Pickens is in a very delicate state of mind, and if you do insist on

---

1. des faits convergents

2. D'une manière ou d'une autre

3. fait marche arrière

4. en fait

5. Tout de même

6. On procédait à son arrestation au commissariat

7. la fin de la procédure

8. poursuivre

9. tomber à un pire moment

1. sous
surveillance
constante
keeping her here, you'd better have her on
constant suicide watch[1], because only last
night—"

Duckworth held up a hand. "I know. I wanted to
ask Ms. Pickens about something that has nothing
to do with her charges. Nothing to do with Rosemary Gaynor."

"Like what?" Natalie said as Duckworth lowered
2. s'asseyait
himself[2] into the chair across from them.

"Marla—is it okay if I call you Marla?"

3. faiblement
The woman nodded weakly[3].

"I know this is hard, but I want to ask you about
your child. The baby."

Natalie said, "Really, this is too upsetting[4] to get
4. pénible
5. pour qu'on en
parle
into[5]."

"Please," Duckworth said gently. "Marla, when
you were pregnant, did you ever give any thought
6. avez-vous
jamais envisagé
de faire adopter
l'enfant
to putting the child up for adoption[6]?"

She blinked her eyes several times. "Adoption?"

"That's right."

Marla shook her head slowly from side to side.
"Never, not for a second. I wanted to have a baby.
I wanted it more than anything in the world."

7. la question
ne s'est jamais
posée
"So it never came up[7]?"

Marla rolled her eyes slowly. "It came up *all the
time*. My mother talked about it. She wanted me
to do that. Well, at first she wanted me to have an
8. que j'avorte
abortion[8]. But I wouldn't do that, and then she
talked about adoption, but I didn't want to do that,
either."

Duckworth lightly strummed his[9] fingers on the
9. tapota des
10. table
tabletop[10]. "You didn't have the baby in the hospital. Your mother's hospital."

"No," she said. "We went to the cabin."

"Isn't that kind of strange? I mean, your mother's in charge of the hospital, and she doesn't want you to have the baby there?"

"There was a thing going around[1]. *C. diff* or something."

"But still. It seems odd to go so far away to have the child."

"It was okay," Marla said, "because Dr. Sturgess was there. Except ..." She looked down at the table. "Except it wasn't okay. The cord[2] got wrapped around[3] the baby's neck, and they couldn't save it."

"It must have been ... horrific," he said.

Marla nodded slowly. "Yeah. Although I was kind of out of it[4] when the baby was actually born[5]. Dr. Sturgess gave me stuff to kill the pain[6]."

"Tell me about that."

Marla shrugged. "That's kind of all there is to say. I was in pain. It wasn't that bad[7], but Dr. Sturgess and my mom said it would get a lot worse[8], so they gave me something. And I never felt it when the baby came out."

"But you saw her after."

Marla nodded. "I did. I don't ... I don't actually remember it ... but I did see her. I touched her fingers and kissed her head."

"But if you don't remember it, how do you know what happened?"

"My mom helped me to remember. Because it was so foggy[9] for me. But she's told me what happened over and over again, so it's like I do remember it."

"Tell me a little more about that."

"Well, it's kind of like ... when I was a baby myself, about one and a half years old, and we were visiting some friends of my parents, and they had a big dog that ran up to me and

---

1. épidémie de quelque chose

2. cordon [ombilical]

3. s'est enroulé

4. un peu dans les vapes

5. vraiment né

6. contre la douleur

7. trop dur

8. que ça allait sérieusement empirer

9. flou

467

1. m'avait fait
tomber

2. s'apprêtait à
me mordre

3. a chassé le
chien

knocked me down[1] and was about to bite me[2], right in the face, when the owner kicked the dog away[3]. I guess I was pretty scared, and cried a lot, but I don't really remember it happening. But my mom and dad have told that story over the years, and I can see it all like a movie, you know? I see myself getting knocked down, the dog jumping on me. I can picture exactly what the dog looks like, even though I really don't know. It's a bit like that. Do you know what I mean?"

Duckworth smiled. "I think maybe I do."

SIXTY-FOUR

David

I didn't have much time to process[1] what Aunt Agnes had to say. Not that she'd said much. But the implications were immense.

By telling me to run, she must have had some idea where I was, and of my situation.

Agnes seemed to know I'd just met up with[2] Dr. Jack Sturgess.

And she wanted me to get away from him as quickly as I could.

A millisecond after Agnes screamed at me, I turned my head left[3] to look at Dr. Sturgess. That arm he'd been keeping close to his side was moving away[4] from his body. I thought I saw something small and cylindrical in his hand. Like a pencil with a metallic point.

No. More like a syringe.

"Shit!" I said, then dropped the phone, threw the column shift[5] into drive[6], and pressed my foot right to the floor[7]. Mom's old Taurus was no Ferrari, but it kicked ahead[8] fast enough to push Sarita back in her seat, spray gravel[9] all over the front

1. intégrer

2. que je venais de voir

3. à gauche
4. s'éloignait

5. poussai le levier de vitesses
6. en position marche
7. écrasai la pédale à fond
8. se propulsa
9. faire gicler des gravillons

469

1. faire sauter Dr Sturgess en arrière

2. dérapa

3. fit une embardée

4. couina

5. pneu

6. touchait le trottoir

7. n'allions pas faire une queue de poisson à un semi-remorque

8. qui tripotait

9. pour en sortir quelque chose

10. Baissez-vous

11. traversai

12. prendre à gauche

13. était peut-être passée sur deux roues

14. s'appuya au tableau de bord

15. croisement

16. à 400 m

17. roulait plus vite que cette guimbarde

of Gaynor's Audi, and make Dr. Sturgess leap backward[1] to keep his feet from getting run over.

"Stop!" he shouted. "Stop!"

The Taurus fishtailed[2] on the gravel, then lurched[3] and squealed[4] as the left back tire[5] connected with pavement[6].

"Who was that?" Sarita cried. "Who called you?"

I couldn't think about answering her question. I glanced back for half a second to make sure we weren't pulling into the path of a tractor-trailer[7], and caught a glimpse of Sturgess fiddling with[8] his jacket, possibly reaching into it[9].

"Get down[10]," I said to Sarita.

"What?"

"Get down!"

I checked my mirror again, worried that the doctor might be carrying more than a syringe. But he wasn't standing there with a gun in his hand. He was running back to Bill Gaynor's Audi.

There was an intersection just ahead. I cut across the lane[11] to make a left[12], the tires complaining loudly. The car felt as though it had gone up on two wheels[13] for half a second. Sarita threw up her hands, braced herself against the dash[14] as we went around the corner.

"What happened?" she asked. "What did you see?"

"He had some kind of needle," I said. "He was holding a syringe. Another second and I think he would have jabbed it into my neck."

There was another cross street[15] only a quarter mile[16] ahead. If I took that, and then the street after that, and even the one after that, I thought I had a good chance of losing them. The Audi could outrun this old clunker[17], no doubt about it. But if they didn't know which way we'd gone, it wasn't going to matter how fast that marvelous piece of German engineering[1] could go.

I reached down beside me, feeling for[2] my cell.

"Where's my phone?" I shouted.

Sarita looked down between the seats. "I see it!"

"Get it!" I said, keeping up my speed[3], glancing in the mirror, not seeing any sign of them yet.

The next cross street was too far away. I feared the Audi would round the bend[4], that Gaynor and Sturgess would catch a glimpse of us before we could make the next turn.

"Hang on," I said.

I slammed on the brakes[5], leaving two long strips of rubber[6] on the road. I could smell it, and smoke billowed out[7] from under the wheel wells[8]. I cut the car hard right[9] and sped into the parking lot of a Wendy's[10]. I drove straight to the back of the property, behind the restaurant, making sure the car was not visible from the street. This fast-food place, and a lot of the other businesses along this stretch[11], had sprung up[12] to serve spillover customers[13] from Five Mountains, and were probably all feeling the pain, now that the park was toast[14].

Not that that was a major concern[15] at the moment. I was just glad for a place to hide.

"What are you doing?" Sarita asked. "Are you *hungry?*"

I sat there for maybe five minutes, then slowly drove down the side of the building and approached the road. I nosed up to the edge[16], looked both ways[17].

No sign of the Audi.

I headed back[18] in the direction we'd come from.

"The phone," I said.

1. petite merveille de l'industrie allemande

2. cherchant de la main

3. sans ralentir

4. allait arriver dans le virage

5. pilai

6. bandes de caoutchouc

7. montait en volute

8. passages de roue

9. braquai à droite

10. [chaîne de fast-foods]

11. le long de cette route

12. poussé comme des champignons

13. l'excédent de clients

14. foutu

15. mon inquiétude principale

16. approchai du bord

17. des deux côtés

18. repartis

1. se remit à fouiller
2. boîte de vitesses

3. me tendit
4. décrocha

5. Ton putain de docteur

6. par téléphone

7. savoir

8. À moins qu'

9. que tu le veuilles ou non

10. faire du stop

Sarita went back to digging[1] between the seat and the transmission hump[2]. "I can't quite ... I got it!"

"Okay," I said. "Go back to the last call and connect me to that number."

She pressed the screen a couple of times, then handed me[3] the phone. "It should be ringing."

Agnes picked up[4] immediately. "David?"

"What the hell's going on, Agnes?" I shouted. "That fucking doctor of yours[5] was ready to jab some needle into me!"

"Did you get away? Are you okay? Where are you?"

"I'm heading back into town. How did you *know*? How did you know what was going to happen?"

"I can't explain over the phone[6]. I ... I can't. I'll meet you at your parents' place. I'll explain. I'll explain it all. Do you have Sarita with you?"

"Jesus, how did you know *that*?"

Were we on satellite surveillance? How could Agnes be aware of[7] everything and everywhere we—

Unless[8] she'd been talking to Sturgess. Or Gaynor.

"David, listen to me," Agnes said. "You have to protect Sarita. I can't explain why now, but—"

"You don't have to," I said. "I think I get it. I'll see you at the house, Agnes. I have to get off the phone. I'm calling Duckworth, whether you like it or not[9]."

"I can't stop what you do." I could hear resignation in her voice.

I ended the call.

"Let me out," Sarita said. "I've told you everything. I have to get away. You can let me out anyplace. I can hitchhike[10]."

I shook my head. "I'm sorry, Sarita. I really am. There's no running away[1] from this."

I glanced down at the phone long enough to hit 911[2].

"I need to talk to Detective Duckworth," I said to the operator. "I need to talk to him right fucking now."

1. Impossible d'échapper

2. [numéro de téléphone de la police]

SIXTY-FIVE

SOMETHING had been nagging at[1] Wanda Therrieult.

The Promise Falls medical examiner[2] had been reviewing[3] the pictures she'd taken during her examination of Rosemary Gaynor. Photos of her entire body, with several close-ups[4] of the marks on her neck and the gash[5] across her abdomen. She had transferred them to the computer and was looking at them shot by shot[6] as she sat at her desk, a cup of specialty[7] coffee—a flavor she could not even pronounce—resting next to the keypad.

She kept coming back to the pictures of the bruising[8] on the woman's neck. The imprint[9] of the thumb on one side, four fingers on the other.

The knife wound[10] that went from one hip to the other. The slight downward curvature toward the center. What Barry Duckworth had said looked like a smile.

She thought back[11] to her very personal demonstration on the detective of how she believed Rosemary Gaynor had been attacked. She recalled how she'd positioned herself behind him, put one hand on his neck, wrapped her other arm around the front of him[12] to illustrate how the knife went in.

Not that easy to reach around[13] Barry.

---

1. préoccupait

2. médecin légiste

3. avait passé en revue

4. gros plans

5. entaille

6. regardait les clichés un par un

7. aromatisé

8. hématome

9. empreinte

10. blessure au couteau

11. repensa

12. enlacé son ventre de son autre bras

13. mettre les bras autour de

They'd known each other a long time—long enough that Wanda could do something like this without it having to mean anything[1]. She loved Barry as a friend and colleague. Sometimes, working where she did, it was just nice to touch a live[2] body once in a while.

The dead bodies she'd always thought of as[3] customers. And she treated them with the utmost[4] respect, because they got to visit her shop only once.

"The customer is always right," she liked to say, because the dead did not lie. The dead, Wanda believed, desperately wanted to speak to her, and what they wanted to tell her was the truth.

Over the years, she'd accepted invitations from a number[5] of groups—Probus[6], Rotary, the local chamber of commerce—to talk about her job.

"I like to think that everyone who ends up[7] on that table is an individual. That each and every one is special. You don't want them all to become a blur[8], if you know what I mean. Even after all these years, I remember every one of them."

Sometimes she'd see something on one victim that brought to mind something she'd seen on another. Ten years back, police were looking for someone who was mugging johns[9] after they'd visited prostitutes in the south end of town. Hitting them in the head with a brick, lifting their wallets[10]. Often he came up with nothing[11], evidently not learning that if you're going to rob someone who's visiting a hooker[12], if you do it prerendez-vous[13], your target[14]'s likely to have a little more money on him.

A couple of these poor bastards ended up dead.

Wanda Therrieult noticed that even though the murders were several weeks apart, the microscopic

1. sans que ça veuille rien dire

2. vivant

3. les considérait toujours comme

4. le plus grand

5. un certain nombre

6. [club de retraités]

7. se retrouve

8. qu'ils se confondent dans votre tête

9. agressait des types

10. leur piquait leur portefeuille

11. n'en retirait rien

12. prostituée

13. avant la passe

14. victime

1. éclats
2. crânes
3. a fait signe de s'arrêter à
4. qui n'avait pas mis son clignotant
5. porte-bon-heur
6. lui rappelait quelque chose
7. très vaguement
8. ça ne lui revenait pas directement
9. revoir un coup de matraque
10. une blessure par balle
11. comme sur une photo
12. dont elle avait entendu parler
13. congé de deux mois
14. important
15. prenait des nouvelles
16. se tenait au courant
17. pour plaisanter
18. aux morts qu'aux mourants
19. affaires
20. écrasée

chips[1] of stone in their skulls[2] were similar. The killer was using the same brick.

One night, police patrolling the south end pulled over[3] a driver for failing to signal[4]. And there, on the front seat, was the brick.

"It was my lucky[5] brick," the man told the judge before being sentenced to fifteen years.

There was something about Rosemary Gaynor's death that was making a bell go off[6], ever so faintly[7], in the back of her head.

Given Wanda's photographic memory for these things, she wondered why it wasn't coming up right away[8]. She could usually close her eyes and call up bludgeonings[9] and gunshot wounds[10] as though they were snapshots[11] from a family album.

What had happened to Rosemary Gaynor reminded her not of something she had seen, but of something she had heard about[12].

Something three or four years ago.

Another murder.

Three years ago, right around this time, she'd taken a two-month leave of absence[13]. Her sister Gilda, in Duluth, had been dying, and Wanda had gone up there to look after her in those final weeks. It had been a sad time, but also profoundly meaningful[14]. It became one of the most important periods in her life. Wanda still made calls back to Promise Falls, checking in[15], catching up[16] on what was going on. Gilda had jokingly[17] accused her at one point of being more interested in the fully dead than the aspiring[18].

Wanda opened another program. Photo files from other cases[19], arranged by date. She went back to the beginning of her leave, opening one file after another.

A five-year-old girl run over[20] by a car.

A forty-eight-year-old roofer[1] who tripped off the top[2] of a church he was reshingling[3].

A nineteen-year-old Thackeray student from Burlington, Vermont, who'd brought his father's Porsche 911 to school for a week, lost control of it, and crashed it into a hundred-year-old oak[4] at eighty miles per hour[5].

A twenty-two-year-old woman who—

Hang on …

Wanda clicked on the file.

Opened up the photos.

Took a sip[6] of her coffee as she studied the images.

"Oh, boy[7]," she said.

1. couvreur

2. tombé du toit

3. dont il refaisait le bardeau

4. chêne centenaire

5. 130 km/h

6. gorgée

7. nom d'un chien

SIXTY-SIX

ONCE Agnes Pickens was finished talking to her nephew, she went up the stairs to her second-floor home office and closed the door. She sat down at her desk, fired up[1] her computer, opened Word, and selected the letter format.

She wanted the margins just right[2]. What she had to write was short, so she didn't want the letter to start too high on the page, which would leave acres of white space at the bottom[3]. It would look unbalanced[4].

So she wrote what she had to say, then selected "print preview[5]" to make sure it looked presentable. It didn't. She had pushed the message too far down on the page. She deleted[6] a few indents[7] above the text, then looked at the preview again, and was happy with how it looked.

She hit "print."

The letter came out, and she read it one more time, looking for typos[8]. That would be so embarrassing, to have a typographical error or a spelling mistake in something of this nature.

Agnes had dated it at the top, then written below:

---

1. démarra

2. parfaites

3. bien trop de blanc en bas de page

4. déséquilibré

5. afficher l'aperçu

6. effaça

7. alinéas

8. fautes de frappe

I hereby resign my position as[1] administrator and general manager of the Promise Falls General Hospital, effective immediately.

She had considered[2], briefly, expanding on it[3]. Perhaps a word about regret. Maybe a line or two about her lifelong commitment to[4] the Promise Falls community and public health. An apology about failing to live up to the high standards[5] she had set for herself. But in the end, a simple, unembellished resignation[6] seemed the way to go[7].

She signed the letter, folded it, and slipped it into an envelope on which she wrote, *To the Promise Falls General Hospital Board.*

She left it on the keyboard[8], then went in search of her husband, Gill. Agnes had thought he was upstairs, perhaps in their bedroom, but she did not find him there. She located him[9] in the basement[10], standing next to the pool table[11], holding a cue[12] in hand vertically, the end touching the floor. The balls were racked[13], but Gill just stood there, staring vacantly[14] across the table.

"Gill," she said.

He turned. "Yes, Agnes."

"I have to go out."

"Have you heard from Natalie?"

"Not since she arrived at the station[15]." She hesitated. "But everything's going to be okay."

Gill set the pool cue on the table. "But if you haven't heard from Natalie—"

"They're going to drop the charges[16] against Marla. Before the day is over, I'd guess."

"How can you know that?"

"I'm just … fairly confident[17]."

Gill said haltingly[18], "About … Carol. I—"

---

1. Par la présente, je démissionne de ma fonction d'

2. envisagé

3. de développer un peu

4. son dévouement de toujours envers

5. ne s'être pas montrée à la hauteur des grandes exigences

6. démission sans fioritures

7. la meilleure solution

8. clavier

9. le trouva

10. au sous-sol

11. billard

12. queue de billard

13. rangées

14. dans le vide

15. commissariat

16. abandonner les poursuites

17. quasi sûre

18. d'un ton hésitant

"I don't care," Agnes said.

"But—"

She raised a hand. "I don't care. Your betrayal[1] is ... nothing, in the overall scheme of things[2]."

"I don't understand," Gill said.

Agnes shook her head ever so slightly[3]. "Be strong for Marla. She's going to need you. Whatever reservations I may have had about you[4], there haven't been any where Marla is concerned. I know you love her very much. The next little while is going to be very difficult for her, but I'm hoping there will be some consolation. That she'll get what she wanted. What was taken from her[5]."

"What are you talking about?"

Agnes turned and walked away.

1. trahison
2. par rapport au reste
3. très légèrement
4. Quelles qu'aient été mes réserves à ton sujet
5. Ce qu'on lui a pris

SIXTY-SEVEN

David

WHO is this?" the 911 operator said.

"David Harwood. Detective Duckworth knows who I am."

"I'm transferring you to a nonemergency[1] line."

"This *is* an—"

But then she was gone. Seconds later a man answered. "Hello?"

"Detective Duckworth?"

"Nope[2]. This is Angus Carlson. You wanna leave a message?"

"Get him[3]. Put him on the phone. Tell him it's David Harwood."

"I'm not sure where he is right now. I just got in[4]. Hang on." Several seconds went by, then: "He's busy right now. What's this about?"

"It's about Marla Pickens. And Rosemary Gaynor. I know what happened."

"Yeah, well, I'm guessing[5] Detective Duckworth does, too," Carlson said. "He's with the Pickens woman right now in interrogation."

"She's been arrested?"

"Yup."

"For the Gaynor thing?"

"No, jaywalking[1]."

"She didn't do it. Marla's innocent."

"So, wait a second," Carlson said. "Are you saying we've arrested the wrong person? I don't think I've ever heard of that happening before."

"Have you ever heard of a cop being a total asshole[2]?" I asked. "That's happening right now."

"Oh, sorry, you're breaking up[3]," he said, as clearly as if he were in the car with me. "Try again later."

Carlson ended the call.

"Dickhead[4]," I said, handing the phone back to Sarita.

"What happened?"

I shook my head, too angry to repeat it. "They've arrested Marla," I said. "She's being questioned now." I paused to let it sink in[5]. "She'll go to jail, Sarita. She'll go to jail if you don't tell the police what you know, and what you did."

"What if they think I did it?" she asked. "I had Ms. Gaynor's blood on me."

"No, they're not going to be looking at you[6]. They're going to be looking at Dr. Sturgess and Mr. Gaynor. Sarita, in five more seconds, Sturgess would have killed me. He was going to stick me with that fucking needle. And then he would have done you[7]. The safest thing for you to do is tell the cops everything you know."

She bit her lower lip, stared out her window again. "Okay," she said, not looking at me. "I will do it. I will help. I won't try to run away."

"Thank you."

"I think ... I think running and hiding would be even harder." She turned, and I saw that she had been crying. "At least there is good news for

---

1. pour traversée hors passage piéton

2. parfait connard

3. je ne vous entends plus

4. Petit trou du cul

5. lui laisser le temps d'intégrer

6. ce n'est pas vous qu'ils vont soupçonner

7. se serait chargé de vous

Marla, yes? She must at least feel good[1] to know her baby is alive."

"She doesn't know," I said. "Not yet."

"What?"

"You didn't actually tell her[2], did you? When you handed Matthew to her?"

Sarita had to think[3]. "I … I guess I didn't. I guess I thought she would just *know*. I mean, all she would have to do is look into the face of that baby and she'd have to know[4] it was hers."

That made me smile. "Marla's not good with faces," I said.

I kept glancing[5] in the rearview mirror all the way home, and never saw the Audi. As soon as I got[6] into the house, I'd try Duckworth again. I'd tell him why Marla was innocent. I'd tell him about Sturgess and Gaynor. What I didn't know, I'd get[7] Sarita to tell him.

There was a lot of it I still did not understand.

If the doctor had somehow tricked Marla into thinking[8] her child was dead so that he could arrange for the Gaynors to have him, how had he been able to trick[9] Agnes?

She'd been right there[10].

Unless she wasn't.

No, Agnes had gone to the cabin. There was no way she wouldn't be totally involved in everything that was going on. Aunt Agnes wasn't someone who was easily fooled[11].

I was hoping to get some answers very soon, provided[12] Agnes showed up[13] at the house as promised.

When I pulled into the driveway, I saw Dad coming out of the side door of the garage, a beer in hand. That wasn't like him[14].

1. être heureuse
2. ne le lui avez pas dit
3. dut y réfléchir
4. saurait forcément
5. jetai fréquemment un coup d'œil
6. j'arriverais
7. demanderais à
8. trouvé le moyen de faire croire à Marla que
9. duper
10. était sur place
11. que l'on menait facilement en bateau
12. à condition qu'
13. se présente
14. ne lui ressemblait pas

1. intrigué

2. en lui tendant
la main

3. je ne sais où
4. s'allonger
5. lui fait mal
6. s'arrêta dans
un crissement
de freins
7. ne prit même
pas la peine
8. tintement
9. contact

10. C'est
forcément
comme ça que

He approached the car as Sarita and I were getting out. He gave Sarita a puzzled[1] look.

"Sarita," I said, "this is my father, Don Harwood."

"Hello," she said, extending a hand[2].

"Uh, yeah," Dad said, accepting it, glancing back
and forth between us. Maybe he was wondering if
I had a new girlfriend. "Nice to meet you. So, how
do you two know each other?"

"Long story, Dad," I said. "Where's Mom?"

"In the house someplace[3]. She might have gone
upstairs to lie down[4]. Her leg's been bugging
her[5]." He looked up the street, his attention caught
by another approaching car. "Hello, what's this?"

It was Agnes. The car screeched to a halt[6]. She
got out so hurriedly she didn't even bother[7] to
close the door. I could hear the chiming[8] of a key
left in the ignition[9]. She came straight to me.

"You're okay," she said.

"Yeah," I said. "You knew."

Her face paled.

"You knew something was going to happen.
That Dr. Sturgess was going to try something. He
had a syringe, Agnes. He was getting ready to jab
the thing—"

She held up a hand. "Please. I know." She set
her eyes on Sarita. "You're the nanny."

Sarita nodded.

"You took the baby to Marla's house. That has to
be how[10] Matthew got there."

Sarita nodded again.

"Because you knew," Agnes said.

A third nod from Sarita.

"Do you know who did it?" my aunt asked her.

"Excuse me?"

"Do you know who killed that woman? It wasn't Marla. It can't have been Marla. Tell me it wasn't her."

I stepped in[1]. "The blood on Marla's door came from Sarita."

1. intervins

"But I did not kill Ms. Gaynor," Sarita said. "I loved Ms. Gaynor. I found her, but I would never hurt her."

"Who, then?" Agnes asked.

Sarita shook her head slowly. "I have ideas, but I don't know."

Agnes looked back at me. "There are things I need to explain."

"No shit[2]," I said.

2. sans déc'

"I never meant[3] … I never could have imagined it would go this far[4]," my aunt said. "I need to tell you … what I did." She took in the three of us[5], as if doing a count[6], and said, "Where's your mother? Where's my sister?"

3. n'ai jamais voulu

4. que ça irait aussi loin

5. nous considéra tous les trois

6. comme si elle nous comptait

"In the house," Dad said. "You shouldn't leave your keys in the car, Agnes."

She was already walking toward the front door. "There's no sense telling this any more times than I have to. Let's find her."

The second we were[7] in the house, Dad shouted, "Arlene!"

7. À la seconde où nous entrâmes

"Upstairs," she said.

"Get on down here[8]! Your sister's here!"

8. Descends voir

"I'll be a minute. I've just got some ice on my leg."

Agnes said, "What happened?"

"Her leg's all swole up[9] since she took a fall[10] yesterday," Dad said.

9. gonflée

10. est tombée

Agnes yelled, "Stay there! I'm coming up."

A convoy of us ascended the stairs. Agnes first, then Dad. I stepped aside to let Sarita go ahead of me[1], and then I went up last.

We found Mom propped up[2] on her bed, on top of the covers, a couple of pillows tucked[3] behind her, one pant leg[4] pulled up above her knee, a thin towel on her leg immediately under[5] the ice pack. There was a half-empty glass of water and an open container[6] of Advil on the bedside table, and a Lisa Gardner[7] paperback[8], spine cracked[9], pages-down on the bedspread.

As one person after another filed in[10], her eyes went wide[11].

"What is all this?" she said. Her face flushed red with embarrassment[12], particularly at the sight of Sarita, a total stranger.

I introduced her, and added, "This woman took the baby to Marla's house."

"What?" Mom said. "So Marla really was telling the truth? Oh, thank God." She looked at her sister apologetically[13]. "Not that I ever doubted her."

Agnes said, "It's okay. It's taken a long time for me to figure out what happened, too. I didn't want to believe Marla had killed that woman and taken her baby, but I knew, the moment I heard where the baby had come from, that it wasn't just some random thing that had happened[14]."

"I don't understand," Mom said.

Sarita said, "Would you like me to look at your leg?"

"What?"

"You should prop it up some[15], get a pillow under it."

"Sarita works at Davidson Place," I said. "She helps people."

---

1. passer devant moi
2. semi-assise
3. calés
4. jambe de pantalon
5. juste sous
6. boîte
7. [auteur de romans policiers]
8. en livre de poche
9. au dos craquelé
10. entrait à la queue leu leu
11. s'écarquillèrent
12. s'empourpra de gêne
13. d'un air d'excuse
14. n'était pas arrivé par hasard
15. la soulever un peu

While Sarita tended to her[1], Mom pressing her back to the headboard[2] as though reluctant to accept help from this stranger[3], she said again, "I don't understand what you're saying, Agnes. What do you mean, it wasn't random?"

Agnes appeared to be struggling[4], so I offered some help. "Because that baby really is Marla's. Matthew is Marla's son."

Mom's jaw dropped an inch[5]. Agnes looked at me, then back at her sister. "He's right." Then, to me: "You found out more[6] than I thought you would. Faster, too."

"But you never wanted me to. If you'd chased me off[7], like Dr. Sturgess tried to do, I'd have wondered why you didn't want my help. That about right?[8]"

Agnes closed her eyes for half a second, as though in pain[9], and nodded. "I kept hoping the police wouldn't really find enough to charge her, but that ... has changed."

"I heard."

"I still don't ..." Mom's voice trailed off[10]. "This isn't making any sense[11]. Don, is this making any sense to you? Do you know about this?"

"Do you want me to get your keys out of the car?" Dad asked Agnes.

Sarita moved out of the way when Agnes indicated[12] she wanted to sit on the edge of the bed.

"I could never be like you," Agnes said to Mom.

"Be like me how?"

"More ... accepting[13]."

"Agnes, please tell me what's going on."

"I've done a horrible, horrible thing," my aunt said. "You have no idea[14]."

Mom slid a hand forward to take hold of[15] her sister's. "Whatever it is, you can tell me."

1. s'occupait d'elle

2. appuyant son dos contre le bois de lit

3. se faisant aider à contrecœur par cette inconnue

4. chercher ses mots

5. en resta bouche bée

6. en a appris plus long

7. m'avais rejeté

8. Je me trompe ?

9. comme si elle souffrait

10. n'acheva pas sa phrase

11. n'a aucun sens

12. fit signe

13. conciliante

14. ne peux pas imaginer

15. saisir

"I can tell you maybe. The question is whether I can tell Marla. I don't know that I can[1]."

Sarita, Dad, and I stood around the bed, barely breathing[2], wondering what Agnes was about to confess. I wanted to call the police station again, try to get Duckworth, but I couldn't tear myself away[3] from this.

She said to Mom, "You've always been able to roll with things[4] better than I could. I have a need to … control things."

Credit to all of us[5]—Sarita excepted, who did not know Agnes the way we did—for not snickering[6].

"It's what's made you successful," Mom told her. "You have to control things. You have a lot of responsibility. You've got the lives of hundreds, even thousands of people in your hands."

"I failed her[7]," she said.

"Failed … Marla?" Mom asked.

"She was determined to have the baby. When that boy got her pregnant, she was determined to have it. I couldn't talk her out of it[8]. I tried to get her to end the pregnancy. Told her this boy wasn't suitable husband material[9], even if he was willing to step up and do the right thing[10]. She had no way to support herself[11] other than this Internet thing she was doing."

Agnes took a moment to breathe, then continued.

"But Marla wouldn't listen. I tried to get her to see reason. She couldn't handle[12] being a mother. She's always been too emotionally immature, too … flighty[13], too needy[14], too distracted to look after a baby. I knew, I just knew that if she had this child, it would fall to me to[15] look after both of them. And I'd had this feeling[16] that she was almost back on two feet again[17], that she was going to move forward with her life, get her act

1. ne m'en sens pas capable
2. osant à peine respirer
3. m'arracher
4. t'adapter
5. Un bon point pour nous tous
6. nous n'avons pas ricané
7. l'ai trahie
8. l'en faire démordre
9. n'était pas bon à marier
10. prêt à agir selon son devoir
11. s'assumer financièrement
12. ne serait pas capable
13. instable
14. en manque d'affection
15. ce serait à moi de
16. avais commencé à croire
17. reprenait le contrôle

together[1]. A child ... it would be an enormous set-back[2] for her."

She dabbed a tear[3] from the corner of her eye. "Do you remember my friend Vera?"

"Vera?"

"She had a tremendous future[4] ahead of her, and then she met this married man, and she got pregnant, and—"

"I remember," Mom said.

"I wasn't going to let that happen to Marla. I raised the idea of adoption. That if she wanted to have the baby, then have it, but let a proper family, with a mother and a father and the financial means[5], raise the child. But Marla would have none of it[6]. She said if her child were put up for adoption, she'd track it down[7], try to get it back[8]."

Gently, Mom said, "Agnes, it was her decision to make[9]."

Agnes focused on the nap of the bedspread[10], ran a palm across it[11]. Softly, she said, "I was coming to accept that[12]. And then an opportunity presented itself. Jack ... Dr. Sturgess told me about a friend of his, Bill Gaynor, who was also a patient.

Bill's wife, Rosemary, too. They'd been trying for a long time to have a baby, but it wasn't possible. And when Rosemary had a hysterectomy, that was the end of it. They'd been trying to adopt, found the process[13] long and difficult and frustrating. Jack said he had an idea, something that would solve[14] not just their problem, and mine and Marla's, but his, too."

"His?" I asked.

"He owed[15] money. A lot of money. He's addicted[16]. He gambles[17]. It's why[18] his wife left him. He worked out a deal[19] months in advance[20] with Bill Gaynor. A hundred thousand dollars and he could

---

1. se prendre en main

2. handicap

3. essuya une larme

4. avenir formidable

5. moyens

6. ne voulait pas en entendre parler

7. le retrouverait

8. le reprendre

9. à elle de prendre cette décision

10. fixa le tissu moelleux du couvre-lit

11. le caressa

12. commençais à l'accepter

13. procédure

14. résoudrait

15. Jack devait

16. C'est un drogué

17. Aux jeux d'argent

18. pour ça que

19. a conclu un accord

20. des mois à l'avance

1. en bonne et
due forme

2. acte de
naissance

3. fait en douce

4. à quel point

5. réglo

6. fait croire à
ma fille

7. que ça s'est
limité à ça

get them a baby. Marla's baby. With a proper[1] birth certificate[2] and everything. Gaynor knew the deal was underhanded[3], but he didn't tell his wife just *how*[4] underhanded. Jack made it all seem legit[5], but to protect the mother's anonymity, he told Rosemary everyone had to believe the child really was hers; that was how it had to be. So for a few months, before … before it was done, she lived in Boston. So no one in Promise Falls would question why she'd never looked pregnant."

"Where is this going, Agnes?" Mom asked. "What did you do?"

Agnes needed several seconds to find the words. "I let my daughter believe[6] her child had died," she said.

Mom pulled her hand away from Agnes's. "My God."

Agnes looked down. "I wish I could say that was the worst of it[7]."

SIXTY-EIGHT

DUCKWORTH went back to his desk, sat down, thought.

There was something not right[1] about any of this[2]. Marla gives birth to a child but has no real memory of the event. This happens at the exact same time Rosemary Gaynor gives birth to a bundle of joy[3].

Except[4] Rosemary Gaynor didn't give birth.

He looked through his notes, found a cell phone number for Bill Gaynor. He picked up the receiver on his landline and dialed.

The phone rang several times, then: "Yes?"

It was just one word, but the man sounded agitated. There was car noise in the background.

"It's Detective Duckworth, Mr. Gaynor. Have I caught you at a bad time[5]?"

"No, no, it's … it's okay. What is it?"

"A couple of things. This may sound like an odd question, but I'm just going over some timeline issues[6], and a few other things."

"Okay," he said tentatively[7].

"About Ms. Gaynor—I was wondering, did she have the baby[8] in Promise Falls?"

A pause. "No, no, she did not. We were out of town[9] at the time."

1. qui ne collait pas
2. dans tout ça
3. bout de chou
4. Sauf que
5. Je vous dérange
6. questions de chronologie
7. d'un ton hésitant
8. est-ce qu'elle a accouché
9. en déplacement

491

"I see. Where was that? Was it Boston? Was the baby born at a hospital in Boston?"

"Well, actually, let me just correct myself about that[1]. Rosemary had Matthew almost the moment we returned. But I'd been working out of the home office in Boston, and I didn't want to leave Rosemary home alone at such a critical time in her pregnancy[2], so we had made arrangements with a hospital in Boston."

"Which hospital was that?"

"Uh, let me think. It'll come to me in a moment[3]."

"Was there one doctor in particular your wife was seeing in Boston?"

A pause. Then: "There were a few. I don't remember all the names off the top of my head[4]. But what I was getting to is,[5] the baby was not actually born there. In Boston."

"So Matthew was, in fact, born in Promise Falls?"

"Yes, exactly. But we were literally back here only minutes when it happened. It was on the drive home[6]; we were almost to Albany, and Rose's contractions started, and I called Dr. Sturgess and he met us as the house and wow, before you knew it[7], the baby was born."

"Dr. Sturgess?" Duckworth asked.

"That's right. Jack Sturgess. Our family physician[8]. And he's been a friend of mine for a long time. Good man[9]."

"Why didn't the doctor tell you to go straight to the hospital? Wouldn't that have been wiser[10]?"

Another pause. It almost sounded as though Gaynor was talking to someone else in the car. "I'm sorry; you were breaking up a bit there[11]. What was the question?"

"I said, wouldn't it have made more sense to go to the hospital?"

---

1. en fait, je me suis mal exprimé

2. à un moment aussi crucial de sa grossesse

3. Ça va me revenir

4. de tête, là comme ça
5. ce que j'allais dire, c'est que

6. sur la route du retour

7. en un clin d'œil

8. médecin de famille
9. Un type bien
10. plus raisonnable

11. la ligne saute un peu

"Well, in retrospect[1], I suppose so. But Rosemary really wanted to be home, and the doctor was already on his way, so … that's what happened. Is there some sort of problem? I mean, I have a proper birth certificate for Matthew, signed by Dr. Sturgess."

"I'm sure you do[2], Mr. Gaynor. Listen, it sounds like you're on the road, and I don't want you getting a ticket[3] for talking on your cell. I'll get back to you[4] later today."

"But I don't understand the point of your questions. I'm happy to help if you'll just enlighten me about[5]—"

"No, that's fine, Mr. Gaynor. I'll be in touch."

Duckworth hung up.

The lying son of a bitch[6].

He sat at his desk, staring at his computer monitor without actually seeing anything. Thought some more[7]. So Dr. Sturgess was not only present for the delivery[8] of Marla's child, but Rosemary Gaynor's, too. Even signed the birth certificate.

Except Rosemary Gaynor did not give birth.

He needed a coffee. He went into the station kitchen, poured a cup for himself[9], and when he returned Carlson was at his temporary desk, a cell phone to his ear. When he saw Duckworth he ended the call, put the phone away.

"Sorry," Carlson said. "Just my mom."

Not caring, Duckworth shrugged[10].

Carlson said, "I checked out all those things you wanted me to. Struck out on[11] the squirrels. No one saw anything. And I couldn't interview those Thackeray students. But I had some luck[12] at Five Mountains. Found where someone cut a hole through the fence. The more I think about it, though, the whole day was a waste of

---

1. avec le recul

2. Je n'en doute pas

3. que vous preniez une amende

4. vous rappellerai

5. voulez bien m'expliquer

6. petit menteur de merde

7. encore

8. naissance

9. se servit une tasse

10. haussa les épaules

11. J'ai commencé par

12. plus de chance

time[1]. No one gives a shit[2] about dead squirrels, Thackeray's security chief took care of[3] that would-be rapist[4], and there was no real harm done[5] at Five Mountains, except for a fence they have to fix[6], which they may not even bother[7] to do, since they're planning to sell off everything that's there. If I'm going to work in this department, give me some real work to do."

Duckworth slowly looked over at him.

"Oh," Carlson said, "you got a call[8] while you were questioning that Pickens woman. Harwood? David Harwood?"

"He called?"

"Yeah. Total asshole[9]."

"What'd he want?"

"He said the Pickens woman didn't do it. Didn't kill the Gaynor woman. Said we'd made a big mistake."

"Why didn't you tell me this sooner?"

"I just did tell you[10]. Right now. You were gone, and I went for coffee, and now I'm back, and I'm telling you."

Duckworth looked through his notebook again, found David Harwood's number. He was pretty sure it was his cell, not a home number.

He made the call.

It rang twice, and then: "Yes?"

"Mr. Harwood? Detective Duckworth here. You were trying to reach me?"

"Marla didn't do it," Harwood said. "Sarita Gomez, the Gaynors' nanny? Well, she didn't do it, either, but she was the one who took[11] the baby to Marla's house. Because Matthew really is Marla's baby."

"How do you know this?"

"Because I found Sarita, and she told me, and she's with me right now."

"And where the hell is that[1]?" Duckworth asked.

1. Mais où, bordel

SIXTY-NINE

David

"MY parents' house," I told Detective Duckworth. "I think you know where that is." He had, after all, been here a few years ago when I was having my other troubles[1].

I put the phone away and said to Agnes, "Sorry. The police are coming."

"Of course they are," she said wearily[2].

"You said that you wished deceiving[3] Marla had been the worst of it," I said. "What could be worse than that?"

"I can answer that," my mother said. "The lie was just the beginning. It was the aftermath[4]. Look what you did to her. Look what you did to your child."

Agnes mumbled[5] something.

"What was that?" Mom asked.

"I thought it was the right thing to do. I was trying to look out for her[6]. I was trying to give Marla a future."

"By driving her mad[7]? Agnes, she tried to steal a baby. You did that to her."

"I know."

1. problèmes

2. d'un ton las
3. que mentir à

4. les suites

5. marmonna

6. la protéger

7. En la rendant folle

496

Mom shook her head slowly, not taking her eyes off[1] her sister. Agnes was still running her palm across the bedspread, studying the nap, but I was betting she could feel my mother's eyes boring into her[2].

"You've always been hard, Agnes," she said, "but I never knew[3] you were a monster."

I said, "But that's not what you were referring to[4], is it, Agnes? When you said there were even worse things."

Her head turned slightly my way. "Jack—Dr. Sturgess—had matters he had to deal with[5]. When things started to unravel[6]. Actions he had to take."

"Like Rosemary Gaynor," I said. "Did Sturgess kill her?"

Agnes shifted around[7] so she could look at me directly. "No, he wouldn't have done that. He … would never have done that. It doesn't fit … It's unthinkable[8]."

"All of this is unthinkable," I said. "But Sarita had figured out[9] what happened, and she told Rosemary." I looked at Sarita. "Isn't that right?"

She nodded. "I told her. She said she didn't believe me, but I think she did."

I continued. "Rosemary had to realize Matthew wasn't a baby someone willingly gave up[10]. The adoption was bogus[11]. If she came forward[12], if she started asking questions, if it came out with what Dr. Sturgess had done, he'd be finished[13]. He'd go to jail. You think he wouldn't do whatever he had to?"

Agnes shook her head adamantly[14]. "No …"

"If not Rosemary, then what are you talking about?"

---

1. sans quitter des yeux

2. la transpercer

3. n'aurais jamais cru
4. de cela que tu parles

5. des problèmes à régler
6. à cafouiller

7. se tourna

8. inconcevable

9. compris

10. donné volontairement
11. bidon
12. se manifestait
13. foutu

14. catégoriquement

1. faire chanter

2. intervint doucement

3. malheur

4. fini

5. s'éclipsa

6. à regret

7. s'appuyer contre moi

8. abritée

9. houleuse

"There was a man—he tried to blackmail[1] Gaynor. Today."

Sarita breathed in[2]. "Marshall. I told him not to do it. I told him—"

"It doesn't matter now," Agnes said. "Jack ... dealt with him."

Sarita put her hands to her mouth. "No, no, no."

Agnes glanced at her. "Was he your boyfriend? He shouldn't have done it. He was the author of his own misfortune[3]. And ... I believe there may have been someone else. An old lady." A strange calm seemed to be coming over her. "It's all over[4]. Everything is over."

There was a hard knock at the front door that we could all hear upstairs.

"Duckworth," I said. "That was fast."

"I'll go," Dad said, and slipped out of the room[5].

"You're going to go to jail," Mom said.

"Yes," Agnes said. "Probably for a long time." Then, almost wistfully[6]: "Or maybe not."

"I don't see how Marla can ever forgive you. I know if it were me, I couldn't."

Agnes said nothing.

I walked over to Sarita, put a hand on each shoulder, and let her lean up against me[7]. She was crying.

So much misery in one room.

Downstairs, I heard the front door open.

Agnes said to Sarita, "You'll tell them?"

Sarita, half shielded[8] by my shoulder, looked at my aunt and said, "I will tell them everything."

Agnes's face looked like it would crack when she smiled. "Thank you for that."

It sounded like there was a heated[9] discussion going on at the front door. I thought I heard Dad say, "Fuck you."

Not the sort of thing I'd have expected Dad to say to a Promise Falls detective.

"Hang on," I said, letting go of Sarita and heading for the bedroom door. As I came into the hall, I became aware of[1] something in the air, as if someone were burning leaves or brush[2] in the neighborhood. Then I saw two heads coming up the stairs. Dad in the lead[3], and Jack Sturgess just behind him. Sturgess's left hand was gripped around[4] my father's right arm. In his right hand was the syringe I'd glimpsed[5] before. He was holding the tip[6] of the needle about an inch away[7] from Dad's neck.

"Agnes!" Sturgess said. "You in there?"

From inside the bedroom, Agnes said, "Jack?"

"Thought that was your car out front." Sturgess and Dad had reached the top of the stairs. I stood, frozen[8], my eyes on the needle.

"It's going to be okay, Dad," I said. "Put the needle down," I told the doctor.

Agnes appeared in the bedroom doorway. "Jack, Jesus Christ."

Sturgess could see into the room. Saw Sarita, Mom on the bed. "What have you told them?" he asked Agnes.

"I can't do this anymore," Agnes said.

"It's over," I told him. "It's all coming out[9]."

Sturgess's eyes seemed to dance, as though he were trying to focus on a swarm of fireflies[10]. The needle wavered[11] by my father's neck.

"Where's the baby?" Agnes asked. "Is Matthew okay?"

"Outside, in the car, with his father," the doctor said, stressing the last word. "His legal father."

"What's Gaynor doing?" I asked. "Waiting for you to come in here and kill the lot of us[12]? How

1. perçus
2. des broussailles
3. devant
4. enserrait
5. aperçue
6. pointe
7. à 3 cm
8. figé
9. L'affaire éclate au grand jour
10. essaim de lucioles
11. vacilla
12. tous nous tuer

many needles you got? You think you can kill everyone here? Is that your plan? Because there's more than just us. The police know, too."

"Shut up," he said. "Think you're smart[1], but not smart enough to hide your fucking car."

He had me there. He knew Mom's Taurus from tailing me[2] minutes earlier, and leaving it out front wasn't the brightest thing I'd done today.

"Put the needle down," Agnes told him. "You're not hurting[3] Don."

I could see the fear in Dad's eyes. He was frozen, scared to make any kind of fast move[4] for fear that needle would be driven straight into him. We didn't have to know what was in it. We knew Sturgess wasn't giving out flu shots[5].

"We have to make a deal," Sturgess said. "Everyone stays quiet, and I won't kill him."

If the situation hadn't been so dire[6], it would have been laughable[7]. "The police are already on their way[8]," I told him. "There aren't any deals to be made."

Sturgess tightened his grip[9] on my father. Moved the needle a few millimeters closer to his neck.

"Then the old man comes with me. I need time. I need time to get away[10]."

I decided to stick with my best argument. "The police will be here before you hit the front door."

"No," Sturgess said. "They're not coming. That's bullshit[11]. We're leaving."

He started to back up[12], carefully pulling my father with him.

"Don!" Mom cried from her spot[13] on the bed. "Please don't take him!"

With all that was going on, I almost hadn't noticed that whatever it was I'd smelled in the hallway a minute ago was getting worse[1]. I had a pretty good idea what it was[2].

"I'm serious," I said. "Detective Duckworth called me a few minutes ago. He's on his way here."

Sturgess yanked[3] even harder on Dad's arm. "Then I guess we'd better go, old—"

The alarm was deafening. The high-pitched squeal[4] went straight to my eardrums[5].

It had to be the smoke detector in the living room, the one outside the door to the kitchen. There was already smoke drifting up[6] from the first floor[7].

I glanced back at my mother, who appeared to mouth[8] the words "pork chops."

1. empirait
2. étais à peu près sûr de ce que c'était
3. tira
4. sonnerie suraiguë
5. me vrilla les tympans
6. qui montait
7. rez-de-chaussée
8. prononcer silencieusement

SEVENTY

David

1. dut se dire

2. dépassé

3. les braillements

4. libéra son bras

5. se rua

6. voulut se lancer sur

7. m'interposer

8. saisis son avant-bras

9. le cognai à toutes forces

10. comme je l'avais espéré

11. Lâche-la

12. se tendit

13. me pressai contre lui

14. me rouler contre lui

15. entrejambe

16. insoutenable

17. reculai en titubant

DAD must have figured[1] this was his only chance.

While Sturgess was briefly distracted and overwhelmed[2] by the wailing[3] of the smoke detector, Dad wrenched his arm free[4] and bolted[5]—almost fell—in my direction.

Sturgess lurched after[6] Dad, but I managed to get between them[7], reaching with both hands for the arm that had the syringe. I grabbed hold of his forearm[8] and slammed it up[9] against the wall, but the syringe didn't fly out of his hand the way I'd hoped it would[10].

"Drop it[11]!" I yelled.

His left hand reached over[12] to try to take the syringe from his right. I shoved my body up against his[13], tried to roll over the front of him[14], block his free arm.

A knee came up out of nowhere and drove hard into my crotch[15], taking my breath away. The pain was excruciating[16], and for a second I lost my grip on Sturgess's right arm. I stumbled back[17].

502

Madly he swung[1] the syringe through the air as though it were a knife. I was jumping back and out of his way[2] as we moved toward the stairs.

Dad came up behind Sturgess and kicked him in the back of his right thigh[3]. The doctor dropped to the floor. I noticed that the syringe was no longer in his hand, but in the confusion I had lost sight of where it had gone[4].

"You son of a bitch!" Dad shouted.

I took advantage of Sturgess while he[5] was down on one knee, and aimed a kick at his chest[6]. I failed to catch him directly, and only knocked him off balance[7]. His shoulder went into[8] the wall. As I closed in on[9] him, he pushed himself off[10] and tackled me around the knees[11].

I went down.

More smoke began to billow its way upstairs[12]. If those pork chops Mom had left untended on the stove were kicking up some flame[13], it was a safe bet[14] that the overhanging cabinets[15] and curtain at the window next to the stove[16] were already ablaze[17].

Sturgess scrambled on top of me[18], straddled me so that he was sitting on my stomach[19], and drove a fist at my[20] head. I turned my face away, felt the fist graze[21] my left ear.

He brought his right hand back up to his left, laced his fingers together[22], getting ready to backhand me[23] hard with a double fist.

This one was going to hurt.

But before he could start the downswing[24], I caught sight[25] of Agnes standing over him.

Something in her hand.

She plunged the syringe into his back, the needle going through suit jacket and shirt.

1. balança
2. hors de sa portée
3. cuisse
4. l'avais perdue de vue
5. profitai de ce que Sturgess
6. tentai de lui décocher un coup de pied dans la poitrine
7. lui fis seulement perdre l'équilibre
8. percuta
9. me rapprochais de
10. se releva
11. me plaqua par les genoux
12. parvint à l'étage
13. avaient pris feu
14. il y avait fort à parier
15. placards en hauteur
16. cuisinière
17. en feu
18. me monta dessus
19. à califourchon sur mon ventre
20. me lança son poing à la
21. râper
22. entremêla ses doigts
23. me coller un revers
24. amorcer le mouvement
25. aperçus

"Shit!" Sturgess said, and stumbled off me[1]. He struggled to his feet[2], looked over his shoulder, trying without success to see the syringe, which was still sticking out[3] of him. He looked at Agnes and said, "Do you know what you've done?"

Agnes nodded.

"I haven't got much time," he said. "I've only got seconds. You have to …" He began to waver[4]. "You have to move fast."

Agnes didn't move.

"Just die," she said. "Just hurry up and die."

Sturgess wavered, stumbled into the wall, back first[5]. We heard a snap[6], and then the syringe, minus[7] the needle, hit the floor.

I looked back into the bedroom. With Sarita's help, Mom was struggling to get off the bed.

"Hurry," I said. "I don't know how bad the fire is[8]."

Dad got around to Mom's other side. The three of them headed for the stairs. Dr. Sturgess was sliding down the wall.

I said to Agnes, "Is there anything you can do?"

She looked at me. "Even if there were … I'm sorry there isn't a second needle. For me."

"We have to get out."

Agnes nodded calmly. Sturgess was on the floor now, but he wasn't dead. His eyelids[9] were fluttering[10]. I leaned over[11] to grab him under the arms so I could drag him down the stairs.

"Trust me," she said. "He won't make it to[12] the front door."

The eyelids stopped moving. I reached for his wrist[13], felt for a pulse[14], found nothing.

"Walk me out[15]," Agnes said.

We went down the stairs together. We could see flames in the kitchen. We found everyone else outside. Dad had grabbed a chair from the front porch and dragged it into the yard so Mom could sit down.

An unmarked police cruiser was screeching to a halt at the curb, Duckworth throwing open the door and getting out. He'd managed to block in[1] the black Audi, where a nervous-looking Bill Gaynor was sitting behind the wheel[2], looking like a cornered mouse[3].

There was someone in the passenger seat of the cruiser.

Marla.

Duckworth, seeing the smoke, ran toward us. "Is there anyone still in the house?"

"Sturgess," I said, propping up my father. "But he's dead."

Duckworth blinked[4]. "From the fire?"

"No," I said. "We need an ambulance for my mom. She can barely[5] walk. My dad may be hurt, too."

Duckworth whipped out[6] his phone, barked out[7] an address, demanded fire engines[8] and paramedics[9]. Neighbors were pouring out[10] of nearby[11] houses to see what all the commotion was[12].

Up[13] the street I saw Ethan, backpack[14] over his shoulder, walking home from school. He began to run.

I saw Agnes walking toward Gaynor's car. She said something to him briefly, pointed a finger of judgment[15] at him, then walked around to the rear passenger door.

Gaynor did nothing to stop her.

Marla was coming out of the passenger side of Duckworth's cruiser, looking at the smoking house, more with wonder[16] than anything else. She was so busy taking it in[17], she didn't notice

1. coincer
2. au volant
3. souris prise au piège
4. cilla
5. à peine
6. sortit vivement
7. aboya
8. des camions de pompiers
9. des ambulanciers
10. sortaient en masse
11. avoisinantes
12. ce que signifiait toute cette agitation
13. Au loin dans
14. son sac à dos
15. doigt accusateur
16. surprise
17. à chercher à comprendre

1. enlever

her mother prying[1] Matthew from the safety seat in the back of the Audi. Once she had the boy in her arms, she started walking toward the unmarked cruiser.

"Dad! Dad!" Ethan cried, running into my arms, a look of horror on his face. "The house!"

2. le pris dans mes bras
3. et l'étreignis
4. se dérouler

"It's okay," I told him. "It's okay." I wrapped my arms around him[2], held on to him tightly[3] as I watched a different drama play out[4] before me.

"Marla," Agnes said.

Marla turned, saw her mother approaching with Matthew in her arms.

5. la voix cassée

"Mama?" she said, her voice breaking[5].

"You know Matthew, of course," Agnes said, and held the child out to her.

"What are you doing?" Marla asked.

"Take him. Hold him. He's yours."

Marla hesitantly took the boy into her own arms. "What do you mean?"

"I mean he's your baby. He's the baby you carried. The baby you gave birth to."

"How … how …"

Marla's eyes filled instantly with tears. Her expression was one of joy mixed with total

6. stupéfaction

bafflement[6].

"Don't worry about that right now," Agnes said, putting her arms around Marla and the child.

"Oh, my God," Marla whispered. "Oh, my God, it can't be true."

"It's true, child. It's true."

7. En larmes

Weeping[7], Marla said, "Thank you, Mom! Thank you so much! Thank you! I love you so much! You're the best mother in the whole world! Thank you for finding him! I don't know how you did it, how it can be possible, but thank you! Thank you for believing me!"

Agnes ended the hug, looked at Marla, and said, "I have to go. You take care[1]."

"Mama?"

I watched Agnes return to her car, the door still open. She got behind the wheel, slowly backed out onto the street, and drove away as Marla took hold of Matthew's tiny wrist so that he could, along with his mother, wave good-bye[2].

1. Prends soin de toi

2. faire au revoir de la main

THE NEXT DAY

SEVENTY-ONE

David

"**SO,** you ready to get started?" Randall Finley asked me.

When I'd seen his name pop up[1] on my cell I should have let it go to message[2]. But like a fool, I answered.

"It's only been twenty-four hours," I told him.

"Yeah, but from what I hear, your sister's in the clear[3]."

"Cousin," I said.

"Cousin, sister, whatever. She's innocent, right?"

"Right. But there are a few other things we still have to deal with."

"Like?"

"A funeral for my aunt, for one[4]," I said.

"Oh, shit, yeah," Finley said. "Fucking hell, I heard about that. She jumped off the falls[5]?"

Right after she drove away from my parents' house.

"Yes," I said.

"My condolences," the former mayor said.

"Plus, I have to find a place to live. There was a fire at my parents' house."

1. s'afficher
2. laisser le répondeur
3. disculpée
4. d'abord
5. cascade

511

"That might be a blessing in disguise[1]. Living with your parents at your age, that's not good."

"They'll be moving in with me while they re-build the kitchen," I said.

"Ouch[2]. Man, you are the poster boy for shit out of luck[3]. So, what do you think? A couple of days? Because soon I want to announce that I'm running[4]. I need to put together[5] a platform[6], shit like that. About how empathetic I am[7], how I feel[8] for the common man."

"It seems so self-evident[9]," I said.

"Yeah, but some people don't pick up the signals[10]. You have to spell it out for them[11]. You know what I'm saying[12]."

"I think so. Why don't I call you toward the end of the week."

Finley sighed. "I suppose. It's a good thing I'm a soft touch[13]. Most employers, they might not take it so well, someone taking time off[14] before they've even started the fucking job."

He ended the call.

I was parked out front of the Pickenses' house. Gill and Marla were inside. She'd be looking after Matthew, and no doubt he was busy making funeral arrangements for Agnes.

The Promise Falls Department of Child and Family Services, pending[15] a more formal review[16] later, decided to let Marla look after Matthew for now, so long as[17] she was living with Gill. Even though the child was hers, and a terrible crime had been perpetrated against her, there was still the issue[18] of her mental stability. She had, after all, tried to kidnap a baby from the hospital. In addition, she'd tried to take her own life[19]. But Marla had agreed to intensive counseling[20] and regular visitations from a caseworker[21].

While Marla was the only one getting professional help, that didn't mean she was the only one who needed it.

My mother was devastated[1].

Her sister was dead. And Agnes might have had her sister's last words to her in mind as she plunged to her death off Promise Falls.

You've always been hard, Agnes, but I never knew you were a monster.

Despite the monstrous things Agnes had done, Mom wished she had said something else.

At some level, I think Mom blamed herself[2]. That maybe if she'd been a better older sibling[3], none of this would have happened.

They found Agnes downriver[4], her body lodged[5] on a rock where the rapids get shallow[6]. She wasn't the first person to die from going off the bridge that spans[7] that rushing cliff of water, and she probably wouldn't be the last. But I doubted anyone before or after had done it with the same sense of purpose[8].

According to witness accounts[9], Agnes walked calmly along the sidewalk to the center of the bridge, set down her purse[10], perched her butt[11] on the railing[12], and gracefully swung[13] both legs around and over[14].

Before anyone else could even react, she was gone.

I couldn't decide whether there was courage in what she did, or colossal cowardice[15]. Maybe some of both. The fact that she never told Marla what she'd done to her tipped me toward[16] the latter.

She'd left that for Gill and others to explain[17].

Considering everything, Ethan was riding this out okay[18]. Moving to a motel for a few nights while I looked for a place for us to live[19] was an

1. effondrée
2. s'en voulait
3. grande sœur
4. en aval
5. coincé
6. moins profonds
7. enjambe
8. une telle détermination
9. les témoignages
10. avait posé son sac à main
11. ses fesses
12. rambarde
13. lancé
14. par-dessus la rambarde et dans le vide
15. lâcheté
16. m'incitait à pencher pour
17. à Gill et aux autres le soin d'expliquer
18. encaissait plutôt bien
19. nous cherchais un logement

adventure. The fire'd been contained[1] before it spread upstairs and destroyed any of his things[2]. The model railroad[3] Dad had built in the basement had gotten soaked[4], but the engines[5] and boxcars[6] and the Promise Falls water tower would dry out eventually[7].

My son had been through worse[8]. We'd get through this together.

I was about to get out of the car to see how Marla and Gill were doing when my cell phone rang. I didn't immediately recognize the number, but at least it wasn't Finley's, so I answered.

"Hello?"

"You son of a bitch."

A woman's voice.

"Sam?" I said. "Is this Samantha?"

"You suckered me right in[9], didn't you? Nicely done[10]. I should have known you were working for them. I knew they wanted Carl back, but I never thought they'd stoop this low[11]."

"Sam, I swear I don't know what you're talking about."

"That was good, fucking me right there in the kitchen where they could look in through the window, get some nice pics[12]. Talk about getting screwed in more ways than one[13]."

Even as my heart pounded[14], I tried to figure out what had happened.

The blue pickup truck with the tinted windows.

"Sam, listen to me—I didn't do anything. I never—"

"I'll get you for this[15]. I will. Don't come knocking on my door again. Next time I'll pull the trigger[16]."

And then she hung up.

1. maîtrisé
2. affaires
3. circuit de train miniature
4. pris l'eau
5. locomotives
6. les wagons
7. finiraient par sécher
8. avait connu pire
9. m'a bien entubée
10. Joli
11. tomberaient aussi bas
12. photos
13. Tu m'as bien baisée dans tous les sens du terme
14. battait la chamade
15. te le ferai payer
16. La prochaine fois, je tire

514

I called her back immediately but she wouldn't answer. When it went to voice mail[1], I said, "Whatever you're thinking I did, I did not do it. I swear. If I've caused you trouble, I'm sorry, but I did not set you up[2]." I hesitated. "The truth is, I want to see you again."

I tried to think of anything else I could say and came up blank[3]. So I ended the call and pocketed the phone.

"Shit," I said under my breath.

Gill opened the door ten seconds after I rang the bell. "David," he said, his voice flat, empty[4]. "Come in."

"I wanted to see how Marla was doing[5]," I said.

"Of course. She's in the kitchen with Matthew. I'm just on the phone, sorting out[6] the details. For Agnes."

I nodded.

"I hope you're not expecting me to thank you[7]," Gill said.

"I'm sorry."

"You were instrumental[8] in getting to the truth. I suppose that's something. But now my wife is dead, and I'm looking after my daughter and a grandson. That's what the truth brought me."

There was nothing I could say.

I followed him into the kitchen. A high chair[9] had been acquired[10] in the last day. Matthew was secured[11] into it with a tiny safety belt that ran around his waist[12]. Marla was sitting in a kitchen chair opposite him, feeding him with a tiny red plastic spoon some green pureed stuff[13] from a small glass jar.

"David!" she said. She put down the baby food, jumped to her feet[14], and threw her arms around

---

1. je tombais sur le répondeur

2. ne t'ai pas piégée

3. ne trouvai rien

4. complètement éteinte

5. allait Marla

6. je règle

7. ne t'attends pas à des remerciements

8. as joué un rôle crucial

9. chaise haute
10. achetée
11. attaché
12. par une petite ceinture de sécurité autour de la taille

13. une espèce de purée verte

14. se leva d'un bond

me. She planted a kiss on my cheek. "It's so good to see you."

"You, too," I said.

Marla sat back down, said, "Grab[1] a chair. I'm just in the middle of giving him his lunch."

I found a chair and sat. "What is that stuff[2]?"

"Peas[3]," she said. "He's Hoovering it[4]." She glanced at me. "Let me ask you a question."

"Sure."

"Do you think I should keep calling him Matthew? I mean, that's the name the Gaynors gave him, but I would have named him something different."

"I don't know," I said.

"Because even though he's little, it's probably already a name he responds to. If I were going to call him something different—and I'm leaning toward[5] Kyle—I'd have to start doing it right now."

"I'm not sure I'm the one to advise you on this. I mean, it might even be a legal matter. There'll probably be a few of those[6]."

Marla nodded, understanding. "You're right. I'm going to talk it over with Mom."

I felt a chill[7]. I glanced over at Gill, who was by the phone, making notes. He looked my way with dead eyes.

"With your mom," I said.

"When she's able to come back[8]," she said. Marla must have seen the look in my eye, and she smiled. "I know what you're thinking. That Mom jumped off the falls. That's what they're all saying." She lowered her voice to a whisper. "But she had to fake her death[9]. She needs time for things to cool off[10]. Then she'll come back and help me."

I was speechless[11].

---

1. Prends-toi
2. ce truc
3. Des petits pois
4. dévore
5. ai une préférence pour
6. Il risque d'il y en avoir pas mal
7. frisson
8. pourra revenir
9. mettre sa mort en scène
10. laisser les choses se calmer
11. muet de stupeur

"They're saying a lot of things about her," Marla continued. "Things that can't possibly be true. That Dr. Sturgess was a very, very bad man. He must have tricked Mom into thinking my baby had died. It was a conspiracy[1]. The Gaynors were part of it. Mom couldn't have been involved in anything like that[2]."

Another smile. Marla slipped a spoonful of peas into Matthew's mouth. Half dribbled down his chin[3].

"Oh, look at you," she said. "Are you a messy boy? You are a messy boy. Isn't he beautiful, David?"

"He is that."

"I think he looks a little like Dad," she said, and then called over to her father, "Don't you see it?"

"If you say so," he said. Then, struggling[4], he added, "I can see some of Agnes in him. In his eyes."

Marla studied her baby. "I see that. I do. I think I actually do, which is pretty amazing for me. Do you see it, David?"

I looked. "Maybe so." I stood. "I'm going to check in on you every once in a while[5], if that's okay."

"I'd love that," Marla said. "It's kind of chaotic around here right now. There's so much to get organized. I might not even go back to my house. At least, not for a few months. When Mom gets back, she'll sort it all out[6]." A grin. "That's what she does, you know. Soon as she walks through that door, she'll take charge[7]."

I gave Marla a hug[8] and said to Gill, "Thanks. See you at the service[9]. I can find my way out."

When I opened the front door to leave, there were two men standing there. A young man I'd

---

1. complot
2. n'aurait pas pu faire un truc pareil
3. lui coula sur le menton
4. avec effort
5. te rendre visite de temps en temps
6. s'occupera de tout
7. prendra les choses en main
8. serrai Marla dans mes bras
9. cérémonie

met before, and an older gentleman who I'd have guessed, from a quick glance[1], was his father.

Derek Cutter had just been about to press the doorbell, and I'd startled him[2].

"Oh!" he said. "Mr. Harwood."

"Hi, Derek."

"Mr. Harwood, this is my dad."

The older man extended a hand. His grip[3] was firm. "Jim Cutter," he said. On the street I spotted a pickup truck with the words "Cutter's Lawn Service" painted on the side.

"Good to meet you. I'm David." I looked at Derek. "You heard[4]."

The Thackeray student nodded. "Marla called me." He swallowed. "I'm a dad after all."

Jim Cutter, standing slightly behind his son, rested his palms on the young man's shoulders. "Not exactly ideal circumstances, but we came to get acquainted[5], just the same[6]."

I called out to Marla that she had visitors, then got in my car and headed home.

1. au premier coup d'œil

2. l'avais pris de court

3. poignée de main

4. avez appris la nouvelle

5. sommes venus faire connaissance

6. quand même

SEVENTY-TWO

THE dead doctor was looking good for it[1].

Motive was certainly not a problem[2], Detective Barry Duckworth thought. If Dr. Jack Sturgess feared that Rosemary Gaynor was going to start asking too many questions about the circumstances surrounding the adoption of Matthew, he might have seen he had no option but to kill her.

He'd certainly shown no hesitation where Marshall Kemper was concerned[3]. Bill Gaynor, who had decided to come clean about[4] everything he knew, had led them to the man's body in the woods. Duckworth had also determined that Sturgess had murdered Kemper's elderly neighbor in a bid to cover his tracks[5].

So the man certainly had it in him[6] to kill when it came to[7] saving himself.

Angus Carlson had been building a timeline[8] of where Sturgess had been the day that Rosemary Gaynor was killed, and there were plenty of gaps in his schedule[9]. So he'd had opportunity. And she would have had no hesitation in letting him into her home. He was her doctor, after all.

But still, there was no actual physical evidence[10] that connected Sturgess to the crime. And the way

1. sans doute le grand coupable

2. La question du mobile ne se posait pas

3. dans le cas de Marshall Kemper

4. confesser

5. dans l'espoir d'effacer ses traces

6. était certainement capable

7. s'agissait de

8. chronologie

9. zones d'ombre dans son emploi du temps

10. de preuve matérielle

the Gaynor woman had been killed didn't seem to fit the doctor's style.

He'd killed Kemper with a fatal injection. He'd attempted to kill David Harwood and his father the same way. He'd smothered[1] Kemper's neighbor with a pillow, but that made some sense[2]. What happened to her might easily have been dismissed[3] as death by natural causes.

But did it follow[4] that a man who killed two people bloodlessly[5] would virtually disembowel[6] somebody? Did a man who used a needle or a pillow carve up[7] a woman like a Halloween pumpkin[8]?

Duckworth had discussed this matter, and others, with Bill Gaynor, who was in custody[9] and facing a slew of charges[10].

"I don't know," Gaynor had told him. "A year ago I wouldn't have believed Jack was capable of what he did this week. I don't know anything anymore. I'm starting to think it's possible."

Gaynor did tell him that he and Sturgess had been able to persuade Rosemary months ago that the adoption of Matthew was legitimate. The doctor told her Matthew's mother was a sixteen-year-old girl from a poor family, that raising this child she was carrying would be more than she or her parents could handle[11]. The girl's identity would have to remain secret, but Sturgess drew up some bogus paperwork[12] for Rosemary to sign that went straight into the Promise Falls General paper shredder[13]. The doctor had persuaded Gaynor that he'd find a way to funnel[14] some of the money[15] to Marla, even though he'd always planned[16] to keep all of it for himself.

1. étouffé
2. c'était assez logique
3. classé
4. s'ensuivait-il
5. sans verser de sang
6. pourrait pratiquement étriper
7. découpait
8. citrouille
9. en garde à vue
10. chapelet d'accusations
11. trop lourd pour elle et ses parents
12. de faux documents
13. déchiqueteuse
14. transmettre
15. une partie de l'argent
16. avait toujours eu l'intention

Chief Rhonda Finderman was eager[1] to see the Gaynor case closed. She wanted one in the win column[2]. And the beauty of this was,[3] Sturgess didn't have to be convicted in a court of law[4].

Duckworth asked her for more time to nail down[5] some of the details.

"Soon," he told her.

The Gaynor case wasn't the only thing troubling him[6].

There were those damn squirrels. The three painted mannequins. That Thackeray student who'd been shot to death by that asshole Clive Duncomb.

The number 23.

Sitting at his desk, he doodled[7] the number several times. There was a very good chance it didn't mean a damn thing.

He thought about the squirrels. Just the squirrels.

Let's say you're some sick bastard[8] trying to make a statement[9]. You decide the way you're going to get your point across[10] is by killing some animals. And that's what you do. But why not ten? Why not a dozen? Maybe twenty-five.

Why do you pick a number like twenty-three?

Duckworth Googled it[11]. The first thing that came up was the Wikipedia entry. "Always a reliable[12] source," Duckworth said under his breath.

It was the ninth prime number[13].

It was the sum of three other consecutive prime numbers: five, seven, and eleven.

It was the atomic number[14] of vanadium, whatever the hell vanadium was. Duckworth thought that might be one of the coffee flavors Wanda had offered him.

It was the number on Michael Jordan's shirt when he played for the Chicago Bulls.

---

1. impatiente
2. mettre l'affaire au tableau des réussites
3. le plus beau, c'était que
4. condamné au pénal
5. tirer au clair
6. qui le préoccupait
7. griffonna
8. un quelconque malade
9. faire passer un message
10. te faire entendre
11. chercha sur Google
12. fiable
13. nombre premier
14. numéro atomique

In one of the *Matrix* movies, Neo was told that—

The phone rang.

"Duckworth."

"It's Wanda."

"Hey, I was just thinking of you. What's vanadium?"

"It's a kind of mineral," she said. "It has some medical applications."

"How do you know that?"

"I took science[1]. You take a bit of that[2] when you become a doctor. Is this important?"

"Probably not. I was just—"

"I don't care what you're doing," the medical examiner said. "Just get your ass over here[3]."

"What were you doing three years ago this month?" Wanda Therrieult asked him after he'd arrived.

"I don't know, offhand[4]," Duckworth said. "Working, I'd guess."

"I'm betting you weren't. I wasn't. I was taking some time to be with my sister, who was in her last few weeks."

"I remember that," Duckworth said. "Duluth."

"That's right."

Duckworth was thinking. "Vacation," he said. "Opening of pickerel season[5]. In Ontario. Went up with a friend to a place called Bobcaygeon. Was gone the better part of ten days[6]."

"Sit down," she said, and pointed to a second chair she'd wheeled over to her desk. She moved the mouse to make the screen come to life. There appeared three autopsy photos.

"I'm guessing these look familiar to you[7]," Wanda said.

Duckworth pointed, keeping his finger away from the screen. They were all close-up shots.

1. ai fait des sciences

2. Faut en faire un peu

3. Ramène ta fraise

4. de tête

5. saison de la pêche au brochet

6. pratiquement dix jours

7. ces photos te disent quelque chose

"Yeah. This is where Rosemary Gaynor was grabbed around the neck. There's the thumb imprint here, the other four fingers here, and that's where he stabbed her. The ... smile. This is all kind of familiar[1], Wanda. It's only been a couple of days."

1. Je reconnais, oui

"This isn't Rosemary Gaynor."

Duckworth moved his tongue around the inside of his teeth. "Go on," he said.

"This is Olivia Fisher." She paused. "You remember Olivia Fisher."

She clicked, brought up[2] a small picture of the dead woman. Young, black hair to her shoulders, smiling into the camera. In the background was Thackeray College, where she had been a student.

2. ouvrit

"Of course," Duckworth said. "But I was never the primary on that[3]. It was Rhonda Finderman. Before she became chief."

3. n'étais pas chargé de cette enquête

"That's why we didn't make the connection[4] right away."

4. rapprochement

"Shit," Duckworth said. "She should have. She's so busy with things that have nothing to do with Promise Falls she doesn't know what's going on in her own backyard[5]."

5. chez elle

Wanda did a few lightning-quick keystrokes and mouse maneuvers[6], and brought up autopsy photos from the Gaynor case, as well as a photo of the woman that had made an online news site[7].

6. pianota et bougea la souris à la vitesse de l'éclair

7. monté un site d'information en ligne

"You're right," Duckworth said. "The wounds are nearly identical." He reached a hand out toward the screen, as though he wanted to touch the face of Rosemary Gaynor.

"Look at her hair, her face," he said. "The black hair, the complexions[8] of the two women."

8. le teint

"Very similar," Wanda said.

Duckworth shook his head slowly. "God, I need a doughnut."

"Who killed Rosemary Gaynor, Barry?"

He hesitated. "Finderman likes the doctor for it[1]."

Wanda pointed at the screen, the two dead women. "You think Sturgess did this?"

Barry Duckworth studied the images. "No."

"Then you know what this means," she said.

Duckworth nodded.

"It means our guy's come back," he said. "Or maybe he never left. Maybe he's always been here."

1. accuserait bien le docteur

SEVENTY-THREE

I feel rested[1].
  Ready to get back at it[2].
  Still so much to do.

1. reposé

2. me remettre au boulot

La collection Yes you can!

Les faux débutants

Linwood Barclay *Broken Promise*

M. C. Beaton *Agatha Raisin and the Quiche of Death*

Michael Connelly *The Black Box*

Michael Connelly *The Burning Room*

Michael Connelly *The Drop*

Ken Follett *The Modigliani Scandal*

Mary Higgins Clark *A Cry in the Night*

Mary Higgins Clark *A Stranger is Watching*

Mary Higgins Clark *Loves Music, Loves to Dance*

Mary Higgins Clark *Where are the Children?*

Anthony Horowitz *The House of Silk*

Ian Rankin *Knots & Crosses*

Nicholas Sparks *Message in a Bottle*

Les intermédiaires

Harlan Coben *Caught*

Harlan Coben *Play Dead*

Harlan Coben *Stay Close*

Harlan Coben *Tell No One*

Harlan Coben *The Woods*

Ken Follett *Paper Money*

Anthony Horowitz *Moriarty*

P. D. James *A Mind to Murder*

P. D. James *Death Comes to Pemberley*

Douglas Kennedy *The Big Picture*

Stephen King *Finders Keepers*

Stephen King *The Green Mile*

John le Carré *A Most Wanted Man*

Yann Martel *Life of Pi*

Les avancés

Paul Auster *Leviathan*
Paul Auster *Oracle Night*
Julian Barnes *The Sense of an Ending*
Michael Cunningham *By Nightfall*
Michael Cunningham *The Hours*
Helen Fielding *Bridget Jones's Diary*
Helen Fielding *Bridget Jones: The Edge of Reason*
Elizabeth George *A Great Deliverance*
Stephen King *Dolores Claiborne*
Stephen King *Misery*

Les classiques

Jane Austen *Pride and Prejudice*
G. K. Chesterton *The Innocence of Father Brown*
Arthur Conan Doyle *The Hound of the Baskervilles*
Francis Scott Fitzgerald *The Great Gatsby*
Mary Shelley *Frankenstein*
Oscar Wilde *The Picture of Dorian Gray*
Virginia Woolf *To the Lighthouse*

HARRAP s'engage pour l'environnement en réduisant l'empreinte carbone de ses livres. Celle de cet exemplaire est de : 1 kg éq. CO$_2$ Rendez-vous sur www.larousse-durable.fr

PAPIER À BASE DE FIBRES CERTIFIÉES

Imprimé par Jouve (France)
Dépôt légal : mai 2018
318962-01/ 11034419-mai 2018
N° 2716886D